Don't miss the first book in the Stargazer series by
Jennifer Echols:

Star Crossed

JENNIFER ECHOLS

Playing Dirty

POCKET BOOKS

New York   London   Toronto   Sydney   New Delhi

Pocket Books
A Division of Simon & Schuster, Inc.
1230 Avenue of the Americas
New York, NY 10020

This book is a work of fiction. Any references to historical events, real people, or real places are used fictitiously. Other names, characters, places, and events are products of the author's imagination, and any resemblance to actual events or places or persons, living or dead, is entirely coincidental.

First Pocket Books paperback edition November 2013

POCKET and colophon are registered trademarks of Simon & Schuster, Inc.

For information about special discounts for bulk purchases, please contact Simon & Schuster Special Sales at 1-866-506-1949 or business@simonandschuster.com.

The Simon & Schuster Speakers Bureau can bring authors to your live event. For more information or to book an event, contact the Simon & Schuster Speakers Bureau at 1-866-248-3049 or visit our website at www.simonspeakers.com.

Cover photograph by Shutterstock

Manufactured in the United States of America

10 9 8 7 6 5 4 3 2 1

ISBN 978-1-4516-7776-8
ISBN 978-1-4516-7778-2 (ebook)

Acknowledgments

Heartfelt thanks to my truly brilliant editors, Lauren McKenna and Emilia Pisani; my tireless literary agent, Laura Bradford; my author friends who cheered me on, Louisa Edwards and Erin Downing; my long-suffering critique partners, Catherine Chant and Victoria Dahl; and my mother, a Gold Life Master.

1

Don't despair, chicky. Try to enjoy your old stomping ground in the Deep South. You'll kick some country butt with your bad pink-haired self and be back in NYC before you know it. Meanwhile, think of me in my maternal suffering. Pregnant women are supposed to glow and I'm glowing, all right. I'm glowing like a nuclear power plant right before the accident.

Wendy Mann
Senior Consultant
Stargazer Public Relations

Sarah grinned at the e-mail on her phone from Wendy, her supervisor at work and best friend since college. This was the first time she'd smiled since the 4 a.m.

call that started her on this journey into the heart of darkness. She only wished she could wrap up business in Alabama and make it back to New York by the time Wendy had the baby. But that didn't seem likely if Sarah's information was correct. Country supergroup the Cheatin' Hearts were in imminent danger of breaking up—before delivering their eagerly anticipated third album—because a love triangle within the band was tearing them apart.

And Stargazer Public Relations had sent Sarah to keep them together.

With a frustrated sigh, she tossed her phone into the passenger seat of her rented BMW convertible. She'd grown up four hours south of Birmingham and hadn't visited the city since a high school track meet. But the green foothills of the Appalachians were familiar to her, such a different landscape from her hometown on the Gulf Coast. The city lay in the valleys and stretched as far as it could reach up the mountains, setting houses and office buildings gingerly on precipices. It was a shame that in a few hours, she would disturb its lush beauty by driving to the Cheatin' Hearts' lead singer's mountaintop mansion, pulling the band out of their basement recording studio, and slapping them to their collective senses with the threats their record company was paying her to deliver.

The statue of Vulcan looming over Sarah from the mountaintop was familiar, too, though changed. He used to hold up a torch with a green light, or a red light if someone had been killed in a car accident in town that day, which she'd found particularly morbid when she was a teenager. Now he'd been refurbished, and he held up a spearhead instead. He was the Roman god of the forge, echoing Birmingham's history as a steel town. But holding the arrow, he looked like an over-grown, butt-ugly Cupid.

What wasn't familiar was the rush hour traffic. While she'd been stuck at a standstill on the highway, she'd had time to read all fifty-five frantic e-mails her assistants at Stargazer had sent her about the Cheatin' Hearts since she'd left LaGuardia. The news was worse and worse. With this traffic, it seemed less and less likely that she'd arrive at the group's publicity office in time to grill the staff for secrets about their employers before they closed for the day.

She'd taken this highway because the radio had said the interstate was blocked, but maybe the de-tour had been a mistake. Just before the intersection on top of Vulcan's mountain, she pulled off to con-sult her GPS and phone directions. At least, that's what she intended. The side road she took kept going up the hill. She inadvertently entered the park sur-rounding the statue. As she stopped in an empty space in the lot, she glanced up and saw a new view of Vulcan above the trees.

As a teen, she'd seen him only from the front as he presided over downtown. He wore a Roman smithy apron that covered his privates in front. The view from the park was not as modest. It had never occurred to her that he was playing peek-a-boo in back. Like David Lee Roth's cutout pants from the infamous "Jump" video, but worse, because there was crack. Alabama wasn't known for its liberal values, and Sarah found it odd that the upstanding citizens of the state's largest city would tolerate this ten-foot-wide iron moon over the skyline.

Shaking off her astonishment, she studied her tiny electronic maps. This highway would lead to the Cheatin' Hearts' publicity office, all right, and so did the interstate she'd abandoned, but there were no other routes. The whole city seemed to be plotting against her. She looked up again and glared suspiciously at Vulcan's nude booty.

Then she returned six calls from Manhattan Music's liaison in charge of communications with the band. She'd tried him on her short layover in Charlotte and again when she touched down in Birmingham, but he'd been unavailable, tied up in a series of frantic meetings about the band. This time his assistant put Sarah through.

"Thank God!" the exec cried.

Sarah cringed. In her eight years at Stargazer, she had counseled many celebrities. She'd been sent on these jobs by a lot of exasperated movie producers, confounded book publishers, and record company executives driven to the edge of sanity. When she contacted them and their first words were, "Thank God!" she knew the job would be a challenge.

In calm tones, she introduced herself and assured the exec he'd done the right thing in calling Stargazer. She would take care of everything. "But the Cheatin' Hearts are a little bit of a mess, aren't they? And they've been that way for quite a while." She opened the Cheatin' Hearts' portfolio beside her on the passenger seat and glanced at a newspaper account of their lead singer, Quentin Cox, overdosing on cocaine in Thailand last month. "What prompted you to hire Stargazer this morning?" In the middle of the night, more like it.

"Someone called me," the exec said. "Someone with inside information on the group."

"Who?" Sarah asked.

"I can't say," he said. "This person swore me to secrecy. You can't even let on to the group that I got a call. All hell will break loose if you do."

"Okay," Sarah said, although it was not okay at all.

"This person said Quentin is about to quit the group because Erin left him!"

"Oh," Sarah said doubtfully, reaching for a printout of the cover of the group's first CD, *In Poor Taste*. The photo showed the lead singer, Quentin, patting the Daisy Dukes–clad booty of the group's trashy bleach-blond fiddle player, Erin, while the drummer and the guitar player looked on. "I read in my material that Quentin and Erin have been on-again and off-again romantically since you signed them to your label a couple of years ago."

"They *have been*," the exec shrieked, "and we've put

up with their shit because it was terrific exposure. Not a week's gone by that they haven't been in the celebrity news cycle for breaking up or getting back together. But *now*, Erin has cheated on Quentin with the drummer. She and the drummer claim they're in love. Quentin is furious. Our source said the band isn't going to survive this. Sarah, they have an album due in *seven days*! They have a nationally televised concert event in *ten days*, on the Fourth of July! Our source said the situation is desperate, and suggested I call Stargazer to ask for the woman who straightened out Lorelei Vogel for us—"

"Wendy Mann," Sarah said. "She just went on maternity leave."

"I know!" the exec exclaimed. "When I called and begged her to help us, she recommended you. She said you're as good as she is at saving stars' careers."

This was a lie. Wendy thrived on challenges and confrontations. Sarah got a thrill from figuring out the psychology of famous, creative people and helping them improve their quality of life, but she didn't enjoy giving tough love. And she definitely wasn't good at it.

The exec added, "But my boss told me *you're* the one who handled Nine Lives."

At the mention of yet another of Manhattan Music's acts, a chill coursed through Sarah in the hot car. Only a few days ago, she'd returned to New York after nine months in Rio with rock star Nine Lives. She'd finally pried his album from his emaciated fingers: triumph! And now he was in a Brazilian jail: fail.

The exec went on, "Wendy told me she's your supervisor, and she'll direct you in handling the Cheatin' Hearts. That was good enough for me. Or . . . at least, the next best thing."

"Thanks." Sarah took a few more notes from the hysterical executive. After hanging up, she texted Wendy.

You told Manhattan Music you would be giving me directions?

She got Wendy's reply almost immediately:

No. Well, yes, I TOLD them that, but I'm not giving you directions. I'm on maternity leave. I'm busy glowing.

Sarah squeezed her eyes shut. Wendy had warned her that she'd had a conference with their superiors at Stargazer. Even though Sarah had just extracted an album from a lunatic, they weren't happy he'd wound up in prison in a different hemisphere afterward, because their client Manhattan Music wasn't happy. Now Sarah's job was in jeopardy. Wendy thought if Sarah took on another act that was a perennial problem for the record company, it would go a long way toward smoothing things over. Wendy had said she'd be on the lookout for a job fitting that description for Sarah.

And this was it? Sarah longed for a nice girl group with no worse problem than big mouths, like she used to handle. Romantic jealousies between band members were the worst work for public relations salvage agents. These crises almost *always* signaled that the band would break up, no matter what the PR agent did. That would be a strike against Sarah, to go along with the one she already had, courtesy of Nine Lives. And nobody at Stargazer—not even Wendy—knew how bad the Nine Lives situation had gotten. Yet. If Nine Lives managed to spring himself from jail and showed up at the Manhattan Music office to enlighten everyone, that would be Sarah's strike three.

She opened her eyes and texted:

> You shouldn't have gotten me into this. It's a bad one. I'm not going to be able to get them out.

Wendy replied:

> You will. You've just lost confidence. Nine Lives is a superfreak and you worked a miracle getting an album out of him. Do the same with the Cheatin' Hearts. Just a lot faster. And maybe keep them out of prison?

With a wistful laugh, Sarah looked up again at Vulcan's bare behind. This was what her life had been reduced to. Her divorce would be final any day now. She had no boyfriend and no prospect of ever having a family of her own. She'd spent the last three quarters of a year in hell. And now, to top it all off, she was about to lose her job, on a hundred-degree day in the Deep South under a statue's naked ass.

She called the band's publicity office and stressed, in her best imitation of Wendy, that they'd better *stay there* until she arrived.

Back on the parking lot Birmingham called a highway, she dialed up a Cheatin' Hearts album and plugged her MP3 player into the car. She hated country music, but business was business. She might as well make use of this downtime to familiarize herself with the wildly popular songs that she'd been sent to secure more of.

Despite her dislike of their genre, she'd definitely heard of the Cheatin' Hearts before her wee-hour assignment. Everyone knew they should have won the Country Music Award for Top New Vocal Group their freshman year but were snubbed because they were an affront to family values. They were also something of an affront to Manhattan Music.

Word around PR circles was that they were conniving as well as raucous. They'd always denied lead singer and bass guitar player Quentin Cox's cocaine addiction, blaming his frequent trips to the emergency room on asthma or allergic reactions. After signing with the record company two years ago, the band immediately started a foundation for pediatric asthma and allergy research at a hospital just down the avenue from the Manhattan Music offices, as if thumbing their noses under the company's watchful eye.

By the time the convertible reached the next mountain on the trek toward the Cheatin' Hearts' publicity office, Sarah had made it through the group's first album and was listening to the second, *Ass Backwards*. She inched the car forward again, then examined a printout of the cover. Erin relaxed in a lawn chair in her Daisy Dukes, considering the muscular backsides of her three nude bandmates. Sarah was surprised Manhattan Music had approved this photo for distribution. Maybe Target plastered a big price sticker over the offending parts.

On the flip side of the cover, each band member was pictured individually, clothed, in a cowboy hat. All were about her age, thirtyish. She shuddered at the thought of *thirtyish*—her thirtieth birthday was coming up fast—then went back to her examination. Quentin had a piece of hay hanging out of his mouth. Erin winked false eyelashes. Could these people get any more cornball?

As if Erin's bleach-blond hair and the wink and the cowboy hat weren't enough to get the point across, she wore heavy eye makeup and a red push-up bra. Owen, the drummer with whom Erin was having her fling, was handsome, huge, and blond. His photo reminded Sarah of the pictures in the football game programs from her high school, with the linebackers trying to appear as tough and emotionless as possible, necks stiff, eyes elsewhere. Martin, the guitar player, apparently the musical genius of the group, looked like a mad scientist in crooked thick-framed glasses, despite the cowboy hat.

Sarah let her gaze return to Quentin's photo. Dark green eyes glared defiantly from under his hat brim. Long lashes framed and softened those eyes. A few boyish brown curls peeked around his ears under the hat. Surely he would have had those curls Photoshopped out if he'd noticed.

Sarah made a mental note to look up the photo on the Internet when she stopped in at her hotel room, and to e-mail it to Wendy, who needed a thrill. She and her husband Daniel had stopped having sex when Wendy was five months pregnant because they had agreed it was like Daniel was making love to a waterbed. Poor Wendy had only wanted to start a family with Daniel. She hadn't counted on the waterbed factor, the nausea, or the crippling sciatic nerve pain like a bullet in the butt cheek (she said) that had come to visit in the second trimester.

And Sarah hadn't been there to help Wendy through any of it, because she'd stupidly volunteered to save Nine Lives. She would have felt better if their friend and former trainee Tom had remained in the office, but he'd shipped off to save a client in Moscow about the same time Sarah left for Brazil.

She still remembered her shock at the way brave Wendy had looked in the LaGuardia ticket lobby when she'd driven Sarah there for the flight to Rio. Overcome with a wave of dizziness, Wendy had sat on a bench by the windows, both arms wrapped protectively around her middle, seeming uncharacteristically lost. She'd called Daniel to come rescue her. And when Sarah had returned from Rio this week, Wendy had been sitting in the same place, in the same position, this time because her feet were swollen, with her arms wrapped the same way around her much bigger tummy.

Sarah could *not* involve Wendy in the trouble she'd found for herself in Rio. She had a band to rescue and her job to save, all by herself.

She focused on the music again. The Cheatin' Hearts' songs were an odd mix. Erin and Owen co-wrote the overblown love ballads. Quentin probably should have seen a more intimate collaboration between the two coming: that Erin would cheat on him with Owen. Martin wrote the most complex and technically demanding songs, which tended to be minor hits and critical favorites. Two of his songs had won Grammys. He'd gotten into fistfights with the losers at the awards after-parties both years.

But their biggest hits were the ridiculous songs by Quentin. Even Sarah had heard these when they crossed over to the pop charts and became the background music in sports arenas. There was "I Want a Leia," about *Star Wars* or sex, according to how much smut your sense of humor could stand. There was "Heavily Sedated," which unfortunately was autobiographical. And then there was their biggest hit of all, "Come to Find Out," a colloquial term in Alabama for making an unexpected discovery: "Come to find out you done done it again / Come to find out I got screwed in the end / Shoulda known better there'd be no doubt / You done the mailman" (or "the mayor," or "all the neighbors," depending on the verse), "come to find out."

But every song had that unmistakable Cheatin' Hearts harmony: Quentin's strong, lazy voice on melody, Erin's high voice an octave above him, Owen singing baritone, and Martin anywhere and everywhere between, his voice transforming the chord mid-syllable. They didn't seem to use backup musicians, and they put out an enormous sound for four people. Sarah turned the car air conditioner down before she realized that it was the music making her hair stand on end.

Finally, *finally*, she pulled the convertible into the parking deck at the Galleria. Besides an enormous shopping mall, the complex featured Sarah's hotel and the building that housed the band's publicity office. She checked her look. Leather bag, ominously organized. High-heeled sandals, strapped on securely. Tight pants, clean and smooth. Cleavage, showing. Makeup . . . She examined her chin in the mirror on the visor. The scar Nine Lives had given her was going to show, but she'd minimized it as much as possible. Hair—

She sighed ruefully as she fingered her hair into place. Hot pink and platinum blond streaks shocked her natural brown. Even now, months after her impulsive makeover that had transformed her from sporty tomboy to vixen, her new look still caught her off guard when she got a glimpse of herself. She had a feeling that, even though her old hometown was a four-hour drive from Birmingham and her mother was rarely in residence, there would be a family reunion during her stay. And her mother would have something dry to say about her hair.

Leaning back against the seat, Sarah tried to relax into the part and channel Natsuko. Natsuko had been the publicist for a Japanese rock band performing with one of Sarah's clients at the Grammys last year. Everyone referred to her in awed tones by that single name, like Madonna, because nobody could pronounce her last name, or—more probably—because Natsuko was a force of nature. She wore low-cut tops, tight pants, killer heels, and blue streaks through her black hair, never afraid to outglitz the genuine stars. When she barked an order, the ultra-cool hipster rock stars who'd hired her snapped to attention and murmured placations to appease her. She was also something of a ho, having hooked up with two of the band members and a top reporter for *Rolling Stone* in the few days Sarah had kept tabs on her.

At first Sarah had been jealous of Natsuko. Then she'd fallen in love. Finally she'd had an epiphany. After years of clients pushing her around and Wendy telling her that dressing for work in something other than athletic wear might help, she knew what she wanted to be when she grew up. A few months later, when her husband told her he wanted a divorce, she'd grown up.

She'd channeled Natsuko for nine months in Rio. The new act had worked better than her old one for threatening rock star assholes, but it still seemed unnatural. This persona was very different from Sarah's normal one. Natsuko didn't have a mother, but had leaped fully armed out of the head of Zeus. She was taller than Sarah and infinitely more sophisticated. Her face revealed nothing, no vulnerability. She only arched one eyebrow when calling a bluff. She used her cleavage and, if necessary, sex appeal as a weapon. Consequently, unlike Sarah, she'd had sex with more than one person in her lifetime.

A car crashed across a seam in the pavement somewhere in the echoing parking deck, and Sarah started around. Then she berated herself, because Natsuko was never startled. Sarah was deathly afraid that Nine Lives would finagle his way out of prison and report to Manhattan Music about what she'd done to him. Worse, he would bypass going after her job and come after *her*. But projecting strength she didn't possess would salvage her job *and*—maybe—keep her safe. She dragged her bag out of the car, kicked the door closed, and walked to the office building entrance with the gait of a no-nonsense bitch used to high heels, humming "Come to Find Out."

～

The guitar dropped out of "Naked Mama." Quentin glanced up from the strings of his bass to see what was going on. Martin had stopped playing and was reaching to a nearby music stand for his cell phone. Now that the rest of the band had stopped playing their instruments, too, Quentin could hear Martin's phone beeping "Stars Fell on Alabama."

With a groan, Owen hurled his drumsticks at Martin and the phone. Quentin jumped backward in reflex, nearly dropping his bass guitar. The sticks narrowly missed Martin and Quentin, flew over Erin's head, and clattered against the glass wall of the sound booth. The album technicians in the control room ducked instinctively.

Quentin was fed up, too. The track had sounded great until they were interrupted. "What the hell," he protested. Then, realizing he'd cussed in front of the elderly couple watching from the control room, he said, "Pardon me, Mr. and Mrs. Timberlane."

The Timberlanes were Quentin's next-door neighbors. Occasionally, when Quentin let them know he'd be home from tour for a few weeks, recording with the Cheatin' Hearts in his basement, the Timberlanes sent their butler to complain about the noise. It was impossible they'd actually been disturbed. The sound booth was so well insulated that the music could hardly be heard in the kitchen upstairs. So Quentin always invited the Timberlanes over to sit in the control room.

Seems he guessed right that they just wanted in on the action. Instead of looking offended at his language, Mrs. Timberlane smiled serenely and Mr. Timberlane winked at Quentin: *Thanks for letting me take my chick on this hot date.*

"It was Rachel," Martin said. As Quentin turned, Martin was straightening his glasses, which immediately fell crooked again, as always. He returned the phone to his music stand. "Our esteemed record company hired one of those crisis management types to keep the band from breaking up. She's at the PR office *right now.*"

"To keep the band from breaking up," Quentin repeated, hoping he sounded incredulous. He lifted off his bass guitar, set it in its stand, and circled his stiff neck to pop it. For the past month, he'd worried constantly about the band breaking up. But that would happen only if the other band members knew what he knew—and that was exactly why he didn't want some specialized public relations consultant poking around.

Erin told Quentin, "This is your fault."

Quentin reached to the wall and turned off the sound into the control room before he challenged her. "Why is it *my* fault? The record company checks on us once in a while."

"This is not a regular record company check-in,"

Martin said ominously. "She honestly thinks the band is breaking up because you two are doing it"—he gestured between Erin and Owen—"and you're jealous." He pointed at Quentin. "You took it too far this time, Q."

"I did not," Quentin protested. After two years, he knew *exactly* how far to take the band's antics, gaining them the new fans he loved and frightening the record company he hated, without the record company sounding the alarm and sending an agent to spy on them.

At least, he'd *thought* he did. Now that the band actually had something to hide from Manhattan Music, maybe they should have behaved themselves for once. But he'd figured that would seem even more suspicious than their usual debauchery. So he'd set up all sorts of mischief for them in the past week.

He'd gambled and lost.

And he'd lost more than this wager. He was losing his edge. His near-death experience in Thailand must have affected him more than he'd thought.

"*You* fired our manager," Owen yelled at him from behind the drums. "*You* made us delay production on the album. *You* engineered this thing between Erin and me. It's too much at one time. Now we've got the Evil Empire up our ass." He stood.

Quentin made a fist, ready for anything.

But Owen passed Quentin without taking a swing at him. He stomped out of the sound booth, slammed the glass door behind him with a sickening *crack*, and jogged up the stairs toward the kitchen.

"That broke something," Quentin said.

"If that didn't," Erin squealed, "this will." Too late, Quentin saw her moving toward him with her hand out. He was used to the sting of her slap, but this time it jammed his glasses painfully into the side of his nose.

Martin came around the drums to catch Erin from behind and pull her crashing into the cymbals.

The Cheatin' Hearts suddenly looked more like professional wrestlers than country music superstars. Which was appropriate, since they'd practiced these moves a thousand times.

Quentin pressed his fingers to his skin to stop the bleeding, wishing the fake fight was a little more fake. Later Erin would claim she'd put on the show for the album technicians in the control room. It was always someone like a technician, supposedly on their side, who was the unnamed source in the tabloid story about the band's behavior. Feeding stories to the tabloids was almost as important to their careers as putting out new music, in Quentin's opinion.

But he suspected that this time, Erin had just wanted to hit him. It had been a hard month.

"You could let me take my glasses off first," he growled at her. Of course, he shouldn't complain. Whenever he fake-fought Owen, he really let Owen have it. Good to get some aggression out. Lord knew they had plenty.

Pulling away from Martin, Erin mouthed behind her hand at Quentin, "I'm sorry," and stuck out her bottom lip.

Quentin laughed and mouthed, "S'okay."

"Let me go fetch Owen and make up for our lovers' quarrel or whatever that was supposed to be." Erin passed Quentin and pulled the door. It didn't budge. She turned to Quentin and said, "The dumbass actually broke it."

With a sigh, Quentin stepped forward to try the door for Erin. It was stuck. He gave it a good jerk and heard glass breaking. One of the technicians got up and was able to open it from the outside. Several shards of glass and a loose screw fell onto the floor.

Erin jogged up the stairs after Owen. Despite the stories they'd leaked to the media, Owen and Erin's brand-new romantic relationship was fake. Even Quentin and Erin's long-term affair was fake. In reality, Erin and Quentin had broken up for good two years ago, before the group had signed with the record company. But that didn't mean he couldn't enjoy the sight of her running up the stairs in very short shorts.

After she disappeared, Quentin remembered the Timberlanes and hoped they weren't horrified at the band's fake violence and real damage to his house. He punched the intercom button. "Mr. and Mrs. Timberlane, would you like some more iced tea?"

They shook their heads. Mrs. Timberlane was smiling and patting Mr. Timberlane's knee like she was thoroughly enjoying this date. Mr. Timberlane kissed her forehead.

Erin led Owen downstairs by the hand. Owen closed the door to the sound booth behind them and unsuccessfully tried the handle, like he didn't believe he'd broken it (typical). The Cheatin' Hearts resumed recording, but the session was ruined because their concentration was lost. They all anticipated Martin's phone playing "Stars Fell on Alabama," signaling more bad news. Finally the call came, and Quentin reached over to turn off the sound to the control room again.

Martin's eyes were wide behind his crooked glasses. He unclapped the hand over his mouth to announce, "The PR chick is enormous and scary, with pink hair."

Owen said, "She sounds like a girl Wookiee."

"She's headed this way," Martin said ominously.

Quentin took off his glasses, rubbed his eyes, touched the wound on the side of his nose, and slid the frames back on. "I guess I'd better go put my contacts in." Part of his job as the band's front man was to look as studly as possible. He hoped his glasses didn't make him look as nutty-professor as Martin, but he knew they made him look nerdy enough, which was why he never wore them when meeting with record company representatives or starting bar fights that would be photographed for the tabloids.

"It's more serious than that, Q," Martin said angrily.

Quentin quickly looked around on the floor for something non-electronic that wouldn't cause a fire when he ripped it up and threw it at Martin. Martin had no right to lecture Quentin about the band's serious troubles.

Luckily, before Quentin could bust up more of his house, Martin was saying, "Okay. Love you, too. Bye."

He clicked the phone off and informed the others, "The Wookiee used the word *imbroglio* in conversation."

"What does that mean?" Erin asked.

"She's onto us," Quentin said.

"It'll be fine," Erin said soothingly. "We'll do the burly hick act."

She was right, of course. They couldn't turn on each other with this PR she-monster approaching. They had to face her head-on. Quentin turned the intercom to the control room back on just long enough to dismiss the technicians for the day. Then he stepped around the piano and over a mass of cables to huddle with the others. "Okay, we'll show her that we're tight-knit, so she'll be satisfied that we're not breaking up, and repulsive, so she'll run screaming from the state and leave us alone."

"Sounds like she doesn't scare easily," Owen said.

"Whose turn is it to get drunk?" Martin asked.

"It's my turn," Quentin said, "but you know me. I'll blow our cover. Let me get drunk at something that doesn't matter so much, like the Fourth of July concert. That means it's Erin's turn."

Erin shook her head. "We were going to record 'Barefoot and Pregnant' tomorrow, Q. I don't want to be hungover when I'm recording something with that much fiddle in it."

"It's for the greater good," Quentin told her.

"It's *your* turn," she responded with more heat than he thought this issue deserved. "You can get a saline IV in the morning and be okay. I'll be sick for two days."

"Fine." He shrugged.

"But don't start laughing and crack us all up," Owen warned him.

"I'm telling y'all," Quentin said, "if I'm getting drunk, you have to be prepared for certain things."

"And remember Rule Three," Martin added.

"You think I'm going to *sleep* with the PR rep sent by the *record company*?" Quentin exclaimed. "She's a Wookiee."

"Let's get to it," Erin said impatiently. "I don't think I have any alcohol in the house. Do y'all?"

"We have a six-pack," Quentin said. "Not enough."

"Do we have time to go to the store?" Owen asked.

Martin said, "She'd already left the Galleria when Rachel called." He glanced at his watch. "Traffic's died down. She'll be here any minute."

Quentin said, "Owen, take the Timberlanes home, and ask them if they have some liquor we can borrow. Martin, find cards and poker chips."

Owen pulled the glass door of the sound booth, which didn't budge. Mr. Timberlane rose from his seat in the control room in slow motion to open it. Then Owen followed Mr. and Mrs. Timberlane up the stairs at a glacial pace. Martin, in a show of forethought that had been rare for him lately, waited with his foot propping the broken door open until Quentin put his own foot in the space.

Quentin watched Martin climb the stairs, then turned to Erin, who was packing her fiddle away. "I'll go put in my contacts." He paused. "You should take your bra off."

"You wish." She sashayed toward him with her fiddle case. "If I take something off, everyone else does, too." She snapped her fingers. "That's it! Strip poker. That'll scare this lady away."

"Excellent," he said, and kissed her forehead. Then, because they were alone now, he added, "Let me see them."

Unperturbed, she batted her eyelashes at him.

"I can't catch any kind of break today," he said dejectedly, holding open the sound booth door until she walked under his arm, then mounting the steps to the kitchen after her. It really was disturbing. No one in the group was allowed to have sex with Erin—that was Rule Two. But she'd pretended to be his girlfriend on and off for the last two years. That had made for a lot of very pleasant PDA. Even in private, if he teased her and asked to see her breasts like he used to when they were dating, she would at least flirt back. After Thailand, he'd told her to pretend to break up with him and choose Owen instead, but he hadn't foreseen that she'd take her fake flirting with her.

They all met a few minutes later on the back patio in the evening heat. Quentin and Martin had taken off their shorts and thrown them in the pool, and Erin had stepped inside the house to take off her bra, by the time Owen arrived with a wooden crate he set on the outdoor table.

He pulled out a small box and tossed it to Quentin.

Over-the-counter sinus medication, expired ten years ago. "Mrs. Timberlane is worried about your allergies," Owen explained. Next came a dozen tomatoes from the Timberlanes' garden. Finally, in the bottom of the crate, Owen reached several dusty bottles of tequila. "The Timberlanes took a trip to Mexico in the seventies." He handed one of the bottles to Quentin. "Get started, Q."

Quentin broke the seal on a bottle, unscrewed the top, took a swig, and grimaced. It was for the greater good, he reminded himself, but he hadn't wanted to get drunk tonight. He'd wanted to have one beer, bake some bread, and retreat to his Fortress of Solitude to read the latest issue of *Clinical Immunology and Allergy Today*.

He was in for a long night.

2

Quentin's a coke fiend, eh? That's too bad. Well, thanks anyway for e-mailing his pic. First impression:

GOOD LORD.

Let me study it. Perhaps I was too hasty.

Okay, GOOD LORD.

Is that a stalk of straw in his mouth? O that I were this straw. Caution be damned, I might just let him sniff coke off my naked belly. Though it would be a long line, because my belly is the size of Brooklyn.

Wendy Mann
Senior Consultant
Stargazer Public Relations

Sarah clicked her phone off and tucked it into her bag, shaking her head. Now in her ninth month of pregnancy, Wendy clearly felt the heat. *There but for the grace of God go I*, thought Sarah, telling herself she wasn't jealous of Wendy.

Sarah had parked in the brick driveway of Quentin's gorgeous old Spanish Colonial mansion. The rest of the group lived elsewhere in town. According to Manhattan Music, they were all staying with Quentin to record the album. In the past, Quentin's girlfriend Erin would have moved in with him while the other two men stayed in the guesthouse out back. But now that Erin had switched boyfriends, she'd also switched residences, staying with the drummer in Quentin's backyard. Judging from the look of Erin in her push-up bra on the album covers, the wonder was that the group hadn't had *more* problems over the years, and that all three men hadn't been tossing her around like a baseball.

Two enormous pickup trucks filled the mansion's garage. A pink Native American dream catcher hung on the rearview mirror of a red Corvette, obviously Erin's, pulled to one side of the driveway. Sarah wondered where the fourth vehicle was. Considering their behavior, one band member or another might have lost his license. But if that were the case, she would have known, because the event would have made the Cheatin' Hearts Death Watch in the Birmingham newspaper.

Sarah had found out about the Death Watch through Rachel, who headed the Cheatin' Hearts'

PR office. A tall African American woman with imposingly long dreads, Rachel looked the part of no-nonsense caretaker of the band's reputation, such as it was. Something had been fishy about her protectiveness of her employers, though. She didn't have much of a poker face. When Sarah had raised one eyebrow at her, she'd confessed that she and Martin had dated in the past.

And when Sarah asked Rachel to fill her in on recent events, Rachel very practically handed Sarah a scrapbook of the Cheatin' Hearts Death Watch, which was more complete and informative than the dossier Stargazer could have compiled with any amount of digging. This feature of the newspaper's entertainment section had started two years before, just as the band made the move from local favorite to national debut act. It had run weekly in the past, but more often lately because there was more material to work with.

Fistfights between the band members broke out onstage with such regularity that some fans reportedly came to witness the violence rather than the billed attraction, as if it were a hockey game. Besides these events, the rundown for the year so far was this:

In January, Erin and Quentin broke up because he had an affair with the band's manager. Quentin overdosed on cocaine—or went into shock after eating an almond, depending on whether you believed the press release—and stayed a day in an Oklahoma City ICU. The band had to reschedule a week's worth of concert dates. Quentin and Erin got back together.

In February, the band embarked on months of overseas tour dates, with plenty of partying in between. Quentin and Erin broke up. Owen was shot in the shoulder in a bar fight in Crete, with more delayed concert dates. Quentin and Erin got back together. Quentin and Erin broke up. Martin was arrested for public indecency in Osaka. Quentin and Erin got back together.

In May, thankfully, the world tour ended before anyone was killed, and the band was scheduled to return to Birmingham to record their third album. Instead, they took a detour to the beach in Thailand. Quentin overdosed on coke again. Or had a life-threatening allergic reaction, whichever. This time he was kept alive on a ventilator for several days. His first act on emerging from the ICU was to fire the band's manager.

Quentin had recovered sufficiently in time for the band to attend the Academy of Country Music Awards. Erin wore a tiara, a bikini, trashy high-heeled wedges, and a beauty contest sash printed with the band's name in glitter. Arguably this was an improvement over her outfit the previous year, a dress from Target.

Last week, Erin had played a Mozart concerto with the Alabama Symphony Orchestra to benefit the Cheatin' Hearts' pediatric asthma and allergy foundation. Even the very worst spoiled stars had a children's foundation, Sarah had grumbled to herself as she read this installment. And every computer-enhanced musician thought she could play with the orchestra. But apparently there really was some substance to Erin's talent. Her concerto drew a sold-out crowd, earned her multiple standing ovations, and garnered local critical acclaim and amazement. Martin attended the performance—without Rachel, so they'd been apart at least since then. Quentin didn't show. Later that night, Erin and Owen were spotted out together at a trendy restaurant, clearly *together*.

Then, two nights ago, as Martin and Quentin were escorted out of a local bar by police, Martin told reporters that the band probably wouldn't make the July 1 deadline for recording their album, due to "malaise."

But of course, after all the negative PR, even this hadn't been the straw that had broken Manhattan Music's back. It had been the phone call tipping them off that Quentin would quit the band, tearing apart this cash cow of a country supergroup, before they delivered their third album. Sarah was beginning to wonder whether the whistle-blower was Quentin himself, heartbroken by his friends' betrayal, lost in a fog of drugs, desperate for help. She was determined to find out.

Steeling herself for her confrontation with the band, she gave herself one last experimental glare in the rearview mirror and stepped out of the convertible with her bag. Shouts and laughter drifted from behind the mansion. They knew she was here because she'd identified herself to an intercom at the gate. She stepped across the driveway, onto slate flagstones between lush plantings that bespoke money, around the side of the mansion, and into a back courtyard with a large pool.

"Welcome to the house of cards," a man called to her from a table where the four band members sat. Then, "Ow! Who kicked me?"

Erin jumped up and hurried toward Sarah with a loud *schlop* of flip-flops. She wore the Daisy Dukes—that wasn't just a costume for the album cover, apparently, but everyday wear—and a minuscule T-shirt with no bra for her ample bosom. And a necklace with a small diamond cross, which Sarah thought understated and strange for a redneck woman.

"Thanks so much for coming!" Erin exclaimed in a chipmunk voice, the high harmony for the group. Sarah could see why the men loved this blond, tiny-voiced, big-breasted girl. And she felt that familiar envy from high school, fresh as yesterday, of beauty queens who were easy with boys.

Erin tilted her head to one side, long blond ponytail curling around one breast. "We're sorry you came all this way for nothing. Everything's great with us. And as you saw when you met Rachel, we don't need any help with publicity."

"Erin," Sarah said pointedly, "the only publicity the Cheatin' Hearts have had this year is bad publicity."

The three men, whom Sarah could see dimly through the dusk, guffawed and clapped appreciatively. One of them yelled, "Better than nothing!"

"I disagree," Sarah called back.

Erin gave Sarah a cute pout. But Sarah thought she detected a calculating look in Erin's blue eyes as she chirped, "Well, have a drink while you're here! Quentin makes a mean margarita." She drew Sarah by the hand to the table. "This is Quentin, and Owen, and Martin," she said.

"I'm Sarah Seville."

The men stared dumbfounded at Sarah. Her heart raced. She was used to meeting celebrities, but it was strange to study them all day, then finally meet them, larger-than-life. Especially stars as handsome as these. And after spending years as a mousy jock and only nine months as a sexy PR diva, she still got a small thrill from being gawked at.

Quentin's eyes met Sarah's, then slid rudely down to her breasts and back up. He meant to intimidate her. But he wasn't doing a very good job. His wide green eyes gave him the look of a small boy at the circus for the first time. She felt her envy of Erin melting away, replaced by power.

All at once, the three men were scraping back their chairs and standing.

"Take mine," a voice said in her ear—the strong melody from the albums, Quentin. A chill coursed from her ear down to her toes. "I'll get you a drink," the melody added.

By the time she'd turned to him, he was walking toward the house, ethereal in the strange light of sunset. All she could see were the ancient deck shoes that looked like he might have bought them the last time they were in style—middle school—and a pair of cargo shorts, and a loose green T-shirt. But she knew from the album cover that an incredible body was hidden underneath the ratty clothes.

"Play with us?" the big blond, Owen, asked in his baritone voice. His shirt was off, baring his muscled chest and the gunshot scar on his shoulder—his souvenir from Crete. He nodded to the table. In addition to margarita glasses in various stages of emptiness, poker chips were piled at each place. The center of the table was crowded with a stack of hundred-dollar bills and Erin's jewelry—everything but the diamond cross.

"How much?" Sarah asked.

"Thousand," Owen said.

Quickly Sarah considered her options. She needed to ensure Quentin's stability and extract an album from the band, pronto. She couldn't afford to waste time drinking with these reprobates. But partying with the stars was often the best way to get to know them and earn their trust. As long as she didn't let things get out of control. And she wouldn't.

Not this time.

Careful not to bat an eye, she sat in Quentin's chair and pulled her checkbook from her bag. She had plenty of money in her account, but it would be nice if she could expense this. Making a mental note to ask Wendy about company policy on expensing bets, she poked her check into the pile of money.

"And when you've lost all your money, stripping," Martin added. His thick-framed glasses were iconically crooked. Oddly, he was wearing a long-sleeved shirt in the sticky humidity, and had opted to take off his shoes instead. Sarah glanced in the other direction and noticed the clothes floating in the pool.

Great. The Cheatin' Hearts were trying to distract her, shock her, do anything with her but discuss their infighting and their missing album. That was okay. She would beat them at their game tonight, which would put her in a better position to threaten them tomorrow.

"All right, but my shoes aren't going in the water," Sarah said. "You don't know what I go through to find comfortable heels."

"Amen." Erin half stood to high-five Sarah across the table.

A sharp *crack* sounded on the flagstones. Sarah's heart skipped a beat. But she managed not to look around wildly for Nine Lives. He was in prison in Rio. He wasn't following her around Birmingham, making loud noises.

Calmly, she turned with the rest of them to see Quentin closing the door to the house with one hand, carrying an empty margarita glass and a full pitcher in the other. He stooped to pick up the folding chair he'd tossed out the door.

"Where are you staying, Sarah?" Martin asked conversationally.

"The hotel at the Galleria," she said. "Closest place to your public relations office."

"I wish *I* could live at the Galleria," Erin said dreamily.

"One more album," Owen said, "and I'll *buy* you the Galleria."

Quentin scowled, but he didn't say a word. He placed the glass on the table in front of Sarah, poured her a margarita from the pitcher, and unfolded his chair beside hers.

After looking uneasily from Owen to Quentin, Erin told Sarah, "I didn't mean before that we don't want you here. It's just that we solve our own problems, as a band. We like Rachel handling our publicity because she knows us. You're an outsider. We're afraid you'll learn some personal stuff about us that we wouldn't want to get out."

"Like what?" Sarah asked.

"If we told you," Quentin said, shuffling the cards and beginning to deal, "it would be got out."

Cards slid one by one into the wet ring on the table in front of Sarah as she sipped her margarita. God, it was good, sweet and sour and cold. After negotiating two airports, driving through traffic, and extracting information from Rachel about this troubled band, the margarita hit the spot. She could already feel the alcohol relaxing her tense muscles. She said casually, "Your employer's contract with *my* employer stipulates that if I reveal private information about you during or after our time together, you can sue my ass off. I do hope you had your employees in the PR office sign the same sort of waiver."

The Cheatin' Hearts blinked at her.

She leaned forward. "Who's the brains of this outfit?" she pressed them. "Did you have your employees sign a waiver—"

"Yes, we did," Owen said.

With one carefully manicured fingernail, Sarah thunked a firefly off her bare shoulder. "Of course, Rachel cares too much about you to cross you, with or without a waiver. I'm surprised the two of you aren't tighter, Martin. I know you're not dating anymore, but she wouldn't tell me why, almost like it's a big secret."

"There's no secret," Erin said, patting Martin's hand protectively. "They just don't want to talk about it with a stranger."

Maybe Erin didn't know the secret, either. But Sarah saw the panicked look Martin shot Quentin. Quentin didn't return the look. He was either too smart to react and give away whatever the secret was, or too stupid to know there was a problem.

Sarah suspected the latter. As Quentin picked up his cards, he asked her, "How d'you like the big ol' salty 'Ham?" He spoke in a thick Southern drawl similar to her mother's, but without the class.

"You mean your lovely little town?" Sarah sipped her delicious margarita. Mmmmm. "I can stand the heat." She looked at her cards. Nothing. She threw away three and asked Quentin to deal her three more. Still nothing. Erin, Owen, and Martin folded. Sarah raised.

Now Quentin stared her down, trying to decide

whether she was bluffing. She met his gaze and got the chance to study him in person for the first time. His T-shirt was printed with a fire-breathing dragon, the mascot for the local university. Some people were fans of a college's athletic teams without ever attending school, she supposed. The shirt was so well loved that a layer of faded white fuzz showed on top of the green material. His eyes had looked intense on the album cover, but against this shirt, in only the weak floodlights from the mansion now that the sun had set, she could have sworn his eyes were *dark* green, like a Southern pine forest. With the alcohol massaging her skin and this handsome hick speeding up her heartbeat, she liked her job a lot more than she had for the past nine months.

"Call," he said, throwing in his chips. "Let me see them." This must have been an inside joke because, inexplicably, Erin slapped his shoulder.

Sarah turned up her cards, and he turned up his. Drat, he'd won. She wished *she'd* won the first hand, setting the tone for her relationship with the band. No matter, though. She'd be winning before they were through.

Quentin raked the chips toward himself and winked at her. "Good start. I wonder how many clothes I'll get off you by the end of the night."

She smiled. She knew he was a cocaine addict from the country. The stars who'd never had money were the ones who got into the most trouble when they suddenly made it big. And he was flirting with her to get even with Erin. Erin took him back again and again, and would again, as soon as she tired of Owen. If the band didn't break up first.

But Quentin had an infectious pleasantness about him. Even now, as he half propositioned Sarah, he didn't gaze at her in narrow-eyed lechery. His face was open and friendly and focused, and he looked absolutely *delighted* to be sitting next to her. She almost wouldn't mind losing this game to him.

Almost. Soon it was her turn to deal, and she enjoyed the Cheatin' Hearts' stares again as she flipped the cards expertly. She'd played quite a bit of poker in her career as babysitter to the stars, and she was the daughter of bridge players. Before long, Martin's socks, Owen's shoes, and Erin's ponytail holder were bobbing in the pool, and Sarah hadn't lost so much as an earring. Quentin hadn't lost any clothes, either, but now Sarah had most of the chips.

They were an easy take. Erin kept asking Owen what to do. She was either a novice or a coquette. She also pretended to be more drunk than she was. In fact, Sarah wasn't sure Erin was drinking at all. She put her margarita to her lips occasionally, but the level in the glass never changed. Owen was constantly distracted by Erin. His eyes slid to her after every play.

Martin did seem to make an effort at winning hands, and his face fell every time he lost. Sarah wondered again about the long-sleeved shirt he still wore in the oppressively hot night. He was awfully thin, too. She'd seen every bit of his well-formed posterior on the cover of *Ass Backwards*, and he'd probably lost twenty pounds since that photo shoot.

And then there was Quentin, who seemed considerably more drunk than the other three. As the night went on, he paused longer and longer before making decisions, as if his already slow brain was slowing more.

Finally, Erin called for a bathroom break. Owen followed her inside the mansion. After the door closed, Quentin said smoothly, "So, Susan," grabbing both Sarah's wrists in his big hands.

"Sarah," she corrected him, trying to conceal her disappointment that he'd forgotten her name. Of course he was just another drugged-up singing star, but she was crushing hard on him by now. She twisted her wrists in his grasp gently to extricate herself without causing a fuss.

He let her go and settled for holding her hand loosely on her knee, his fingers always moving, rubbing up and down her fingers and circling on her palm. Electricity shot up her arm. "What's your favorite Cheatin' Hearts song?" he asked her.

"You want me to name one you wrote," she said coyly.

He kept drilling his dark green eyes into her and electrifying the palm of her hand.

She was enjoying him a bit too much. She could hold her liquor, but that margarita was clouding her judgment, if flirting with this out-of-control celebrity seemed like a good idea. The time had arrived to back him off. She said, "'Come to Find Out' is pretty amusing. It's unusual to hear a country song about backdoor action." When he gave her a confused look, she prompted him, "'Come to find out I got screwed in the end'?"

He let her go in surprise. "I never thought about it that way," he said slowly.

Now Sarah missed the constant tease of his hand on her hand. She knew she was feeling the margarita, but she couldn't stop herself. She hadn't had this much fun in a long while. She baited him, "Do you come up with your album titles and covers? Are you an ass man? Because that seems to be a recurring theme."

"I am now." His gaze flicked down to the region of her thigh. He cocked his head to let her know he was considering her bottom. Then his gaze returned to her face.

"Good God," Martin grumbled. "I have to be more drunk than this before I like to watch." He poured himself a margarita out of the pitcher.

Sarah came back down to earth. "Excuse me," she said, recovering her dignity. She clopped across the flagstones in her heels and passed Erin and Owen tickling each other on their way out of the mansion.

In the bathroom, Sarah clung to the marble counter and stared into the mirror at her pink highlights. She needed to concentrate, remember why she was here, and develop a plan. Without calling Wendy. She didn't want to drag Wendy any further into the mess she'd made for herself at Stargazer.

So. She wasn't getting the feeling she'd expected from the group. She'd thought at first that the drunken party would quickly devolve into a three-way fight among Quentin, Erin, and Owen, with seemingly levelheaded Martin refereeing.

Tension definitely filled the air. But some of it was a result of Sarah's presence and the fact that Quentin was coming on to her. It made sense that the others in the group would want to stop Quentin from hooking up with a PR expert sent by the record company, which would create even more tension. They were about to be in hot water for missing their album deadline, whether they broke up or not.

What was absent, other than the one time Erin had slapped Quentin on the shoulder for no apparent reason, was tension directly between Quentin and Erin. Likely there *was* sexual tension between them, and Sarah wasn't detecting it, despite her honed senses. She'd gone through this with bands before. The members spent so much time together, knew each other so well, and were such good friends or archenemies, that they conveyed messages to each other without saying a word.

Or Quentin could be just as close to leaving the group as the mysterious caller had warned Manhattan Music, but the band was covering up their troubles to get rid of her.

At any rate, she would get to the bottom of it. She could use Quentin's passing attraction to her to edge closer to him and find out what was going on.

The problem with this plan was that she liked Quentin a little too much. Enjoyed his cheesy pickup lines. Thrilled each time he touched her hand. She couldn't be sure at this point, but she didn't *think* it was all because of the tequila.

She convinced herself that she was doing a great job for Stargazer. Natsuko would act aloof from the likes of Nine Lives, but upon encountering someone handsome and friendly like Quentin, she would flirt. Seduce. Make a pretense of following through.

Sarah would never actually sleep with a drug addict. Or anyone she'd just met, for that matter. Natsuko might not, either, but she would at least respond to Quentin and lead him on. Otherwise, the whole band might sense that Sarah wasn't a scary bitch after all, but a marathon runner who'd just learned to apply makeup at age twenty-nine.

She knew how she could make this work. Quentin hadn't been drunk when she got there. But she'd taken note of every sip he'd consumed since she'd arrived, and by now he was more inebriated than such a big man should have been. He couldn't hold his liquor at all—which was the opposite of what she usually saw in hard-partying musicians. Whatever the reason, she intended to take advantage. After a few shots of tequila, it would be lights out for him. Just before that happened, she intended to be very much in his way.

She took a deep breath and let it out slowly, watching her badass and not entirely familiar reflection in the mirror. A year ago, she wouldn't have dreamed of cooking up a scheme like this or placing herself so dangerously close to a star. Even nine months ago, after her makeover, she wouldn't have done it. But her experience with Nine Lives in Rio had changed her. She had no husband, no social life—and if she didn't make a bold move to save her job, nothing left to lose.

She headed back out to the game, pausing in the kitchen. Through the glass-paned door, she glimpsed Erin walking along the pool's edge. Erin watched the men to make sure they weren't paying her any attention. She held her margarita glass low and behind her, then dumped its entire contents into the water.

What the hell was going on here? Too much to figure out in one night. Best to file it away for later: *Erin hides sobriety from men.* Sarah let Erin think she'd gotten away with it. She waited until Erin sat back down with the men before she exited the kitchen and returned to the poker game herself.

As Sarah took her seat, Quentin touched her hand. "I was about to come in there after you."

"I'm fine," she assured him. "And ready to get you undressed."

He smiled at her as he dealt. In fact, he couldn't seem to tear his eyes away from her for long. Cards fluttered onto the flagstones and into Erin's lap amid shouts of, "Q! Earth to Q!"

The others folded. Sarah squared off against Quentin again. He stared at her long and hard, considering whether to call her bluff.

"You've been awfully quiet tonight, Q," Erin remarked. Perhaps she was jealous of Quentin's attentions to Sarah.

"Strategery," Quentin said with a straight face. Sarah couldn't tell whether he'd seen the *Saturday Night Live* imitation of George W. Bush or he really thought it was a word.

He looked at his cards, then looked at Sarah. His dark green eyes pierced her eyes, caressed her cheek, paused over her lips, stroked her neck, lingered at her cleavage. He had the audacity to tilt his head to make sure she knew he was contemplating her ass again. This was good for her bluff, though. The longer he stared at her, the closer she came to forgetting she held only a pair of threes.

"'Let the Wookiee win,'" Owen quoted *Star Wars* in a bad British accent.

"I fold," Quentin said finally, throwing two eights on the table.

Sarah turned her cards over.

"Oh!" the others moaned, and Quentin laughed. And laughed, and laughed, and started everyone else laughing because he was laughing so long. Sarah recognized that infectious laugh. A full thirty seconds of his laugh ended the album *In Poor Taste*.

"*Damn*, woman," he said finally, brushing away the tears at the corners of his eyes. "That's some poker face. I got lucky the first time, and no luck since."

"Story of your life," Owen said. Erin giggled more loudly. Quentin's eyes flickered toward them.

"You bluff well, too," Sarah told Quentin, although she suspected it was easy for a blissful ignoramus to look noncommittal.

"Course, you ain't as inebriated as we are," he said, pouring her another margarita. He paused. "Inebri— Is that a word?" Now he faced her full-on, knee to knee with her. He stroked his fingers from her scalp all the way down to the ends of her locks.

She shuddered under his touch but didn't dodge it. Flirting with this intense man was exciting and frightening and something Old Sarah never would have done. The tequila helped, too.

"I really like your hair," he growled. "Did you know that?"

She shook her head, but not hard enough to shake her hair out of his hand.

"It changes when you move." He slid his fingers down a blond strand and held it next to her cheek. "You're a blonde." He did the same with a brown strand. "You're a brunette." She suppressed shivers of anticipation as he touched her scalp one more time and selected a pink strand. "I don't know what you call *this*." He smiled at her. "I ain't never seen nothing like it."

"It's pretty normal in New York," she assured him.

"Let me clue you in on something," Owen said. "Pink hair isn't normal *anywhere*."

Erin hit Owen's chest and said, "Rude," at the same time Quentin said, "Do you mind, dumbass? I've got something going on over here."

"That's what worries us," Martin said.

Ignoring Martin, Quentin stroked Sarah's hair again. "It's like that ice cream with all the flavors. Napoleon."

"*Neapolitan*," laughed Erin, Owen, and Martin. Now Quentin was laughing, too, and Sarah laughed along. She wasn't *really* Natsuko, and never would be. She had no *real* designs on Quentin. But wouldn't Wendy just die if Sarah ended her yearlong celibacy by having a fling with this handsome idiot, bringing the grand total of her sexual partners to two in her lifetime? If only everything were different. If only he wasn't a coke addict, he wasn't a stupid hick, she wasn't trying to keep him together with his band, and she wasn't contracted to his record company, she would have had the most delightful decision to make: to ho or not to ho.

~

Martin's mouth was moving. Quentin switched off the blender so he could hear what Martin was saying.

"—the matter with you?" Martin asked, leaning against the kitchen counter. "Drunk?"

"It's hard to play dumb this long at a stretch," Quentin said. "I may go cross-eyed." Of course, he *was* also drunk, and he knew it when, pouring margaritas from the blender into the pitcher, he asked Martin casually, "Would you do her?"

"I *knew* it," Martin scolded him. "You can't do her. Rule Three."

"I'm not going to *do* her," Quentin said, putting down the pitcher and holding up his hands. He shouldn't be pursuing this at all, but he was so full of this girl, this beautiful pink-haired manga she-villain. "I'm just asking, hypothetically, would you?"

"Yeah," Martin said quickly as Owen stumbled in from the bathroom.

"Yeah, what?" Owen asked.

Quentin turned to Owen. "Would you do her?"

Owen looked shocked. "Who?"

"The Wookiee, dumbass," Martin said. "Who did you think? *Erin*?"

"I can't do Erin," Owen said self-righteously. "Rule Two."

"So," Quentin pressed, "hypothetically, would you do her?"

Owen asked, "Who?"

Quentin and Martin looked at each other.

Owen clarified, "The Wookiee?"

"Yes!" Quentin and Martin said.

"Oh. Yeah, I'd do the *Wookiee*." Owen picked up the pitcher and walked toward the door to the patio. "But she's frightening."

As Owen passed through the doorway, Erin came in. The two of them rubbed against each other and laughed in a way that made Quentin uncomfortable. If he asked, they would say they were touching because Sarah could see them from the table outside. But Quentin wasn't so sure. He and Erin had played lovers and yet resisted each other for two years. Surely Erin and Owen had been able to resist each other for a week of pretending? Of course, when Quentin had faked a relationship with Erin, he'd also had the band manager on the side. Owen hadn't been in a steady relationship in a couple of years.

Erin snapped Quentin out of his thoughts by asking sharply, "What have you boys been talking about in here?" Then, in a complete failure at an imitation of a man's deep voice, she asked, "Would you do her?"

Martin laughed and went outside, leaving them alone, as Quentin told Erin, "*No*, that's not what we were talking about, and I'm offended that you would assume such a thing. We're not shallow. We were talking about the potential impact of current unemployment figures on US Treasury note prices."

Erin grinned. "If you're not interested in Sarah, then you won't want to hear what she said about you."

Quentin's gaze darted outside to Sarah at the table. She and Erin must have had a girl talk. Oh God. "What'd she say?"

"It looks good for you," Erin teased him. "It's a shame you're not allowed to have sex with her."

"*What'd she say?*"

"She said you're cute. You remind her of Ernie from *Sesame Street*."

"Ernie," Quentin said, nodding. "Good guy. Jolly prankster." He paused. "Not the sexiest fellow."

Erin smiled smugly. "Better than Bert."

"Speaking of Bert," Quentin said, searching her innocent blue eyes, "you're not breaking Rule Two with Owen, are you?"

She grimaced and stuck her finger in her mouth, as if to say *Gag me*. Then she asked brightly, "Did we fool you? We've been working hard on it." She tilted her head and considered him. "You're drunk."

He gave up. "I guess."

"Come on." She took him by the hand and led him back outside to Sarah.

Sarah. Sexy white high-heeled sandals. White pants that flared at the bottom and tapered up to hug her perfect ass. A black blouse that pooled in the front to reveal her cleavage, and in the back—well, there *was* no back, just some thin strings keeping the front on. He could have reached behind her and bared her with a few tugs. Clearly no bra. Red lips. Crazy hair.

With a twist. She gave the first impression of being tall, unattainable, hardened. But he'd studied her while calling her bluff. She was average height or smaller. The longer he gazed at her, the smaller and softer she got. Her eyes were brown and gentle. And her name: *Sarah*, like a sigh.

And the way she said his name. Not *Quentin*, enunciating every consonant. Soft and lazy and half-gone, *Que'n*. He detected the slightest Southern drag on her voice, from somewhere far south. Maybe Mobile, with old money.

And a nasty scar following the line just under her

chin, as if the soft girl playing hard had gotten in over her head at least once.

He was sure the punk Amazon attitude was an act. Despite the fact that most of her was showing, he didn't see a tattoo on her anywhere. If she were who she'd seemed at first, there would have been a heart in flames on her lower back. He didn't feel annoyed or threatened by her deception. He was thrilled that she'd attempted to play a player.

And he was eternally thankful that he had the good luck to be single. He was the logical one to pair off with Sarah, whereas two weeks ago, when he was still pretending to be with Erin, it would have been Owen who was unengaged. As he thought this, Quentin balled his fists—then realized what he was doing and tried to relax. He needed to stand down. Neither he nor Owen could be with Sarah, ever, because that was against Rule Three. But still.

He'd had the idea to hand Erin off to Owen last year, reasoning that a love triangle among the band members would be terrific tabloid fodder. But he hadn't insisted on it until he'd decided to fire their manager, Karen, so she wouldn't find out about Martin's drug use and spill the beans. They'd never let her in on the band rules. She'd believed Quentin and Erin were (mostly) together. This had kept her at arm's length, expecting nothing but a good time with him.

Karen had been beautiful. Karen had been smart. Karen had even been a pretty good manager. She'd been able to steer the band through all the crises they'd made up, and some they hadn't. Karen had been an excellent lay. But Karen didn't have that—

As he sat down beside Sarah at the table, she looked up at him with those dark-fringed brown eyes and smiled.

—*spark*. "I swear you're just as sober as you were when you got here," he told her, making sure she could hear his disappointment.

"Tequila doesn't make me stupid, I'll give you that." She touched his knee. "It does make me loose. How about a shot?"

Quentin raked back his chair again and ran inside. He brought out one of the bottles of tequila and two shot glasses and poured for each of them, ignoring the looks he was getting from Erin and, you know, whomever. Who cared?

"To loose," he toasted Sarah.

She clinked his glass with hers and said, "Lautrec."

Toulouse-Lautrec, 1864 to 1901, he remembered from a college art history class twelve years before as he downed the shot. He had to be careful or something like that would come out, and then they'd be forced to build an even more elaborate facade to explain to Sarah that he was some kind of idiot savant.

She picked up the bottle of tequila and examined the label curiously, but she didn't seem drunk. She was beating everyone at poker. Of course, *he* was drunk, and during the next hand he lost to her again and had to throw his shirt into the pool, yet he was still coming in second. But that was because Martin sucked at poker, try as he might to keep his long-sleeved shirt on. Erin was pretending to suck at poker. And Owen, on top of sucking at poker, was pretending—at least he'd *better* be just pretending—to give all his attention to Erin.

After a few more hands, Quentin told Sarah, "I hope you're still getting loose, because you ain't getting stupid, far as I can tell."

She winked at him over her cards. "Tolerance. I spent the past nine months in Rio with Nine Lives."

"Oh boy," Quentin said. He wished she'd mentioned this when he first brought out the shot glasses.

"The rock star?" Martin asked. "I thought I read in the paper that he's in jail down there."

Owen gave Sarah a thumbs-up. "Good job." Erin hit him.

"He went to jail on day two hundred seventy-five." Sarah sounded irritated. "I kept him out of jail for the first two hundred seventy-four. You try it."

"I feel better," Quentin said.

Sarah poured two more shots, downed hers, and pointed at Quentin's. "Are you going to drink that?"

"What do you call him?" he asked her. "Nine, or Mr. Lives?" He knocked back his shot.

"Either, if you're having sex with him."

Quentin spit out his shot, just managing to hit the patio rather than Erin's bare leg.

Erin squealed, "Gross!"

Unfazed, Sarah refilled Quentin's glass. "If you're not, Bill."

Quentin knocked back the shot again and said, "You ain't answered the question. What do *you* call him?"

She grinned at Quentin. "Bill."

He let his eyes travel lazily from her crazy hair down her curves to her high heels. "That's a little hard to swallow."

Erin stood up. "Q, I'm on empty. Come help me make more margaritas."

Quentin sighed. Usually he didn't mind cooking, but these people acted like they couldn't even make themselves a ham sandwich. And he was busy getting in Sarah's pants. "Step one," he said, "take lime juice from freezer— Ow!" Erin was pulling his hair. "Don't move," he called to Sarah as he followed his hair into the kitchen.

Erin pushed him against the oven and stood with her hands on her hips. "What are you doing? Are you trying to break Rule Three and get kicked out of the band and leave me with these two nutcases?"

"Y'all have got to let me break Rule Three," he pleaded. "Just this once. You have to admit this is special."

"*You* made the rules," Erin said. "If the rest of us can't break them, *you* sure as hell can't."

Quentin sighed. "But she's so pretty."

"I know." Erin patted his chest sympathetically. "And it's so cute to see you happy. You're staring at her like you can't *believe* it."

He laughed at the accuracy of that statement. And kept laughing.

"Lay off the shots," Erin said. "We shouldn't have made you get drunk."

"It's too late now." He laughed.

The door opened. Sarah walked in behind Erin and leaned against the refrigerator. Quentin stepped toward her.

Erin scowled at both of them, then went back out to the pool, wiggling three fingers above her head.

Sarah touched the side of her nose and asked him, "What happened right here?"

He touched his own nose, feeling the fresh scab from earlier that evening. "Erin slapped me. What happened right here?" He traced a line under his chin equivalent to her jagged scar.

She didn't touch her own chin.

Holy cow. A shadow descended over her as he watched. He reached out to her scar. She turned her head away, murmuring, "Don't."

Fascinated to find a genuine hard part in the soft girl, he bent to kiss her.

She opened her mouth for his. She tasted of tequila and sweetness, and he wanted more. He held her against the cold steel of the refrigerator and let his lips travel down to her neck, around to her ear. When she shivered, he pressed his whole body against her to warm her.

He didn't stop when the kitchen door opened and Martin called back outside to the others, "Q's kissing the Wookiee."

Sarah tried to pull away from Quentin, but against the refrigerator, she didn't have anywhere to go, and Quentin was determined to stay with her.

Owen shoved his shoulder hard, sending him into the middle of the kitchen.

"Owen," said Quentin in warning.

"Quentin," said Owen in the same tone.

"Owen," Quentin said again, and burst out laughing. Owen rolled his eyes.

"I'll make margaritas," Quentin suggested, vaguely remembering the pretense Erin had used to bring him into the kitchen. He waited for Owen and Martin to back slowly out the door. Then, as he gathered ingredients, he explained to Sarah, "They don't want anything to happen between us. The record company sent you, and our relationship with the record company is contentious."

What was he saying? As he got more drunk, he was having a hard time editing out words longer than five letters. But maybe Sarah wouldn't notice, because his drawl got worse and made him sound more backwoods the more he drank. Or so he'd been told. Like he could tell.

She edged up to him while he ran the blender. When he flicked off the icy roar, she put her hand to the waistband of his shorts and slipped one finger inside. "I don't want to be a Wookiee," she said seductively. "I want to be Leia. Like in your song."

Oh shit, she was *coming on* to him!

He glanced outside through the glass-paned kitchen door and saw Erin, Owen, and Martin each holding up three fingers. *Rule Three.*

"Let's go finish these guys off," he said, filling the pitcher and grabbing Sarah's hand.

It didn't take long. Martin was clinging to his long-sleeved shirt for the time being, but Owen was down to his tighty-whities. Erin must have decided it was time to intimidate Sarah with her nakedness, because she threw the next hand and lost her shorts.

Quentin knew from experience that the sight of Erin wriggling out of her shorts was pornographic. He shielded his eyes and turned toward Sarah.

Sarah smiled. "You can look."

"That's right generous of you," Quentin said, "but I'd get slapped. Again." After the shorts flew into the pool and Erin safely sat down again, he turned back to the table.

Erin also lost the next hand. "T-shirt, thong?" she asked. "It's not really a choice."

"Why don't you take a dip in the pool, and we'll count that," Quentin suggested.

"Good idea," Martin said.

Owen looked like he was going to murder everyone.

They all turned to watch Erin walk slowly, seductively down the pool steps, swim underwater to the side, and climb slowly, seductively up the ladder, long blond hair slicked back, soaked T-shirt clinging to her breasts. She called, "Does this mean I'm all in?"

"I think we *all* are," Martin said.

Now they were watching Quentin expectantly. Right. The burly hick act. He was supposed to start a fight. "I'd like to *get* all into that," he called to Erin. It was a lame line, but the best he could come up with under the circumstances.

Owen jumped up, fists balled. "That's it! Come on!" he hollered at Quentin, sounding and looking as threatening as he could manage in his underwear. Martin ducked away from the table. Erin splashed out of the pool to pull on Owen's arm.

Quentin stood and said quietly to Sarah beside him, "Move, please." With a quick push on the edge, he heaved the table over.

Instead of dashing its contents across the patio like it was supposed to, the table kept going, and the whole thing fell into the pool. It floated there upside down for a few seconds, then sank.

"Well, *that's* never happened," he said, then started to laugh. He didn't mean to laugh when they were supposed to be fighting, but Owen looked so *serious* that it was hilarious.

"Oh no," someone said.

He kept laughing and couldn't stop. Then Owen laughed, and Erin grinned, and Martin shook his head, and Sarah looked at them like they were all from Dagobah.

Erin jumped back into the pool, swam deep down, and brought up handfuls of chips and money and jewelry, which she dumped at the edge.

"Oh, honey, you don't have to do that," Quentin said, leaning over the side. "I'll do it. Or maybe it'll come up in the filter."

"It's okay," she said. "I'm already wet. Back away from the side, Q, before you fall in." She went under again.

"I should go," Sarah called.

"Oh no!" Quentin jumped up, nearly fell down, and braced himself on her shoulder. He was damned if he was going to get drunk and make a fool of himself and be hungover tomorrow for nothing. His beautiful pink-haired girl, gone. "You shouldn't drive."

Martin sifted through the growing mound Erin had retrieved from the pool bottom. He handed a short, soggy stack of bills to Quentin and a thick stack to Sarah, along with a torn check.

Sarah waved her wet hundreds at Quentin. "Taxi," she said.

"No, no. If it comes to that, I'll call my car service for you." He put his hands on her shoulders and bent to whisper in her ear, "It doesn't have to come to that. Stay the night with me."

She shook her head no. "I was tempted earlier, but I don't think you're truly as attracted to me as you've led me to believe. You just tried your best to start a fight over your ex-girlfriend."

"That was out of habit," he insisted. "I was only pretending to look surprised when the table fell in the pool. This is what we always do at parties. At Christmas we throw a sofa in the pool. For Thanksgiving we put a chair in the bathtub. You should come back for St. Patrick's Day one year."

They both backed away from the pool as Erin climbed up the ladder.

"Let's get you out of those wet clothes," Owen said, ogling Erin's boobs and exchanging a fake look of desire with her that Quentin found too convincing.

As Owen pushed her toward the guesthouse, Erin stopped to whisper in Martin's ear, her hair streaming water on the flagstones.

"How am I supposed to do that?" Martin asked her. They were talking about Quentin.

Erin whispered to Martin again, then let Owen direct her toward the guesthouse with his hand on her thong.

"Stay with me," Quentin repeated to Sarah.

"Quentin," Martin said in warning.

Quentin said in the same tone, "Martin." Martin had a lot of nerve reminding Quentin not to break Rule Three. They both knew Martin would break Rule One sometime in the next eight hours. Quentin attempted to give Martin the evil eye, and ended up laughing instead. Oh well. "Come on, beautiful," he said, tugging Sarah's hand.

"I can't," she said. "I mean, I can't do *that*. But maybe I could stay awhile longer, and we could talk."

"Talk?" Quentin puzzled.

"Or sing," she said. "I haven't heard you sing in person, after I've come all this way to save your band."

"My band doesn't need saving," he lied.

"Oh, come on." She squeezed his hand. "Don't you love to sing? Why else would you make a career out of it?"

"Hm." They both took several steps back to avoid the splash as Martin dove into the pool, still wearing his boxers and long-sleeved shirt. After a few seconds, he appeared in the shallow end with the table in tow and attempted to wrestle it up the steps.

Suddenly, after all the lies the band had told to Sarah and each other tonight, Quentin felt compelled to tell her the truth. Or he was so drunk, he was afraid he'd get caught if he told another lie. "I love to sing with the band," he admitted. "I love performing for a crowd, the bigger the better. I thrive on the energy."

He must have been grinning like a jackass eating sawbriars, because she nodded expectantly and gave him the most beautiful smile.

"But I don't serenade nice young ladies one-on-one," he explained. "That would be weirdly vain of me. I'd rather find out more about *you*."

"I guess I'll go back to my hotel, then." She reached for her bag slung over the back of her chair.

"But for you, I'll make an exception," he said quickly. He tugged her by the hand toward the house—more gently this time, so he wouldn't scare her—and called over his shoulder, "Good night, Martin. Good luck with that."

"Fuck you," Martin called back.

Quentin led Sarah through the kitchen and down

the stairs to the control room. By the time they landed
on basement level, he had the first few lines and a tune
in his head. He amazed himself by still remembering
to flick off the control room light before he pulled her
into the sound booth, so the glow around the edges of
the door upstairs wouldn't give away to Martin where
they'd hidden themselves. He wanted to impress this
beautiful woman. He wished he could do more, but it
was enough that she wasn't leaving yet.

It couldn't have impressed her, though, that he didn't
have perfect pitch like Martin. He sang, "You lost your
shirt / I ain't lost nothinnnnnnnnnnnn," holding out the
"nnnnnnnnnnn" and fumbling around the piano keys
until he figured out the note he sang was a G. Great!
He and the key of G-major were buddies. "Sit down,"
he told Sarah, taking his hand off the high end of the
keyboard to pat the piano bench beside him. When he
felt her warmth at his elbow, he played and sang what
was in his head, a simple progression of one chord, four,
five, one, repeat, with pretty fills between the lines.

> *I lost my shirt.*
> *You ain't lost nothing.*
> *I lost my shoes.*
> *You ain't lost a thing.*

He glanced at her. She watched him with serious
eyes. Serious called for replacing the major ones in the
middle with minor sixes, so sad.

I want to go
Up into my bedroom.
You had to choose.
We ain't had a fling.

Now a money note in the melody, up to the higher G.

I want to know
Why I can't get lucky.
Need the queen of hearts
Always draw a king.

Now the end. The first line repeated the melody he'd established, but the other three lines took a detour into quiet darkness, stopping on a question mark of a major four that made audiences uncomfortable and won Grammys.

I lost my heart
To a lady from the city.
I asked you to dance.
You asked me to sing.

The vibration of the piano strings lifted, leaving him and Sarah alone together.

"I love the way it ends, down low," she said softly, sexily, nearly a whisper. "I didn't expect it to go there."

"Yeah. You try not to get too repetitive. Go in the opposite direction from what your instincts tell you, to shake it up. Martin taught me that." Martin had taught him a lot in the twelve years they'd been friends. And now that Martin really needed him, Quentin hadn't been able to do shit.

"Is it on the new album?" Sarah asked.

"This song? I doubt I'll remember it in the morning." That said, Quentin started through the chord progression again. If he could commit it to his sloshed memory, maybe Martin could do something with it.

"You mean you made that up while we've been sitting here?"

"Sure, can't you tell?" he asked over the chords.

"In retrospect, yes. As I was hearing it, I was just thinking it was very appropriate to the situation."

"Very appropriate, and it sounds super drunk. 'Strip Poker Blues' ought to be a jaunty two-step. This is a melancholy ballad." He looked over at her. Her brown eyes were huge, and her hair in every color fell soft around her heart-shaped face. "Because you turned me down."

She smiled kindly. "We can't hook up, Quentin. I get the distinct impression that would drive the band apart. I'm here to keep you together."

"We're not breaking up," he said to his hands spread across a four-octave B-minor chord. He wished this were true.

"You know what?" she asked. "Let's call it a night. You seem really tired."

He laughed. "I seem really drunk. I'm so sorry. I'm a terrible drinker. They made me get drunk because it was my turn."

She was standing beside him then, with one small hand on his shoulder. "I'll help you to your room."

He grinned up at her.

"And that's all," she said sternly. "Promise me, Quentin. I've had a client before who wouldn't take no for an answer."

"Is that where you got that scar?" he asked.

Her big eyes, so soft before, were two cold points boring into him now.

"Sarah," he said gently. "Nobody in this band will hurt you. There are a lot of things wrong with us, but that isn't one of them. You're safe here."

"I feel safe here," she said.

"Good."

After a pause, he felt her tugging on his upper arm. "Well, I said I'd help you," she murmured, "and I will, like I would help a sumo wrestler."

"Sorry. I'll help you help me." He stood, braced himself against the piano with a smashing of the lowest octave, and held out his hand for the door to the control room. He reached the handle and pulled. The door didn't budge.

"Fuck," he exclaimed. "I love Owen. I love him like a brother. I do not want to murder him."

"Problem?" Sarah asked.

"It's a mantra I repeat to myself in the hope it will come true someday," he said. "Owen broke my door. We're locked in."

"Oh." Sarah stepped forward and pulled the handle herself. He didn't blame her for not believing him, after he'd tried to seduce her repeatedly. "Isn't there an intercom to the control room?" she asked.

"Yes." He hit the button. "MAAAAAAARTIIIIIIIN," he hollered, but he knew it was futile. "The speaker's turned off out there, though. And Martin's gone to bed"—*or was shooting up*—"in a guest room on the ground floor on the other side of the house, so I doubt he'd hear us even if the speaker was on." Quentin turned to her with an apologetic grimace. "What a shitty welcome to Birmingham."

"Oh, hush, it's fine," she said with such grace that he almost believed her. He wondered again whether she was Southern, and tried in vain to remember what had given him this impression in the first place. She was moving around the room, gathering the pads that draped over the stands and drum set and piano while the band was away on tour. She made a pallet in the corner and held out both hands to him. "Here."

He stumbled immediately, but Sarah had him, and somehow maneuvered him until he was lying in softness and squeezing his eyes shut against the bright light overhead. He heard her whisper, "Hold on." He felt rather than saw the lights go out. A cymbal crashed as she tripped in the darkness. Then she was stretching out beside him. He inhaled the sweet smell of her hair and spread his hands across her skin.

3

Sarah started awake.

At least, she thought she did. Her eyes felt wide open, but the room was black. Her nightmares hadn't been dreams after all. Nine Lives had locked her up where she'd never be found—

And then she remembered where she was as Quentin sighed behind her. His hand, which had settled inside the waistband of her pants and electrified her as she dozed off, now moved lower. His fingertips stopped at the edge of her mound.

She took a deep breath through her nose, careful not to move enough to wake him, and exhaled, relaxing into his arms. The heat from his bare chest burned her skin where her shirt parted in the back. She'd told him a few hours ago that she felt safe with him, and she did. He'd assured her he wouldn't hurt her, and she believed him.

But that didn't mean her heart was safe. His song for her—a song rendered sad not by their missed hookup, but his depression about Erin, she was sure—was regardless the sweetest thing a man had ever said to her. Which didn't say much for her seven years of marriage to Harold, she realized. The tingling in her lips from his expert kisses earlier in the night hadn't faded, either. As she listened to his deep, even breathing behind her, she half wished, perhaps three-fourths wished, that everything were different, and that they had made love.

He was good-looking. He was funny. He was vibrant, emanating a life force that had penetrated her and made her feel more alive, too, as she sat next to him getting drunk. Or maybe that was the alcohol. No, she'd never felt the life force while drinking vodka with Nine Lives.

She would have enjoyed hanging out with a good-looking, funny, vibrant man in any case. But it was Quentin's gentle control that reached inside her and pushed her buttons. He'd tried to hide it from her, but she'd understood the group dynamic by the end of the night. Owen, Erin, and Martin looked to Quentin before making a move. He didn't return their looks, but everything pointed to him as the group's leader.

Which must have made the betrayal hurt that much more when Erin cheated on him with Owen.

He was accustomed to controlling them. And he controlled himself. Sarah thought back to the near fight, when he turned over the table. He'd clearly gotten drunker than he was used to—he'd told her later it was "his turn." He'd been in a rage, understandably jealous as Erin and Owen flaunted their new love in front of him. And he *still* had the wherewithal and the courtesy to say to her, "Move, please," before he threw the table into the pool.

Move, please. Maybe he was worried about more than her physical safety. Maybe he could tell how far gone she already was. In his direction.

Or toward the Alabama coastal town where she'd grown up. He reminded her of the high school boys who wore cheap cologne and long bangs and ironed jeans with their shirts tucked in when they dressed up special for dates. Not that Quentin had long bangs. His haircut was such an unstudied mess of brown waves that it couldn't technically be considered a haircut.

It was more the Southern drawl that was familiar, and the insolence with which he eyed her. She'd seen that look many times, but it had never been directed at her, and she'd wanted it. She'd wanted one of those cheap cologne dates and had never had one. She'd smelled the boys when they played basketball with her, smelled their hot sweat. Then, on Saturday night, she would go to the movies with her friends. The boys would be there with their dates, wearing their cologne, eyeing those other, luckier girls lustfully. The scent would stab through her.

No, she told herself. Sex with Quentin would be a disaster. She was trying to stabilize him, not wreck the band. The Erin situation was precarious. And Sarah was beginning to believe the band's problems ran even deeper than she'd been told. The only reason she could think of that Martin would hold on to a long-sleeved shirt from hot night to strip poker to pool was that he needed to hide his track marks. Tomorrow morning she would have a talk with Quentin about Martin's drug use. And Erin. And every lie he'd told her.

But for now . . . Now that she'd lain asleep with Quentin, she was afraid she'd fallen even further for him. She'd lived with Harold for so many lonely nights. Even their most romantic evenings together had ended with them parting ways perfunctorily and leaving the middle of the bed empty. Harold claimed Sarah had the metabolism of a racehorse and made him hot—in a bad way—if he held her while they slept. A man had never held her in the dark, embracing her like he treasured her, sliding his fingers closer to her sex as the night grew older.

The placement of Quentin's hand gave her an idea for how to shock him into telling her the truth in the morning. But here in the dark, disoriented without her phone and lost in time, she might as well enjoy it. She slid her own hand on top of her fly until it covered his hand beneath the material.

Her blood heated as his fingers curled against her.

She wondered if she could stir the passion in him that he'd felt for her at first. Carefully she pressed her ass against his groin—and then tried not to gasp as he nuzzled her neck in his sleep and dragged a rough kiss along her jaw.

He grew still again, holding her more tightly than before. She didn't dare make another move lest she get more of what she wanted than she was bargaining for. She simply enjoyed the sensation of being caught in his heat, because she would never get so lucky again.

~

"Q! Where's breakfast?"

This time, Sarah knew she was awake. The sound booth was brightly lit. She recognized the acoustic tile on the walls. She'd grown familiar with the feel of Quentin's hand in her intimate area.

And, looking up toward the voice that had woken her—looking way, way up—she saw a very irate Erin standing over them, fists on her hips, her eyes on Quentin's wrist disappearing into Sarah's pants.

An emotion passed across Erin's pretty face. Sarah knew fear when she saw it.

And then Erin was padding across the sound booth in her bare feet. A music stand scraped across the floor. Erin dragged it into the doorway to prop the door open. She jogged up the stairs, calling, "They're both down here. I told you."

Sarah was surprised that even with all the noise and the lights flicked on overhead, Quentin hadn't moved. His fingertips burned her mound, setting her body on fire. She felt guilty that she was enjoying his touch so much—especially after seeing Erin's horrified look. Erin did not want to lose Quentin. Not for good.

But Sarah's guilt quickly turned into defiance. Erin *had* chosen Owen over Quentin, at least for the time being. Sarah *was* almost divorced. She and Quentin were both single, practically speaking, and they could sleep together if they wanted, even if it was only on the sound booth floor.

She sat up carefully so his hand stayed in place but she could look over at him.

He breathed evenly through his nose, one muscled arm flung above his head. He looked boylike, innocent. And there wasn't a tattoo on him. If he were who he seemed, there would have been barbed wire around his biceps.

She reached down and moved her fingers gently across his hot skin, tucking a stray curl behind his ear and feeling a flash of protectiveness for him. She hoped she could help him with his drug problem. Although the thought wrenched her aching heart, she sincerely hoped she could help him get back together with Erin. His repeated breakups with Erin over the past few months must have torn him up inside and fed his desire to escape into drugs—which, ironically, might have led Erin to choose Owen instead. Sarah stroked Quentin's handsome face, his features at peace for a few moments more, as she plotted exactly what she would say to him.

He woke. His stubble scraped her palm, and his lashes fluttered open against her fingers. He gazed at her sleepily, smiling a slow, beautiful smile.

All at once he pulled his hand out of her pants and

gaped up at her in shock. "I'm in big trouble," he muttered.

"I hope not," Sarah said. "We didn't use a condom."

He stared at her, uncomprehending. "That's crazy," he mumbled. "I always . . ." He closed one eye, squinting at her. Then switched eyes, with no better luck. Then pressed his fingertips to his brow. Finally he said, "Hold that thought," and rolled to his feet. He held out one hand to her and pulled her up from the floor.

He let her go to navigate her own way across the tiny room packed with equipment, and up the stairs. Someone had brought in her leather bag from outside and hung it on the back of a barstool in the kitchen. She snagged it as they passed, despite the fact that Erin and Owen glared at them from a few stools down.

"What were you thinking, Q?" Owen demanded. "What if you'd needed your inhaler while you were stuck down there with no way out?"

Halfway through the den that adjoined the kitchen, Quentin turned to shout at Owen in outrage, "What if you hadn't *broken my door*?" He held out one arm to Sarah, almost protectively, and waited for her to pass him. "Here," he said quietly behind her.

Obediently she turned and mounted another staircase to a hallway and kept walking past bedrooms and bathrooms.

"This is me," he said, stopping in a bedroom doorway behind her. "Just let me take my contacts out and we'll talk."

She pointed to a bathroom across the hall. "I'll slip in here for a second and meet you there."

He gave her the smallest nod. A troubled look crossed his face, as if he were angry with himself for not extending her that courtesy first. But now her imagination was running wild. Of all the unexpected things she thought he was and wasn't, it was too outlandish to think he was a gentleman.

She ducked into the bathroom and checked her phone. Wendy was worried about her. Sarah texted back, "I'm okay. More soon," then brushed her teeth and removed her makeup—the bare minimum of maintenance, because she was afraid of what Quentin might be snorting while she left him alone.

In his bedroom, she locked the door behind her, kicked off her sexy shoes, and settled in the middle of his luxuriously soft bed. Morning sunlight bathed her, and happy birds sang in the crepe myrtle outside the window. Over their chirps, from down a short corridor to the master bath, she could hear pills rattle in a bottle. Water ran. She heard no prolonged sniffs.

And then Quentin caught her off guard. He walked into the room with his shorts off, wearing only boxers printed with dog bones, plus wire-framed glasses that made him look studious. Ha. And strangely vulnerable, despite his muscular body.

He sat beside her on the bed and pulled her into his lap, with her legs straddling his waist. She was very aware that only his boxers and her pants and a wisp of panties separated her center from his naked groin. She tamped down her mixture of excitement and alarm. It made sense for him to touch her this way if he believed they'd had sex last night—which was exactly what she wanted.

He kissed the top of her hair and said soothingly, "I'm sorry. I have a headache. Let's start over. Tell me how you feel about the morning-after pill. I can call my car service for us, and we can go to the pharmacy right now. Actually, no, the paparazzi will follow us. We'll figure it out, though. You tell me what you want to do." He hugged her hard. "I'm so sorry. I'm a really bad drunk."

She felt horribly guilty for lying to him. It was the only way she knew to shove him off balance. And she needed him off balance for the talk they were about to have. But *oh*, it was even worse to deceive a playboy who turned out to be a decent guy, or at least talked the talk. She didn't like this side of Natsuko.

She looked him in the eye. "Quentin."

He gazed back at her, green eyes sorrowful now through his glasses.

She couldn't bring herself to say it.

"I know this is an important moment and all," he whispered finally, "but if we're just going to stare at each other, do you mind if I lie down?" He flopped back onto the bed and pressed the palm of his hand to his temple.

"Quentin," she started again.

"Ma'am."

"We didn't do it. You were asleep in five seconds."

After a few moments of silence, he said calmly, "That's a cold game of gotcha you've got going." He sat up and said, "Excuse me while I go scrape my heart off the bathroom floor!" His hand was still pressed to his temple, shielding one eye. His other green eye pierced her.

Then he started to laugh, because he felt relieved, or because he could laugh at just about anything, it seemed. "What is the *matter* with you?" he asked.

"I was just trying to wake you up—"

"It worked!"

"—and give you back some of what you've been dishing out. You served me a big margarita glass full of bullshit last night." She tried not to cringe at her own metaphor. Her mother would be horrified at the imagery.

Now he put down his hand and watched her with both green eyes wary. "What do you mean?"

"I mean, if you're a regular heavy drinker, I'm a horse's ass. And I'm not a horse's ass."

"So you drank me under the table," he said defensively. "But like you said, you've been drinking with Nine Lives, who eats brimstone for lunch and brushes his teeth with Drano."

She raised one eyebrow at him. "I'm going to give you thirty seconds to come clean with me. And then I'm going to call Manhattan Music and tell them there's no way you can have this album completed by

July first. I'm going to tell them that they should look around for a more dependable country act that can deliver as per contract."

"Okay," he said quickly. He grabbed her hand and stroked his thumb across her palm as he spoke. This was strange. Usually when she had the inevitable adversarial conversation with a rogue musician, the musician backed away from her emotionally, even physically. Quentin came after her, drawing her closer.

It was also strange because she usually felt revulsion at these spoiled stars and their chemical dependencies. This one definitely wasn't revolting. She tingled at the touch of his callused thumb.

"Normally we drink some," he said. "Not a lot. We take turns drinking at big events."

"I'm flattered that I qualify as a big event." She considered grilling him about Erin not drinking at all. But she was reasonably sure he didn't know this. She asked, "Why all the subterfuge?"

He looked confused. "Subter—"

"Why the big production of pretending to be an alcoholic and acting like a dumb hick who can't tie his own shoes? You may not be a rocket scientist, Quentin, but that song you wrote in two minutes last night while you were plastered is going to earn you several million dollars. Why put on this elaborate show for me?"

Now, finally, he drew away from her, dropping her hand and folding his big arms across his pecs. "Because the record company sent you."

"You want Manhattan Music to think you're red-neck drunks?"

"Of *course.*" He lay slowly back down on the bed with the muscle control gained from a million sit-ups. Then he patted the bed. Obediently she lay on her side. Now that her surprise attack was over, she ought to move to the leather chair across the room while they had this discussion. But if he felt comfortable with her this close, she supposed she could stand it.

Finding her hand again, he used his thumb to rub and gently tug the sensitive skin between her thumb and forefinger as he explained, "The band got together about five years ago. We worked at our day jobs all week and played gigs on the weekends. We scored festivals where we knew the record company scouts would be, and we sent in demo tapes, and it wasn't enough. We had this terrific, sexy fiddle player—"

Sarah's stomach turned over with jealousy. But this is what she wanted: for Quentin to be in love with Erin. This was good. It was part of the plan. *Let go*, said Natsuko.

"—and good songs," he continued, "and a great sound, and we still couldn't break down the door.

"Now, let me back up and say that my granddad was a banjo player, and my grandma played guitar. They toured all the honky-tonks in the South in the 1950s. Granddad always told me playing music wasn't enough to bring people in. He and Grandma did some grandstanding. They might never have made it big, but because of their showmanship, they got on as studio musicians in Nashville.

"Course, that still wasn't much of a living, and my dad resented getting dragged around the country and growing up poor. He always told me since my mom died from allergic asthma and I have the same problem, I didn't have any business trying to make it with a band. I needed to hold down a steady job, get health insurance, and take care of myself. A little over two years ago, I was so frustrated with trying to get a recording contract I was about ready to agree with what my dad had always told me and quit the band. Then somebody in the front row at a show smoked a cigarette, and I had an asthma attack."

"Oh no," Sarah said gamely. She wasn't for a second buying this asthma story the band had been feeding the press. Downstairs, Owen had mentioned Quentin's inhaler. Probably more preplanned subterfuge. But she didn't stop Quentin from telling her this tale. To protect the one lie, he might just reveal everything else.

"I had to go to the hospital," he said. "A rumor started that I was on coke. All of a sudden, we got attention. More people came out to see us play. The newspaper wanted to interview us. I kept telling the truth, but of course the louder I said I have asthma and allergies, the surer everybody was that I was on coke."

"Bastards," she said sympathetically.

"Well, that's what I would have thought if I was still listening to my dad," he admitted. "But my grand-dad had just died a few months before. I could see his whole career, this long span where he *almost* made it big. I could hear him in my head, talking me into it, telling me a little showmanship never hurt nobody."

"Uh-oh," Sarah said.

Quentin nodded. "We decided if you can't beat 'em, join 'em. If people wanted a hot mess with their country music, that's what we'd be. We started getting drunk and staging a fight at every concert."

"Staging a fight?" she repeated. "You mean the table in the pool?"

He took a deep breath, watching her, realizing he'd given something else away, and calculating how to back out of the admission.

She raised one eyebrow.

He sighed, giving in. "Have you ever heard of Mad 'Red' Mud?"

"The professional wrestler?"

"Yeah. He used to work at the steel mill over in Fairfield with Martin's uncle. He taught us some moves. We just try to keep Erin from getting hurt." Quentin shrugged. "Usually it goes more smoothly than last night. I *told* them I shouldn't get drunk while you were here. I tend to start laughing and lose my threatening scowl. Watch."

He showed her such a ridiculous scowl that she laughed herself.

"When we started setting up fights," he said, "our

local fan base increased, because we weren't just getting the country music fans anymore. We were getting the monster truck fans, too, the kind of folks who
pay cash money to watch shit crash. That's when the
local paper started a column called the Cheatin' Hearts
Death Watch. Have you seen it?"

"Yes, I've seen it. You act like you're proud of it."

"I *am*," he insisted. "That was a big break, because it
got Nashville's attention, and then Manhattan Music
came calling. Don't look at me like that. Put your eyebrow down." He reached out to touch her brow.

His other hand already held her hand captive in
a tingling dance. But something happened when he
reached toward her face and touched her gently. His
own expression changed. His green eyes turned serious
and dark.

Then he was kissing her. Astonishingly, she was kissing him back. She couldn't resist. His mouth took her
mouth. His tongue tangled with her tongue and slicked
across her teeth. She was embarrassed that she gasped a
little. Natsuko most likely had made out with someone
else this year and was used to this sort of thing.

He rolled on top of her, pinning her beneath him
with his weight. She started to push him off, remembering that she hardly knew him and he could be dangerous, despite how he'd reassured her last night—and
then his glasses fell onto her forehead. He laughed,
sounding embarrassed for the first time. He seemed
so young and vulnerable at that moment that she
laughed, too, to make him feel better.

He moved her wrists close together above her head so he could hold them with one hand while he tossed his glasses onto the bedside table with the other.

"So we got the contract with the record company," he said, and pressed his lips hard on hers again.

"But it was a tough fight," he whispered, biting at the corner of her mouth.

"And then we had to reneg— What's the word?" Through his cotton boxers and her silk shirt, his cock moved against her belly.

"Renegotiate," she breathed. "Stop the act. You know the word *renegotiate*."

He grinned like the devil. "We had to reneg—what you said—between the first and the second album." His tongue was inside her mouth again. Between this insistent pleasure and the pressure of the bulge shifting against her down below, Sarah had a hard time following what he was telling her.

He stopped kissing her to say, "And we're damn tired of giving the lawyers all the crumbs Manhattan Music throws us. We want to seem crazy enough that the record company is scared to mess with us. But not crazy enough that the record company sends you down here to spy on us."

His kisses deepened. Her body had never enjoyed a man's body more, but her mind spun with realization. He'd just called her a spy. He seemed to take perverse pleasure in keeping her wrists captive above her head while he tortured her. He thought he had her right where he wanted her when the reverse was true. Her job, her whole life as she knew it, was riding on what she did next.

She whispered against his lips, "What about Martin?"

He stopped stock-still on top of her for several seconds, then kissed her cheek, close to her ear. "I'm calling your bluff," he murmured. "What *about* Martin?"

"What is he doing? Heroin?"

~

Quentin rolled off Sarah and pressed his hand to his temple so his eyeball didn't fall out. He had one mother of a headache, which had gotten worse each of the many times in the past half hour that Sarah had threatened to ruin his life. It had gotten better each time he put his hands on her.

He'd almost kicked her out of the house after she told him they did it, and then told him they didn't. That was coldhearted of her. But it was hard to stay too mad at her when he *had* been laying the hick act on thick. And he didn't feel the least bit guilty about getting as close to doing her as she'd let him without actually doing her.

Funny to think he'd gone into the bathroom to take out his sticky contacts and put on his glasses so he could see the woman he might be having a child with. He'd been terrified that she was an ugly chick he'd just laid because he was drunk. He'd never had a one-night stand before, but he'd heard stories.

Well, as far as he was concerned, the one-night

stand with an ugly chick might be an urban myth. The night before, she'd seemed unreal, like an impossibly sexy comic book villainess from another universe. This morning, she was still a gorgeous pink-haired girl, only real, and warm, and barefoot in his bed.

And with superhuman powers of perception. He wondered what could have given Martin away. Maybe the long-sleeved shirt—it had been eighty-five degrees last night. He should talk Martin into linen. No, that would be enabling. But wasn't that better than—

"Do you want me to get you some painkillers?" Sarah whispered. She sounded genuinely concerned.

"I already had some." He looked sideways at her. "Please don't tell Erin and Owen about Martin. They'll kick him out of the band. We have a rule about that. No drugs."

"Really. Then why don't they kick *you* out?"

"Because I'm not a cokehead." Ironic that having asthma had lost them a potential contract two years ago, whereas his fake drug use had made them famous. And now that the band was established, he was willing to admit he had asthma, yet he was in trouble with her for using drugs.

She clearly didn't believe him, but that wasn't what concerned her now. Her dark eyes stared off. He could tell she was doing the algebra in her head. Cheatin' Hearts with Martin on heroin? Or Cheatin' Hearts without Martin? Which would make the record company more money?

She said, "Maybe getting kicked out would help Martin."

Like you care, Quentin thought, but it was important not to let her see how much he hated her. Or the record company that had sent her, at least. He rolled on his side and propped his head on one hand so he could look at her and hold his eyeball in his skull at the same time. With his other hand, he reached over and traced around her belly button where her shirt had fallen away. She jumped at first, then relaxed against his fingers.

"I've threatened Martin," he told her. "He promised me he'd clean up while we're in Birmingham, before the next tour. It's gotten worse instead. He has a steady dealer in town. But if I told Erin and Owen and we kicked him out, that wouldn't help *him*. He'd get depressed and use more. Believe me, I've given this a lot of thought. Martin had a girlfriend—"

"Rachel," Sarah said.

"Yeah," Quentin acknowledged, "but he lost her because of the drugs. There are only three things left he cares about in life." He tapped his thumb. "Music." He tapped his pointer finger. "The band." He tapped his middle finger. "Heroin. This isn't the first time Martin's gone off the deep end. I made drug use against band rules for a reason. At first it was the only way I would stay in the band with him. Now it's the only way Erin and Owen will stay. If they find out he's been using, they will *shit*. We'll have to kick him out of the band, and what's he got left?" Quentin put his thumb and pointer finger down.

Sarah stared at his extended middle finger, which represented heroin. Suddenly he realized he was shooting her the bird. He drew his hand back, but she caught it and held it in both her hands. Her brows knitted as she watched him. "I can tell Martin means a lot to you."

"Well, we've been friends since—"

He stopped himself before he said that they'd been assigned as dorm roommates when Quentin was a freshman in college and Martin was a sophomore. Or that they'd shared a tiny apartment on Birmingham's Southside when Martin was earning his master's in nursing and Quentin was starting work as a respiratory therapist. The record company thought Quentin was an uneducated hick. He sure wasn't going to show her his hand now.

"—since before the band got together," he finished. He smoothed his hand under her shirt. She didn't back away, so he cupped her breast and flicked his thumb back and forth across her nipple. She only parted her lips and breathed more deeply.

"Listen," he whispered, "I'd appreciate it if you didn't tell the record company about *any* of this. But I guess that's too much to ask. And I don't suppose there's anything I could do to persuade you." If she took him up on this proposition, he was going to be in trouble, since he had no intention of breaking Rule Three now that he was sober. But he was pretty sure she was playing him, after that pregnancy threat.

"It's sweet of you to offer." She shifted so that her breast edged away from his hand.

"I wouldn't take it as a hardship. I'm feeling real close to you right now. Five minutes ago, I thought you might be having my baby." He slid his hand back down to her flat belly to drive home his point.

Her face fell. "I'm truly sorry. Like I said, I was just trying to give you a wake-up call. As you woke up."

"Well, tit for tat. Except that your tit *was* a damn sight bigger than my tat." He chuckled. "I'm sorry, Susan. That sounds vulgar, doesn't it?"

If her face had fallen before, now it was utterly flattened. Her brown eyes wouldn't meet his eyes. He could see only her long, dark lashes. She pushed his hand off her belly and corrected him. "Sarah."

"Right, sorry again. Sarah." He hadn't expected her to react quite this way. He'd wanted to put her in her place, not crush her. He reached out to the scar under her chin.

Before he could touch her, she sat up in the bed. "Quentin," she said, all business now, "there *is* something you can do to persuade me not to tell on you."

"I'm listening." He expected the worst.

"Let me help you get back together with Erin."

He laughed. He stopped laughing when he saw that she was serious. He said, "That may be harder than it looks."

"I don't think so," she said. "You should have seen the look on Erin's face this morning when she discovered us in the sound booth with your hand down my pants."

He didn't need to see the look. He was going to have some explaining to do to the band about that. But he wasn't sure why that was any of Sarah's concern. "What do you care?"

"I don't care so much about *you*," she said. He wondered whether this was true, or whether she was getting revenge on him for apparently forgetting her name.

She went on, "I care about millions of dollars for Manhattan Music. The Cheatin' Hearts are about to hit the height of popularity. If Erin and Owen remain a couple and you quit the group, which you will, you'll say at first there are no hard feelings. You'll allow the group to continue to play your songs in concert. But eventually you'll refuse, and they'll fight it, and you'll drag them into court. Suddenly the Cheatin' Hearts are number one on a TV special about the biggest band fights ever, and a group of has-beens."

"I can't picture us suing each other."

"Band members never can at first. You're still together. When it sinks in that you're watching your childhood friend screw your girlfriend, you'll think differently."

He reasoned, "Then won't you be worried that Owen will quit the band?"

"No, he hasn't been with Erin nearly as long. Also, frankly, we're not as worried about him quitting as we are about the band breaking up completely, or about *you* quitting. You're the front man. And you wrote 'Come to Find Out.' Can you imagine a Cheatin' Hearts concert without 'Come to Find Out'?"

Actually, Quentin could. In Japan. The Japanese preferred Erin and Owen's ballads of unrequited love. But he saw where Sarah was coming from. And he understood now that the rest of the band had been right. The record company was terrified. He'd pushed too far.

"Owen has co-written all his songs with Erin," Sarah was saying, "which would give the band a stronger leg to stand on if you had to sue him for the right to perform them."

This all would make such perfect sense if it were true that Quentin, head throbbing, was almost starting to believe it. "What if I promised that we'll finish the album on time? Not that I'm trying to get rid of you. But we really don't like being watched. What if I gave you my word that everything's okay?"

"Your word?" she repeated. "Your *word*? Quentin, everything is *not* okay. Martin's addicted to heroin. You overdosed on cocaine, you fired your manager, and Erin cheated on you with Owen, all in the space of a month. And your album is due in six days, Quentin, *six days*, and the Nationally Televised Holiday Concert Event in support of said nonexistent album is three days after that."

"The tele— What?"

"Your Fourth of July concert at the statue of Vulcan."

"I'm sure it'll be fine," he said, stretching again. "We've recorded albums before. We play concerts all the time."

"That's not good enough." She tucked her pink

locks behind her ears and leaned toward him. "Let me explain something to you. Nine months ago, I volunteered for a job overseas. I thought that if I threw myself into it, I might finally get a promotion out of it. Instead, I botched it. Manhattan Music got Nine Lives' album, but I lost Nine Lives for them. He's in prison.

"My supervisor at Stargazer told me there was talk of firing me over this. She thought if I took another job for Manhattan Music and did well this time, it might salvage my rep and save my job. You give me my album, you have a nice Fourth of July concert, you make it look like you and Erin are on the mend, and I'll get my job security back. And then I'll be out of your hair."

Quentin closed his eyes. His head hurt.

"You *do* want Erin back, don't you?" she asked.

"Of course I do!" He was alarmed at the thought that she might suspect the deceit. He sure hoped his alarm sounded more like desperation. "I'm just not sure it's possible."

"The best predictor of future behavior is past behavior," Sarah said. "You and Erin belong together. You've shown that over the years. Naturally you'll make up. The only reason things are different this time is that the balance of power has changed. You always had your manager to run to when you and Erin broke up. Erin didn't have anybody. Now that you've fired your manager, *you* don't have anybody, and Erin has Owen. I know that makes your blood boil."

The thought of Erin and Owen together *did* make his blood boil, but not because he was jealous. He didn't want Owen taking advantage of Erin, and he didn't want a breakup fight between the two of them tearing the band apart. That's what Rule Two was for. He hoped again their playacting was as innocent as they claimed.

He had half a mind to tell Sarah all of this, to get rid of her. But he understood now she wouldn't go. Not until she got her album and they played the concert. And he was terrified she would drive Martin to rehab before he was willing, breaking up the band in the process. For good.

If her price for staying quiet was getting him back together with Erin, he would pay it.

"Right." He sat up despite his headache. "What's the plan?"

"We should let Erin think that we slept together last night, and that we're continuing to sleep together while I'm here. You'll feel like you've gotten some of your usual power back. She'll get more jealous as time goes on. I'll bet once you've gotten through this rough patch, you'll make up and your relationship will be better than ever. But my concern is that the band is stabilized long enough to record your album and play your concert. Stick with me until then. Can you do that?"

"I can do that."

He exchanged a long look with Sarah. After all that had transpired in the last hour, not to mention last night, she was as cool as ever, and as beautiful. Her hair was different now, glowing in the morning light and tousled in new directions. More blond than pink. With her face scrubbed clean of makeup, she looked younger, innocent, despite the crazy hair. Her soft brown eyes were the same.

He went to his dresser to pull out some clothes, then looked over his shoulder at her. She lay on her stomach on the bed with her elbows propped up and her chin in her hands, watching the show, one foot kicked up and swaying lazily in the air behind her.

"You had this planned all along," he said casually as he got dressed.

"Pretty much," he heard her say.

"Were you going to do me?" He hated to put it to her the way he put it to his friends, but he had to stay in character. He looked over his shoulder again for her reaction.

Even without his glasses, he could see well enough to tell that she didn't flinch. "I had a good idea you'd pass out," she said. "I have some experience with this."

"You wanted me to pass out," he accused her. "You suggested the shots."

She shrugged, refusing to deny it.

"What if I hadn't passed out, and we'd been awake, locked in the sound booth together, all night long?"

"Look, I don't think it's a good idea for us to sleep together," she said sagely. "We agree on this now that we're sober, right? We *are* trying to get you back with Erin."

"Fair enough," he said, glad for this excuse not to have sex with her. He couldn't explain Rule Three to her, that he couldn't have sex with record company spies, because that might give away Rule Two, that band members didn't sleep together. And he couldn't give her that. Then all his leverage to protect Martin would be gone.

"But you like to sidestep my questions." He crossed the room, knelt in front of her, and looked into her soft brown eyes. "Were you going to do me?"

Her eyes turned hard. He saw strong desire there, and frustration.

She looked down and away as she said, "Don't be cute, Quentin. You can tell how I feel about you."

He wanted more than anything to lean in and kiss those soft lips, kiss them into a smile again. But if he started, he wouldn't be able to stop. He stood, pulled his glasses off the bedside table, and left the room in a hurry.

As he was closing the door behind him, she called, "Quentin, one more thing."

He looked around the door at her.

"About the coke."

He said without emotion, "I don't do coke."

"Seriously. You stay clean until after the concert."

"I will."

"Great." She smiled at him, friendly, nonjudgmental.

He paused in the hall to collect himself before going downstairs, running both hands back through his hair. Besides the intense headache, he felt off balance, with every atom of his world turned upside down. Like when he got out of the ICU last month. But he also felt lucky that he hadn't made love to her, so he wouldn't get kicked out of the band.

And so he didn't know what he was missing.

4

Yes, if you'd had gambling losses, you could have expensed them, but only if the gambling had led to consummation. See the employee handbook, section 2, paragraph 6, "Copulation with the Stars of New Country."

And no, you should not have hinted to that nice coke addict that you might be pregnant. I don't care what he did to deserve it or how it advanced your position in your battle of wits with him. You're going to hell.

Wendy Mann
Senior Consultant
Stargazer Public Relations

It was difficult to close the e-mail on a cell phone *really hard*, but Sarah tried her best, giving the screen a jab with one long fingernail. Wendy was always funny and supportive right up until she wasn't anymore. And somewhere under the sarcasm, she was almost always right.

What irked Sarah most, besides the haunting tingle when Quentin took her in his strong arms and comforted his supposed one-night stand, was the idea that she'd turned him off to her. He'd been content enough to toy with her on the bed. But by the time they'd finished with each other, he was more agreeable with the plan not to have sex than she would have liked.

There was no way she would get involved with a coke addict. It was for the best. But she didn't want *him* to think so.

That was her job, though. She'd suspected before that he'd been the one who made the call for help to Manhattan Music. Her suspicion was stronger now. He'd been right to do it, too. She could definitely keep the players in this band playing. She might get herself heartbroken in the process, but not if she had no heart left.

To distract herself from her desire for Quentin and from Wendy's opinion of her destination in the afterlife—with which she heartily agreed—she checked Quentin's story by googling *banjo* and *Cox* on her phone. Several articles popped up on Ernest and Velma Cox, honky-tonk musicians during the 1950s who later became studio artists and joined the regular band at the Grand Ole Opry. From the black-and-white photos posted of the couple, playing their instruments with their mouths wide open, singing their hearts out, it was clear to Sarah that part of their "showmanship," as Quentin called it, was dressing Velma up in a sequined leotard and fishnet stockings.

"Grandma!" she exclaimed.

There was also a story, with sketchy details because all the eyewitnesses remembered it differently, about Ernest and Velma shooting off a Civil War cannon to draw a crowd to their opening night at a bar in Eclectic, Alabama, and accidentally burning down the church next door.

Some of what Quentin had told her was true, then. The only question was, which part? In her eight years working for Stargazer Public Relations, she'd never had a celebrity tell her the truth when he promised her, "I'm not on cocaine." If the subject of cocaine came up, the star was on it.

She studied Quentin's bedroom in the daylight. What she was looking for besides dope, she wasn't sure. She would know it when she saw it. She'd felt last night that something was off about the band. She'd persuaded Quentin to tell her some secrets, but there were more. He'd told her what he'd told her *very carefully*. This was disconcerting. She'd been able to read Nine Lives like a book. Right up until the last few weeks in Rio, which she hadn't seen coming.

But there wasn't much to find in Quentin's room. As with the rest of the house, it looked like a rich bachelor had called an interior designer and said, "Furnish my house," with no further instructions. Each piece of furniture was expensive and elegant and modern and black or brown or tan.

Feeling guilty, and assuring herself that she was just gathering information as part of her job, she opened every drawer in his room. Most of them were empty. A few contained clothes. She slid a hand down the sides and into the corners, searching for small vials or plastic bags of coke. Nothing.

The last drawer she opened was full of boxer shorts. She'd figured Quentin had worn his dog bone boxers because he was playing strip poker, but no. Here was an entire collection of joke boxers. Halloween boxers with ghosts and bats, football boxers, a pair covered in bottles of hot sauce. If he'd bought all these himself, it would be extremely odd. She wondered whether he had sisters who gave him funny underwear every birthday. She and Wendy had given quite a few joke neckties to Tom, their protégé at work.

It did make sense, Sarah decided. Quentin was fun-loving. Liked to wear funny boxers. Liked to do a little cocaine at parties, thought he could handle it, until one day it turned sinister on him.

Straightening, she noticed six chessboards with games in play were positioned on top of the dresser and armoire. Odd. She knew Quentin liked games, but he didn't strike her as a chess man. He was talented, yes, but no intellectual. He was more of a checkers man, Chinese checkers at best. She was afraid that in chess, he'd forget which way the horse went. Otherwise, the room was empty of his signature.

She peeked into his closet. One suit and two shirts hung there, but the space was mostly filled with large, stacked boxes marked *Q*, likely because he was always on tour and hadn't stayed home long enough to unpack in the two years since he'd bought the mansion.

The bathroom was tan marble, with nothing on the clean countertop. Nine Lives had kept his flask of vodka in the water-filled back of the toilet and his meth in a manicure kit in a bathroom drawer. So, again, Sarah forced herself to be nosy. She found nothing but Quentin's bottles of pills that were *not* on her list of prescriptions stars used to sneak a high. She puzzled over the bottles . . . but of course he would have these on hand to bolster his cover story about asthma and allergies. This was how rich and famous addicts worked.

Though, if he was using, it *was* strange he hadn't suggested to her last night that he pull out his secret stash for them to share.

No. She was making excuses for him now. That's what she got for falling for a star. She put the bottles back.

Luckily she'd packed her bag with fresh clothes and toiletries in case her luggage had been lost on the flight. After her shower, she clopped downstairs in her high heels and ballsy-bitch uniform.

Erin and Owen sat close together on the U-shaped

sectional sofa. They watched a NASCAR race. Erin beamed at Sarah, a one-eighty from her look of alarm earlier. She said brightly, "Good morning," and then glanced at Quentin lying on the opposite side of the U. "For some of us."

Quentin had an IV stuck in his arm. The tubes were attached to the almost empty IV bag, which hung on a metal stand next to the sofa.

Sarah nearly sprinted from the room. She'd been sliced across the chin and treated in a Brazilian hospital recently. She wasn't too keen on needles. She managed to remark calmly, "After Rio, I never thought I'd say it, but this is a new one on me."

"It's just saline," Quentin said, lifting his head to gaze at her sleepily. "Rich man's hangover cure."

She gazed doubtfully at the contraption. "It's all very Michael Jackson."

Erin rounded the coffee table to Quentin and pulled the IV needle from his arm as if she knew what she was doing. "Do you want one, Sarah? I know Q's a lightweight."

"I'm not a hundred percent," Sarah admitted. "But that will just make it easier to do my job, which this morning is to lecture that publicist of yours some more."

"Rachel," Quentin said firmly.

"Rachel," Sarah agreed, eyeing him. She felt herself flush under his intense gaze. The green camo T-shirt he wore, a marker of supreme hickdom for the boys in her high school, also highlighted his green eyes behind his glasses.

It was so unfair for him to give her that sexy, piercing gaze when he wasn't acting remotely like they'd slept together. This would never do. He was going to give them away to Erin.

Sarah leaned over the back of the sofa to ask him, "What's with the attitude? Was it no good for you?"

Feeling Erin's and Owen's eyes on her, she tried to ignore them and focus on Quentin. Slowly Owen went back to watching TV, Erin to taking down the IV bag.

Pressing his fingers to the wound on his arm, Quentin sat up to face Sarah. "Rachel is a friend of ours," he explained gently. "She's put up with a lot." He grinned as he stood. "It was okay for me."

Still unsatisfied, Sarah followed the three of them across the open room to the kitchen and slid onto a stool on the opposite end of the bar from Owen. They watched Erin cook breakfast, with Quentin helping. Sarah was even more deeply disappointed at this. Erin was a floozy, and a fantastic musician, and was able to hold her own around all the testosterone in the band. She had watched as her naked bandmates paraded in front of her on the cover of *Ass Backwards*. She had thrown back everything the men dished out last night. Sarah had thought Erin had more fire in her than to serve the men bacon for breakfast in addition to the wet T-shirt at night.

Then Quentin appeared from inside the pantry, supporting a tall stack of ingredients with his hands and balancing it with his chin. By stages Sarah realized that

Erin was just handing utensils, assisting the surgeon. Quentin was the one cooking. Cooking like a chef, chopping onion quickly and evenly, cracking eggs with one hand. He'd obviously worked in a kitchen before he was able to make a living with the Cheatin' Hearts.

"May I help?" Sarah asked, because she wanted to keep up the facade that she and Quentin were lovers. *Not* because Quentin watched Erin's ass as she bent to retrieve a bowl under the counter.

Quentin made a shooing motion to Erin, who rounded the counter to sit beside Owen at the bar. Sarah took Erin's place in the kitchen and suppressed the urge to stick out her tongue at Erin.

Quentin snapped his fingers as if he'd forgotten something. "More flour," he said, taking Sarah by the shoulders and pointing her back toward the pantry without so much as a surreptitious pat on the bottom.

Sarah stood inside the pantry and stared at the boxes and bottles. This was the pantry of a cook, with all the basics, plus jars and boxes with colorful labels in foreign languages. It was a far cry from her own pantry: granola bars and ramen noodles. She found the flour and turned.

Inside the pantry door, a handwritten note was taped:

Gate code
7712
Use the force
DUMBASS

Now she could come and go from the mansion as she pleased, and if they misbehaved, she could catch them in the act.

Keeping her poker face would be difficult after a scoop like that. To hide the expression in her eyes, she obediently slid the flour onto the counter next to Quentin, then searched for some kind of cooking activity to busy herself with. Quentin tended the sizzling pans on the stove. It seemed he'd forgotten to close the lid on the waffle iron with four circles of dough—batter?—in the center, so she made herself useful.

Quentin turned at the deafening hiss and gave her a look through his glinting glasses. "You close the lid on waffles," he told her. "With the little squares. These are pancakes."

"Oh."

He patted her head as if she were a misguided child rather than a sexy diva who couldn't cook. "Go sit down," he ordered her. Opening the smoking griddle, he muttered, "Crêpes."

She took her place at the bar beside Erin, who was trying and failing to suppress a self-righteous smile.

Quentin slid a mug of coffee across the bar to Sarah. He asked her dryly, "Black?"

Sarah preferred lots of cream and sugar. He was right, though: Natsuko would take hers black. She sipped the rich, expensive coffee he handed her, which without sweetener tasted like rich, expensive nail polish remover.

Quentin transferred omelets and bacon onto several plates and wrapped them in foil. He said to Owen, "Call the Timberlanes' butler, would you?"

As Owen fished his phone from his pocket, Sarah asked, "Who are the Timberlanes?"

"Q's next-door neighbors." Erin smiled. "Q has a thing for old people."

Quentin said without looking up again from the stove, "I just hope I'm that wily when I'm a codger. If I live long enough to be a codger."

Owen rolled his eyes and said disgustedly, "Oh *God*." Erin took the fiddle from her lap and played a low dirge.

Quentin glared at both of them. "Are you *making fun* of me for *Thailand*? I'm going to make fun of you when *you* have a near-death experience."

He might have been annoyed with them, but he fed them well anyway—so well that it almost made up for Sarah's coffee. The pancakes were fluffy, the eggs were perfection, and the fruit was fresh and cold. It probably was the best breakfast Sarah had ever eaten. Which wasn't saying much, because her mother wasn't known for her culinary skills, either. The other three made no comment, as if they ate like this every morning. What *luxury*. Sarah ate until she was stuffed. Owen and Quentin were still eating when the doorbell rang.

Quentin put down his food and took the foil-wrapped plates to the front door. They heard him exclaim from several rooms away, "Hot damn!"

"The Timberlanes have a garden," Erin explained to Sarah.

Quentin returned carrying a large grocery sack. "I got some corn. See? It pays to be nice to people. I'll make this for lunch, and I'm not giving you any." He gestured to Erin and Owen. "You remember that the next time you make fun of me for being on a ventilator."

Owen asked, "How long are you going to milk this ventilator thing?"

"I was near death!"

"It's hard to feel too sorry for you," Sarah couldn't help commenting. "You OD'd on coke. You did it to yourself."

"No he didn't," Owen told Sarah at the same time Erin said, "He has food allergies that close up his airway and make him go into shock unless he gets his medicine in time."

"She doesn't believe you," Quentin said simply. He turned to Sarah. "No corn for you, either."

Was he so stupid that he'd already *completely* forgotten they were supposed to be lovers?

The doorbell rang again, and three long-haired men reeking of cigarette smoke let themselves in the door from the garage, waved briefly into the kitchen, and stomped down the stairs to the studio. They were followed immediately by a grizzled man with an impressively laden tool belt. "Came to fix your door?" Quentin pointed him down the stairs, too.

Sarah had never felt so sad about a door being repaired.

"I guess we'd *all* better get to work," she remarked.

So there would be no mistaking her message, she pointed at Quentin, then pointed toward the garage. She waved good-bye to Erin and Owen as she slid off the stool. Erin waved back. Owen stared. Sarah heard them whispering behind her as she rounded the corner.

She met Quentin at the door to the garage. "You're not very good at this," she whispered acidly. "You act like you love fresh corn and that waffle iron more than me."

"It's a pancake griddle," he whispered back. "You told Erin last night that I remind you of Ernie from *Sesame Street*. That's not good for business, either."

"Touché." Sarah laughed.

"Let's try again to make Erin jealous," he said softly, stepping closer and slipping his hand under her shirt. "We'll do a better job this time."

Her whole body tingled at his touch. She pulled off his glasses just before their lips met.

At first, she let him kiss her. Then she broke the kiss. When he stopped in surprise, she licked his lips with the tip of her tongue and simultaneously rubbed her thigh across his groin.

He had exactly the reaction she'd been counting on strategically, and aching for physically, all through breakfast. He took in a gasp, let out a small groan, and kissed her hard, with drive.

That's when she put her hand on his chest and pushed him away. "Better." She settled his glasses back across his nose.

He opened the door to the garage for her. She was such a masterful femme fatale that she managed to hold his hungry gaze without tripping in her heels while she descended the two steps. "I want my album," she said.

"I'm going to give it to you," he said darkly.

Maneuvering between the pickup trucks in the garage, headed for her BMW out on the driveway, she heard the door to the kitchen close behind her. Then a soft thud. Then a faint curse. She smiled to herself and kept on walking.

~

Quentin collapsed with his back against the door. And banged his head in frustration. And cussed.

"*Did you break Rule Three?*" his bandmates hollered from the kitchen bar. Even Martin had finally dragged himself up from the guest room/opium den to confront Quentin about Sarah.

"You think I'd be beating my head against the door if I'd broken Rule Three?" Quentin exclaimed. With effort, he pushed away from the door and returned to the kitchen under their accusing glares. He started an omelet for Martin like everything was normal, even though he knew Martin wouldn't eat it.

When he looked up from the pan, they still stared grimly at him over the bar. They didn't believe him. Nobody believed him today.

"I swear to *God* I didn't," he said.

Their looks didn't change. They were going to kick him out of the band.

"I swear on the statue of Vishnu in my daddy's front yard," he said desperately. "Erin, you believed me earlier!"

"That was before *she* came downstairs," Erin told him. "There was definitely a vibe between you two."

"Well, I was *going* to," he confessed. "I had full intention of breaking Rule Three." He laughed nervously. "And then I passed out."

Owen exploded in laughter, and Erin clapped.

Martin said quietly, "If you'd broken Rule Three, being drunk wouldn't have been an excuse. A rule is a rule."

Quentin said, "Yeah, but—"

"There's no 'but' if you break a rule."

Martin was really beginning to piss off Quentin with his hypocrisy. Martin was *high*, for Pete's sake, his pupils pinpoints behind his glasses.

"Y'all *made* me get drunk!" Quentin protested.

"It was your turn," Owen said.

"Yeah, but we could have skipped me and moved to Erin if we'd known Chewbacca was a hot chick." He reached across the bar to poke Martin's chest with the eggy spatula. "Why didn't you stop me?"

"Because you acted like you were going to hit me," Martin reasoned.

"I've hit you before and you survived."

"And anyway," Martin said, "the three of us agreed you were going to pass out before you could make a move on her."

"Then what the hell's the problem?" Quentin smacked the omelet onto a plate and shoved it across the bar at Martin.

"The problem is that there was a *vibe* between you and Sarah," Erin repeated. "You know I know you, Q. You know I know the vibe."

Quentin glanced at Owen, expecting to see him jealous. But Owen didn't emote much, and his face was the usual blank. Quentin could have sworn he'd sensed something real between Erin and Owen last night. But he'd been drunk. Or he was just no good at detecting the *vibe*.

He confessed, "Sarah wants to fake a thing with me until the concert, to get me back with Erin."

Martin grumbled, "What *kind* of thing?" and Owen cursed, but Erin's voice rose high above theirs. "What have you gotten yourself into? What have you gotten *us* into? Don't you remember what's at stake here? Owen, tell him what's at stake."

Owen recited the sales figures for *In Poor Taste*, the portion of profit that went to the Cheatin' Hearts, the large portion that went to the record company, and the *other* large portion that went to the lawyers. Then the figures for *Ass Backwards* with the profit breakdowns for the band, the record company, and the lawyers.

After he finished, Erin declared, "I'm not fighting the record company and signing my life away to the lawyers again. I'm not going to do it, Q. This double life we're leading isn't worth the money." Her diatribe escalated into a wail. "My grandmother thinks I'm a slattern!"

Quentin decided this was not the time to point out that they still had an awful lot of money. He allowed them to complete the ritual. Erin lectured and Owen recited the sales figures every time Quentin made a decision they didn't like. That was fine if it made them feel better.

Then he said, "We don't have much choice. Sarah's a Jedi. She figured out the burly hick act is a put-on." He explained the deal he'd arranged with Sarah, deleting their discussion of Martin's heroin use. Also omitting Sarah's opinion that Owen didn't matter as much to the band as Quentin did. Owen was thin-skinned. Also editing out that his dreams last night had been filled with making love to Sarah, which was probably why he'd woken with his hand in her pants.

"That bitch!" Erin exclaimed.

"She makes me *very* nervous," Owen agreed.

"That's what she's here for," Quentin said to Owen. He gave Erin a reproving look. "And she's not a bitch. She took a page out of *our* book. Look, y'all, I *didn't* break a rule. I won't get drunk again. I'll pretend—*pretend*—to be doing the deed with her to make Erin jealous, just like Erin and Owen are *pretending* to do it to make me jealous. Hell, *none* of us are getting any. No wonder we're all on edge."

Martin stared at his untouched food. Owen laughed nervously, and Erin watched her fingers flying on the neck of her fiddle.

"We'll put our energy into the album," Quentin went on. "Come the Fourth of July, Erin and I will pretend to get back together. The Wookiee will see that the band's not breaking up, and she'll go back to New York or Tatooine or wherever the hell she's from."

He turned to Erin. "So you act jealous." He turned to Owen. "And you . . . continue to say as little as possible. Grunt if you must."

Owen grunted.

Quentin said, "And I'll beat my head against the wall for nine more days."

~

Late that afternoon, while Martin and Erin worked in the studio on Erin's solo for "Barefoot and Pregnant," Quentin and Owen lay on opposite sides of the sectional sofa in the den, watching Owen's DVD of an old *Masterpiece Theatre* production of *Crime and Punishment*. Quentin had argued about this at first because he wanted to watch *World Poker Tournament*, but he'd relented after a few minutes. He'd come so close to getting kicked out of the band this morning that he figured he'd better tread lightly for a few days. Or just hours, maybe, depending on how things went.

Now he was sorry he'd given in. He'd only skimmed *Crime and Punishment* in college because he'd had a calculus midterm that same week. He'd convinced his girlfriend at the time to fill him in on the details of the novel so he could ace the test. Owen had started the DVD on episode two, and Quentin was thoroughly confused. He couldn't remember how Raskolnikov had gotten himself into this guilt-ridden fix in the first place. Quentin hated being confused. "Why'd he whack those old ladies?" he asked Owen.

"Shut up," Owen said without taking his eyes off the screen.

Martin appeared behind them with his phone in his hand. "Excuse me, Porfiry Petrovich."

"Which one?" Quentin asked.

"Rachel just called," Martin told them. "We got an offer to be on a late-night talk show in a few days, and Sarah turned it down."

Owen actually peeled his eyes from the TV and turned to Quentin. "You see? That's exactly why we don't get involved with the record company."

"I'm sure she had some reason," Quentin said, strangely defensive of the pink-haired girl yet again. "She doesn't want us to do badly. The record company brought her in, and they want us to have good sales. That's how they make money."

"Doesn't matter," Owen said. "We want to sell albums on *our* terms. She's manipulating us on their behalf, and you're letting her."

Quentin held his hand backward so Martin could give him the phone. "I'll call her and find out what's going on."

Martin's steps sounded back down the stairs to the studio, and Owen and Quentin were reabsorbed by

Crime and Punishment. Quentin found the story revolting but hard to stop watching. Like a particularly nasty gunshot wound to the abdomen with intestines spilling out that had come into the emergency room on his shift once. Anyway, it was a lot easier to watch this poor sod torture himself with guilt than to think about Sarah, the problem with Sarah, what he was going to do about Sarah.

"Call her," Owen insisted, eyes glued to the TV.

"I have it under control," Quentin said. It was early evening, and he half expected the phone in his hand to ring with the signal that she was at the gate in her car. He'd hoped all day, hoped and dreaded, that she would come back over to check on their progress on "her" album.

"Chop-chop! Where's my album?" she said behind them, startling him. The phone flew out of his hand and hit Owen on the nose.

"Under control, eh?" Owen muttered, flinging the phone back at Quentin.

Quentin deflected it instinctively with his forearm. It flew in a high lob behind the sectional, where Sarah amazingly caught it with one hand. Quentin thought she'd spin it on her finger like a basketball next, but she just tossed it onto the kitchen counter.

She was wearing a tight. Red. Low-cut. Shirt.

"Good evening," she said pointedly to Quentin. She gestured with her eyes. He got the message. She wanted him to kiss her hello in front of Owen.

He knelt on the cushion, pulled her as close as he

could get her with the back of the sofa between them, and showed her that he'd missed her all day.

Finally she pushed him away. "I missed you, too," she whispered, breathing light and fast.

"You figured out the gate code," he said.

"I have eyes in the back of my head," she said ominously. Then she laughed. "That's my mother's line. She always knows more than she's supposed to."

"That's creepy," said Quentin.

"You have a mother?" Owen asked.

Sarah didn't answer. Her eyes had fallen on the TV. "When you're through watching this, you can borrow my copy of *Anna Karenina*."

Owen didn't understand Sarah's sarcasm. "The one with Helen McCrory or Nicola Pagett?" he asked. If he was *going* to understand that membership in a redneck country band was not consistent with an interest in nineteenth-century Russian literature, he was going to come to this understanding very, very slowly.

Quentin said only, "Owen, you dumbass." Then, to distract Sarah, he grabbed her around the waist in a wrestling hold, lifted her over the back of the sofa, and threw her bouncing onto the cushions. It was a rude move that seemed ruder performed on a sophisticated woman like Sarah, which was why he did it. He slid her across the leather to trap her against the arm of the sectional.

"We hear you turned down a late-night talk show for us," he said softly. Sitting close beside her, he stroked his thumb slowly down the open neckline of her shirt, dipped cheekily into her cleavage, and stroked slowly up the other side. Then he turned his thumb and stroked her in the same places using his callus from holding down his guitar string. She'd seemed to enjoy the touch of his thumb in his bedroom that morning.

She gasped a little. "I did," she breathed.

"Well, we think you must be nuts," he told her gently, retracing the tender path of his thumb. "That would have been great publicity."

"We didn't need you to come down from New York to do something inane," Owen added.

Inane, Quentin thought in alarm. The Cheatin' Hearts didn't know the word *inane*. But Owen was too inane to realize this.

"I want my album," Sarah said stubbornly, despite Quentin's thumb in her cleavage. "The album is the most important thing. If you don't have an album, you don't have anything to publicize."

"We could fly up there, do the show, and fly back down that night," Quentin suggested, moving his whole hand to cup the part of her breast that was bare in her neckline.

"I know it's never that simple with you," she said. "There's no telling what kind of stunt you'd pull, and that poor TV host has had heart surgery." She slapped Quentin's hand away and tried to stand. "I can't believe Rachel told you about this. I'm going to have a talk with her."

"You're not going anywhere until we settle this," Quentin said with authority. He stood over her, his hands on the sofa so she couldn't escape.

She raised one eyebrow, asking him, *Are you bluffing?*

He was not. The band was too important. He kept his eyes on hers. But he had his contacts in, and he would have to blink sooner or later. So he said, "You need a spanking."

"You have to catch me first," she said. She feinted left under his caging arm, then dashed right. She slipped through his grasp.

"Thanks for taking care of it," Owen called as Quentin ran after Sarah into the dining room.

She was on the far side of the pool table. "Elegantly appointed dining room," she commented, patting the felt. Her voice echoed weirdly against the marble walls and the painted ceiling. The evening light from the window danced in the chandelier and shot shadowed dots across her face and chest.

He took one slow step to the left, and she moved to the right. He stepped to the right, and she moved to the left. He bent as if to slide under the pool table. She scrambled over it.

Too easy. He caught her, laid her down on the felt, and kissed her. His hand crept across her pants to the inside of her thigh.

She took a deep breath and said low, "I mean it. You're stretched too thin right now. The talk show will ask you back after the Nationally Televised Holiday Concert Event."

He kissed her neck, carefully avoiding the scar under

her chin because he didn't want her to shy. "From now on," he said, "I want you to discuss it with me before you decide something like that." He bit her earlobe.

"Okay."

Now he ran his tongue lightly inside her ear, and it seemed from her reaction that he really did have everything under control. He told her, "If you were my girlfriend, I'd make love to you right now."

"I'm not your girlfriend," she whispered.

"You feel like my girlfriend," he said. "Let's see if you sound like my girlfriend." Despite her protests and her feeble attempts to tickle his ribs, he lifted her onto his shoulder. Registering with a quick glance into the next room that Erin and Martin were leaning over the sofa in discussion with Owen, he climbed up the stairs to his bedroom.

He shut and locked the door behind him, tossed her onto the leather armchair by the window, and pushed the chair over to the door with her in it.

"I thought we agreed that we're not going to do this," she said, sitting up.

"We're not." He noted with supreme interest that she looked disappointed. "But we want Erin to think we are. Right?"

"Right," she said uncertainly.

"So make it sound like we are." He folded his arms. "Show me what you've got."

She looked at him dubiously, then laughed, nervous. Her cheeks had turned bright pink, the same shade as a wayward lock of hair that half hid one of her big, dark eyes.

"Come on, now," he scolded her. "This is for your *job security*."

She got serious, squaring her shoulders. "Don't watch me."

He looked away while she uttered a pitiful imitation.

Turning back to her, he shook his head. "Every fake orgasm from now until the end of time is going to sound like *When Harry Met Sally*." He picked her up, sat down in the leather chair himself, and settled her in his lap with her back to him. After cranking up the footrest so they reclined comfortably together, he deftly unbuttoned and unzipped her pants and slipped his hand inside, past the delicate lace of her panties.

"This isn't a good idea," she said in warning, clutching his hand. "I have to go to the office tonight to get some more work done, and I don't want my clothes to be all wrinkled."

He laughed shortly. "I've never heard that one before. And that's the worst excuse I've heard in probably a decade." He removed his hand from her panties and pulled down on the waistband of her pants.

"Quentin," she scolded him, slapping his hands. "My trousers are headed in the wrong direction."

"Relax." He slipped out from under her and stood up so he could get more leverage on the pants leg. "Are your clothes always this hard to get off?"

"When my shoes are on."

"I don't want you to take your shoes off. I really like you in those shoes. Oh!" he exclaimed in relief, finally coming away with the pants. He made a great show of smoothing them and folding them carefully before dropping them in a heap on the carpet. Now that she was cooperating, he handled her shirt with one good tug. He crumpled it on the floor beside the pants. Then he sat on the footrest to look at her.

Red lace bra. Red lace panties, some stylish kind that sat low on her hips and cut straight across her ass in back. Underneath, creamy skin stretched taut over the hard muscles of an athlete.

He said sincerely, "You are *so beautiful.*"

"Thank you!" She smiled, brown eyes big.

"I *really* like being in cahoots with you."

"Me, too."

He moved to the chair and pulled her back against him again, positioning her so she could feel his erection. This time when he pushed his hand into her panties and she began to protest, he was ready. He clamped his other hand over her mouth. She'd been talking like she wanted to stay in control. But instinct told him if she thought she wanted control in the bedroom, nobody had ever shown her what she really wanted.

"We need to get down to business," he whispered. "We're wasting time. Don't say anything else until you've got a good moan ready. You understand me?"

In answer, she bit his hand gently. He put his fingers in her mouth.

He worked on her, his middle finger circling and

stroking her clit. She pressed against him. His cock complied, swelling further. At the same time, she raised her hips, giving him better access to her mound. He wanted to push his fingers into her, and he figured that's what she wanted, too. But he didn't dare, because once he knew what she felt like inside, he wasn't sure he could keep himself from snatching down her panties and taking her from the back.

So he tried to content himself with feeling the pressure of her ass against his cock, and circling his finger on her clit. The rest of her body relaxed, but her sex grew tense. And he thought, *What am I doing?* Sex with his ex-manager Karen had been one thing. Karen had been casual. There was nothing casual about this. Sarah's pink hair and red bra and red panties turned his mood dead serious.

Several exquisite minutes passed this way. The room grew hot. Finally she pulled her mouth away from his hand and rested her cheek on his shoulder, pleading to him, eyes half-closed. "Don't make me."

"A beautiful woman like you," he murmured. "I don't understand why you need this so bad. I have to make you, for your own good."

Still gazing at him, she seemed to stop seeing, and shuddered under his hand. He kept circling, pressing more firmly. She dug her high heels into the footrest and arched her back, raising herself off the leather and nearer to his hand. He circled and she shuddered. Then came the long, loud moan he'd been waiting for. And then she cried, "Que'n!"

He pressed her mouth with his mouth. His fingers still circled as she sparked and finally vibrated to a halt. He forced his tongue past her teeth, sweeping inside her mouth, showing her the way he wanted to make love to her.

But now he was thinking, *What have I done?* Making her come had seemed like a good idea while he was chasing her around the pool table. But they'd just transformed their business relationship into something a lot more complicated.

She broke the kiss and said, "I'd better go."

"You'd better," he agreed grimly.

She couldn't get her clothes on fast enough. She cursed as she tried to pull the pants on over her shoes and got the legs caught on her high heels. He handed the small red shirt to her.

They went downstairs. The TV room was empty. As they walked through the kitchen, Quentin pointed to the open door that led downstairs to the studio and put his finger to his lips: the band was still listening.

By the time they stopped at the door out to the garage, Quentin had finally recovered himself enough for salvage operations. He put his hand on her elbow. "This isn't the end of the world," he whispered.

Sarah said gravely, "We need to remember that we're just doing this to make Erin jealous."

"I guarantee you Erin doesn't have any problem about what she does with Owen," Quentin said. This had better not be true. "It's okay to have fun," he went on, rubbing Sarah's arm. "Come back tomorrow." He kissed her tenderly, letting his lips linger on hers.

"I don't think we should go this far anymore," she breathed.

"We'll see," he said.

He watched her walk all the way through the garage in her tight pants. Then he closed the door and banged his head against it.

Martin's voice traveled up the stairwell from the studio. "I'm assuming from the *thud* that you didn't break Rule Three."

Martin was usually more savvy than this. Quentin was shocked that Martin would give away one of their rules to the technicians in the control room. Then, calculating from the fading light outside, he realized that it was later than he'd thought. The technicians had gone home for the night. Time flew when you were having fun. Or pleasuring a woman who was out-of-bounds. Either one.

Quentin said wearily, "No, I didn't."

Owen's voice came echoing up next. "It sounded like you were breaking Rule Three."

"I had to do *something*," Quentin said in his defense. "You should see this woman's *underwear*."

"Don't get too close to her, Q," Erin warned him.

"Erin, I'm sure your underwear is very nice, too," Quentin called down to her. "The finest Target has to offer."

Last came Mrs. Timberlane's weak voice. "Did you use a condom?"

Without comment, Quentin closed the door to the stairs and opened the door to the pantry. He'd feel better if he made some tarka dal. But the lentils had to simmer for a whole hour. Or jehangiri shorba.

That's when he saw the note he'd taped inside the pantry door to remind Owen of the code so he could let the pizza guy in the security gate.

Sarah didn't have eyes the back of her head. She just had eyes.

Well, Owen might not be able to remember the gate code, but he was good with gadgets. He probably knew how to *change* the gate code, so that Sarah couldn't come over at will.

But Sarah had liked popping in. And Quentin liked that she had popped in. If she had to wait at the bottom of the driveway for someone to open the gate for her, maybe she wouldn't come over as often.

He wouldn't change a thing.

5

I wonder if they have e-mail in jail in Rio

Love
Nine Lives

Good question, Sarah thought as her muscles tensed and her body flushed with adrenaline, ready for fight or flight. Staring at the innocent-looking e-mail message on her laptop in her hotel room, heart racing, she thought back to Rio several weeks ago. Her impression of the jail was fuzzy. When she was there, she hadn't slept in two days. But she didn't think inmates would have access to e-mail. As a general rule, there was no e-mail access in a facility smelling that strongly of urine.

Nine Lives could have gotten his bodyguard or his driver or another member of his entourage to e-mail her. But that would mean they were all at leisure to worry about *her* rather than *jail*.

If he was still in, he wouldn't be there long.

Now that the first rush of panic had lifted, she shivered. After she'd left Quentin's mansion last night, a rainy front had moved through, ushering in a rare cool June day. Natsuko couldn't show vulnerability by shivering, even in her thin, revealing blouses, so all morning Sarah had moved through the office punching buttons on the computer and the telephone with icy fingers.

She resisted the urge to soak in a warm bath to regain her circulation. She couldn't receive this implied threat from Nine Lives lying down and babying herself. She had to take care of herself, and take action.

The action she was thinking of involved Quentin. But of course she did *not* want to see him, and she was *not* going to repeat last night's dangerous walk on the wild side. She would use him and be through.

Half an hour later, as she stepped carefully into Quentin's kitchen so her high heels wouldn't clop on the marble, the bite of spice hung in the air. He was bent under the cabinets, putting away pans.

"Working hard on my album?" she asked sarcastically.

He started up against the counter, brushing against a colorful jar of some foreign ingredient. It fell and broke on the floor with a *pop*.

He turned. She could tell from his expression that he was prepared to make a sarcastic remark in reply.

But when he saw her, his face changed to concern. "What's the matter?"

"Nothing," she said casually. "What excuse were you about to make for not working on my album?"

"I *am* working on *your* album." He grinned, scooping up the broken jar with a wad of paper towels and dumping it into the garbage.

"You say that every time I come over here. And every time I come over here, you're getting drunk, or watching *Masterpiece Theatre*, or cleaning your kitchen. All of which makes you a fairly well-rounded person, but not a person especially inclined to finish an album in five days."

He took a step toward her.

She took a step backward.

He looked disappointed. "Does it feel cold in here to you?" he asked. When she nodded, he moved to one side of the kitchen and adjusted the thermostat on the wall. "*Somebody's* working on the album. When it comes to recording, I've got the easy part. Bass guitar and lead vocals are straightforward. It's the other instruments and the background vocals that change how the song sounds, and that's what has to get planned out." He turned back to her. "Tell me what's wrong."

Not able to meet his green eyes, she looked past him into the kitchen. "What have you been cooking?"

"You mean food? Indian."

"Indian! What kind?"

"Baingan bartha. Want some?"

Despite yesterday's delicious breakfast and the current mouthwatering smell, Sarah was dubious of the hunky hick's skills with Indian. Besides, she'd already eaten a granola bar for lunch. She asked, "Isn't that a professional wrestler?"

"Big Baingan Bartha? Yeah, I think he had a meet with Mad 'Red' Mud in Tallahassee one time. Come with me."

He pulled her by the hand to the sofa and vaulted over the back of it, onto the cushions. She'd noticed that there wasn't much room to move at the open end of the sectional, nearest the TV. Quentin seemed content to vault over the back of the furniture. Bachelors. He'd be sorry when he wore out the springs underneath the leather. Or not. He was rich. And he was rarely here.

Too late it occurred to her that Quentin was playing an encore of last night's performance. He pulled her tumbling across the back of the sofa and pinned her to the cushions. His hands were heavy on her wrists, his green eyes were hungry, and the red T-shirt he wore made him look handsomely evil. When his lips brushed hers, it took everything she had to turn her head and put the freeze on him.

It had been a good plan. It was still a good plan. It was working. Erin had been decidedly uneasy at breakfast yesterday, and had whispered angrily with the others when Quentin took Sarah upstairs last night.

Sarah might just pull this off. She might get Erin back with Quentin, keep the group together, get out of this mess with Nine Lives, keep her job, and live happily ever after.

Or as happily as possible with a broken heart, if she fell for Quentin in the meantime. She could put the freeze on him all she wanted, but Quentin melted her.

Since she wouldn't give him her lips, he chose her neck instead, nipping deliciously. He growled in her ear, "If you were my girlfriend, I'd take you upstairs again."

A wave of desire swept over her, so strong that it actually forced her up to meet him. That had been one *excellent* orgasm, and she needed another.

He was offering to give her another, as if it were nothing. Because it was nothing to him. *She* was nothing to him. She might let him kiss her and fondle her, but she would always remember what it meant: nothing.

Now a shiver coursed through her and she pushed him off. "I'm not your girlfriend."

"You look like my girlfriend," he said stubbornly. Then he seemed puzzled. "Or do you? You look different." He ran his hands through her hair, flopping her locks this way and that. "No, that's not it," he concluded. "Tell me what's wrong."

She folded her arms and tried to rub away the chill bumps with her hands. "Nothing's wrong."

He edged closer to her. "Tell me what's wrong or I'll hold you down and make you come right here." He stood and reached to the coffee table for the TV remote control. "I'll make you come while we watch NASCAR."

She asked him quickly, "Do you know anything about guns?"

He sat down beside her again. "I live in Alabama, don't I?"

She took a deep breath and asked, "Would you go with me to buy a gun? I have no idea what I'm doing."

He eyed her. "Sounds like a good reason not to buy a gun."

"This had crossed my mind," she admitted. "You can teach me how to shoot it. Do you know how to shoot one?"

"Everybody in Alabama learns to shoot a gun when they're ten years old."

"Well, maybe boys do."

Now he looked at her hard. She was sure she'd given herself away. He was going to call her bluff and tell her she'd grown up in Alabama.

But what he said next caught her totally off guard. "Tell me what happened to you in Rio."

She suppressed another shiver. "No," she said with finality.

He continued to give her that hard look, trying to read her. "If I take you to a firing range," he asked eventually, "will you wear a bikini?"

He had to be joking. He didn't look like he was joking. And Sarah didn't own a bikini. But if Quentin would teach her to shoot, she might buy a bikini. She might shoot in the nude if he would just teach her.

"Never mind," he said before she could respond. "I can't ask you to do that. The firing range is out in the woods, and there are chiggers." He looked at his watch. "I've got something I need to do in a minute, and then I'm laying down some tracks with Martin. But when we're done, I'll take you to the firing range. We'll bring Martin. He's a much better shot than I am."

"Can't you see that I'm serious about this?" she cried.

Quentin put a heavy, warm, calming hand on her thigh, saying, "He should be sober by then."

A cell phone rang. He pulled his from his back pocket, glanced at it, then used the remote to turn the TV to the channel that showed the feed from the camera at the security gate. "Oh, it's Rachel." Lowering his voice, he told Sarah, "I'm going to run down there and have a word with her about Martin before she drives up." He handed Sarah his phone. "Don't press seven to open the gate until I wave to you." He jogged through the kitchen. She heard the door to the garage close behind him.

She shivered once more, hugged herself, and pessimistically surveyed the utilitarian room for a blanket. Then a movement on the TV screen caught her eye. She recognized the flash of cargo shorts and strong leg as the camera caught a glimpse of Quentin climbing over the high fence.

This didn't say much for security at the mansion.

As he jumped down from the fence, Rachel smiled up at him. He let himself into the passenger side of her car. Their faces grew serious as they talked with their heads close together. Rachel appeared to be pleading with him, brows knitted. He shook his head no. Rachel reached forward, put her hands around his neck, and pretended to choke him. Sarah knew the feeling.

Behind her, "Stars Fell on Alabama" beeped on another cell phone. Martin called from the control room stairs, "Someone's at the gate, wanting in. Has anybody looked at the TV feed? Oh, greetings, Sarah." She turned around to face him. With his phone still beeping in his hand, he stared past Sarah at Quentin and Rachel on the TV.

And he was gone again, running out of the room and slamming the door to the garage behind him.

Sarah wasn't sure what was going on, so she stayed put, waiting for Quentin's signal to open the gate. As she watched, a flash of jeans leg signaled that Martin was climbing the fence. Quentin glanced up at him. Rachel called to him.

Even though Quentin probably had two inches and forty pounds on him, Martin put his hands on Quentin and hauled him backward through the open window, over the closed door, out of the car, and onto the pavement.

White lights flashed in the bushes beside the gate. The paparazzi. With cameras.

Sarah pulled off her heels, dashed to the bag she'd left on the counter, dug out her billfold, and sprinted out the door and down the driveway on bare feet.

She knew she had thirty hundred-dollar bills, washed and dried and looking somewhat the worse for wear after their dip in the pool, but spendable nev-

ertheless. That wouldn't have been nearly enough for
the professional paparazzi in Rio, but it might suffice
for the ragtag crew working Birmingham. If not, she
had her checkbook. She couldn't use a Stargazer check
because the company didn't want to be linked to a
traceable payoff, but maybe the paparazzi would take
a personal check. And maybe Sarah could expense it.
She should check with Wendy about expensing bribes.

At the end of the steep driveway mottled with
shade, the tall gate was open. Rachel was out of her
convertible, screaming at Martin—which seemed very
strange to Sarah. She'd hardly been able to make out
Rachel's demure voice at the office. Martin sat on the
hood of the car, breathing hard, taking it.

Quentin stood to one side, breathing hard, too,
hands on his hips, a streak of dirt across his red shirt,
dried leaves in his hair, as if there had been a scuffle in
the landscaping. When Rachel took a breath, Quentin broke in to holler at Martin, "Why in God's name
would you think Rachel and I were cheating on you?"

Martin might have been shamed into silence by Rachel, but he obviously didn't feel the same way about
Quentin. "Because *that* isn't against *band rules*!" he
shouted back bitterly.

Sarah had no time for this. Quentin said, "Hey,"
as she dashed behind him, but she didn't slow down.
She ran past him to where the cameras in the bushes
still flashed. She opened her billfold before she even
stopped.

Quentin swept her up from behind and threw her over his shoulder. When she struggled, he simply adjusted his hold so that she was completely immobile. He hiked up the driveway with her as if she were a roll of carpet.

"The deal is off!" she told his very nice butt. "I'll consult you about doing late-night talk shows. But if you won't let me bribe your way out of trouble, I can't do my job!"

"Let me explain something to you," Quentin huffed, still catching his breath. "I work hard to plant stories. We've got to give the newspaper material for the Cheatin' Hearts Death Watch. When the newswire picks it up, it can make every newspaper in the country, all for free. But if we don't give them anything to gab about, they bump us and fill that bottom corner of page C1 with a recap of last night's reality shows. You think I want you to erase a story I didn't even have to work on?"

"But you're trying to get Erin back!" Sarah reminded him, her voice sounding hollow now that they'd entered the garage. "She'll see your fight with Martin in the newspaper and think you were coming on to Rachel!"

"No she won't. She knows I wouldn't do that to Martin and Rachel." He opened the door and carried Sarah into the kitchen.

Sarah wasn't following his logic. Erin would know his intentions were honorable, after all Erin and Quentin's nasty breakups in the past? Sarah was losing her battle of wits with him because she couldn't even see the battlefield. "Put me down," she said suddenly. "I don't like it when you pick me up and toss me around."

Effortlessly he flipped her off his shoulder and set her lightly on the marble floor. "You don't?"

"No. It makes me feel like I'm out of control." Which she was.

"I could have sworn you liked it. Is it cold in here to you?" He bent to peer at the thermostat on the wall again. "I turned this up already, didn't I?" He faced her. "You think I have the hots for *Rachel*?" he asked incredulously.

"No . . ." Sarah slipped her feet back into her high heels. "But Martin seemed pretty convinced of it when he ran down there and hauled you out of the car."

"Martin's on heroin," Quentin said dismissively. "He hasn't seen Rachel all week, because she won't come over here while he's using. I had a devil of a time getting her to show up today. That's what I was talking to her about. I tried to convince her to come all the way up to the house, make Martin win her back, make him realize what matters."

"Properly executed, that's called an intervention," Sarah informed him acidly.

"I *told* you." Quentin's voice rose for the first time. "Erin and Owen will kick him out of the band. And the band and Rachel are all that's keeping Martin on this earth right now."

Sarah didn't ask again why Quentin hadn't gotten

kicked out of the band for using coke, because she knew the answer. Quentin was different. Quentin could get away with anything. That was part of his problem.

The door from the garage into the kitchen slammed. Quentin went on in the same loud tone, "Anyway, I'm glad Martin and I put on a good show for the cameras. But he's not really mad. Are you, Martin?"

Martin, glasses even further askew than usual, indicated that he *was*, in fact, angry with Quentin and Rachel for sneaking around and plotting behind his back. He directed a stream of obscenities toward Quentin that would have made Nine Lives' driver blush. Then he stomped down the stairs to the control room.

"I'd better go record your album," Quentin told Sarah. "Please tell me *you're* not really mad."

Sarah folded her arms against the cold. "Are we still on?"

"Of *course* we're still on! I never meant—"

She threw her billfold at her bag on the counter. "Where's Erin?"

He jerked his thumb toward the guesthouse. When Sarah stepped through the door to the patio outside, he leaned through the doorway and called after her, "Why? What are you doing?"

"Going fishing."

"I haven't restocked the pool in a while," he said uneasily.

Sarah heard another barrage of curses from Martin

drift up the stairs. Quentin closed the door and disappeared from the window.

For the first time, she walked around the pool at a leisurely pace. *Cool* was a relative term in the Alabama summer, but at least there was some relief today from the previously unrelenting heat: a more gentle sun, lower humidity, a breeze meandering under the enormous oaks.

She paused at the edge of the patio and looked toward the back of the mansion. She'd seen the inside of only six or seven rooms, but the house was vast, way more square footage than Quentin needed. She supposed he'd bought it for the basement that he'd converted into a studio, the security gate of questionable effectiveness, the guesthouse, the pool, and the view through the trees of the Birmingham skyline in the valley far below.

The mansion towered above her and fell away below her. The steep bank was planted with white crepe myrtles buzzing with bees. A screened porch protruded off the lowest story. She took a step closer and made out a magazine folded open on a lounge chair, a coffee cup on a side table, and the glint of Quentin's glasses.

Erin intruded, as always. The *plink* of a piano recording began to cascade from her guesthouse, across the patio. As Sarah walked nearer, she noted that all the doors and windows were thrown open to the pool, and she recognized the first movement of Bach's Italian Concerto in F Major.

She nearly tripped on the flagstones with a rush of

déjà vu. Her father had loved Bach, and her mother sometimes opened all the windows for a few hours on a summer morning, replacing the air-conditioning with the breeze off Mobile Bay—an act that bespoke money above any other, because her parents' ancestral antebellum house was hard to cool. Sarah would return from a run to hear a piano piece trickling out the windows just like this, alternately whispering and inaudible under the breeze in the trees.

Pausing in the open doorway to the guesthouse, she saw Erin with her back turned, playing a grand piano expertly in a tight tank top and Daisy Dukes, barefoot.

And Owen across the colorful, stylishly furnished room, sitting on a flight of stairs, hidden from Erin by the angle of the wall. When he saw Sarah, he glared at her for a moment, then disappeared upstairs.

This shook Sarah. Something was wrong. Owen didn't want Erin to catch him listening to her play. As if he wasn't supposed to be in love with her.

And the look he'd shot Sarah was pure hatred. He knew she was trying to get Erin back together with Quentin.

This simply couldn't be. Blond, muscle-bound Owen didn't strike Sarah as perspicacious. His friends referred to him as *dumbass*.

But maybe *he* had been the mysterious caller to Manhattan Music, desperate for help in keeping Quentin with the band?

No. Owen was so into Erin that he valued his relationship with her more than the band. Otherwise he wouldn't have started the affair with her. He wouldn't have called Manhattan Music for help in keeping Quentin around. Sarah must have been mistaken.

As the piano stopped abruptly and Erin leaned forward with a pencil to mark a measure on the sheet music, Sarah knocked on the open door. "Planning to play a piano concerto with the symphony next?"

"Oh, no," Erin said with her chipmunk giggle. She patted a soft upholstered chair next to the piano bench for Sarah. "The violin concerto didn't work out too well."

Sarah couldn't believe hold-her-own Erin would stoop to this level of self-deprecation. "Everyone else seemed to think so," she said as she sat down. "It made the entertainment news on TV."

"Yeah, but Q got really mad about it," Erin said sadly. "Q wants me to remember the difference between fiddle"—she placed her left hand on the piano bench—"and violin"—she put down her right hand—"and he says I'm a fiddle player. Q has to have his way. And that's why we broke up."

Sarah was searching for an in to explore this topic when Erin went on, "No, I'm just fooling around, trying to chill out. I spent the whole morning alone in the studio with Martin. Lately he's so loopy. Exhausted from the tour, I guess. It's nice to come back here to my pretty house and hide, and play an easy little Bach. Bach makes such good sense."

"It *is* a pretty house." Sarah smiled. "Quentin has better taste than I thought."

"Oh, it came this way," Erin said. "I figure the old man he bought his mansion from must have kept a mistress."

Sarah nodded, carefully controlling her poker face. She would *not* give away to Erin how much the idea of Quentin keeping a mistress bothered her. "Why don't you guys hang out here?" she asked. "This house is so much homier than the mansion."

"The studio's over there, and Q cooks. And like I say, I prefer to go over there and get what I need and retreat, you know? Martin and Quentin are high-strung. They make me tired."

Despite the warm colors in the pretty house, and Erin's big blue eyes and very sweet face, Sarah couldn't shake the cold and sick feeling. She had the nagging suspicion that she and Erin would make terrific friends if they could just keep Quentin out of it.

Just as Sarah and Quentin would make terrific lovers if they could just keep Erin out of it.

But there it was. Rather than skirting the issue, maybe it would be best to face it head-on. Sarah said, "Listen, I'm sorry about all the public displays of affection with Quentin. You seem really happy with Owen, but I know you and Quentin broke up only recently."

"Oh! Don't worry about that," Erin said, waving her hand and sounding sincere. "I'm used to it. He acted the same way with our manager."

Sarah couldn't feel any sicker and colder without needing a hot toddy of Pepto-Bismol. Maybe the problem was that Erin wasn't jealous. She really believed Sarah was just another of Quentin's dalliances, like the band's former manager. If Erin thought Sarah and Quentin were getting serious, things might change. Sarah decided then that she and Quentin would get some extended time alone the next day.

Suddenly Quentin himself breezed in on a shady draft from the patio. His presence filled the room. He caught Sarah around the waist, lifted her off her feet, and ran outside with her, without giving her a chance to say good-bye to Erin.

"Let's go do some shooting," he said. "Yee-haw!"

Suddenly he stopped on the patio and put her down. "Sorry. I forgot you don't like to play caveman." He brushed some imaginary dust off her shoulder.

"I thought you were recording," she scolded him.

"I was. We finished."

"That was quick," she said suspiciously.

"It doesn't take long when you get it right the first time. Course, I'm talking about *recording*. Other things might take me all afternoon," he informed her provocatively, wrapping his warm hand around her icy one.

As they crossed the flagstones, Sarah glanced back toward Erin's house, Bach drifting out the open door again. *She* was the one who was jealous, not Erin. Quentin might have his coke, and Martin his heroin, and Owen his nineteenth-century Russian literature fetish, but they all were strong men ready to defend

Erin in her stylish little castle. Nothing bad could happen to Erin. Unless one of her men did it to her.

Sarah had no one to defend her. Not while her friend Tom from Stargazer was in Moscow, convincing a Hollywood movie star to make a commercial for vodka rather than drink it all. Well, there was Wendy's husband, Daniel, too. Wendy might talk Daniel into committing murder if Sarah really needed protection. But Daniel was the press secretary for a senator, and somehow Sarah didn't think his murder conviction on her behalf would make for good political PR. Wendy might not forgive her.

Besides, Sarah couldn't drag Wendy anywhere near Nine Lives. Quentin would help Sarah get her very own gun, and then she could defend herself. He swung her hand as they passed under the crepe myrtle trees buzzing with bees. She thawed a little in the sunshine.

~

That night, Quentin sipped his beer and tried to concentrate on peanut antigens and the cytokine response. So much had been discovered in the two years he'd been on tour. Now he was refreshing his memory with the most recent issues of *Clinical Immunology and Allergy Today*.

He hadn't had trouble concentrating for the last few weeks. It was pleasant out here at night on the secluded screened porch, his Fortress of Solitude. The ceiling fan faked a breeze in the still dark, and tree frogs chanted in the forest. He hadn't even had trouble concentrating last night, after he'd made Sarah come and then cooked jehangiri shorba.

Tonight he was having trouble. Maybe because he was looking forward to a definite date with Sarah tomorrow night. She'd whispered to him as she left this evening that they should go out alone tomorrow to give Erin the willies.

More likely it was the cold shoulder he'd gotten from Sarah that was bothering him now. He suspected she'd only come over in the afternoon because she wanted a gun. And he couldn't convince her to stay after they returned from the firing range.

He shouldn't have messed around with her last night. He'd pushed her too far too fast, and now she was shying away. Which was smart of her, because they couldn't be together. Right.

Owen walked onto the porch without knocking, with Martin behind him. Owen snatched the copy of *Clinical Immunology and Allergy Today* away from Quentin and threw it at Martin, then collapsed into a wicker chair that creaked under his weight. Martin sat in the chair on Quentin's other side. Quentin was cornered.

"I didn't break Rule Three," Quentin said automatically.

"We know Erin will go ballistic," Owen assured him. "This is just between us."

"I *still* didn't break Rule Three," Quentin insisted.

Owen and Martin looked at each other.

"Don't I look frustrated?" Quentin asked.

"But you *will* break Rule Three," Martin said.

"No I won't." Quentin rubbed his eyes behind his glasses. "There are only eight more days until the concert."

Owen said, "We want you to go ahead and cut her loose."

Quentin had to tread carefully here, so they wouldn't see his desperation. "I can't do that," he reasoned. "There wouldn't be any way to explain it to her without telling her that the thing between Erin and me is fake."

Martin suggested, "You could get back with Erin early."

"I don't think that's a good idea," Owen said quickly.

Reaching for his beer, Quentin gave Owen a knowing glance. Owen looked appropriately uncomfortable. Aha. Ammunition. But Quentin didn't want this kind of ammunition. If Owen fell for Erin, the band would be in a world of trouble. That's what Rule Two was for. Maybe Quentin *should* get back with Erin early.

And lose Sarah? No way.

After a sip of beer, Quentin said, "Me, neither. If Erin switches around too much, the press will lose interest. It has to be a big deal when she changes hands."

Owen looked like the wind had died out of his sails. Martin wasn't as intent as Owen, anyway. Martin had never been a plotter, and it was almost impossible to get him involved in band politics when he was on a drug binge.

"I don't know what y'all are complaining about," Quentin went on. "There's nothing in Rule Three that says Sarah can't hang around. For that matter, there's nothing in the rule that says I can't cop a feel."

Owen woke up to this challenge. "The spirit of the rule is that you can't cop a feel."

"We've never established separation of power," Quentin pointed out, "so you don't have the right to interpret the spirit of the rule."

"Logically," Martin said, "you wrote the rule, Q, so you're legislative. Someone else gets to be judicial."

"I'm appointing myself executive," Quentin told them, "and I'm ordering you the hell out of my Fortress of Solitude!"

Owen and Martin looked at each other again, and Owen motioned with his head. They got up and left with more creaking of wicker.

"Martin!" Quentin called after them. "*Clinical Immunology and Allergy Today.*" He caught the magazine as it flew through the doorway at him.

He downed the rest of his beer, then thumbed back through the magazine. And looked at his watch. He wondered what time Sarah would show up tomorrow night, where they'd go, and whether they'd get some privacy. If privacy wasn't part of Sarah's plan, maybe Quentin could convince her.

Martin reappeared on the porch and pulled a chair close to Quentin for a conference.

Quentin said, "I didn't break Rule Three in the last five minutes."

Martin fixed Quentin with an anxious stare, eyes owlish behind the thick glasses. "I didn't try to explain it to Owen," he said low, "but I've changed my mind since he and I talked about it this morning. I don't think you should cut Sarah loose."

"That makes two of us."

"I think you should keep her closer," Martin said ominously. "Or go with her to buy a gun, like she wanted."

"Have you lost your mind?" Quentin laughed. "You saw her at the firing range. She nearly capped me while I was standing next to her. I've never seen anyone's hands shake that badly, outside the hospital."

"She's scared because she thinks she'll have to use that gun."

Quentin bit the bait. "On whom?"

"Nine Lives. You know he's in jail for assault."

Quentin could see that Martin was genuinely concerned for Sarah. But heroin made Martin paranoid. "You don't know that it was assault on *Sarah*," Quentin said. "Why *would* Nine Lives have assaulted her? It wasn't a lovers' quarrel. She said she didn't have sex with him."

"You say she's not having sex with you, either, and look at you. Completely whipped. She's been here three days and you're about to implode. She was down there—what'd she say?—months and months."

Quentin saw Martin's point. But he still thought Martin was blowing the issue out of proportion. "It's a good thing Nine Lives is safe in a Brazilian prison."

"That guy has more money than the four of us put together," Martin said. "How long do you think he'll *stay* in a Brazilian prison?"

Quentin started to protest, but Martin put up his hand. "I don't want to hear it. You're so caught up in your games, like that shit you pulled with Rachel today, that you're not paying attention. I know I've got my problems, Q, but at least I'm paying attention. Sarah needs to feel like someone's got her back, and she's not getting that from you."

Martin rose to leave. He paused in the doorway to say, "She has a fresh three-inch scar under her chin, Q. She really wanted that gun."

~

Martin's words were still echoing in Quentin's head the next morning. *She really wanted that gun.* And Quentin wanted to find out why she wanted it. A little revenge wouldn't hurt, either, for the phone to Owen's nose and the jar of garam masala broken on the floor. His hired car had driven him to the Galleria, and he'd sweet-talked the hotel desk clerk, a fan, into giving him a key card.

Sarah's room was dark and, not surprisingly after the way she'd treated him yesterday, cold. The bathtub was dry, so she hadn't taken a shower that morning.

He felt a flash of worry for her, which justified scanning her room and checking out her closet. Everything was in neat order. Nothing was wrong.

She always looked immaculate. Not a wrinkle in her clothes, not a hair out of place—until he got a hold of her. He doubted she would let anyone see her at breakfast in the hotel restaurant before she'd taken a shower. But underneath her soft skin, her muscles were rock-hard. If he had to guess, he'd say she was exercising now.

He resisted the urge to sift through her things, looking for the reason she felt so threatened. He quashed the even stronger desire to examine all her underwear. He consulted the hotel map on the bedside table and found the gym.

She was the gym's only patron, jogging on a treadmill among the rows of white machines. As soon as he stepped off the elevator, he recognized the pink streak in her ponytail through the gym's glass wall. Her back was turned to him, and she wore her earbuds plugged into her MP3 player, so she didn't see or hear him. He sat in a chair just outside the elevator. He would watch her for a few minutes before entering the gym to surprise her.

She was a runner. He knew that right away. She was no dilettante. Her tank top and shorts were soaked through with sweat, as if she'd been here for a long time. Yet she showed no signs of being the least bit winded, or of stopping anytime soon. He wished he could see her face.

He wondered what she was running toward, or running from.

Martin's words came back to him yet again. *She really wanted that gun.* This was the first time Quentin had seen her when she wasn't on parade. She thought no one was looking, and her drive was raw and undisguised. *She really wanted that gun.* She had a problem, and she would take care of it. If not this way, another way, wheels always turning. Quentin understood this completely.

What he didn't understand was how she was *still jogging*, her running shoes padding on the treadmill in time with his heartbeat. He had to exercise in short bursts each morning to keep from wheezing. He was actually jealous that she was healthy and athletic, probably going on ten miles by now.

Suddenly she jumped from the treadmill without turning it off and jogged to the water fountain in the corner. Quentin was poised to go either forward to greet her, or back into the elevator, before she discovered him. Then she bent over to drink from the fountain, and he decided to stay where he was. Discovery or no, if he died right now of an asthma attack, at least he'd had a view of Sarah Seville bent over in her running shorts.

She jumped back onto the treadmill without looking in his direction. He was invisible.

This was stupid. It was like he had a crush on her, which hadn't happened to him since Vonnie Conner in high school. There was almost no resemblance between Sarah and Vonnie Conner. Vonnie had been blond and busty, like Erin. A cheerleader. Only the feelings of lust, wistfulness, and loss that Vonnie and Sarah evoked were similar. The feeling that *he had to have this* and *he could not have this*.

He couldn't have Vonnie Conner because in high school, he'd been lanky, glasses-clad, and asthmatic, without a truck. There hadn't been much he could do about that. Sarah he could do something about. He could quit the Cheatin' Hearts.

No he couldn't. The band was counting on him. And what would happen to Martin?

What would happen to *him*?

He could convince her to quit *her* job. Maybe Martin was right. If Sarah felt she needed a gun to protect herself against a rock star in jail in a different hemisphere, it didn't say much for her job satisfaction.

But this didn't feel right, either. She *did* love her job. Maybe not that part of it, but she wanted to keep it badly enough that she was willing to tackle Quentin. She came on to him hesitantly, as if she wasn't used to being sexy—though she seemed comfortable enough in those low-cut shirts and high heels. She put on a show because she loved her job. Like Quentin loved his.

The need to go to her, bring her down off that treadmill, and take her was so strong that he could feel the blood shifting in his veins with the gravitational pull.

It was too much.

And Quentin knew now Sarah was holding her cards too close to the vest. He wouldn't find out why she felt so threatened until she decided to tell him herself. He slipped back onto the elevator and headed for home.

6

Sweetie, I just got your e-mail from several days ago. I am not as "wired" as you are. I have been in Birmingham all week at the Vulcan Regional Duplicate Bridge Tournament. Please come to the evening session after you finish work today. I am sorry that I will not be able to see you on your birthday. I am flying out early tomorrow morning for the Lake Taneycomo Regional Duplicate Bridge Tournament in Branson, Missouri.

Love,
Mom

Sarah stepped out of the shower still invigorated from her run and a long set of Cheatin' Hearts on her playlist. Running had always helped her handle the stress of Nine Lives. Running with Quentin's strong, lazy melody in her ears was at once relaxing and terribly exciting. There was no way she could miss her date with him tonight, mother or no mother.

She toweled off and began her hundred-step beauty routine. Before her Natsuko-style transformation, she hadn't worn much makeup. Natsuko required sultry eyes and clear skin. She called her mother on her cell phone and tried to blow her off between the moisturizer and the liquid foundation.

Her mother asked sharply, "Are you telling me that you cannot spare three hours per year to spend with your aging mother?"

Sarah was overwhelmed with anger that her mother manipulated her, guilt that her mother was right, anxiety that her mother would see her hair, and love. The mirror reflected her hand pressed to her cheek. Her mother's cheek. The older she got, the more she looked like her mother. The pink hair did not fix that.

"I'm babysitting this band," she explained weakly.

"The Cheatin' Hearts," her mother said. "After you e-mailed me, I looked them up on your Internet. I've heard a song of theirs, 'Come to Find Out.' Catchy, if risqué."

"That pretty much describes them," Sarah acknowledged. "Mom, I don't want to dis you, but I'm swamped with work today. And tonight, I'm supposed to keep up with one of the band members, who causes problems when left unattended."

"The one with the green eyes?"

"Since when do you notice?" Sarah asked suspiciously.

"I'm old," said her mother. "I'm not dead."

"They're really more hazel," Sarah lied.

"Bring him to bridge. He can *hang out*, as you say."

"Look, Mom, I'm not mixing business with mother," Sarah said with finality. She needed to see her mother. She *needed* to see Quentin.

After she hung up, she considered the implications. Her mother would want her to stay for dinner at the hotel after the bridge session. Strangely, Quentin seemed to have passable table manners. There had been no table when he'd stood in the kitchen to eat breakfast, but he'd chewed with his mouth closed. She called Quentin's cell phone.

He sounded like he was standing in a blender full of margaritas. "Are you in your car?" she asked. She only became more confused when he said yes. They had made their ill-fated trip to the firing range last night in Martin's truck, with Martin driving. She'd concluded Quentin was the Cheatin' Heart without wheels. "Are you driving?"

"No," he said.

"Who's driving?" she asked in a panic. He'd better not be with Erin.

"The guy I hire to drive me."

Oh. "But in *your* car?"

"Well, in the car I hire to go with the driver."

Right, the car service he'd mentioned several times. Sarah was exasperated. She was trying to put together the puzzle of the Cheatin' Hearts, but he was hiding the pieces from her. "Quentin, why don't you drive yourself?"

"Because I don't have a driver's license."

"Why *not*?"

"Because I don't need one when I'm hiring someone to drive me."

"You've been rich for two years," Sarah said. "How did you get around before that?"

"I lived on the bus line." He paused, then said, "Good morning, sunshine," and laughed and laughed until she laughed.

"I'm sorry," she said. "I just hate it when you hold out on me."

"I understand," he said, still holding out.

"Why aren't you recording my album?" she asked.

"That's where I'm headed."

"Really? Then where have you *been* this early in the morning?"

"Fishing."

She sighed. He was so friendly and open, mostly, but when he chose to close down, it was like talking to a wall. "Quentin," she said, "I don't want to cancel our date tonight—"

"You'd better not," he warned her.

Suddenly she was aware that she was standing naked in front of the bathroom mirror. She slid her thumb slowly across her nipple. Shuddered. Reached for her bathrobe.

"I don't want to," she repeated huskily, "but something's come up. I have to play bridge. You can still go with me so Erin thinks we have a date, but you'll just be sitting there while I play bridge. Is this too uncool for you? Would it ruin you if a photo ran in the Cheatin' Hearts Death Watch that showed you with me while I played bridge?"

"Unless I'm at one of my usual bars, or in the town where I grew up, I don't get recognized. We're careful to keep our hats on when we're performing." Slow on the uptake, he asked, "Bridge, the card game?"

If she didn't tell him the whole story, he'd keep asking. She lay on the bed and hugged herself into a ball. "About four years ago, my dad retired, and he and my mom set off on a bridge tour of the United States. I never understood it myself. I guess some retired couples have their RVs, or their gardens, or their grandchildren, and my parents had bridge. Then, about two years ago, my dad died of a heart attack."

Quentin was saying he was sorry, but Sarah didn't want to hear it, only wanted to get this story out and over with. She interrupted him, "And then my mother started her solo bridge tour of the United States. I know what she's doing. She's looking for my dad. You'll hear her. She has a different partner every time, and every one drops tricks or passes her forcing bid. She wore her poker face at the funeral, didn't shed a tear. I know this is it. This is the tears. This is her sick style of mourning. She left so fast that I had to clean up her house after the wake."

Sarah was spilling this story maniacally. She forced

herself to take a deep breath before finishing slowly, "My mother never comes to see me. She hardly ever goes home. We usually see each other at Christmas, but not last year. I was in Rio."

"So, you're her bridge partner for a few hours," Quentin said, accepting casually, which Sarah appreciated.

"It doesn't even make that much sense," she admitted. "Beulah has been her partner for the whole tournament, even though the very first morning, Beulah put Mom in slam missing two aces. I'm sure you'll hear all about this, too. But Mom's made a commitment to Beulah until the end of tonight's session, and she won't break it. Besides, she and I had a little altercation when I was thirteen, which I won't get into, and I swore I'd never be her partner again.

"No, I have to go to the partnership table and get paired with someone. There are a few normal people. And some people who eat paste. And some hardcore people like my mother. Luck of the draw."

Quentin said, "I play bridge."

"You do not."

"I play all the games."

You sure do, Sarah thought. She arranged to pick up Quentin for the bridge tournament that night. Then she called her mother back. "Now, listen, Ethel. This band is worth millions of dollars to Manhattan Music, and therefore, it's worth my job to me. Please remember that when you foil me."

"You could always get a job at the Fairhope Country Club," her mother drawled elegantly. "They need a public relations expert. Their Cobb salad is an absolute shame."

Sarah tapped one fingernail on her phone in irritation. Yesterday she'd handled the *New York Times* and *Vanity Fair*, but she couldn't handle her own mother.

"I'm just joshing, sweetie," her mother finally said. "Stop tapping."

"Do not *josh* me about this. If you want me to play bridge, you have to help me keep up the image to Quentin that I'm a tough New Yorker."

"And *I'm* supposed to be a New Yorker?"

Her mother was right. That was ridiculous. "I've never specified that I grew up in New York City. I could hail from somewhere else in the area. Maybe Schenectady."

"Gracious, how do you expect me to pull *that* off? I'm bound to slip up and order a glass of iced tea. Couldn't you move us to Louisville, or Richmond?"

"Richmond doesn't exactly have that hard rockin' edge I was looking for."

"*Schenectady*," her mother repeated. "You might as well have made me from *Los Angeles*."

"*You* don't have to be from Schenectady," Sarah explained. "You grew up in Alabama, but you moved to Schenectady when you were—"

"Twenty," her mother finished. "And had you right away. That would make me fifty now."

"I'm glad you're into the fantasy," Sarah said dryly.

"And I've moved back to Fairhope to live out my

days in quiet solitude, without my only child interloping at inopportune times, such as Christmas."

"I was in *Rio*!"

"They have airplanes in Rio."

Theoretically, Sarah thought.

~

That night, she drove Quentin to the hotel where the bridge tournament was held. She marveled that in the car, he never once complained about the strange turn their date had taken. When they registered in the lobby, he towered over the women and stooped elderly men wandering about, yet he seemed completely comfortable. The uncomfortable one was Sarah.

The moment came. Her mother stood at the edge of the lobby, watching for Sarah, silver hair coifed in its neat bob, chic pantsuit impeccable. Her mother didn't recognize her.

Sarah took Quentin's hand and pulled him toward the inevitable. Her mother noticed them then, but she seemed to recognize Quentin first. Only then did she turn her gaze to Sarah. She wore her poker face, without even the raised eyebrow. Absolutely no reaction. It was almost worse than screams of *What have you done to your hair?* which was why, as a teenager, Sarah had never attempted to shock her mother.

Then they embraced, and Sarah introduced her charming mother to charming Quentin. For a few moments, she could almost imagine that she had a normal, loving mother. Even the mother she'd had before her dad died, though not normal, would do. She could almost imagine that she was introducing her normal mother to her handsome boyfriend, who was not in love with someone else.

Her real mother returned. "I never thought I'd say this," she drawled, "but I do believe I'll be glad when this tournament is over tonight. In one hand during the afternoon session, Beulah didn't lead my suit after I bid it three times!" She glanced at her watch, then toward the ballroom filled with card tables. "Almost time!" She patted Quentin's arm. "Have fun!" She swept into the ballroom as if she owned it and her partner, cowering at a table, was her maid.

Quentin stood directly in front of Sarah and looked down at her. "I see where you get your poker face," he said. "But you kept yours, too. You took it real good."

"Thanks." She looked up into his beautiful green eyes and wished she could spend the evening in his arms. Without even having sex. She just wanted to be held by him. "I hate bridge."

They took their assigned places at one of the tables and played for three tedious hours, with their opponents rotating to new tables every so often. Most of the other players seemed to be of the paste-eating variety, and some of the women and all of the men alternately stared at Sarah's hair and ogled her cleavage. Natsuko would have accepted this as part of the territory, but Sarah minded.

And it wasn't even any fun to play bridge with Quentin. Playing poker with novices was difficult for Sarah, because she never knew whether they were making a savvy move or just getting lucky as they bungled their way through the game. Bridge was similar, except that in bridge, Quentin was supposed to be her partner. It was almost impossible to play this partner game by herself. Now she knew how her mother felt.

A collective gasp echoed in the ballroom. Sarah looked over to see a large elderly lady at another table melt out of her chair and puddle onto the floor. Instantly a man was on top of her, pressing her chest and giving her mouth-to-mouth.

"Your turn," the west player said.

With a shocked look at Quentin, Sarah set down a spade, then glanced back at the woman and the man performing CPR. Other people watched, too, and were periodically hounded by their opponents to keep playing their hands.

The east player suggested, "We should move our table so the stretcher can get through." The four of them picked up the table and shifted it toward the wall to clear a path on the ballroom floor.

"Your turn," West said again to Sarah.

The hand ended. They had to wait for the other tables, slowed by rubberneckers, to finish before their opponents could rotate to different tables.

Quentin stood and stretched. "I'm taking a little break."

Sarah nodded. Probably he needed a moment in the lobby, or a drink from the bar, to collect himself after witnessing the shadow of death, or the Vulcan Regional Duplicate Bridge Tournament's crassness in the shadow of death.

Instead, he walked to the supine woman, tapped the now slowing man on the shoulder as if cutting in at a ball, and took his turn pressing the lady's chest and giving her mouth-to-mouth.

West asked East, "How does Annabelle look?" East shook his head.

"Is she a friend of yours?" Sarah asked in horror.

"A dear friend," East said. "But she was doing what she loved to do." He turned to West. "You really should have led the three of diamonds on that hand."

The ballroom doors burst open and two paramedics rolled a stretcher in. It took both of them plus Quentin to lift the lady onto the stretcher, and it was Quentin rather than one of the paramedics who placed an oxygen mask over her face. Finally, as the paramedics wheeled the burdened stretcher out, Sarah thought she heard one of them call to Quentin, "Queen to king two."

The ballroom door closed behind them. The hand ended. The east-west pairs switched tables, with the bustle more animated now that there was something to talk about. Several people patted Quentin's back as he made his way to Sarah, sweat glistening at his temples.

Sarah asked a passing waiter to bring Quentin a glass of water. She was going to hug him, but he bent over to look into her eyes first. "Are you okay?" he whispered. "Your dad didn't die playing bridge, did he?"

"Oh, no," Sarah assured him. "Sitting at home in his favorite chair, listening to Bach." She shook off a sob. "Is she going to be okay?"

"No," Quentin said with finality. "She was already dead when I took over."

"Then why'd you keep trying?" Sarah whispered, flashing back to Quentin's strong arms pressing the dead chest.

"You have to try," he said calmly. "You never can tell."

Sarah turned to the closed ballroom doors. "Did you know that paramedic?"

"Yeah," Quentin acknowledged. "When the Cheatin' Hearts hit the big time, I was working at the hospital."

She murmured, "That explains your cavalier attitude toward IVs."

Lost in thought, he looked through Sarah. "Did he say queen to king two?" He swore. Then he focused on her again. "We've had a chess game going for three years."

He moved past her to pull out the chairs for their last opponents, Sarah's mother and Beulah. Sarah's mother asked, "So, enjoying this geriatric excitement?" as Quentin scooted her up to the table.

"You mean sitting around playing bridge for kicks, right?" Sarah said reproachfully. "I know you're not making a joke about that poor woman."

"I suppose I'm inured," her mother said. "It happens so often. It happened to my partner at the Fort Custer Regional Duplicate Bridge Tournament in Kalamazoo last year."

Beulah eyed Sarah's mother uneasily.

Sarah exclaimed, "Oh my God, Mom! What did you do when she died?"

"Don't take the Lord's name in vain, sweetie. It's not polite. I was able to find another partner by the afternoon session."

Quentin made a noise, about to burst into laughter. He covered it by clearing his throat.

"It's because you're all so sedentary," Sarah told her mother. "You need to get your butts off these extremely uncomfortable chairs and go for a jog."

"*Sarah*," her mother scolded scathingly.

Sarah realized what she'd said. "*Butt* is not a curse word," she defended herself. Remembering an argument with her mother from fifteen years before, she added, "And neither is *snot*."

Playfully her mother reached over to cover one of Quentin's ears. "Please don't use that kind of language around me, even to make a point," she said. "Your marathon isn't the answer to everything."

"Neither is bridge."

Quentin was dummy on this hand, appropriately enough. He laid down his cards for Sarah to choose from and watched her intently as she played. Sometimes he scrutinized Sarah's face, then her mother's, then hers, fascinated or—if he shared Sarah's opinion—alarmed at the likeness.

Sarah was able to contain herself while she controlled the cards, but when she finished and the bidding began for the next hand, she couldn't stand it. She hardly ever sat still for this long. Just one more hand. Hyped from her run that morning, she tapped her feet under the table.

"Don't fidget, sweetie," her mother said as Beulah, the dummy for this hand, left the table. Sarah had noticed during the session that Beulah seemed to take a break from Sarah's mother every time she was dummy, which didn't surprise Sarah in the least.

"Don't scold, Mom," Sarah said. "It doesn't become you." Then, as she watched her mother rearrange Beulah's cards to her liking with busy efficiency, she asked, "Has Beulah done any better this session?"

"Beulah," her mother said derisively, "just took me to four with only five points in her hand, as you can see, and we're vulnerable."

"Maybe you should play poker instead of bridge," Quentin suggested, the first words he'd spoken other than bridge bids since Sarah's mother sat down. "Poker and bridge are a lot alike. Your poker face would come in handy. And you wouldn't have to count on anybody but yourself."

"Mmmm-hmmm," her mother said dismissively, studying her cards.

Quentin said, "Of course, poker's more of a man's game."

Sitting back in her chair with an amused smile and one eyebrow arched, Sarah's mother examined Quentin like a tiger looking over a piece of meat. "Is it, now."

"Yes, ma'am," he said guilelessly.

Sarah's mother leaned toward the table again and began to play the hand. "Perhaps it's you who needs to play bridge instead of poker. If your whole life is poker, playing the game isn't fun."

Quentin shot Sarah an alarmed look. Sarah shrugged. Her mother liked to scare people.

Her mother scared Quentin again at the end of the session when she asked him to accompany her to the teller machine in the lobby as her bodyguard. She asked Sarah to get them a table for dinner in the restaurant. Clearly this was a ploy to grill or threaten Quentin alone, but Sarah knew that attempts to dissuade her mother weren't worth the effort. She moved to a table in the restaurant and waited obediently.

Quentin looked stricken when they returned, but he managed to pull out the chair for Sarah's mother before informing Sarah that he'd be waiting for her at the bar.

"Won't you join us for dinner?" Sarah's mother asked, sounding genuinely disappointed.

"Oh, no, ma'am," he said. "I already et." He actually said *et*. "I'm sorry you missed the barbecue I grilled up earlier."

"You were supposed to be working on my album," Sarah said.

"I did that, too. I was multi—" He ran out of words.

"Multitasking?" Sarah suggested.

"You amaze me with your book learning." He leaned down to kiss her lips softly, then held her gaze with his green eyes for a few seconds, giving her strength, before crossing the room and easing onto a barstool.

Sarah didn't blame him. It could be that he'd already eaten, or that he wanted to give her time alone with her mother. Most likely, fifteen minutes of Sarah and her mother sparring was all he could stand. Sarah knew the feeling.

"Happy early birthday, sweetie," her mother said, passing her five hundred-dollar bills under the table, as if she was afraid they'd be mugged in the hotel restaurant. Sarah tried to accept the gift graciously. She didn't mention that she still had three thousand dollars in poker winnings in her bag.

They chatted for a few minutes about relatives, and Sarah's lying, cheating, soon-to-be-ex-husband, and Wendy, whom Sarah's mother had met several times and disapproved of as "brazen." But Sarah's mother had nothing but praise for Quentin.

"Such a gentleman," she said between dainty sips of she-crab bisque. "And so *handsome*. If only we could get him out of that faded T-shirt." She glanced up at Sarah. "So to speak."

"He's not exactly the corporate mogul you always said you wanted for me, Mom," Sarah pointed out. "And he's very talented, but he doesn't seem all that bright. This is one of those times you'd be telling your bridge friends, 'Thank goodness intelligence descends through the mother.'"

"Brains aren't everything," her mother said. This was counter to everything else her mother had ever said in her life. "But he might be smarter than you think."

"Mom, he acts *so dumb* sometimes. He'd have to be absolutely brilliant to play dumb that well."

Her mother raised one eyebrow. "Well, he pushed us into five spades and then doubled us, and the only reason we made the contract was that you threw away your eight of diamonds."

"You're saying he *knows what he's doing*? I thought he was overbidding."

"Sarah," her mother lectured her, "the first step to winning at bridge is to know your partner."

"The other thing *you* don't know about my partner is that whatever he may formerly have had of a brain, he's fried with coke." She saw the wheels turning in her mother's head. "No, not like RC Cola," she clarified. "*Cocaine.*"

Her mother frowned. "He doesn't seem—what do you call it?—*wasted.*"

"He's not high right now," Sarah admitted. In fact, he hadn't used in the four days Sarah had been in Birmingham.

"The lobe that plays bridge is still working," her mother declared.

"Mom," Sarah sighed, watching her mother pick happily at a Caesar salad. Her mother hadn't pitched a boy this hard since Harvey Marvel, whose daddy owned the bank. Or maybe her mother wanted Quentin for herself. "Quentin is not canceling his next world tour to accompany you on your bridge tour."

"He might." Her mother winked. "Does he obey you?"

Sarah laughed out loud at the very idea. "Do you *want* him to obey?"

"I want him to follow the bidding conventions."

Sarah said carefully, "Dad didn't."

"And if he had," her mother said almost angrily, "I might have made Grand Life Master by now."

Sarah changed the subject somewhat. "Quentin cooks, though."

Now her mother was *really* interested. "Cooks what?"

"Breakfast. Indian food."

"Can he make quiche?"

"I don't know," Sarah said, rolling her eyes. "Do you want me to send you his résumé? I can make a good guess at it. Six years, prep cook at a restaurant. Six years, hospital orderly. Clearly he knows CPR. He probably knows the Heimlich maneuver, too, so if you choke on his cooking, you're covered. Do you want me to ask him whether quiche is in his repertoire?"

Her mother shushed her escalating tone before whispering, "That's not necessary, dear. It's just that I'm not terribly fond of Indian cuisine. I once had an unfortunate experience with some curried potatoes." She took another dainty bite and smiled sweetly.

"You know what I think?" Sarah asked. "I think you're making excuses for a pair of intense green eyes."

"Don't be ridiculous, sweetie. I told you, I'm *old.*" She dabbed at the corners of her mouth with her napkin and folded it neatly. "Although I have to admit that it's fun to be goaded again."

"Goaded?" Sarah asked blankly. "About playing poker? I don't think he was goading you. He's a chauvinist. Or he was warning you that other men are chauvinists, as if you didn't already know."

"I'm telling you, he was goading me. There was a gleam in his eye."

"I didn't see any gleam."

"I saw gleam," he mother insisted. "What's known in poker as a *tell*. I've played bridge for fifty-three years, and I know a gleam when I see one."

"You've played bridge since you were negative three years old?"

Her mother looked puzzled. *That* didn't happen often.

"Because you're only fifty now, remember?" Sarah explained. "You're no good at living the lie."

Her mother's eyebrow went up. "Speaking of living the lie," she said, "I don't approve of your look."

Sarah frowned. "No kidding."

Her mother held up one hand for silence. "I don't approve of the look, but I have to say that it's put together well. You pull it off. Now you may say, 'Thank you, kind Mother.'"

"Right."

"Use your birthday money to buy yourself more of these"—she paused purposefully—"garments. Or more of whatever chemicals cause your pretty brunette hair to turn those colors. Your Quentin seems to like the look very much."

Sarah had had enough. She put down her fork and leaned forward in her seat. "Mom. Seriously, now. Please don't press this and mention 'my Quentin' like he's the one who got away every time we talk for the rest of our lives. I would be tempted. I *am* tempted. But he's in love with that girl from the band."

Her mother finally heard her. She gazed at Sarah sadly. "Does he make you happy?"

"Yes," Sarah said without hesitation.

Her mother looked away. "Does he make you laugh?"

Sarah had thought since the funeral that everything would be okay if her mother could just drop the poker face for a moment and mourn. Now that tears shone in her mother's eyes, Sarah wanted her mother's mask back in place, because her heart was being torn out. She reached across the table and took her mother's hand.

Glancing past her mother's shoulder, toward the bar, she saw Quentin's green eyes on her even at this distance. He might have been watching them the whole time. Out of deference, he swiveled on his barstool and turned back to the bartender.

~

The statue of Vulcan, clothed front view, watched from atop Red Mountain as Sarah entered the expressway and the lights of downtown fell away on either side of the BMW. "Are you sure you won't drive?" she asked Quentin. "I almost got us lost on the way over here. Would you drive us back to your house?"

"I've had a drink," he said, "and the last thing I need is a DUI with no license."

Lame excuse. He might not be much of a drinker, but right now he was a far cry from DUI. She tried to conceal her frustration as she switched lanes and took the exit. She was afraid that if she pressed him further, he'd press her back, and she'd reveal her own roots. Quentin and Owen were from a small town south of Birmingham. Their high school football team had come down to kick her high school's ass in the state playoffs one year.

She knew from experience that if you grew up in a small town in Alabama, you had a car. If you were of driving age, you had a car. If you were poor and lived in the projects, you had a car. If you had to sell one of your kidneys to get it, you had a car. There just wasn't any public transportation to speak of. You had to have a car. *Especially* if you were a lusty teenage boy.

It made no sense that Quentin, thirtyish, didn't have a license. She would get to the bottom of this. She began to plan.

Quentin interrupted her thoughts. "Your mama's nice."

"You have got to be joking."

"Nope. Our manager's mama—wow, what a piece

of work. The key is, could you stand to spend Christmas with her without staying drunk the whole time? And I think your mama passes that test."

"You'd like to spend Christmas with my mom?"

"Yeah, I bet it would be nice," he said. "I bet she lives in an old house, and everything is all decorated and fixed. I bet the house is big enough that you can kind of get lost in it if you want to be by yourself. And then, when you're ready to go downstairs, I bet there's lots of bridge."

Sarah laughed, because he was right.

He went on, "I bet it gets to be a problem that there's three people instead of four, or seven people instead of eight, and you have to round up somebody to play bridge with you. And it's always somebody that doesn't fit in, like the next door neighbor's addled aunt Emmy."

Sarah was cracking up. "No, it's my mother's gardener's brother-in-law. When my mother can't find a partner for the bridge club in Fairhope, she pays him to play with her, because otherwise he won't go."

"Exactly," Quentin said triumphantly. "And I bet your mama isn't much of a cook because she'd rather play bridge, but she knows all the best caterers, so the food is always great. And then, this is Fairhope, so when you get tired of food and bridge and relatives, you can go sit in the park and look out over Mobile Bay."

Sarah glanced at him, but she couldn't see his face in the shadows between streetlights. "How do you know all that?"

"I've been to Fairhope," he said. "When the band started out, we used to work all week and play gigs at every honky-tonk in the Southeast on the weekends."

Sarah said, "I meant about my mother."

"She's a lot like you."

Which means you know all about *me*, Sarah thought. And he had known her four days.

"Seems like you and your mama don't get along great, though," he said. "You're trying to work something out. And it isn't bridge."

"My dad played peacemaker." Sarah sighed. "Or distracted us from our arguments. It's hard for us to relate to each other without Dad standing between us."

"He was a real funny guy?"

"Yeah." Sarah smiled as she parked the BMW beside Erin's Corvette. She left the motor running.

Before she could prepare herself for this, Quentin pulled her across the seat and into his lap. She demurred, pushing halfheartedly against his chest. He quickly pinioned both her wrists behind her back with one of his big hands.

The kiss was a tranquilizer. Any fight she'd had left in her escaped suddenly, and she opened her mouth for his.

Then she felt his thumb on her scar.

"Don't!" she cried, jerking her hands free, backing up against the car door.

"Does it still hurt?" His low voice vibrated through her.

The house floodlights were off. She couldn't see his face clearly in the darkness.

He asked, "Did you go to the doctor when it happened?"

She didn't even process the question. She was busy thinking *Why did he have to do that?* Her body still wanted him.

"Let me look at it," he said.

"No!" she said. "Get out."

"I want to get close to you."

"I don't," she insisted. This was a lie. "I do," she admitted, "but there's this thing between us." The thing's name was Erin.

He laughed. "I liked it better two nights ago, when there was a thing between us and I made you come anyway."

She turned forward, gripping the steering wheel. "Thanks for putting up with bridge and all."

She could feel his eyes on her, watching her, waiting for her to say something else.

Finally he reasoned, "We're adults. We can talk this out. This is all real high school."

"If it were high school, you'd be driving."

He slid his big frame out of the car and slammed the door.

She drove as fast as she could down the driveway, away from his touch on her chin.

7

Quentin stood in the driveway, watching the retreating taillights of Sarah's BMW, considering her scar. At registration for the bridge tournament, she'd quickly called dibs on the north position. When her mother sat down at the table with them, he'd realized why: her mother played west. Sarah's scar faced away from her mother.

But Sarah's mother didn't miss a thing. When he'd walked with her to the teller machine, she'd said with a hard grin, "You're made, mister."

"Ma'am?" It was all he could do to keep from laughing while the elegant pentagenarian raised one eyebrow at him just like Sarah, calling his bluff. She suspected he was putting on the hick act. But he didn't laugh. If she really made him, that would be a serious problem. Unless she kept it from Sarah. It seemed that she and Sarah didn't communicate.

She pulled her teller card and the cash from the machine and tucked them in her purse, then turned back to him with her arms folded. "How did she get that mark on her chin?"

"I don't know, ma'am. She had it when I met her."

Sarah's mother raised that eyebrow again as she glared at him. "You look after her."

"Yes, ma'am," he'd promised. But he couldn't keep that promise if Sarah wouldn't let him.

It was *so frustrating*. He walked through the garage to his house, closed the door behind him, and was about to bang his head when Owen bounded up the stairs from the studio, looking alarmed.

Owen saw Quentin and sighed with relief. "I thought you were Sarah."

"What if it *had* been Sarah?" Quentin asked, walking into the next room, where the TV was tuned to an orchestra performance. "When we're not watching TV, we need to keep it on NASCAR."

"That's not what I was worried about." Owen called across the room in a sharp tone Quentin rarely heard from him, "Erin!"

Erin started up from the couch. She'd been lying curled with her back to Martin.

"What if Sarah comes in?" Owen asked Erin. "Sarah's not going to be convinced you and I are together if you're sleeping with Martin."

This hadn't occurred to Quentin. Erin and Martin took naps together occasionally. He'd never thought much about it. They all were lonely.

Erin sleepily wandered around the coffee table and flopped onto the opposite side of the sectional. "I want a vacation," she groaned. "I want one day, just *one day*, when I don't have to *fake* anything."

Quentin was about to make an orgasm joke when Owen said, "That's what the trip to Thailand was supposed to be for."

"Okay." She sighed. "I want one day when I don't have to fake anything *and* nobody ends up on a ventilator."

Owen turned to descend into the studio again, but Quentin pulled him into the kitchen and whispered, "You can't break a rule with her."

"I was going to remind you about the same thing," Owen whispered back. "You've been gone with Sarah for hours."

Quentin still wasn't one hundred percent sure that what he suspected between Owen and Erin was really going on. He said in warning, "Owen."

"Quentin," Owen said in the same tone.

"Owen." Quentin laughed, because this wouldn't get them anywhere. Owen wouldn't admit anything, if there was anything to admit. All Quentin could do was wait and see, while the world crumbled around them. He couldn't sense that *vibe* like Erin could. He suspected, but there wasn't any way to find out for sure.

Or was there? Owen went back down to the studio, and Martin disappeared in the direction of the bathroom. Erin was alone on the couch, elbow on the armrest and head in her hand, blond curls cascading over the leather, watching the orchestra through half-closed eyes.

Quentin jumped over the back of the sectional and sat beside her. He took her hand and rubbed her callused fingertips and her fingernails cut down to the quick for fiddle playing, so different from Sarah's careful manicure. He said honestly, "I've been meaning to tell you all week. I feel terrible. I should have gone to your concert with the orchestra."

She gazed at him coldly. "You said you had to stay home so it would look like we were in a fight, to set up the thing between Owen and me."

"I should have figured out a way to go," he said. "I really regret missing it. I know how important it was to you, and I wanted to see you do it. I'm sorry."

"Well, I'm still mad," she said stubbornly. "Check with me in another week. And I don't want to flash you, and it's not funny, so don't even ask."

He stared hard at her. Something in her eyes was different. She'd turned him down before, but she'd at least flirted back. Tonight she was aloof.

He gave her his best teasing smirk. "Let me see them."

He recognized a flash of real anger in her face before she slapped him, hard. She flounced out the door to the patio, headed for her house.

Oh *no*. She and Owen were lovers.

Martin stood in the bathroom doorway, laughing. "If you have *ever* deserved to be slapped," he said, "that was it."

Quentin rubbed his cheek, thankful Martin found it funny. Martin hadn't figured out yet that Erin and Owen were breaking Rule Two. Maybe he never would. Maybe he'd never get off heroin, either. The whole thing was hopeless.

Quentin sighed, "Want to go to Five Points?"

"I'm there."

~

The hip bar had an older clientele and an elegant feel. That's why Quentin liked to create a disturbance there. Martin starting a fight there made more of an impact than Martin starting a fight in a sports bar out on Highway 280. Quentin listened carefully to Martin's shouts from the kitchen over the noise of laughter in the crowded room, but the altercation hadn't escalated enough yet.

In the meantime, he wished a beautiful woman would sit next to him and make inane conversation with him to take his mind off his problems until Martin punched someone. He didn't know what to do about Owen and Erin, and he was *so frustrated* about Sarah.

Sarah slid onto the barstool next to Quentin. "Buy me a drink?" she asked.

Swallowing his surprise, he murmured, "I was just

thinking about you," and retrieved the kiss he'd intended to have in the car. Hands on her face, he let his thumb linger at the corner of her mouth. She hesitated, but her eyes were hard on him with wanting, and a woman couldn't fake that look. As if *this* helped his predicament.

He liked a little intrigue in case the Cheatin' Hearts Death Watch was observing, but this kiss quickly flamed too hot for a public place, even for him. Her lips were too soft and too open, and he was getting too hard. He ordered her a drink, picked up his own, took her hand, and led her through the press of the crowd to a small booth against the wall. "How'd you find me?"

"I have a mole in all your haunts." She laughed. "Please tell me you're not getting drunk again."

"Oh, no," he assured her. "Martin and I act like we've had quite a few before we get here. Then I sit at the bar and make passes at hot chicks. Just for show," he added when a hurt look flitted across her face. "Martin goes in the back and gets in a fight with the kitchen staff. We try to call the car to pick us up before the cops come. Sometimes our timing is off."

Sarah pressed her thumb to the corner of her mouth, where Quentin's thumb had been. This was unconscious, surely. And that was strange, because Sarah didn't do much of anything unconsciously. Then her thumb moved across her cheek to the scar on her chin, and he *knew* that was unconscious.

"What's the matter?" she asked uneasily. "Why'd you come down here?"

"Had a fight with Erin."

"What about?"

He took a big swig of his drink. "Flirted with her and she got mad."

Sarah raised one eyebrow. "Flirted with her, how?"

"Asked her to show me her tits."

Sarah scowled at him. He winked at her, so she'd see it was all in fun. She sat back against her high leather seat.

Uh-oh. She really liked him.

She *had* really liked him, and now he'd screwed himself.

He said weakly, "She slapped me. She never slaps me. I mean, not for *that*."

"Maybe she's serious with Owen," Sarah suggested.

Just what Quentin was afraid of.

Sarah went on, "Maybe she realizes you've reached an age where you can't use each other as inflatable dolls anymore."

"Are you saying I'm immature?"

Sarah shrugged. "Most people do want to settle down at some point, and you're still sniffing coke and asking to see women's breasts. Maybe Owen looks more stable to her."

"I don't do coke," Quentin said halfheartedly.

Frowning, Sarah looked deep into his eyes, like she might just believe him. But all she said was, "Maybe you should take a hint. *We* need to get more serious."

Suddenly the turn of events seemed less dire to Quentin.

"I'll pick you up tomorrow," Sarah said. "We'll disappear again, this time when you have plans for recording, so Erin feels really inconvenienced. In fact, let's go in the morning, so Martin is high and he jumps up and down on Erin's last nerve."

Quentin swirled the ice in his glass. This sounded to him like a terrific plan. Any plan involving disappearing with Sarah sounded terrific. But the band would be genuinely angry with him if he skipped out on a recording session. "What about the album?"

"To help the band stay together, it's worth it. But you'll have to refrain from goofing off another day. I want my album."

A crash in the kitchen overwhelmed even the noise of the bar. "Time to go," Quentin said, sliding his phone out of his pocket. "I'll call my driver."

"I'll drive you," Sarah offered.

Now there were shouts, and the kitchen doors burst open. Three of the cooks herded Martin in front of them, out the door of the bar.

By the time Quentin and Sarah reached the street, the Birmingham paparazzi had swooped down on them. A grizzled freelance photographer took color stills for the newspaper. Two teenage boys from the Alabama School of Fine Arts shot footage they sold to the local news stations. They were always hitting on the two black-clad college girls working on a senior project for their photography studio. Quentin had spent a couple of hours at a bar once with the art school girls, letting them take his picture, pretending to get drunk, and pretending not to be interested in the social commentary underlying their paparazzi project.

He winked at one of the girls and then, for the benefit of the cameras as well as his own satisfaction, kissed Sarah hard on the mouth. Or started to. A police siren wailed somewhere on the dark mountain. He jerked Martin away from the irate cooks and shoved him into the backseat of Sarah's BMW amid the flash of cameras. Quentin hopped into the front passenger seat. With a squeal of tires, Sarah pulled away from the curb.

Quentin leaned over and whispered, "Erin would be so pissed if you came in the house with me."

With a sidelong glance at him, Sarah nodded. Score!

He spent the ride home touching Sarah's hand on the gearshift and watching her perfect breasts heave in her plunging shirt. And, oh yeah, making small talk with a half-drunk Martin. Which didn't stop him from fantasizing about what he would do to Sarah when he got her into his bedroom again. After all the kissing and flirting they'd done, he hadn't even seen her bare breasts. Something had to give.

But when they pulled into the driveway, Erin's car was gone. Damn.

"Where's Erin?" Sarah asked, sounding almost disappointed.

Quentin sighed. "I'll bet she went home. Mostly she lives with her grandma in Irondale. Even if we're working on an album, she leaves when she gets sick of us."

"This late? Will she be back tonight?"

"Probably not," Quentin said before he thought. Damn again! He should have waffled, and then maybe Sarah would have waited around to make Erin jealous, and ended up staying all night.

"Thanks for the ride, Sarah," Martin said as he slid out of the backseat and closed the door.

Sarah turned to Quentin. "I think we're still in good shape. We have tomorrow morning. And surely Martin and Owen will tell Erin they saw us together tonight."

"Owen?" Quentin asked.

Owen sat on the tailgate of his truck in the garage, glowering at Quentin.

Quentin cursed.

"What's the matter?" Sarah asked.

"I don't know," Quentin said, stepping out of the car, "but I've got a feeling I'm about to find out."

Owen didn't let Quentin stand up straight before he lunged at him. He knocked Quentin into the fence beside the driveway and held him there with an under-cut, then another. The last time they'd fought this hard was before Thailand. Quentin couldn't get his breath.

Sarah and Martin were nearby, sitting on Sarah's BMW. Sarah asked, "Are you sure they've practiced this fake fighting enough? Because that looks like it really hurts."

"This isn't fake," Martin told her.

"I'll say," Quentin forced out as he finally mustered the strength to shove Owen away from him. Luckily, Owen lost his balance and smacked onto the pavement. Normally Quentin wouldn't take advantage, but Owen had taken advantage of him first. He kicked Owen in the ribs. Not as hard as he could, but pretty damn hard.

"How do you get them to stop?" Sarah asked.

"They'll stop soon," Martin told her. "Q can't go for too long at a stretch."

"Ah, a little stamina problem," Sarah said knowingly.

"What?" Quentin exclaimed, turning toward her.

But before he could demand clarification on exactly what Sarah and Martin meant, Owen yanked his leg out from under him. He hit the concrete flat on his back and lost his breath again.

Martin was telling Sarah, "You should know best."

Quentin scrambled up. As Owen tried to stand, too, Quentin caught him with a left hook to the jaw, which usually made Owen call uncle. But this time it didn't even slow him down. Quentin wasn't sure what happened next, but he found himself upside down against the fence.

He rolled backward and slowly staggered up. "I'm thirty," he groaned.

Martin called, "You're only as old as you feel."

"Then I'm eighty," Quentin declared, looking around for Owen. Now that the headlights of Sarah's BMW were off, it took him a moment to find Owen in the darkness. He was back in the garage, reaching into the payload of his pickup.

He came out brandishing a four-foot-long wooden beam.

Sarah gasped at the same moment that Martin called, "Time!"

Owen was still coming for Quentin, and Quentin braced himself.

"Owen, time!" Martin said, stepping into Owen's path. "That's egregious."

Owen dropped the board.

The Cheatin' Hearts wouldn't know the word *egregious*, Quentin was thinking, so he wouldn't have to contemplate just yet that his best friend since kindergarten had been ready to kill him. Then he saw the blood. "Owen."

Owen pulled off his T-shirt and held it to his gushing forehead. Martin reached up, peeled the T-shirt back, and examined the wound. "Stitches," he proclaimed.

"I'm not going back to the hospital right now!" Owen yelled at Quentin. "I'm sick of the hospital!"

"Me, too," Quentin said. "I'll sew it up."

Sarah called from the hood of the BMW, "You're not *really* going to give Owen stitches, are you? Come on."

Quentin shrugged. "I've done it before."

"In that case, I'm leaving." She slid down from the hood.

"Oh, please don't leave," he said, going to her. He hesitated to hug her because he was soaked with sweat. "You keep leaving." Sensing Owen behind him, he whirled and socked him with another left hook to the jaw. This time Owen went down in a heap on the driveway. Quentin turned back to Sarah, shaking out his sore hand. "You can stay over at Erin's house until the bloodcurdling screams die down."

Sarah waved toward the woods at the edge of the driveway, where cameras flashed from behind the fence. "I have to get to the office to take care of this new PR fiasco."

He stepped closer to her, despite his sweat. He took her hand and stroked down one slender finger to her perfect smooth nail. "If you were my girlfriend, you'd stay and take care of me because I got my ass kicked."

Sarah looked down at Owen on the driveway, who might have been unconscious. Martin was slapping him to revive him. She looked back at Quentin pointedly. Then she leaned to his ear and hissed, "If I were your girlfriend, the more I thought about how you came on to Erin, the angrier I'd be." She slammed the door of her BMW and sped down the driveway in a huff for the second time that night.

Owen was six foot four, but Quentin and Martin managed to drag him into the house and dump him over the back of the couch and onto the cushions. Of course he snapped wide awake when Quentin gave him a shot of anesthetic at the edge of his scalp. He started cussing.

"This needle is nothing compared to that chunk of wood you were about to whack me with," Quentin grumbled. He adjusted the lampshade so he could see better, and Martin handed him the needle carrier with the needle and suture material.

"I wasn't going to whack you with it."

Quentin pulled the first suture taut before he said, "Owen, you suck at poker. I saw the look on your face. You were going to *take me out* with that two-by-four!"

"Didn't you want me to pretend to be doing Erin?" Owen protested. "If you ask her to flash you her tits, shouldn't I act pissed?"

"Owen, you dumbass. No one knew about that except Erin and me, and maybe Martin. You don't have to fake being pissed at me for something no one knows I did." Of course, Sarah knew, but Owen didn't know she knew.

"Well, there's no reason for you to fake being an asshole," Owen griped. "It's so much easier for us to publicize how you're an asshole in real life. *Ow!* How many drinks have you had?"

"Two."

Owen groaned, and Martin asked, "Do you want me to sew it up?"

"How many drinks have *you* had?" Quentin asked Martin.

"More than two."

"Then, no." Quentin pulled several more sutures taut, and Owen calmed.

Finally Owen asked quietly, "Are you in *love* with Erin?"

"Of course not," Quentin said. "I mean, I love her like you love a friend. A friend with a really nice rack."

Martin asked Owen, "Are *you* in love with Erin?"

"No," Owen said emphatically. "She's beautiful, but she's high-maintenance."

Quentin felt some relief at the verisimilitude of this statement. He'd come to the same conclusion when he and Erin had broken up two years before.

But he would have felt better if Owen had been able to look Martin and him in the eye when he said it.

8

I'm having contractions, but apparently my discomfort is not sufficient for me to be admitted to the hospital just yet. Sarah, we did both agree to get pregnant. I went into this with my eyes open. I know it's not your fault that things didn't work out on your end. I'm not blaming you. But when the contractions come, I like you less than before. I can't help it. If I happen to text you some curse words in the next few days, please consider it my way of including my best friend in this joyful experience.

Much love,
Wendy Mann
Senior Consultant
Stargazer Public Relations

Sarah arrived at the mansion in the morning and peeked into the kitchen. Mouthwatering smells hung in the air, but the counters were clean. Breakfast was over. Listening for a moment at the door down to the studio, she heard Erin's fiddle, but not Quentin's bass guitar.

On a hunch, she stepped as quietly as she could out the back door and across the patio, past the pool, to stop under the crepe myrtles buzzing loudly with bees. She looked down the slope toward the screened porch off the lower story. Sure enough, Quentin sat in the lounge chair, intent on a magazine open on his knees, occasionally sipping coffee.

His hair was still damp and wavy from his shower. He wore his glasses, but no shirt, and the sight of his tanned muscles made her fight down a wave of heat. He looked like a commercial for outdoor furniture, or glasses frames, or exercise equipment. He could have sold her just about anything.

She reentered the house and explored the depths, unexpectedly discovering Martin's bedroom, a small movie theater, and a sauna on the bottom story before she walked through an unfurnished, blank white room to the screened porch.

She jerked the door open and asked, "Where's my album?"

Immediately she was sorry, because Quentin jumped a foot off the lounge chair and the magazine went flying. They were both lucky he hadn't been holding his coffee.

"Didn't anybody ever tell you it's rude to walk in on people without knocking?" he asked angrily with his hand over his heart.

She called up anger to match his. "You owe me an album. Until I get my album, you shouldn't do anything over here that you don't want me to know about."

He cracked a smile then. "*Anything?*" he asked suggestively.

She bent to pick up the magazine, making sure that he got the full view of her back end. "Anything," she said emphatically. She held up the magazine and waited for an explanation.

He shrugged. "I lifted it from the waiting room the last time I saw the allergist."

She raised one eyebrow. "You stole a copy of *Clinical Immunology and Allergy Today*?"

"They were out of *Fish and Field*." He ran his hands through his hair as he did when flustered—she was finally able to read him a little. He said, "I didn't expect you. Clearly."

"I thought we had a date."

"You left so late, and you acted all mad," he accused her.

"*You* may be mad at *me* by the time our date is over. Tit for tat, as we like to say."

"That's vulgar." He smiled.

While waiting for him to put in his contacts and find a shirt and the dilapidated deck shoes, she got into her BMW and put the top up. The ordeal promised to be traumatic enough for him. She didn't want to make it worse by keeping the top down. Then she waited on the hood for him.

"Where are we headed?" he asked, rounding automatically to the passenger side.

"You tell me." She tossed him the keys.

Instead of catching the keys, he watched them fly through the air and land in the bushes.

She'd expected this might be difficult. Patiently she walked around the car and retrieved the keys—again bending over with his view of her in mind. Then she straightened and dangled the key ring from one finger. "Take me for a ride, and I'll take you for one."

He didn't smile, just leaned back against the hood of the BMW with his arms crossed. "That's a nice package you're offering. But there is nothing you or anybody could give me that would make me drive a car."

"Why not?"

"I don't drive."

She didn't want to have *this* conversation again. "It isn't just about driving," she said. "It's for the good of the band. Driving will help you in the long run, because it will start to detangle some of the disabling codependence you have with your bandmates."

"The dis— What?"

"Disabling codependence," she repeated slowly. "You act like a dysfunctional family. You all make Erin feel sexy so she doesn't need to seek a stable relationship outside the band. You think for Owen and allow him to be a dumbass. You function for Martin so he can do heroin."

Quentin glanced toward the house. "Erin and Owen don't even know about Martin," he whispered.

"But they've unwittingly created an environment where it's safe for him to be an addict," Sarah said. "And *you* know. You're the primary enabler."

Now Quentin looked angry again, so she finished quickly, "And they drive you around, or allow you to hire a car without questioning you. Not to mention your diabolical leadership style. You play the rest of them like pawns in your chess game.

"None of you has a mental problem, except Martin's addiction, which he might get over with help. Potentially, you could function very well together. But you'd have to learn to come together as a band, as a job, and then go home to your separate lives."

Quentin glared at her. "I thought you wanted me to get back with Erin."

"Yes, we want to keep that part," Sarah said despite the knot in her stomach, "but the rest has to go."

"We got this way because we're always together. We're always on tour."

She shrugged. "Then maybe you shouldn't tour so much."

He gave her a look of disbelief. "The record company wants us to tour, to promote our albums."

"The record company wants the band to stay together and put out more albums," she corrected him. "So get in the driver's seat."

He shifted against the hood of the car and recrossed his arms, as if he planned to stay put.

She'd been afraid of this. It was time she put her Southern heritage to use. She knew how to phrase the proposal in terms a Southern male couldn't refuse. "Be a man, Quentin."

He gaped at her. "Oh, Sarah," he finally said, "don't play that card. Only my sick old granddaddy was allowed to play that card."

"Be a man."

He cursed, slid into the driver's seat, and slammed the door. Quickly she got in with him. He snatched the keys she held in front of his face, shoved them into the ignition, turned the engine over, and burst into reverse. He stomped the brakes.

She instructed him, "You need to gently—"

"I know how to drive," he snapped, jerking the car backward again. Finally he'd reversed and stomped the brakes enough times that he had room to pull forward down the driveway. He stomped the brakes again while the gate opened, then jerked the car onto the avenue.

Sarah was alarmed, but she didn't want to alarm him in turn. After all, she *had* asked for this. "Where are we going?"

Although the morning was still cool and the avenue was shady, beads of sweat stood out on his forehead. "We're going . . . to die."

He *looked* like death. It occurred to Sarah that he might not have recovered fully from his illness in Thailand. Maybe people looked like this during a heart attack, face pale. She hadn't been there when her dad died.

"Quentin," she said. "You're going to die of a cocaine overdose. Or an allergic reaction, right? And I'm going to die at the hands of a crazed rock star." The words were harsh, she knew, but her tone was soothing. "We're perfectly safe in this car."

She expressed more confidence than she felt, especially when she saw that he was merging onto the crowded highway. She watched for oncoming traffic so she could scream out in panic for him to hit the brakes if necessary. But he looked out for cars in the proper direction. If he could keep from screeching to a halt in another car's path, she thought they would stay alive. As he'd said, he really did know how to drive. He just didn't do it.

She settled back in the passenger seat, hoping she appeared relaxed, and pressed buttons on her phone to view her e-mail messages.

He protested, "If I can cut out on the band for this bullshit, you can cut out on *People* magazine." Sweat wet his hair and forced it into curls at his nape.

"I'm not working," she said. "I'm just checking on my pregnant friend."

"How far along?"

The question struck Sarah as strange. Wendy's husband Daniel had seemed well-informed and very sympathetic about Wendy's condition. But most men in Sarah's experience thought pregnant was pregnant until the baby appeared.

"To hear her talk, about thirteen months." Sarah found Wendy's latest message, chuckled at it, and clicked the phone off.

"What'd she say?" Quentin glanced nervously in the rearview mirror.

"She's still at home having contractions, it's not time to get an epidural yet, and this is all my fault."

"*Your* fault! It's been a while since high school biology, but—"

"It's a long story. A long, passive-aggressive story."

"I've got some time," Quentin said. He glanced again and again at the rearview mirror. Sarah turned around in her seat to see an eighteen-wheeler behind them, tailgating. Birmingham traffic was like this, and Quentin needed to get used to it.

She watched him carefully. Except for the frequent glances at the rearview mirror, he was motionless. He seemed to be driving fine now, but he stiff-armed the steering wheel, and his knuckles were white. She had to distract him.

"It's not really my fault," she said. "It was a collaborative effort. About this time last year, my friend and I were doing well at work, and we were about to turn twenty-nine. We decided that we didn't want to wake up one day, forty-five years old, professionally successful, and barren. We made a pact to go home that night and inform our husbands that it was time to get pregnant."

"*Husband?*" Quentin grabbed her hand and yanked

it in front of him so he could look for a ring while keeping his eyes on the road. At least he'd forgotten about the eighteen-wheeler for now.

She wondered whether he was putting on a show or he really cared she wasn't quite single. How delicious! But she managed to withdraw her hand. She wanted him to keep both hands on the wheel. "A few months later, Wendy was pregnant, and I was getting a divorce. My husband, Harold, got a girlfriend."

Quentin glanced at her, then into the rearview mirror, and tapped the brakes in warning. The eighteen-wheeler backed off. He glanced at her again. He said in disbelief, "You had a husband, and he cheated on you and divorced you because he didn't want to have a baby with you? He didn't want to be with you, when you look like *that*?"

"I didn't look like this," Sarah explained. "This isn't my natural hair color."

"Really? I thought you were the love child of Nicki Minaj and Ronald McDonald."

"Hey," Sarah said. "I'd enter a bridge tournament if I wanted my mother's opinion. I'm making myself vulnerable here to take your mind off driving and help you with your disabling codependence, and this is the thanks I get?"

He raked one hand back through his hair, but it got tangled in his curls. He gave up and put his hand on the steering wheel. "I'm really sorry. I'm a little tense. The story helps. Go on."

"About the time Harold moved out, Manhattan Music started getting reports that Nine Lives was self-destructing in Brazil. Before my breakup, I would have hidden in the bathroom until some other fool was assigned to the job. But I didn't want to be that person anymore. I could see myself becoming that childless, and now husbandless, professional forty-five-year-old. My friend Wendy and I had a college professor who wore red socks with her purple Birkenstocks and cooked for her dogs. I didn't want to be that woman. She seemed very bitter. I couldn't do anything about being childless and husbandless just then, but I didn't have to devolve into a shapeless mass. So I volunteered to tackle Nine Lives.

"I'd been pretty successful looking like I did, which basically was like a marathon runner after a shower. But I'd never gone up against someone like Nine Lives. Wendy kept warning me he would eat me for lunch if I wasn't careful. So I gave myself a makeover. As a result, Wendy tried to make me an appointment with her therapist. And Harold decided that he wanted me back."

"Whoa," Quentin said. She thought he was about to hit the brakes. Then she realized that he was commenting on her story. He asked, "What did you say to Harold?"

Sarah recited for Quentin the stream of epithets she'd offered Harold.

Quentin laughed and laughed, until Sarah laughed,

too. He laughed so hard that he had to wipe tears from his eyes. Slowly his laughter subsided. Finally he asked her almost seriously, "Did you love him?"

"I thought I loved him," she answered honestly, "but now I realize I didn't. I loved being married. Or the *idea* of being married. I liked having someone to do stuff with and plan with. I wanted to have kids. You know? I enjoyed the partnership."

Quentin probably couldn't fathom such a thing. He stared through the windshield and asked the next logical question: "Are you glad you didn't get back with him?"

Sarah sighed. "I'd been with him all through college. I thought marriage would be more exciting, but it got to be kind of a rut. And now . . . Well, I wouldn't say I've been happy, but I'm definitely not in a rut."

Quentin nodded. "And then what happened?" he asked. "What happened in Rio? You said you're going to die at the hands of a crazed rock star. That sounds fairly serious."

Sarah went cold despite the warm sun streaming through the windshield. Reaching down to adjust the air conditioner, she said, "Figure of speech. Enough about me. *You* tell *me* a secret. Let's talk about what happened to you in Thailand, and why you fired your manager, and why Erin ran to Owen."

"Let's not," he said.

"Why not?"

He pulled off the highway to park at an overlook,

with downtown Birmingham spread out below them, skyscrapers and warehouses and the complex of university hospitals. He punched the button to open the convertible top, letting in a rush of fresh, warm air.

Then he turned to Sarah and grinned maniacally. "I can drive."

"You can drive!" She clapped for him.

"I can drive," he said, still smiling, "and I'm having a great time with you, and the last thing I want to do right now is to go back to Thailand. You know where I want to go? You know where I want to *drive*, I mean?"

"Where do you want to *drive*?" she asked happily.

"I want to *drive* back to my house, and I want you to take me for that ride you promised."

"I won't back out on my promise," she said. "But we agreed from the beginning that we weren't going to . . ." Searching for a term, she gestured with her palms out.

He imitated her gesture. "Do it?"

"Right," she said, relieved. "So what kind of ride are we talking about?"

"Let's go upstairs and discuss it."

"Okay." She giggled in an unsophisticated manner as Quentin backed out of the overlook, without stomping the brakes this time, and drove smoothly across Birmingham. She'd acted angry the night before about Quentin asking Erin to flash him, and—well, she *had* been. But she'd wanted him to touch her anyway. If it hadn't been for the prospect of watching Owen get stitches, she would have gone with him to his room then. Now she got that electric feeling again at the thought that he would drive her to his room and touch her.

And she was genuinely happy that she'd convinced him to drive. It was good for her job security that she'd broken through at least this one obstacle barring the band from healthy human relations. Moreover, it was good for her friend, Quentin. It was a hot and beautiful day.

He sped up the driveway of the mansion and skidded to a stop just shy of Erin's Corvette. Holding Sarah's hand, he led her into the house. She'd forgotten, and she suspected that he'd forgotten, too, that he'd cut out on a recording session for their date. The door downstairs to the studio stood open. As they came in, the band bustled up the stairs like sleepy parents after curfew.

"We had this session planned with the four of us, Q!" Erin squealed. "Where the hell have you been?"

He beamed at them. "Sarah got me to drive."

Obviously this news had been a long time coming, because it took a few seconds of silence to sink in. Then, with the first genuine smile Sarah had ever seen on his face, Owen said, "Q, that's great!" at the same time Erin bit out, "Sarah, you have *no idea* what you're doing to us. Why would you put Quentin through that?"

Everyone watched Quentin, who gave Erin a withering look. "Stay out of it."

Erin seemed unsure, her eyes darting from Quentin to Martin to Owen and back. But only for a moment. "I'm glad you're driving, Q. But can't you see that Sarah's just shooting into trees to see what falls out? All I've done is hint at what happened to your mother, and you've gone stark white. That's why *we've* never made you drive."

Sarah asked Quentin, "What happened to your mother? Why wouldn't you tell me what was going on?"

He turned on her. "And you've been completely honest with *me*."

Sarah had just bared some of her biggest secrets to him—things she realized she should never have revealed, because now she seemed weak. She hoped the look she gave him showed him how hurt she was. But gazing into his black-green eyes, she knew he couldn't see her pain. He wasn't even in there.

"This is not about me," she said quietly. "This is about you, and the fact that you left out a pertinent piece of information when I took you for a drive on the busy highway."

"What'd you think I was going to do? Have a flashback, freak out, cross the median, and kill us both?"

"Q," Martin said, putting a hand on Quentin's shoulder.

Quentin shrugged Martin off violently. He turned through the open doorway and stomped down the stairwell, calling back over his shoulder, "I don't want to talk about it, *Erin*. It was half my life ago." The door to the sound booth squealed open and clicked shut.

The kitchen was silent again. Owen looked troubled, a moody Frankenstein's monster with a row of neat stitches following the curve of his hairline. Martin looked sick. And Erin glared at Sarah, accusing and self-satisfied, defending her territory. She had managed to take a triumph for Quentin and turn it into trash.

Sarah forgot her job. She forgot Natsuko. In a wave of hatred for the chokehold all of them had on each other, and especially for the talons that Erin had in Quentin, a defensive little freshman on the high school track team stepped up and took over.

She yelled in Erin's face, "Don't give me that look, girlfriend. *You're* the one who cheated on him. Don't act like you give a shit about him *now*."

She escaped into the garage and slammed the kitchen door as hard as she could, without her customary kiss good-bye from Quentin. She was certain she'd never get that kiss again.

~

Quentin looked forward to Sarah popping back in that day and startling him. She didn't show. He downright pined for her to pop in that night. Still she didn't show. When she didn't pop in the following morning, he finally got the message. She was through with them. With *him*. Well, he wouldn't let her get away with *that*. He drove to the Galleria and let himself into her hotel room.

The room was steamy and the shower vent still

roared, which made it easier for him to sneak inside unheard. But she wasn't in the bathroom. Wrapped in a bathrobe, she lay on the bed, facing the window, with her back to him.

He walked softly around the bed, aiming to startle her. He still wanted a little revenge for the phone to Owen's nose and the jar of garam masala and, now, the copy of *Clinical Immunology and Allergy Today*.

She was curled in a ball, asleep. The morning sunlight streaming through the window lit her fair skin and glinted in her wet hair, still dark from her shower so there wasn't much difference among the brown, blond, and pink strands. Fist under her cheek, she looked like a normal, beautiful girl. Except for the red scar under her chin, livid without makeup dabbed over it.

He longed to touch her soft cheek and caress her awake. But three enormous bouquets of flowers in vases on the dresser caught his attention. Several mornings ago he'd watched her run. It seemed strange to him that she'd nap instead at the same hour. The flowers might have something to do with it.

He stepped over to the first bouquet, blooms in vibrant colors. He found an envelope tucked among the stems and read the card, which he supposed was from Sarah's pregnant friend.

> You may be 30, but at least
> you're not knocked up.
> Love, Wendy & Daniel

Ouch, her thirtieth birthday. That was rough for women. He was already planning to work a weeklong break into the tour on either side of Erin's thirtieth birthday this fall so he wouldn't have to be in the same state with her. No wonder Sarah had curled into the fetal position and given up on the day.

The second bouquet was two dozen red roses. The card for this one read,

> Birthday wish granted.
> Harold

Harold. Her ex-husband. Folded inside the card was a form. Glancing once at Sarah, who still breathed evenly, Quentin unfolded it. A copy of a divorce decree from a New York court, dated yesterday. *Harold Fawn v. Sarah Seville.*

Quentin stood for a full minute, staring at the paper, staring at the sleeping Sarah, going back to the paper. She'd told him yesterday that her husband had cheated on her when she said she wanted a baby. And that this was before she had pink hair and showed her cleavage. But Quentin simply couldn't picture Sarah married to a jackass, no matter how she was dressed. She wouldn't stand for it.

Would she?

He wondered how Rio fit into this.

Now he studied the third bouquet warily. If the messages got worse as he went down the dresser, he wasn't sure he wanted to open the last one. The bou-quiet itself didn't instill confidence. There were flowers, but they all seemed to have thorns, and some green stalks thrown in couldn't have been anything but briars. And—was that a Venus flytrap? He reached for the card and withdrew his hand carefully, half expecting to be bitten.

> Happy b-day
> See you soon
> Nine Lives

He detected movement out the corner of his eye and whirled around just in time to see Sarah, a terrified expression on her face, start toward him.

He backed away from her, toward the door. "Sarah," he began in explanation.

He'd almost reached the door when she slapped his cheek with enough force to turn him around sideways. While he was still off balance and stunned, she pulled open the door and shoved him into the hall.

The door slammed. The dead bolt clicked.

He rubbed his stinging cheek, staring dumbfounded at her door. Then he crossed the hall and knocked.

There was a pause. She was breathing hard. "Who is it?" she called sarcastically.

"It's your friendly neighborhood country music legend, Quentin Cox." When she didn't respond, he went on, "You may know me for hit songs like 'Slap My Face and Slam the Door.'" Still there was no response but her breathing.

He backed a few paces away and sang a medium-tempo ballad at full volume:

> *Slap my face and slam the door.*
> *You never done that way before.*
> *I feel bad I scared you so*
> *But now I don't want to go.*
> *I'm just standing in the hall*
> *Singing to you through the wall.*
> *You done shook me to the core.*
> *Slap my face and slam the door.*

As he sang, several hotel patrons down the hall peeked out of their rooms. When he finished, there was a smattering of applause. He tipped an imaginary hat. "Thank you very much," he said in his Elvis impression.

The lock clicked open, and Sarah threw herself into his arms and buried her face against his chest. She said into his T-shirt, "I don't recall hearing that song."

"There's always room for one more on *your* album."

Without loosening her hold around him, she looked up into his eyes. "That was really good. I can't *believe* you made that up standing here."

He shrugged. "It ain't brain surgery." He stroked his hand through her wet locks. "Are you going to let me in?"

"Oh." She seemed to realize only now that she was standing in the hotel hallway in her bathrobe with, he thought with pleasure, nothing on underneath. She pulled him into the room and closed the door.

"Why don't you lock this from now on?" he asked as he turned the dead bolt. "In case the Grand Ole Opry comes calling unannounced."

"Usually I'm careful," she said. "I must have forgotten the last time. People kept knocking on the door this morning, bringing me ominous flowers." She put a hand up to his cheek. "It's really red. I'm so sorry."

"That's okay. I'm used to it." He laughed. "I have that effect on women. Though I have to say, Erin's slap is more like a love pat next to yours. Yours will make a man think twice."

She smiled guiltily. "How did you get a key?"

"You're not the only one with connections," he said mysteriously. "You're always busting into my house unannounced, so I thought I'd return the favor. I didn't mean to scare you that bad." In turn, he put a hand to her chin, not quite touching her scar. "What happened to you in Rio?"

Predictably, she pulled away from him and closed herself in the bathroom. When she came back out, she wore a tank top and running shorts. And she'd regained her composure. Damn. He wondered what it would take for her to tell him what had spooked her in Rio.

He tried once more to throw her off. Sitting casually on her bed, he said, "So. You're turning thirty, your divorce came through, and Nine Lives wants to see you."

Her smile vanished. "You read the cards."

"I did," he admitted, "but I wouldn't have done it

if I'd known our relationship was this antagonistic."
Oops. He added, "Antagon— Is that a word?" Still
she frowned at him, so he held out his arms for her.
"Come here. You've had a bad enough morning."

She collapsed onto the bed, put her head against
his chest again, and allowed him to rub her back and
to finger her damp hair. She wailed, "It's not just that.
Did they tell you what I said to Erin yesterday?"

He chuckled. "Don't worry about that."

"Do they all hate me?"

"No, but they think you went to a rough New York
high school." He didn't believe she'd been to high
school in New York at all, but he wanted to test her
reaction.

"Rough track team," she qualified.

He traced patterns on her smooth shoulder. "Erin
gets mad, and sooner or later she gets over it. I've got
a lot of experience with this. Anyway, right after you
left, Martin told Erin that she'd met her match, and
Erin got mad at Martin. Then Owen tried to jump
between them, and Erin got mad at Owen. Then they
all came downstairs to the studio and yelled at *me*. So
you probably weren't out of the driveway before we'd
forgotten about you and were mad at each other, just
like normal."

Immediately he wanted to correct this statement.
He certainly hadn't forgotten about her. He'd hardly
thought of anything else in the five days he'd known
her. But he didn't point this out, since he couldn't
do her. It was bad enough that he was sitting on her

bed, marveling at how beautiful she looked with no makeup and wet hair.

Trying to appear unconcerned, he wove a blond section of her hair into a pink section as he asked her, "Is Nine Lives out of jail?"

Sounding utterly exhausted, she said into his chest, "Would you *please* go with me to buy a gun?"

"Sarah—" he started.

"I don't want another of your lectures on gun safety. I won't shoot it. Just go with me to pick one."

"Sarah, hear me out, now. You are the poorest shot I've ever seen. *Owen* is a better shot than you, and Owen once shot his own hound dog."

"Oh no! Was he okay?"

"Well, he was upset—"

"I meant the *dog*."

"Oh. Sure. It just grazed him. But since you're this poor a shot, and you want a gun this badly, I'd say you need to go to the police. Or tell me what happened in Rio, at the very least."

"You're right." She sat up with a forced smile. "It's not that bad. He's probably still in jail. He could have had one of his employees send the flowers."

This made sense to Quentin. But whether or not Nine Lives was out of jail, he wasn't going away. He'd remembered Sarah's birthday, and he'd bothered to send her flowers. Sooner or later, Sarah would be forced to deal with him again.

Quentin knew he'd tried too hard to get her to confess, and that she'd drawn way back, when she asked, "Why aren't you working on my album?"

"We're taking the day off," he told her. "We're going down to the lake, and you're going with us."

"The hell you're taking the day off!" she said. "My album is due in two days. I've got a courier coming!"

"We're almost done with it." He reached out to play with her hair again, lacing a brown section into a pink section, despite the look she gave him. "You don't want the last two cuts to stink, do you? We need to take a break and blow off steam today. We'll work late tomorrow and be done with it in the afternoon of July first, easy, in plenty of time." He shrugged. "The others have already left. Nothing we can do about it now. And it's your birthday."

She said grudgingly, "I don't have a bathing suit."

He gazed at her skeptically. "You just spent nine months in Rio and you don't have a bathing suit?"

"Nine Lives got up when the sun went down." She licked her lips as if she had a bad taste in her mouth. Then she brightened. "I know where I can get a bathing suit on our way out. Erin shops there for all her evening wear."

"Great." He rubbed his hands together. "Now I just need a place where I can get you a birthday present. You messed up this time, because if you were my girlfriend, you would've told me it was your birthday."

"No I wouldn't."

He gave her a look.

"Okay, maybe I would."

"Mmmm-hmmm," he said knowingly. "Get your stuff together." He fished his cell phone out of his pocket and headed into the hallway, dialing Mr. Timberlane, who would know the right jewelry store.

She followed him to the doorway. "Where are you going? What are you doing?"

"I'm ordering you a birthday present," he said patiently. "What do you like? Diamonds? You seem like an emerald kind of girl."

She blinked at him, taken aback. It almost made him sick to think that this Harold Fawn jackass never bought her anything.

She said, "Quentin, seriously, I can't let you do that."

"You would if you were my girlfriend."

"No I wouldn't."

He gave her the look again.

"Okay, maybe I would." She grinned.

He rolled his eyes. "Don't fasten the dead bolt. I'll let myself back in."

9

En route to hospital. So far this is not the magical experience promised by all the books we read on childbirth, but I'm sure any second now I will have sunshine and rainbows streaming out of my vagina.

Wendy Mann
Senior Consultant
Stargazer Public Relations

"No working today," Quentin demanded, reaching for Sarah's phone.

"Keep your eyes on the road." She exited her e-mail. "I'm not working. Just checking on my pregnant friend. Hey . . ." She squinted at the truck pulling onto the highway in front of them. "Is that Owen? They must have been in Target, too."

"They were. I wasn't really interested in the Taylor Swift posters. I distracted you while they bought you some birthday presents."

"Aren't you busy." This was one of her mother's favorite derogatory phrases. She patted the big bench seat of his truck cab. "Looks like you were busy yesterday, too."

"I was. We finished the big bad recording session in two takes, after all that hullabaloo, because I am so freaking good. And then I went to get my driver's license. Do you want to see it?"

"I'd love to." He handed her his wallet, and she examined his laughing photo. "This is the happiest driver's license I've ever seen." She handed it back to him. "And then you bought this . . . truck."

"You don't like my big-ass truck?" he asked in mock disappointment.

She turned to the rear window. "Why does it have a gun rack? You don't carry rifles around."

"It's for effect."

"And why'd you buy a used truck? Surely you can afford a new one."

"Effect," he said again, and started laughing, and laughed and laughed. "If you plan to show reporters my big-ass truck for an article, let me know so I can spill some beer in it."

Sarah looked in the glove compartment. "I notice you have an economy pack of condoms."

"Came with the big-ass truck."

"I've seen condoms in your bathroom. These are your brand."

"They're for *effect*!"

She laughed along with him. She had decided to cut him a break, and cut herself a break, and make this her best birthday ever. It wouldn't be difficult. Her mother had a habit of giving her frilly dresses for her birthday, as if rubbing in what Sarah wasn't. And Harold had always managed to turn the day around and make it about *him*.

Earlier that morning, before the parade of bouquets, she'd thought it was damned depressing to be divorced at age thirty. After the note from Nine Lives and the visit from Quentin, she'd changed her mind. How delightful to spend one last day on earth at a sunny lake with her fake boyfriend.

She asked gleefully, "Do you think Erin's going to be jealous when she sees my birthday present?"

Quentin chuckled. "She'll be nice in front of you, but I guarantee she'll let me have it later."

"Really? That's great! What did you get her for her birthday last year?"

"Rosin. We were on tour up north, and she was out of this special German rosin that had changed her life. She couldn't remember the name of it. She'd know it if she saw it, but the music store in St. Paul didn't have it, and the store in Madison didn't have it, and the store in Lansing didn't have it. I finally got online and figured out what it was, and had it delivered to our gig in Indianapolis."

"That was thoughtful. Costly?"

"About thirty dollars."

"I see. What did you get your manager for her birthday?"

Quentin looked at Sarah blankly, then snapped his fingers. "No *wonder* she was so pissed at me in Austin! Oh well. Too late now. Watch this."

He pulled into the passing lane and blew past Owen's truck. Sarah waved, and Erin in the passenger seat waved back cheerfully enough. Maybe they could skip the catfight after all.

"Where's Martin?" Sarah asked.

"In the back of the club cab, asleep. He's depressed about Rachel and he used more than he should have this morning. I went down to his room and argued with him about it but . . ." Quentin glanced over at Sarah. "I know. It's bogus to argue with your best friend about using heroin in moderation. But you can't send somebody to rehab until they want to go. It doesn't take. And when I've suggested it to him, he's disappeared for a couple days. He's going to do it. Better for him to do it at my house than in some abandoned building on the north side. At home, at least I can catch him if he falls."

She shook her head. "It seems really obvious to me. I don't understand how Erin and Owen haven't figured it out. I mean, he's high in the back of their truck."

"It's only been this bad since we got back from Thailand. Thailand left us all a little crazy. And you've seen drug abuse before, so you know what it looks like. I understand him better than they do, because I've roomed with him off and on since I was eighteen. And Erin's innocent, and Owen's a dumbass. Martin still has more sense when he's high than Owen and Erin have put together, sober."

"For now."

"Right. And that may be what it takes. When he can't write music anymore, then he'll let me help him." Quentin's tone brightened. "Speaking of which. Do you read music? Then look in the glove compartment and get the staff paper and a pen. No, under the condoms. Write this down so I can show it to Martin." He sang easily, "Slap my face and slam the door / You never done that way before."

"*Door* and *before*?" Sarah looked up from scribbling. "You're not going to keep that, are you?"

"You said at the hotel that you liked it! You acted all amazed and shit!"

"It's a great song. But that rhyme's been used a million times, not the least of which is 'Ruby, Don't Take Your Love to Town.'"

Quentin cleared his throat. "Pardon me. How many hit singles have *you* written?"

"Point taken."

"Trust me on this. Folks don't want to think too hard when they're drinking margaritas and line-dancing. They're liable to get a lime stuck in their two-step."

Small towns, green forests, and kudzu-covered hills spun by as Sarah jotted down five verses of "Slap My Face and Slam the Door" for Quentin. Despite his lack of sophistication, or perhaps because of it, he was a master at composing catchy tunes and rhymes about the mundane. The third album would be a success and Sarah's job security assured if the music had anything to do with it. She kicked off her running shoes and stuck her feet out the window, crossing her ankles on the doorframe. What a relief, a whole day without high heels. The warm wind tickled between her toes.

An hour later, Quentin maneuvered his truck into an empty space in the nearly full parking lot next to a rambling brick restaurant, with Owen's truck close behind.

"The Highway 280 Steak House," Sarah read from the sign. "Did you eat here a lot growing up?"

"You could say that." He took her hand and led her through a side door and between crowded tables, as if he knew the place well. Sarah wondered whether he'd worked here.

"I don't see anyone eating steak," she observed.

"They only serve steak on Wednesday night, after church. The rest of the time, they serve chicken. Except special occasions, when they serve Indian food."

"Indian?" Small Alabama towns had no taste for the exotic. "Why Indian food?"

"Because my stepmother's from Delhi," he called over his shoulder as he pushed open a swinging door into the enormous, bustling kitchen.

Several women and men came away from their pots and knives to hug or shake hands with Quentin and shout greetings at him over the foreign pop music with strange percussion. A beautiful older Indian lady in a purple sari approached him, talking in heavily accented English or a foreign dialect—Sarah couldn't tell which with the music blaring.

Quentin gave the lady a long hug. He said loudly over the music, "This is Sarah."

The lady eyed Sarah's hair. Then, smiling broadly, she leaned close. "You made Quentin drive." She hugged Sarah hard, talking over Sarah's head to Quentin in what Sarah assumed was Hindi.

Quentin responded, "No," then, "Yes," then, "Oh yeah? How many hit singles have *you* written? Everybody's a critic today."

Muttering something, Quentin's stepmother released Sarah, then ladled stew out of a nearby pot and handed Sarah a plate and fork. Sarah politely prepared to try it.

"Don't eat that," Quentin warned her.

Sarah didn't want to be rude. She opened her mouth.

Quentin took the plate and fork away from her and dumped the stew into the garbage. He handed the plate and fork to a passing worker, who took them without comment and headed for a dishwasher the size of a car. "When I tell you not to eat something that my step-mother gives you," Quentin said, "don't eat it. People from Schenectady don't eat that part of the animal."

"What is it?" Sarah asked, horrified. "An Indian delicacy?"

"Soul food. She makes it for Owen."

Quentin's stepmother unceremoniously plopped an enormous pile of wet herbs on the counter in front of him. Sarah didn't know what they were, because she didn't know one herb from another. He took a knife from a nearby block and began separating leaves from stems and chopping expertly.

"So this is how you learned to cook," Sarah said, watching from his non-chopping side.

He laughed shortly. "There were seven of us, and I was the only one old enough to be of any use. And the restaurant didn't do so well at first. Let's just say I earned my keep." He glanced at her. "Well, it wasn't *that* bad. I was sixteen by then. I would call Owen to come get me and we'd go drink beer. When I dragged myself home again, she'd slap me in the back of the head, but it wouldn't hurt so much."

Sarah leaned closer, inhaling the spice of the herbs and watching his poker face. "You're trying to tell me something, but you're layering the jokes so thick that I don't know what you mean. Was it bad or not?"

He stopped chopping and turned to her with a strange look. Finally he said, "It was good. I just didn't know it at the time."

The open moment passed. He scooped up the herbs and threw them into two bowls at the back of the counter. "This is baingan bartha in progress," he told her. "One for me and one for the lightweights. Do you like yours hot?"

Sarah nodded, because Natsuko probably loved spicy food, the hotter the better. She watched uneasily as he chopped very small peppers and scooped them off the cutting board with the blade of the knife. He raked them, seeds and all, into the small bowl, and stirred. Tearing off pieces from a nearby pile of nan, he dipped out some for Sarah and some for himself.

It was delicious. Five seconds later, it was the hottest thing Sarah had ever put in her mouth. It was all she could do to keep from wincing.

"Not hot enough," Quentin said. Sarah watched in horror as he chopped more peppers and dipped out a taste for them again. This time it was all she could do to keep from spitting it out in self-preservation. She realized now that Quentin was getting her back for the tequila shots that first night.

"I just can't get it hot enough," he complained innocently, chopping up more peppers and stirring them into the bowl.

Quentin's stepmother reappeared, put her hand on Sarah's shoulder, and scolded Quentin. Sarah feared the burn in her mouth might have charred part of the circuitry of her brain. But she thought Quentin was giving his stepmother lip in slow, deliberate Hindi with an Alabama accent. His stepmother reached up and slapped him hard on the back of the head.

"All right!" Quentin said. He put down the knife and motioned for Sarah to follow him to a huge refrigerator. He handed her a small carton of milk. She opened the carton and started drinking, watching him over the top. How could *he* stand the heat? Finally, with a wry smile, he reached in for his own carton of milk.

Sarah didn't stop drinking until the milk was gone and some feeling had returned to her mouth. She gasped, "What did your stepmother say?"

He crumpled his empty carton in his fist. "Uh . . . 'What are you doing to the pink-haired woman . . . Don't you want her to have your babies . . . Get the hell out of my kitchen.' Basically."

Sarah laughed heartily. "That's a hot game of gotcha you've got going."

"Tit for tat." He threw away the milk cartons and pulled her out of the kitchen, through the large, open restaurant, to a front entry with a counter and cash register.

Sarah would have recognized Quentin's father right away, even if he hadn't been passing into the dining room to seat customers. He was a few inches shorter than Quentin and had dark hair, but their muscular builds were similar and their green eyes were the same. When he saw Quentin, he beamed at him and nodded to a group of customers coming out of the dining room. Someone needed to ring up their check. Quentin slipped behind the counter and worked the cash register as if it was second nature.

While she waited, Sarah moved around the small room, examining the Cheatin' Hearts memorabilia decorating the walls. In the most prominent spot was a huge poster of the back cover of *Ass Backwards*, signed by all four band members. Sarah agreed that this was a good choice for the restaurant, despite Erin's red push-up bra, because it showed the band members' faces and no naked butt.

She made her way around to the counter. Quentin watched her while she examined a framed family photo. A teenage Quentin, tall and thin, light brown curls even wilder than now, wearing spectacles. Holding his fingers in rabbit ears above his father's head. His father with his arm around Quentin's sari-clad stepmother. Two blond preteen girls and four small, black-haired children.

"You *are* the oldest," Sarah murmured, fascinated. "I had you pegged for the youngest."

"Why?"

"Because youngest children are the ones who join sex-crazed country bands. Oldest children and only children are the responsible ones with steady jobs. They tend to—"

"Dye their hair pink and move to Rio," he said, pulling her ponytail. "Hey," he called over her head to his father. Sarah stood back as the two of them embraced and Quentin's father slapped him on the back.

"This is Sarah," Quentin said.

His father took both Sarah's hands and looked down into her eyes.

"Did that package show up?" Quentin asked.

"They just delivered it," his father said without taking his eyes off Sarah. He motioned with his head toward a door behind the counter. "It's in the office."

"I'm going to check right quick," Quentin told Sarah, "and make sure I got you what I think I got you for your birthday." He disappeared through the doorway.

His father held Sarah still with his green eyes. He asked, fascinated, "How'd you get him to drive?"

"Dumb luck," Sarah explained. She wanted to ask him what Quentin's problem had been, but she didn't quite dare bring it up and ruin the happy moment.

Quentin's father raked his hands back through his hair in the motion of Quentin's that Sarah was growing to love. "I've been trying to get him to drive for—" Quentin's father shook his head, then threw his arms around her and hugged her hard. "Thank you."

"Gross," Quentin said beside them. "I start driving and everyone turns to mush."

A large group came in and Quentin's father went to seat them. Quentin led Sarah to a table where Erin and Owen leaned together in intimate conversation. Martin sat beside them, arms folded on the table, chin on hands, eyes closed. He stirred, then closed his eyes again as Quentin's stepmother appeared with a cart of food and handed bowls to Quentin to pass around the table.

Sarah still felt apprehensive about facing the Cheatin' Hearts again after her outburst the day before, but bravely she moved forward, pulled out a chair, and sat beside Erin. Then, partly because she wanted to test how angry Erin was, and partly because she really was completely confused, she asked Erin quietly, "Does Quentin speak Hindi?"

Erin giggled. "It's pretty weird hearing that come out of his mouth, isn't it?" But she took a bowl Quentin's stepmother passed her and didn't elaborate, as if an uneducated country boy speaking Hindi was weird, but not *that* weird. She elbowed Martin and tried to hand him the bowl. "Are you going to sleep all day?"

"No," he said matter-of-factly, sitting up and rubbing his eyes.

To change the subject from Martin's conspicuous napping, Sarah said truthfully, "This food is so delicious. Amazing."

"Isn't it?" Erin agreed. "It's even better than Q's."

"I know," said Quentin. "I think my stepmom's holding out on me. She's putting something in it that she isn't telling me about."

"Why would she do that?" Erin asked.

Sarah said, "She wants you to keep coming back."

She felt Quentin staring at her. When she glanced up at him, he looked like she'd given him a revelation. She smiled and resumed eating.

Then she felt Erin staring at her from the other side. Erin was pissed. Sarah filed this information for future use. Erin minded a little when Sarah touched Quentin, but she minded a lot when Sarah made inroads or gained insight that Erin didn't have. Convincing him to drive. Commenting on his stepmother. It was okay with Erin for him to have sex with someone else. It wasn't okay for him to fall in love.

Sarah thought it wise to concentrate on her food. This was another rare occasion when she ate until she was stuffed. She wasn't sure what most of the Indian dishes were, but Quentin didn't stop her again, so she figured they were safe to eat. Later, when Quentin and Owen finally finished, Quentin's stepmother cleared away the empty bowls and brought out a white birthday cake decorated with Sarah's name. Quentin's stepmother and father sat down at the end of the table.

Erin and Owen handed Target-wrapped gifts down the table to Sarah. Erin's was straw stacked heels that tied around the ankle—the countriest, sluttiest shoes Sarah had ever seen. "Welcome to my side of the fence," Erin said with a wink.

Owen's gift was a silver toe ring with heart cutouts. Sarah thought Erin must have picked it out, but Owen actually smiled at Sarah when she opened it, as if he wished her well for once. She wasn't sure what to do. What the hell? She stood and hugged him. Kindly he whispered, "Happy birthday," in her ear.

She sat down to a small, flat box. This must be the emerald from Quentin. He leaned over expectantly, watching her. She opened what she thought would be a gold chain with a small emerald pendant.

Everyone gasped.

The whole thing was emeralds. Lots of emeralds, large and small, set in circles. The necklace was narrower in the back, cascading to a pendant in front.

Erin looked grim.

Owen's sarcasm returned. "Look, the royalties for 'Come to Find Out.'" He slapped Quentin on the back. "Good thinking."

Sarah looked to Quentin in horror. Quentin shook his head and smiled. When he motioned, she turned around obediently so he could clasp the heavy necklace around her neck.

"Looks great with your tank top," he said.

She put her lips to his ear and whispered, "I can't take this."

"I'm rich," he whispered back. "If you were my girlfriend, you'd shut up and kiss me."

She sat back to gaze into his laughing green eyes. Then she put her arms around his neck and kissed him like a girlfriend who'd just gotten a very expensive, very beautiful birthday present.

Quentin's father leaned over Sarah to flick a lighter to the candles on the birthday cake. Just as Sarah was taking a breath to blow them out, Quentin's stepmother said something in Hindi.

"I was just thinking the same thing," Sarah said. This day seemed so foreign and yet so right.

Quentin laughed and laughed his musical laugh. Finally he choked out, "Make a wish."

Sarah looked around at the faces smiling at her. Her eyes lingered on Quentin. She wished that he wasn't

in love with Erin, and that he and Sarah could be together. She blew out the candles.

~

They spent the afternoon at a huge modern house
tucked among shady trees along the lake. Sarah was
apprehensive about changing into her bathing suit
along with Erin in the bathroom. She was afraid Erin
would take the opportunity alone with Sarah to share
exactly what she thought of her and the emerald necklace.

But the tension melted when they saw that the red
bikini Sarah had bought at Target was identical to the
one Erin wore, and with their country heels and toe
rings on, they looked comically like they'd planned to
dress as twins.

Erin giggled. "I guess country floozy and rock 'n'
roll floozy aren't all that different."

Sarah agreed, "Not in a bikini."

Laughing together, they passed Martin sleeping
on the living room couch and walked down the lush
lawn to a sandy beach and a pier. Quentin and Owen
were setting a large ice chest down on the wood. Owen
reached in for a beer.

"I thought it was Erin's turn to get drunk," Quentin
said.

"I traded with Owen," Erin said.

Sarah thought again, uneasily, *Erin hides sobriety
from men.*

"Look at you," Quentin said to Sarah. He held her

arms away from her body and examined her midriff, then her breasts. He took her hand. "Come with me into the lake," he growled at her, "or I'm going to pick you up."

Sarah rather wanted to be picked up. But she let him pull her into the water, which was clear in the shallows and warm as a bath. Then he picked her up anyway, wrapped her legs around his waist, and kissed her deeply.

They kissed for a long time, standing in the lake, dappled in bright sun and shade from the overhanging trees. Quentin was erect against Sarah, underwater where no one could see. She got a thrill rubbing against him with Erin and Owen lying in the heat on the dock twenty feet away, and with motorboats passing by out in the river channel. She wondered if he caught the buzz, too.

"This is great," she said, voicing all her appreciation for the long, heady crotch rub with her handsome friend on her birthday. "Is the house yours?"

Quentin was kissing just above her bikini on her chest. He said without raising his head, "Owen bought it for his parents."

"Where are they?"

He kissed above her other breast. "Last week he sent them to Australia for their anniversary." Kiss. "At least, that's what he said." Kiss. "I think he just wanted to get them out of town because of Erin."

Her eyes darted to Erin, lying unaware on the pier with her hand on Owen's back. "Why?" Sarah asked. "What about Erin?"

Quentin kissed his way up Sarah's neck. "Erin in general. Parents don't like Erin."

"Owen's parents, or your parents?"

"*All* parents," Quentin said in her ear. "I wish you could have heard what my stepmom said about her at the restaurant. Of course, you *did* hear it. I'm glad y'all don't speak Hindi." He sucked Sarah's earlobe.

"Why don't parents like Erin?"

He stopped and gazed over at the pier. "Are you kidding? Look at her. She *looks* like trouble." He turned back to Sarah and slid his hands down to her ass. "Of course, my stepmom only had nice things to say about you, and look at *you*. This is how I like my women. Barefoot, pink ponytails, bikini, emerald necklace." He stuck his tongue in her ear.

They spent the long, hot afternoon alternately lying on inflatable rafts in the water and lying on towels on the pier, spreading sunblock provocatively on each other's hot skin, making out, and talking. The sun sank lower in the sky, and the four of them devoured the leftovers Quentin's stepmother had packed from lunch.

Then Quentin and Sarah lay down together on the pier once more, and Sarah reviewed what she'd found out in the last few hours. They liked the same TV shows—and he told her about a few intriguing ones that had debuted while she'd been in Rio. They liked the same movies. They had voted for all the same presidential candidates. She had hidden her surprise that Quentin had voted. If she hadn't known better, she would have basked in the glow of falling in love with him. She'd felt this way at first with Harold, except they'd never had the intense physical connection she and Quentin shared to back up the mental one.

And that was the problem, wasn't it? She and Quentin might have similar tastes, but they weren't intellectually compatible. She couldn't pretend she'd really be happy long-term with Quentin. What if intelligence *didn't* descend through the mother? She would wake up in the morning to the sound of birds chirping in the crepe myrtle and the children running into the walls.

Not that brains were everything. As her mother had pointed out, one had to weigh brains with such things as ability to play bridge and make quiche. And as Sarah and Quentin began to talk again, she forgot their differences, because they seemed to agree on everything that meant the world to her. They both wanted kids— and they laughed uncomfortably about the phantom baby Sarah had threatened Quentin with their first morning together—but they also wanted to keep their busy careers, and they weren't sure how to balance this.

"I don't know," Sarah said. "I think I would make an excellent mother. I think I could do a better job than my mother. But my mother did a pretty good job. We misunderstood each other when I was a teenager. And our relationship hasn't been good lately because life came calling. I mean, death. You know."

She uttered this in a nonchalant way, with her eyes closed to the sun, so that he could take it or leave it.

But he was quiet so long that she thought she'd offended him, even pushed him into defensive anger like the day before.

"Exactly," he finally said. "My dad and I misunderstood each other, and death came calling, and it wasn't his fault. I know that. But it's hard to let go."

She opened one eye and saw that his eyes were closed. She closed her eyes again. It was so much easier to talk with their eyes closed in the massaging sun.

"Your mom died of allergic asthma," she said carefully.

"Yeah."

"What happened?"

"They were never sure whether it was something she ate or something she inhaled as we drove by in the car. They'd adjusted some of her medicines so the side effects wouldn't be as bad. They probably shouldn't have."

Sarah asked, "You were driving?"

"She was giving me a driving lesson."

"Oh." Sarah sighed. "You were fifteen." She took his silence for a yes. Poor Quentin. No wonder he'd never gotten over it.

"I managed to drive her to the hospital," he said without emotion.

"But they couldn't help her?"

"She was already dead."

There was another long silence, punctuated by a speedboat zipping close on the lake, the lapping of waves against the shore, and Erin's chipmunk giggle.

Sarah ventured, "You felt betrayed when your dad got remarried."

"I did," he said. "My dad and I made a pact to be strong for my sisters and keep ourselves together. And the next thing I knew, he'd brought five strangers into the house."

She heard him moving and opened her eyes to watch him turn his beautiful body from his tanned back to his tanned stomach on the towel, eyes still closed.

"I mean, I get along fine with my stepbrothers and stepsisters now," he said. "But back then, it was hard."

"You see the parallel with the band, don't you?"

He opened his eyes. "No."

"Why you need such tight control of them, so they don't betray you."

He blinked.

"And the first time you lost control was in the car with your mother."

Without taking his eyes from hers, he found her hand on the towel and took it in his. "It wasn't my fault. There was nothing I could do."

"Of course not."

"But I feel guilty just for being there. Just for being alive."

"I understand," Sarah said.

"I know you do." He brought her hand up to his lips and kissed her fingers. Then he smiled sadly. "This is awfully heavy for your thirtieth birthday." His green eyes were as bright as ever, but for the first time she noticed the laugh lines at the corners.

He was a few months older than her, she knew, but suddenly he seemed older still. He wasn't just the fun-loving playboy next door that he'd seemed at first. He was a man who had been through hell at a very young age and still struggled to make lemonade out of lemons.

And as she watched him, her whole perspective on him shifted. He definitely wasn't on drugs. Everyone and everything told her this. She knew all the signs of drug abuse. He displayed none.

And he wasn't stupid, either. He was oddly eloquent through the colloquialisms. He was smart enough not only to make up hit songs off the top of his head but also to impress her mother at bridge and converse in Hindi. And to manipulate his band's public relations campaign masterfully. He might even be cultured. He and Owen had both seemed awfully absorbed in Dostoyevsky the day she walked in on them.

He was putting on an act with her. Playing a game. Which meant he was a lot closer to being the man of her dreams than she wanted to admit.

But to him, she was still the enemy, the public relations rescue worker for the record company. He was only passing the time with her while they fixed his relationship with Erin.

Just like Sarah had promised him.

"Uh-oh," he said. The lines around his eyes deepened as he squinted at her.

"What's the matter?"

"You've changed your mind about something."

She stroked his fingers as if she weren't alarmed. She must have dropped her poker face for a moment. "Like what?" she asked.

"You tell me."

That would do neither of them any good. She changed the subject by sitting up and shading her eyes with one hand. "Let's swim out to that island across the lake."

"I can't make it that far." He turned his head away from her on the towel. "Have you been lying still too long? You go run around the house a thousand times and come back."

"You're a big, strong man. What do you mean, you can't make it that far?"

"I have asthma," he said without opening his eyes.

She supposed he really did.

"I'm not saving you, Q," Erin called. "I'm officially off 911 duty for today."

"I'm drunk," Owen said. "I'm ready for Chimney Rock." He and Erin began to gather towels from the pier and put them in the motorboat floating at the end. Quentin stood with a groan and pulled Sarah up.

"What's Chimney Rock?" she asked.

"A tradition whenever Owen's drunk," Quentin said. "Good publicity. Candid shots by onlookers make it into the Cheatin' Hearts Death Watch." He glanced uneasily toward the house.

She reached up and smoothed her hand over Quentin's hot shoulder. "I'll go get Martin."

Quentin said quietly, "I'll go. You shouldn't have to deal with him when he's like this."

"It's part of my job," she said. "You deserve a break." She walked up the pier and across the lawn, toward the house. She turned around once. Quentin was watching her. Even though she knew he wasn't playing for keeps, she felt a hot flush of pleasure at seeing his gaze on her. She rode that warm wave into the house freezing with air-conditioning.

Martin lay on the sofa, just as he had when Erin and Sarah passed him earlier. But he was awake now, staring at the vaulted ceiling.

Sarah knelt beside him on the carpet and took his hand. She said gently, "Martin, if you OD before you finish my album, I may lose my job."

"What do you mean—" Then their eyes met. "Okay," he said, defeated. "Don't tell Erin or Owen. They'll kick me out of the band."

"So I've heard," Sarah said. "You're making things very difficult for Quentin."

"I know," Martin said. "Q doesn't understand evil like you and I do."

Sarah went still. She heard her own heart beating. Yes, she'd seen evil in Rio. Somehow Martin sensed this. And he was in a similar evil place now, battling his drug cravings.

He drew her hand onto his chest and held it open with both his hands, rubbing his thumbs over the lines as if reading her palm. "I have a birthday present for you," he said gravely. "There's a gun. In my room. In

the top left-hand drawer of my dresser. It's unregis-
tered. It can't be traced back to me. Or to you."

They watched each other for a few long moments.
Martin was *not* Nine Lives, yet he'd guessed at another
man's drug-fueled obsession with Sarah.

And he was afraid for her.

"The gun's there for you if you ever need it." He
smoothed his thumb across her palm one last time,
erasing the dark future he saw there.

She squeezed his hand, trying to give him a lot
more comfort than she felt herself. "Come on, let's
go get some sunshine." She pulled him until he reluctantly got up from the sofa and followed her down to
the motorboat, where the others waited. And she tried
to leave that feeling of foreboding behind.

But now Erin caught Sarah's eye and patted the
empty seat beside her in the bow. Sarah smiled and
climbed into the boat, over Owen, toward the inevitable. Quentin backed the craft away from the pier
and sped across the glinting water. Crouched below
the lip of the boat, Sarah and Erin could hear each
other perfectly, while the men couldn't hear them at
all above the roar. Here it came.

Sarah went first. "I'm sorry about what I said to
you yesterday. It was a gut reaction. I didn't know why
Quentin wasn't driving, but I thought it was important for him to get over it. And I thought his friends
would be happy for him," she added, hoping to induce
a guilt trip.

Erin wasn't falling for it. "I know it's not my place

to say, because Q and I aren't together anymore. But it pisses me off that you come in here and try to fix everything and act like you know what's going on, because you don't."

"He clearly had a problem. I helped him solve it. How can that possibly get under your skin?" Sarah asked, knowing exactly how.

"You have no idea," Erin said. "He gets mad at us for mothering him, especially me, but I can't help it. I've known him five years, and I've sat with him in the ICU twice this year, thinking he was a goner. I've sat with him in the hospital a bunch more times. I don't know how many times I've been with him to the emergency room and they let him go the same day. We do that so often, it doesn't even register."

"You feel protective of each other." Sarah nodded. "But there's a point at which protectiveness becomes codependence."

"I don't think that's bad," Erin said. "Q provides the master plan, and comic relief, and food. Owen manages the money."

Sarah wondered at the wisdom of putting the dumbass in charge of the money.

"Martin has the final say on the music," Erin went on. "And I—"

Erin didn't verbalize it, but Sarah was thinking it, and she figured Erin was, too. Every village needed a whore.

Erin brushed her blond hair out of her face against the wind. "I agree that we're dysfunctional. But we're functional, too, in our way. It's taken an enormous effort for us to record two albums and go on two world tours in two years. We've done mostly what we didn't want to do, when we didn't want to do it. We've been unnatural."

Erin was trying to tell her something. Sarah glanced up at Quentin behind the wheel of the boat. He might have been watching them, but she couldn't see his eyes behind his sunglasses. He wore his poker face.

"I'm glad you convinced Q to drive," Erin said. "It's not that. It's everything. We've built our relationship as a band over five years, and you want to unravel it in a week."

Sarah had no idea what Erin was trying to convey to her. She said, "It would help me avoid stepping on toes if all of you would be honest with me and tell me what's going on, so I don't have to figure it out piecemeal."

"We can't do that," Erin said stubbornly. "I mean, we all like you, Sarah. I know Q *really* likes you. But you were sent here by the record company. We had a hard time getting a contract with them, and then we had a tough negotiation between the first and second albums. We don't trust them as far as we could throw them, and that extends to you. I'd like us to be friends, but that's how it is. Truce?"

Sarah took the hand Erin offered and shook it. "Truce," she agreed, feeling relieved that she and Erin had made peace. At least for now.

As the boat slowed, they both sat up on the bow

seat. Ahead, a high rock formation covered in colorful graffiti broke the expanse of dark green forest lining the lake. Gathered at the base of the rock were perhaps a hundred pontoon boats and ski boats, with a few sailboats thrown in for good measure. Some were tied together in flotillas. Others wove in and around, drifting away on the current and maneuvering back to see the display. Every few minutes, someone jumped from the highest point of the rock formation amid applause and whistles.

Quentin cut the engine and let the boat drift silently into the mass. A splash signaled that Owen was overboard. They watched his broad back as he swam toward the shore.

Erin asked, "Q, how tight did you tie those knots in his scalp?"

"Not tight enough that his brain should stop working," Quentin said. "He's not jumping off Chimney Rock because of that. He's jumping off Chimney Rock for the same reason he always does. He's a dumbass."

Erin said, "I was more concerned that the stitches might come out when he hits the water."

"Good point," Quentin said without concern.

Despite the truce, Sarah felt uncomfortable sitting next to Erin. And she missed Quentin. She walked out of the bow and stood next to him at the steering wheel, watching Owen swim toward shore. She asked Quentin, "Did you ever jump off?"

He looked at her over his sunglasses and smiled. His eyes were light green. "When I was a teenager."

"But you don't anymore? Did you have a bad experience?"

"Nothing like that." He wrapped his arm around her waist. "By now, I've been near death enough times that I don't jump off cliffs."

They watched Owen climb onto the base of the rock formation. He disappeared into the woods. A few minutes later, he reappeared on top of the rocks. A murmur ran through the crowd: "Owen McDonough, Cheatin' Hearts." People around them glanced toward their boat and toasted Quentin with their beer cans. A group of boys in a dilapidated boat emblazoned with Greek fraternity letters chanted, "O-wen! O-wen!" Even silent Martin, zonked on heroin or pouting about Rachel or both, sat up in his seat to watch.

Owen held up one arm like a gymnast ready for competition, then leaped into the air. He howled all the way down and landed with an enormous splash. The howl and the splash echoed against the rocks.

Quentin let Sarah go and leaned over the side of the boat, watching the water. Owen didn't surface. Quentin swore and pulled off his shirt, preparing to jump in. Just in time, Owen appeared, gulping air, and stroked toward the boat. The crowd cheered again.

"Come on." Sarah reached behind her neck to unclasp the emerald necklace. She passed it to Erin without looking at her, not wanting to rub it in right now. She had other things on her mind.

"What?" Quentin eyed her warily.

"I'm going to jump, and I want you to jump with me."

"No," Quentin said.

"Owen went off," Sarah taunted him.

"Have we told you that Owen's a dumbass?"

"I believe someone did mention that," Sarah said. "But it's my birthday."

Quentin ran his hands back through his hair and then said, "Okay."

"It looks like love to me," Erin sang from the bow.

"It looks like a compression fracture to me," Quentin said. With a grimace, he jumped into the lake with Sarah.

They swam through the water, cool at this depth, and passed Owen swimming back. Owen stopped and treaded water, watching them in surprise. "My God," he said to Sarah, "Q would follow you anywhere."

Sarah laughed as she and Quentin swam the rest of the way to the shore and hauled themselves up onto the rocks. Barefoot, they picked their way up the steep path through the woods. They passed a group of giggling girls and a group of men shoving each other on their way down, jumper wannabes who had chickened out.

Quentin said over his shoulder, "If I jump, you're going to owe me."

"I don't owe you *anything* after those peppers," she shot back.

They emerged from the trees and walked across the warm, flat rock to the edge. "I mean it," he said. "If

I do this, you owe me, and I'm going to come get it tonight."

"Do you promise?" She curved her hands around his back and looked up at him. She'd never seen him so handsome. His green eyes laughed, and his muscular, tanned chest was naked to the setting sun.

He kissed her deeply, his tongue gently exploring her mouth. Far below him, the fraternity boys chanted, "Quen-tin! Quen-tin!" Thirty was not so bad, Sarah thought, pressing her palms to his hard biceps and feeling his hands slide down to her bare waist. Even if this was lust with Quentin and could never be love, she sure was enjoying it. If it weren't for the threat of Nine Lives coming for her, thirty would be okay after all.

They moved toward the edge of the rock to look over. Sarah started back.

"Don't look," Quentin said. "Don't think about it. On the count of three. One, two—"

Natsuko pushed Sarah off.

~

Quentin made it the last few one-armed strokes to the boat, released Sarah from the lifesaving hold around her chest, and lifted her up. Owen grabbed her under her arms. She still coughed and laughed simultaneously.

"What's the matter?" Erin asked, bending over her as Owen laid her on the floor of the boat.

"I got water up my nose," she coughed out. "*Way* up my nose."

"At least it's clean water," Quentin assured her, climbing up the ladder and into the boat. "They tested it. It's cleaner than New York City's drinking water."

"I don't know what they tested for," Sarah said, "but in my experience, New York City's drinking water isn't green and full of mud."

"You know what's good for that?" Quentin asked.

"If you say *peppers*—"

Owen handed her a beer from the cooler. She held it to her face, under her eye.

A cell phone rang. All five of them looked around for it while Erin announced, "No working today."

"Mine," Sarah said. Still lying down, she drew her phone out from under a pile of towels. "Hello? What? Oh, Wendy!" She squealed and stamped her feet on the floor of the boat.

The others stared at Sarah, then at Quentin.

"Her friend must have had her baby," Quentin explained.

"She has a friend?" Owen asked. At Quentin's look, Owen said, "Kidding. I'm kidding."

Quentin started the boat and piloted it fast across the rush of lake reflecting the pink sunset. Occasionally he glanced sideways at Sarah, whom he couldn't hear over the roar of the motor, talking animatedly with her friend. He'd liked her hair before, but the punked-out schoolgirl look with two pink ponytails at her nape really moved him. He let his eyes travel to her perfectly polished toenails, up her long legs to her strong, smooth thighs, and he wished for the millionth time that he could make love to her.

As he cut the engine and coasted into the pier at the marina, Sarah was saying into the phone, "I just jumped off a cliff into a lake. Got water up my sinuses and can't get it out. Which is not nearly as bad as your experience this morning. Or perhaps somewhat similar."

"Vonnie Conner sighting," Owen called to Quentin.

Quentin saw the still-buxom still-a-blonde standing at the top of the hill, under the pine trees, with her arms crossed. "She's up there *waiting* for us?" he asked in disbelief.

Sarah clicked her phone off. "Who's Vonnie Conner? High school sweetheart?"

Owen said, "Vonnie Conner broke up with Q when he tried to get his driver's license but couldn't get into the car. Because of course a girl can't date a guy who can't drive."

"I wouldn't mention that if I were you," Erin warned Owen.

"Doesn't matter that the guy's mother had just died," Owen went on. "Vonnie Conner is such a *bitch*!" He said the last word loudly enough that it echoed across the lake.

At the top of the hill, Vonnie couldn't have heard the first part of the sentence, but she heard the last word, and she knew who Owen meant. She uncrossed her arms.

"Owen, you dumbass," Quentin said. "Thanks for telling PR more than she needs to know. Again."

"Hey," Sarah said, turning Quentin's chin so that he had to look down into her eyes. She whispered, "Just because it happened when you were young doesn't mean it didn't hurt."

Quentin shook his head to clear it. Sarah was right. He shouldn't be too mad at Owen. He could tell by the way Owen looked through him that Owen was fabulously drunk. And Owen *hated* Vonnie Conner on Quentin's behalf.

Quentin even managed a smile for Sarah. "Vonnie Conner is in charge of Hank on the Banks, which is the annual Hank Williams festival here at the amphitheater. So we always crash it." He helped Sarah out of the boat, then sauntered up the pier and up the hill with her.

As they walked, Sarah leaned into him. She slid her hand down his shirt and around the waistband of his bathing suit. She bent his head down so she could nibble his ear. She took his hand and guided it under the string of her bikini bottoms, which . . . Jesus, it was getting hard to concentrate on Vonnie Conner.

They stopped as Vonnie stepped into their path. "Quentin Cox, you're not supposed to be here!" she hollered. "Owen," she called as Owen and Martin passed carrying the ice chest, blankets, and lawn chairs, but Owen kept right on going.

"I've got every right to be here," Quentin told Vonnie. "The judge threw out that restraining order." Sarah kissed his jaw.

"Only because you were in chess club with the judge in high school," Vonnie snapped.

Quentin covered Sarah's ears with his hands. He appreciated that Sarah giggled like an idiot. "Do you mind?" Quentin asked Vonnie. "You don't have to go spreading that around."

Vonnie was royally peeved. "If you're going to come to Hank on the Banks anyway, why don't the Cheatin' Hearts play? Next year we could arrange—"

Quentin interrupted her. "On the Fourth of July, we have a Nationally— Tell her, Sarah."

Sarah took her lips away from his ear just long enough to recite obediently, "Nationally Televised Holiday Concert Event."

"What she said," Quentin continued, "and you think we have time to drive down here to your two-bit local festival?"

In an unusual show of aptitude, Vonnie seemed to appreciate the irony. She asked, "Is this about the tenth grade?"

Quentin winked at her and slipped his arm around Sarah's waist to lead her away.

Vonnie flung after them, "Nice hair."

"It's Napoleon," Sarah called over her shoulder. "Like the ice cream."

Quentin glanced at her uneasily. Had her mother

told her that he'd been made? Surely not. Sarah would have said something about it before now.

He rubbed his hand appreciatively across the smooth skin of her bare back. "Thank you," he whispered to her.

"No problem," she said flatly.

He leaned out to assess her expression as they walked, but she wore the poker face. He said quickly, "I didn't mean to— I'm not after Vonnie, you know. She's married. I'm just settling an old score."

Sarah smiled at him, thank God. "I get it. Glad to be of service."

They reached the top of the hill and looked down at the stage loud with country music. The audience sat on blankets or in lawn chairs radiating outward in the grass.

Sarah asked confusedly, "This is the amphitheater?"

"People around here call this the amphitheater," Quentin said. "To New York City, it may look like a sloping field. But it's not just any old sloping field. It's close to the original lake cabin that a local car dealer loaned to Hank Williams after he was fired from the Grand Ole Opry for drunkenness. He wrote 'Your Cheatin' Heart' here right before he died."

"Really!" Sarah exclaimed. "How sad. His whole life was a country song. And that's why you're the Cheatin' Hearts? Local provenance?"

"I wanted to be the Sow-Bellied Syrup Soppers," Quentin said, "but Erin didn't want to be a sow. Or be accused of sopping." Owen was hiking determinedly in their direction. "Oh boy, Owen's drunk, and Erin can't dance with him because she's in line to buy a funnel cake. I hope *you* like to dance."

Owen grabbed Sarah's hand and pulled her toward the stage. She glanced back at Quentin in alarm. Quentin shrugged at her. He sat down in a lawn chair next to Martin and watched Owen dance with Sarah. Owen could cut a rug, and he was patiently teaching Sarah some steps.

Quentin felt so relieved. Owen had been nice to Sarah all day. It wasn't like Owen had the hots for Sarah. It was like the dark cloud of Owen's intense emotion, seeming to desire Erin and detest Sarah, had lifted. All that was left was the big, blond, easygoing Owen whom Quentin had known his whole life. Owen wasn't breaking Rule Two with Erin after all.

"That's some necklace," Martin remarked.

It was almost the first thing Quentin had heard Martin say all day. Quentin chose his words carefully. "I had to keep up the image that we're really together. If I didn't give her a nice gift on her birthday, she'd think something was up."

Martin turned toward him. "Q, Sarah is one cool chick. I'm afraid of what Nine Lives is going to do to her."

Quentin fought down his flash of anger at Martin's drug-induced paranoia.

"But she's still the record company," Martin was saying. "Her presence here is antithetical to everything we've worked for."

"Martin, it's just a necklace," Quentin protested. "I've got the money. I don't spend it on anything but the foundation. And the occasional big-ass truck."

"We know you're smart, Q," Martin growled. "We know you're smarter than we are. But that doesn't mean we're stupid."

"She was feeling down this morning," Quentin said innocently. "She's away from her family and friends on her thirtieth birthday. I wanted to cheer her up. I like her."

"You told her," Martin accused him.

Great. When she went into the house, Sarah must have revealed to Martin that she knew about the heroin.

Quentin said, "I haven't told anyone. Sarah saw through you the first time she laid eyes on you." He sighed. "Come on, Martin. We're supposed to be taking the day off, remember?"

Martin didn't respond. But when, after four songs, Owen finally brought Sarah back and traded her for Erin, Martin led Sarah down to the stage for a dance. Quentin watched them with pleasure. Sarah looked carefree.

She was having so much fun that even Quentin had to dance with her. He wasn't much of a dancer, but he'd played enough honky-tonks that he couldn't avoid picking up a few steps. Then Owen danced with Sarah while Quentin danced with his AP chemistry teacher. Martin danced with Sarah while Quentin danced with the wife of his math team coach.

It was getting late, and the featured band started its last set. If they were going to crash the festival, they needed to go ahead. He called Owen, Martin, and Erin over to discuss it.

A few minutes later, Sarah bounded over and poked her head in between them. "You look like you're in a football huddle," she said. "What's up?"

"Come with me," Quentin said. He emptied the ice chest and piled her with blankets and a few lawn chairs.

"The concert isn't over," she pouted as she followed him down the hill to the boat. "Why are we packing up?"

"So we'll be right ready to go when the police come." He threw the ice chest into the boat, then took the chairs and blankets from her and threw them into the boat. Then, because she was so beautiful with the full moonlight filtering through her crazy hair, he threw *her* into the boat.

He sat down in a seat and pulled her into his lap. She straddled him in her very small bikini. He kissed her to distract her while he pulled at the string around her neck to release the bathing suit top.

This was quite a sight: Sarah with pink ponytails, the emerald necklace, her breasts bare in the soft light.

"It's a marina," she said. "Someone else is going to come down to their boat and see—"

Her protest transformed into a gasp as he put his mouth on her nipple. He sucked at her first, then bit her gently, then laved her with his tongue, testing her reaction to see which she liked best. She liked being bitten. Interesting. But when she began sliding the crotch of her very small bikini up and down on his erection, he forgot about the scientific method in a dark rush.

The night was black. The lake was black but for a few reflected lights from houses far across the lake, rippling in the water. He had his mouth on this pale girl. God, he was going to have to make love to her soon. He couldn't, but how could he *not* make love to this woman?

Finally he moved to her other breast to be fair. He shouldn't have let her go. She had the opportunity to ask, "Is this to make Vonnie Conner jealous, or to make Erin jealous?"

"No one can see us. This is for me," he said, his lips still brushing her. He pulled away and glanced at his watch. "We have to go crash Hank on the Banks in five minutes. See me tomorrow morning about finishing this. Until then, live a little. It's your birthday."

That seemed to satisfy her for the time being. He suckled her, teased her, and held her as she groaned. Pressed her down on his erection. Thoroughly enjoyed himself. But thought the entire time how much better it would be if he knew he could have it again, and again, and again. He had to have her. Oh God.

They ran a few minutes over. By the time they dashed hand in hand to the top of the amphitheater, Owen had already climbed onstage and muscled the mike away from the band's lead singer. And Vonnie Conner was already headed in Quentin's direction.

"I called the police, Quentin," she shrieked. "You get Owen McDonough off my stage!"

"He doesn't come when I call him," Quentin said calmly. "Sarah, hon, be a dear and run get Owen off the stage."

"Do think it would help if I took my top off?" Sarah asked vacuously, batting her eyelashes at him.

"Yes," he said. "But not right now." He swatted her ass as she bounced down to the stage.

"Where did you get *her*?" Vonnie asked him acidly.

"Fairhope," he said, watching Sarah go. The crowd applauded and hooted and yelled, "O-wen!" as Owen made love to the microphone. He crooned to Erin, who stood at the foot of the stage with Martin's arm around her shoulders. The song, appropriately, was "Lake Day Love," with Owen's lyrics and Erin's tune.

"Why do you come here every year?" Vonnie complained, near tears. "How long am I going to have to pay for the goddamned tenth grade?"

He faced her and said, "This is the last time." Of course she didn't believe him, and she flounced away. But this would be his last visit to Hank on the Banks, at least as a party crasher. He hadn't been romantically interested in Vonnie Conner since high school. He *had* taken great pleasure in getting her goat. Well, she could keep her goat from now on. The idea of being with Sarah this time next year was so cool. And impossible. But he knew that after Sarah, it was going to be hard for Vonnie Conner or anyone else to hold his attention.

Sarah leaped easily onto the stage. Her striking appearance elicited a barrage of catcalls from the audience, and she did a little curtsy. Then she rubbed Owen's upper arm and said something to him. He gave her a big, drunk grin and kept singing. The irate band they'd interrupted, including a couple of big guys, had been holding their own football huddle and began to move in Owen's direction.

Quentin waved until he got Owen's attention, then moved his finger in a circle. Owen said into the microphone, "Thank you very much," in his own Elvis impression, jumped down from the stage, and helped Sarah down. The two of them plus Erin and Martin held hands and maneuvered slowly up the hill between blankets on the grass, singing "Lake Day Love." The band onstage began playing again but was all but drowned out by "Lake Day Love" as the audience joined in.

Quentin jogged down the grass and took Sarah's hand at the end of the line. Rather than sing along, he listened to her soft, pretty voice. He'd never heard her sing. She sounded happy. She *looked* happy. He hoped it had been a good birthday.

As they crested the hill, a police siren chirped. Quentin spotted the blue lights between the pine trees. "Run!" he yelled. Owen threw a squealing Erin over his shoulder. They all barreled down the hill and into the boat, and roared away in the moonlight.

~

"Sleepy?" Quentin asked as Sarah laid her head on his thigh in the big-ass truck.

"That funnel cake did me in." She moved her manicured hand to stroke lightly inside his thigh. "Quentin, would it be okay if I spent the night with you from now on? To make Erin mad."

It was more than okay with Quentin. But he thought there was more to it than Erin, especially because of the timing. Martin was right. Sarah was afraid of Nine Lives.

And he had his own problems. Sooner or later he would wake up to an asthma attack. This didn't help attract women.

"I sleep in the nude," he warned her.

"So do I."

This gave him a hard-on. He wasn't sure he'd ever driven through Socapatoy with a hard-on. Come to think of it, he'd hardly ever driven, so this was a no-brainer.

It would make a good song. "Driving through Socapatoy with a hard-on." He could name a new town on Highway 280 for each verse: "Driving through Goodwater with a hard-on," "Driving through Sylacauga with a hard-on." He could call the song—how far was it from the lake to Birmingham?—"Eighty-Mile Hard-On."

He laughed out loud, because the big-ass truck gave him a new lease on life. Sarah shifted her head on his thigh and murmured a cussword at him. This made his erection, which had been calming down some, swell again. He put his hand absently in her soft hair and continued to think through this. The song might not make it onto the third album, but they could put it on a special X-rated album. They probably had enough of Quentin's discarded songs for one of these right now.

If Sarah stayed around much longer, they could make it a double album.

10

The rough rock scraped under Sarah's bare feet as she leaped into the air. A hundred colorful boats floated below her on the green lake, each loaded with people waving, holding up their beer cans. The setting sun was warm. The wind rushed up. Her stomach left her—a dizzy, first-date feeling.

Too soon she smacked into the water and plunged deep under, where it was dark and cold. Her skin stung from the impact. Her head felt tight, full of fluid. She swam upward toward the yellow sunbeams filtering through the green darkness.

She had almost reached the surface. She was running out of air. She should have reached the surface by now. She ran out of air. She clawed toward the surface.

Something deep below her grabbed her ankle. She looked down into Nine Lives' catlike eyes.

~

She sat up, gasping, bewildered, in the dark room. Then she saw Quentin's silhouette as he turned on the bathroom light, just before he closed and locked the door. She knew where she was, but not what was happening. Through the door, she heard his coughs, and then a terrible sound, like he couldn't breathe at all.

She fell out of bed and ran to bang on the door. "Let me in!"

He coughed and coughed.

"Are you okay? Damn it, Quentin, let me in!"

The terrible sound returned.

Now came a knock on Quentin's bedroom door. Sarah went cold, and realized that she was naked but for the weight of the emerald chain on her collarbone. She'd pulled off her clothes and flung them somewhere when Quentin had set her down in bed earlier in the night, because she'd vaguely recollected that she'd lied to him that she slept in the nude. Now she snatched one of his long-sleeved shirts out of his closet, shrugged it on, and opened the bedroom door for Martin.

In a T-shirt and sweatpants, hair mussed but the ubiquitous glasses on, Martin strode past her and knocked quietly on the bathroom door. "Q," he said. The door opened, Martin slipped in, and the door locked behind him.

Sarah stood in the dark with her arms folded across her breasts, staring at the locked door. She didn't want to put her ear to the door, but she didn't want to be left out, either. It hurt so much to be snubbed. She didn't belong to Quentin, and he didn't belong to her, but she cared about him. She deserved to know what was going on.

There was more coughing and more of the terrible sound, and Martin speaking low. Then the door opened, spilling light into the hallway and making her blink. Martin put his hand on her shoulder and squeezed briefly. "He's okay, kid," he told her. "Go back to bed." He padded across the carpet and closed the bedroom door softly behind him.

The bathroom light clicked off and Quentin met her in the dark. "I'm okay," he choked in a strange, gravelly voice. He pushed her in front of him to the bed and drew her under the covers beside him. "You sleep in the nude," he said, claiming the shirt she wore and throwing it across the room.

"You're supposed to, too," she protested, feeling a T-shirt and boxers on him.

"I may have to get up again"—he stopped, pounded his chest, and cleared his throat several times—"and cough up my other lung."

Her eyes hadn't readjusted to the dark. She couldn't see his face. She reached out to put her hand on his chest, over his heart. "Is this the asthma?"

"This is the asthma." He cleared his throat again. "Sexy, isn't it?"

Maybe he was still thinking this way, that their relationship was all sex appeal and business, but Sarah had moved way beyond this. She didn't want to care so much about him. But there it was. She rubbed his chest soothingly. "Don't lock the door on me."

"I have to."

"Why?"

"Don't get too close to me," he said. "The record company sent you."

"If I were your girlfriend, you'd let me in."

"You're not my girlfriend," he said, and coughed. Then his body convulsed in a coughing fit.

She pressed her body to his quaking chest and curved her arms around him. His coughing subsided.

He said roughly, "I wish you were."

She scratched his scalp with her fingernails and stroked the waves of his hair, tugging her fingers through the tight curls at his nape. He settled his head against her chest and let her hold him. Soon he was asleep.

~

She lay awake for hours, listening to his healthy, even breathing. Finally she fell back asleep. But immediately, it seemed, she awoke again in the room bright with morning light, and listened to Quentin's shower.

When the hissing water shut off, she stumbled out of bed to wash the lake out of her hair. They passed each other in the hallway to the bathroom, her naked but for the necklace, him naked and beautiful, with wet curls. As his arm brushed against her arm, he said, "Gulp."

She stepped into the hot shower and slowly came back to life. This meant that her brain began functioning again, but also that her nipples hardened and her sex ached for the naked man she'd just passed, and passed up.

She slicked the shampoo out of her hair and opened her eyes. His dark, blurred form leaned against the wall outside the shower, arms crossed, watching her. He couldn't have seen much because the shower door was translucent glass, but her body thrilled that he was watching her at all. She stepped close to the glass and slowly passed her breasts near it, where they'd be clear through the mottling, as if she were innocently rinsing under the shower stream. Seeing him shift positions uncomfortably, she suppressed a laugh. And rolled the door open. "You had your turn," she said.

He wore cargo shorts and the green camo T-shirt. His eyes were still on her breasts. With effort he lifted his green eyes to her face. "I had my turn in the shower. I didn't have my turn at *you*." He stepped forward to take her mouth with his.

She drew him into the shower stream, then reached out to roll the door closed behind him. His T-shirt darkened and stuck to his solid chest.

He pushed her out of the hot stream and against the cold marble wall. His soft lips massaged hers, then traveled to her ear, making her shiver. His hand slicked down her torso, traveled around to her front, and cupped her mound. "If you were my girlfriend," he said in her ear, raising more goose bumps, "I'd put my mouth right here." He worked his thumb on her clit to emphasize his point.

"I'm not your girlfriend," she said weakly.

"You look like my girlfriend. Let's see if you taste like my girlfriend."

He went down on his knees and still had to bend a little to get under her. Spreading her thighs with his warm hands, he began to tease her with his tongue, and then to suck her. And then she wasn't sure what he was doing, because she'd never experienced anything like it. She felt herself open.

He stopped. "Sarah," he said gently.

"More!"

"Breathe," he ordered her.

She took in a ragged gasp, but it was hard to worry about pesky things like breathing when her center radiated heat. He must have sensed that she was too dizzy to stand, because he held her with both strong arms and laid her on the marble floor of the shower. Sliding his forearm underneath her buttocks so he had her just where he wanted her, he gave her the most intimate kiss.

The feeling was incredible. It was so good that she could hardly stand it. But she could and did stand it, because when she tried to shift away from his hungry mouth, he held her more firmly. She had no choice.

Then came a moment when she was hyperaware of everything touching her: hot water splashing over her breasts, cold marble under her back, warm arm under her ass, Quentin's hot tongue. She knew she was about to come. She put her hands in his hair. That wasn't enough. She wanted to give back what he gave. But when she reached toward his shorts, he took both her wrists in one hand in that familiar, delicious grip.

There was no release but her screams. She bucked under him. Still he held her. He pressed his mouth to her until she stopped.

Moving to the inside of her thigh, he kissed her even then, as if he regretted it was over. She took a shuddering breath of wet air.

A pounding sounded out in the bedroom, on the bedroom door. Erin's voice called, "Q, where's breakfast?"

Quentin bit down on Sarah's thigh so hard that it almost hurt. "I'm gonna skin me a fiddle player," he grumbled. Then he rolled open the shower door and called, "Step one, take eggs from refrigerator. I'm in the shower."

"That's the point!" Erin said.

Sarah whispered, "She heard me. She knows we're in here together."

He rolled the shower door shut. But by this time, cold air from the room whirled in the shower, mixing with the hot spray. Sarah shivered and weakly tried to sit up. He pulled her into his lap and warmed her with his strong hug. "There's no reason to feel caught," he whispered. "This is what we wanted, to make her jealous."

Sarah giggled nervously. "Don't you feel caught?"

"Yeah, but I'm not sure it's a bad thing." He kissed

her gently, his tongue playing at the corners of her mouth, as if he planned to do this all morning.

With a reluctant sigh, Sarah said, "You need to go after Erin. You're supposed to get her back. You have to go after her and string her along." Sarah reached down to unbutton and unzip his shorts, this time without resistance. She reached her hand past his boxers and around his big, solid cock. "But first, I could return the favor."

He closed his eyes, took in a deep breath through his nose, and exhaled. "I can't let you do that," he said, pushing her hands out of his shorts.

"Why not?" she coaxed him.

"Because my self-control has limits. If you got me off in this shower, I'd have to have you right here. Or maybe I'd bend you over the bathroom counter, depending on how things worked out. And you don't want *that*." He rolled the shower door open again. She shivered in the cold draft.

Defrosting in the warm water, she thought, *That's exactly what I want.*

~

At the muffled galloping noise, Quentin looked up from the stove. Sarah ran down the stairs from his bedroom in her high heels. In a high mood. He noted with amusement that the more comfortable she became with him, the less sophisticated she got, with the athlete showing through.

"Good morning," she sang to Erin, hugging her

on her barstool. "Good morning," she sang to Owen, reaching up to pat his head. "Good morning," she sang to Martin, pinching his cheek.

She clopped into the kitchen. "Good morning," she purred suggestively to Quentin. She still wore the emerald necklace, this time with a plunging white shirt.

He knew he was grinning, and his bandmates were glaring at him, but he couldn't help it. He put his hands on Sarah's ass and kissed her. "What do you want for breakfast?"

"Can't eat breakfast. Goofed off all day yesterday. Got to get to the office. I already called your driver and he's probably waiting for me."

"You have to eat breakfast," he protested, calculating how long it would take to make her a breakfast burrito to go.

"Office," she repeated, already pulling away and clopping toward the door to the garage.

Following her, he backed her against the door and kissed her again, deeply, doing to her tongue what he had done to the rest of her earlier. She shuddered under his hands, and he couldn't help breaking the kiss and laughing.

She smiled, too, and cupped his chin in her small hand, then clopped down the steps into the garage. As she reached the bright sunlight outside, she turned back to him and smiled one last time. A secret smile: *more to come*.

But he felt the band glaring at him all the while. He knew that this lover routine would go over like a lead zeppelin. He returned to the stove and feigned surprise at the expressions on their faces. "*Now* what?"

"There was no *thud*," Martin said. "You didn't bang your head against the door in frustration. That's a bad sign."

Quentin pointed at him. "I did not. Have. Sexual relations with that woman," he said in his Bill Clinton impression.

Owen said, "We all know by now that Clinton needed to define *sexual relations*."

"Well . . ." Quentin paused to think. "I may have touched her inappropriately."

"Q!" Erin wailed.

He banged the frying pan down on the stove and said in a rush, "It's been five days and I haven't broken Rule Three! I've been so good! You expect me not to touch her boobs? Come on! Erin won't even let me *look* at her boobs. I don't know what the world's coming to. Y'all never let me have any fun. A month ago, I was in the ICU—"

Martin groaned.

"—about to die—"

"You used that one already," Erin said. She set down her fork and drew the bow across her fiddle in another funeral tune.

"You have to call off this thing with Sarah, trying to make Erin jealous," Owen said.

"How am I supposed to do that?"

"Just tell her the truth," Owen suggested. "You don't really think she'd tell the Evil Empire, do you?"

"Yes," Martin and Erin said together.

"Yes, I do," Quentin agreed. "She botched the Nine Lives job, and now she needs a big success or she'll get fired. She's using us. If she knew we've been screwing with her, she'd tell the Empire so they'd see what a difficult case we are and what a great job she's done." He wasn't sure whether he believed this, but it didn't matter. He was just trying to get them off his back for five more days.

"But here's an idea," he said, running his hands through his damp hair. "I could break Rule Three with her, and then she'd feel loyalty to the band, to me, and *then* we could tell her."

Again they gave him that collective silent stare of disapproval that was as familiar to him as his own face.

"Y'all seemed cool with her yesterday," he complained. "Why are y'all pissed about her today?"

Erin said acidly, "Because she has moved in with you."

"That's just to make you mad," Quentin said lightly. "And she's scared of Nine Lives." He glanced at Martin. If Owen asked later, Martin would back him up on this. "Nine Lives is in jail in Rio, but for some reason, Sarah seems to think he's going to get out and come kill her."

Owen said, "I know how he feels."

"Okay, okay," Quentin said, holding up his hands in defeat. "I probably won't even see her today, except at the photo shoot. Tomorrow I'll hardly see her because we're finishing the album. July second, she'll be stuck in the office all day doing PR for the concert. We have rehearsal for the concert on the third. On the fourth, after the concert, she'll leave." Fighting down his panic at the thought, he managed to shrug. "I can keep from breaking Rule Three with her for five more days."

He sighed. "I really want to, though." He looked to Martin for camaraderie. "Did you see her in those *pants*?"

"Yeah," Martin said sympathetically.

"Which ones?" Owen asked.

"The red ones," Quentin and Martin said together.

"Oh yeah," Owen said knowingly.

Quentin watched Erin carefully, but she didn't glare jealously at Owen, thank God. She glared only at Quentin.

"Okay, Erin, I said okay."

11

> *I know you don't want to be bothered with this right now,*

Are you kidding? What the hell else am I going to do while breast-feeding 24/7? Your drama with the country star is at least as entertaining as any of these reality shows about rednecks. You're welcome.

> *acting like I was with Quentin to make Erin jealous, so that she'd want to get back with him. But we haven't had sex*

My only question here would be, WHY NOT?

> *because he's still in love with her*

Right. Damn.

> *emerald necklace that must have cost a fortune. I'm*

sure it's just to keep up the facade, and of course I'll give it back to him when he makes up with Erin

Whatever.

> orgasm in the shower. Not your run-of-the-mill "unh"-and-I'm-done orgasm, either. This orgasm extended for miles either way down the highway. They probably felt this thing in Tuscaloosa.

Wow, this is better than reality shows about rednecks.

> wrong, wrong, wrong, wrong

It's not wrong. All you've ever had is Harold Fawn. You deserve some hot-boiled 'Bama love.

> what if I fell for him?

Oh, hell, Sarah, let him go down on you if he wants.

Wendy Mann
Senior Consultant
Stargazer Public Relations

Late that afternoon, Sarah drove Rachel and two new employees she'd hired to the photo shoot for the album cover at the statue of Vulcan. The Cheatin' Hearts were already there, lying in lounge chairs in the bed of Quentin's truck, watching the photographers set up their tripods around the wall at the base of the statue. Quentin jumped down from his truck and met Sarah at her car door.

He kissed her briefly, softly on the lips. "I missed you today."

"I missed you, too." She smiled up at him. This was the understatement of the year. Normally she loved the office work of her job, in which she dotted all the *i*'s, crossed all the *t*'s, made sure everything came together, and networked in a friendly way with the media. Even back when she thought she was in love with Harold, daydreams of him never distracted her from her job.

Quentin was a different story. Sarah had known she was good at multitasking, but she'd amazed even herself at her ability to give statements to the press about the band and the album release and the upcoming concert while simultaneously fantasizing about making Quentin come.

He glanced toward the new employees climbing out of the backseat of her BMW. "Since when do you give rides to the paparazzi?"

"The Cheatin' Hearts' star is still rising. After your concert, Rachel's going to need more help. These ladies were hanging around at the bottom of your driveway, and they seemed perfect for the job, so I asked them to keep doing what they were doing but report your movements to me as well as the media. That's how I knew you'd gone to the bar at Five Points with Martin the other night."

Quentin's eyes followed the women across the parking lot. "You hired the art school girls?"

Sarah laughed at his name for them. "They're well qualified. They have lots of experience following you around. And Beige will graduate from college in August. Amber will, too, if she can manage to pass geology."

In the same surprised tone, he asked, "Their names are Beige and Amber?"

"I thought it was weird, too, that they have such neutral names to go with their black garb. You'd think they'd be Drucella and . . . I don't know."

"Noir," Quentin suggested. He drew Sarah by the hand toward his truck. Erin stood nearby, with a makeup artist touching up her lipstick. Owen and Martin still lay in chairs in the payload. Martin wore long sleeves in the heat.

Sarah looked back at her car and motioned for Rachel to join them. Rachel shook her head almost imperceptibly and sat on the hood of the BMW.

Quentin lifted Sarah onto the tailgate of his truck, hopped up beside her, and draped one heavy arm around her shoulders. "You look tired. You should have eaten breakfast."

"I had the first course," she whispered.

He gave her a lopsided smile, green eyes sparkling. "Maybe that's why you're tired."

"Then I could get used to being tired." She sighed with satisfaction.

He rubbed her arm. "I'm sorry. You're tired because I woke you up in the middle of the night."

"Don't be sorry. I always have trouble sleeping. And anyway, how do you know I was awake? *You* were asleep."

"I could feel you tossing and turning." His voice softened. "I dreamed about you." He wrapped both arms around her from behind.

She tried to enjoy it. Just drop all the schemes and worries and enjoy it for a moment: the hot sunshine, the fresh summer breeze slightly cool at this altitude, and Quentin's protective embrace, almost as if he loved her. Of course, he didn't love her, and fantasies aside, Natsuko insisted that Sarah keep this in mind.

And then he kissed the top of her head, absently, asking nothing in return. As if he loved her.

It was all for show, she reminded herself. For Erin, who watched them from a few yards away as one man pulled at her hair and another coated it with hairspray.

To distract herself so she wouldn't cry, Sarah asked Quentin, "What's the name of my album?"

Quentin said, "*Buns of Steel*."

Sarah squinted up at Vulcan high on his pedestal. "I thought the statue was made of iron."

"*Buns of Iron* ain't funny," he told her with exaggerated patience.

The crew moved away from Erin's hair. "Your turn, Q," she called from underneath her enormous coif.

"I'm not going to wear makeup," Quentin said stubbornly. "We go through this every time. I won't be facing the camera anyway. I have an idea."

Erin looked apprehensive, Martin groaned, and Owen cursed.

Quentin released Sarah from his hug and slid off the tailgate. She noticed for the first time that his faded black T-shirt was emblazoned with white words: *Will cook for sex.*

Sarah said, "You dressed up for the cover shoot, I see."

He looked down at his shirt, then back up at her. "I can honestly say that I gave it no thought whatsoever. Anyhow, I had some idea I might get naked."

"Naked?"

He took off his shirt.

"Quentin," Sarah warned him.

"Bear with me." The pun struck him, and he laughed so hard that he had difficulty unbuttoning his shorts. Between spasms, he said low enough that only Sarah could hear, "You want some more, don't you."

"Who could resist an ego like that?"

He dropped his shorts and boxers together.

"Quentin!" she gasped. "The park's still open!"

"We got permission to be here," he reminded her, kicking off his shoes. "Surely they expected something like this. Everybody in Birmingham knows we get naked. It's art, right?" He pointed to the art school girls for confirmation, and they nodded.

Erin called, "We've been arrested for public indecency so many times—"

Quentin finished, "We should set up the Jefferson County court system to debit our account." He walked over to the photographers, who moved back ever so slightly. He pointed and framed with his hands, explaining his vision. Erin, Owen, and Martin went to sit on the retaining wall.

Then Quentin, with his back to Sarah and the photographers, struck a pose exactly like Vulcan, one arm raised to the sky. Sarah understood the picture now: Quentin as Vulcan in the foreground, his bandmates behind him on the wall, and the real Vulcan above them and in the background. The cameras flashed, and a ring of spectators began to form.

After a few minutes, Quentin relaxed and motioned to Owen. The two of them came toward the truck, Quentin still naked. They opened the doors and rummaged in the cab.

Now that Martin was at a safe distance, Rachel had joined Sarah on the tailgate. As Quentin and Owen found what they wanted in the truck and walked by again, Rachel commented in her demure voice, "You *do* get used to it."

Sarah doubted this.

Quentin slid his boxers from the tailgate as he passed—pink boxers printed with little red hearts and the words *Kiss me.* He pulled them on and sat by Erin on the wall.

Now Owen stripped amid murmurs from the crowd. When he took the Vulcan pose, he held up one drumstick like Vulcan's spear.

As the cameras quietly snapped, Sarah looked at Rachel beside her. Rachel's gaze was fixed on Martin.

Sarah said conversationally, "I know Martin's thirty-one, but when I first saw him without his glasses as we drove up, I thought Erin had acquired a twenty-one-year-old boy toy." Sarah didn't add that she'd been alarmed at first. Alarmed for her plan to make Erin jealous, and excited at her new prospects with Quentin if Erin were otherwise occupied and out of the picture. And then she'd realized it was Martin.

Rachel said, "He looks young because he's lost so much weight."

"That, too," Sarah admitted. She went on cheerfully, "But I'd never noticed that he has dark blond hair, or handsome dark eyes. The glasses overwhelm him."

"He can't see a foot in front of his face without them," Rachel told her, nodding slowly. "That's why he has them off. He knew I'd be here. He doesn't want to see me looking at him."

What Sarah had read as Rachel's reserve, she now realized was profound sadness. She said quietly, "With your experience, I could put in a good word and get you a job doing publicity for another group signed with Manhattan Music. Get you away from here."

"Thanks." Rachel kept her eyes on Martin, who sat beside Erin on the wall, zoning out. "I might take you up on that. But not yet. I'm not quite through here yet."

Owen relaxed his pose. Quentin asked the crowd, "Which one looks better, me or Owen?"

Erin said, "You look more like Vulcan."

Quentin craned his neck to look backward and up at the statue. "I'm not sure how to take that."

Erin said, "Uh. You're shorter. In height?"

Owen asked, "Well, which one do you *prefer*?"

"We won't see your front in the photo, right?" Erin asked. "Because all I'm getting is the front, if you know what I mean."

Sarah predicted that they'd ask Erin to pronounce judgment on the front view next. Then there would be a fight, wooden beams, and stitches.

"Okay, that's it," Sarah called, walking toward them. "Wrap this up and put your clothes back on." Out of the corner of her eye, she noticed a local news van setting up in the parking lot.

"This is great publicity," Quentin told her through his teeth.

"If you get arrested tonight," Sarah pointed out, "you might not make the album deadline tomorrow."

Owen dove for his clothes.

"It's still not quite right," Quentin said. "Martin, you want to try it with a guitar pick? Is that insulting? No, a *guitar*!"

"That's okay," Martin said. He looked toward Rachel, then looked away. "I'm not in the mood."

"Well, I'm going to try one more time," Quentin said.

As Owen put his clothes on and sat down, Quentin stripped. Then, cocking his head and looking up at the statue, Quentin slipped his ancient deck shoes back on because Vulcan wore Roman sandals. He pulled his T-shirt back on because Vulcan wore a smithy apron. He held the microphone he'd fished from his truck like Vulcan's spear. Then he resumed the pose, butt still bare to the warm sun and the mountaintop breeze.

"What are the rest of us supposed to do?" Erin called to no one in particular. "Get an eyeful?" She ogled Quentin. "Just sit here and look pretty?" She smiled sweetly for the camera.

"Shield your eyes," Owen suggested. He and Martin shielded their eyes while Erin continued to look pretty. The camera flashed, and Sarah knew that this was the album cover.

The photographers kept working, capturing the scene from every possible angle with every available light setting. Sarah sat back down on the tailgate of the truck, next to Rachel. She'd known Rachel only a few days, but she felt for her. She put her arm around her.

"I was right to break up with Martin," Rachel whispered.

"Of course you were," Sarah said. "You couldn't stay with an addict. You owed that to yourself."

Rachel's eyes widened. "How long have you known?"

"Since I got here."

Rachel sighed. "I don't know what to do anymore."

"He needs to go to rehab, plain and simple."

"But Quentin says, and I know it's true, that Erin and Owen will kick him out of the band if they find out. Then he'll think he has nothing to live for. That's what will happen if we do an intervention. Quentin says we just have to wait for Martin to make the call. Then we can invent an excuse for Erin and Owen and get him the help he needs in secret. But what if Martin never makes that call, or makes it too late?"

Sarah rubbed her hand soothingly across Rachel's back. "Don't give up on Martin yet. I think you should hang tight, wait and see, because the band can't go on like this much longer. Something's going to give. Can't you feel it?" She glanced at Rachel's placid face hiding such sadness. "No, you can't feel anything but Martin." She glanced at Quentin's bare butt. "And they all *look* relaxed enough. But trust me. *I* can feel it. Something's about to happen."

The photographers finished with Quentin and switched their attention to Erin, who stood on the wall and let a large fan blow her skirt up like Marilyn Monroe for the back cover of the album. Quentin shuffled over to Sarah. He was still bare from the waist down but for the deck shoes. Rachel wisely went to sit in the BMW. The show was over.

Sarah would have to leave soon, too, and she couldn't stand the thought of spending hours and hours more fantasizing about Quentin without some promise of fruition. She said, "About this morning."

He said quickly, "Please don't give me a hard-on while I'm naked in public."

"Put. Your. Clothes. On."

He slid the *Kiss me* boxers from the tailgate and pulled them on. Over at the wall, the other Cheatin' Hearts applauded. "Put it on, Q!" they called.

Sarah asked, "Did your sisters give you those boxers?"

"How'd you know?" He pulled on his shorts.

Sarah eyed the *Will cook for sex* T-shirt. "Where'd you get that shirt?"

"Erin, I think. Women give me weird clothes."

"Because you *wear* them," Sarah laughed. "They think it's funny that you actually wear them."

"Where else am I supposed to get my clothes?"

"From the store?"

"I don't shop," he said simply. "Now. About this morning." He stepped closer to her and held both her hands in his. "I want to try it again and see if I can do better this time. But we're recording until late tonight."

"I'm staying late at the office, too."

"Then let's make a date for tomorrow morning."

"It's time to switch," she said. "Let me see if I can do a better job than you."

He stared at her, but not with the raw want she expected. There was desire, but also mature concern, as if she'd just propositioned her high school track coach.

"This gives you pause," she said.

He shook his head. "I can't let you do that. I promised you from the start that we wouldn't have sex. If you make me come, I may have to break my promise. *I'll* make *you* come again. Let me tell you what I'm going to do."

He leaned down and whispered the dirtiest thing she'd ever heard in her life, then continued to detail where he would put his tongue. She watched Erin and the others sitting on the wall, talking together, oblivious, while Quentin turned her nipples hard and sparked a pulse between her legs just by whispering in her ear.

She said, "We'll see."

~

She came in so late from the office that he was already in bed. Disrobing, she slid into the luxurious sheets beside him. She curled up against him, her breasts to his back, her mound to his buttocks, and her arm around his warm chest.

And couldn't sleep. He was *comatose* and he still made her want him just by existing, naked. Her center burned so brightly that when she finally drifted off and awoke seemingly moments later in the empty bed in the sunlit room, she was sore. She wondered if he'd touched her in the night.

While she listened to his shower hiss, she brushed her hair, then pulled on a pair of see-through white lace panties and Quentin's long-sleeved white shirt from the closet. She still wore the emerald necklace.

The shower shut off. She balled up the sheets in both fists in anticipation. Then, remembering Erin's interruption the morning before, she dashed across the room and locked the bedroom door. She skidded back onto the bed just as he came out of the bathroom.

Wearing a towel around his waist.

Before she could inquire about this newfound and, in her opinion, extremely unfortunate modesty, he stopped by the dresser and told her, "No. I knew you'd do this. I already said no to this. *I'll* make *you* again."

"It's Quentin two, Sarah zero," she complained.

"Or the other way around."

"Either way, I want to even the score." She went to him and led him by the hand to the bed, settling him beside her against the headboard. "If you were my boyfriend, you'd want this."

He laughed. "If you were like most of the girlfriends I've had, I'd be *begging* you to, and you'd say no."

"I'm not your girlfriend."

"I wish you were." He touched his callused thumb softly to her lips. He tucked her hair behind one ear, then behind the other, in the sweetest gesture, as if he really cared about her.

She grabbed his hand and wailed, "I can't believe I'm sitting half-naked on this bed, trying to convince a man to let me give him a hand job!"

He opened the shirt she wore and peered inside at her breast as if examining an engine before purchasing a truck. He closed the shirt again. "Me, neither. But I've told you. Do that to me, and I'm not going to be able to stop myself. And we decided that's not a good idea. Because of Erin."

His mention of Erin should have stopped Sarah cold. He was reminding her that though Sarah might be a fun plaything to toy with for a while, it was Erin he loved. But Sarah had crossed over to a place where she wanted to be Quentin's plaything. She couldn't imagine getting through the rest of this day without taking action. What drove her was mostly lust, but part revenge for Quentin seeing her vulnerable in the shower the morning before, and that night in the chair. And part selfless joy at giving pleasure to her handsome friend.

She said lightly, "I thought you liked games."

"This isn't a game. It may have started out that way, but . . ."

"That's the problem." She slapped away his hands so she could open the towel around his waist. "We'll make it back into a game. I don't have a lot of experience." This was the truth, but she hoped he'd think she was being coy. "You can help me with my technique. Tell me how I'm doing on a scale of one to ten, with one being painful and ten being about to come."

Before he could protest again, she put both hands around his swollen cock.

He gasped, and swore, and swore again. "Sarah."

She used her hands like she wanted to use her center. She slicked her thumb across the fluid at his tip, then gripped him and slid up and down his length. After several minutes of silence but for his breathing, she stopped and looked at his face.

His dark green eyes watched her with a combination of disbelief and horror, which almost made her laugh. But he didn't argue anymore.

She said, "Number, please."

"Ten," he said.

There were several more minutes of silence as she playfully circled the swollen head of his cock with her thumb. She said, "Number every few seconds, please, so I can perfect my technique."

"Ten," he said.

She stroked slowly down one side. Then said softly to remind him, "Quentin."

"Ten," he said.

She stroked slowly up the other side.

"Ten," he said.

"It can't be ten all the time," she scolded him. She slid one hand across his chest, over his heart, to enjoy the rapid rhythm. She gripped him harder with the other hand and stroked more quickly.

"Ah." He laughed. "Eleven." Then, "Ouch, three." Then, "Eleven. Sarah, please don't make me."

His heart raced, and she was as aroused as if *he* were the one pleasuring *her*. She leaned over him, her lips brushing his lips. "Tit for tat," she said, and pumped him hard again.

His hands were in her hair, pulling her, pressing her mouth to his mouth so forcefully that she was frightened, fleetingly. She took back control by stopping.

He broke away from her to say in agony, "Sarah!"

She gave him what he needed, as he had given it to her. She didn't stop again until his come covered her belly and his grip on her hair slowly relaxed.

~

He watched his beautiful pink-haired girl slide her hands off his still-erect cock and kiss her way down in that direction, then slowly back up his stomach toward his face, the emerald necklace sliding cold across his skin and making him flinch. All he could think was, *Oh no*.

She kissed his neck, his chin, his mouth, and looked into his eyes with her big, dark eyes. "Did I do it right?" she asked, disappointed.

He nodded slowly.

"I guess I've never seen you speechless before. Is it a good thing or a bad thing?"

He shook his head, because that's all he could manage.

She sat back on her heels. Her shirt—that is, his shirt—fell open to expose tempting white lace panties, flat belly, beautiful breasts. "This is not the response I was expecting," she said, annoyed now. "I expected unmitigated jubilance."

He began, "What does that mean, unmit—"

Clearly disgusted, she disappeared into the bathroom. He heard the water running briefly, and she returned naked. "Is there a gym somewhere in this house?" she asked without looking at him as she rummaged in the dresser drawer he'd cleared out for her.

"Yeah," he said. "There's a bowling alley, too."

She turned around to look at him as she pulled a sports bra over her breasts. "Really? Where?"

"Not sure."

She stamped her bare foot impatiently. "Well, where's the gym?"

"On the main floor, down the hall, to the right."

She put on her tank top and shorts before she left, but she took her socks and running shoes with her, bundled together with her music player and earbuds, as if she couldn't stand to stay in the room with him any longer.

The door clicked shut behind her. He stared at it, feeling numb, thinking, *Oh no, oh no.*

Finally he stumbled downstairs. He cooked breakfast for the Timberlanes and called their butler to come get it. He cooked breakfast for Martin and Owen and left it on the counter because they were already in the studio. The band should have plenty of time to finish the album by the afternoon, hours ahead of the midnight deadline that would cause them to break the contract with the record company. But Martin was paranoid and Owen was a dumbass, so they were getting an early start. Because of the time of day, Martin must be profoundly high right now. Quentin was glad Owen was down there rather than him.

Except that he had to do his best to pretend that everything was okay when Erin came in and sat at the bar for breakfast. And when Sarah eventually appeared from her run, wet tank top hugging her breasts, and sat beside Erin.

Munching bacon, Erin laughed uneasily. "Sarah, what did you do to Q this morning? He acts like a zombie."

"I know," Sarah said. "I've never seen a man act so grumpy after a hand job."

His grip slipped. Before he could catch it, an entire carton of eggs dashed onto the floor.

"I wouldn't press it, Sarah," Erin said evenly. "He's about to crack."

As he wiped up the puddle of yolk, Quentin stared at Sarah, because it was better than staring at Erin. But Sarah, ignoring him now, inhaled pancakes like it was her last meal. He had to keep cooking for her. Some exertion had made her ravenous. Running five miles on the treadmill. Or jerking him off. Or making him fall in love with her.

Finally she dabbed at her pink mouth with her napkin and slid off the stool. "Thanks for breakfast, Quentin. I want to make sure you know I *appreciate* what you do for me." She galloped up the stairs to his room.

Erin was giving him a long, long, long look.

He cleaned up the kitchen automatically, then sat on the sectional. Erin lay on the opposite side with her eyes closed, practicing fingerings on her fiddle. It was a matter of time before she asked him a pointed question, and he wasn't sure he could bluff her into believing that nothing serious had happened between him and Sarah. She knew him a little too well.

If only his Leia hadn't clopped onto the patio ten days ago with the intimidating presence of a seven-foot-tall Wookiee. If only he hadn't brought her down here to spy on them with all his public relations engineering.

What she'd said to him the day she convinced

to drive was dead-on. He played his friends like chess pieces, and he knew it. The solution, she'd said, was to develop relationships outside the band. Well, *she* was his solution. But he'd put his own solution out of reach by writing Rule Three.

Suppressing the insistent *Oh no, oh no* in his head, he tried to work out a logical plan of action. The others would know when he left the tour to make a booty call in New York. He had to tell them. And leave the band.

He couldn't ask Sarah to quit her job, because her job was part of what made her alive. He suspected that his job did the same for him. He knew the band made him happy, kept him buoyant, got him through the day.

It did the same for Martin, and he couldn't abandon Martin. In his current state, without the band, Martin would do himself in.

Quentin wouldn't. If he didn't have the band, he could beg the medical school to let him in two years after he'd been admitted. In fact, since Thailand, the need to return to his medical career had been gnawing at him.

But he knew that without the band to distract him, he let the sick kids he treated at work and his own health problems and the specter of death get him down. He brooded, and as Owen and Martin had pointed out to him countless times in college, before they started the band, he was difficult to be around. Like now. If he got stuck like this, Sarah wouldn't want him anyway, and he would have given up the band for nothing.

So even if he found a solution to Martin's problem, there was no solution to his own.

He was thirty years old. If he lived to be a hundred—which he rather doubted, after Thailand—he would pine every day for the beautiful pink-haired girl. He was a character in a sad country song. *Oh no*.

With an exasperated sigh at himself, he looked up for the first time and noticed that the TV was tuned to the *World Poker Tournament*. He told Erin, "Sarah's here. Turn it to NASCAR."

"I'm watching this." Erin sat up with her fiddle in her lap. "Hell's Belle is racking up. She claims this is her first time playing poker, and she just wandered into the tournament. But she's putting all the men to shame. Except that she has a Southern accent, this chick could be Sarah's mother, right down to raising one eyebrow."

Quentin said, "That *is* Sarah's mother."

12

I honestly can't say. It's been so long since I had a sexual encounter of ANY KIND WHATSOEVER. Theoretically, no, Daniel wouldn't be silent afterward, because he's sweet-talking me, angling for a victory lap. He's all, "Don't think I'm done with you, dirty girl." Ah, to hear those sweet words again. But I digress. Maybe Quentin wanted to horse around with you, then go back to Erin. He warned you not to push him over the edge. You pushed him anyway. He's acting funny because now he wants you instead of Erin, and he doesn't know what to do.

Wendy Mann
Senior Consultant
Stargazer Public Relations

Sarah was on step ninety-nine of her hundred-step beauty routine when Quentin called to her. If it had been anyone else, she would have applied her red lipstick before responding. But Quentin had never yelled her name before.

Alarmed, she descended the stairs in a controlled fall. Quentin and Erin lounged on the sofas, eyes glued to the TV.

"Where's my album?" Sarah exclaimed. "The courier will be here at noon."

Quentin gestured to the television. Sarah walked around the sectional so she could see the *World Poker Tournament*. Her mother sat at the poker table, looking very pretty in her gray suit, wearing earrings Sarah had given her, gazing at her cards. The announcer explained that Tennessee Frank was currently the chip leader, with the amateur Ethel Seville, a.k.a. Hell's Belle, now a close second. Hell's Belle shook her head at this hand and threw away her cards. Rising, she excused herself to the men, who all half stood politely as she left the table.

Sarah pulled out her cell phone. Punching her mother's number, she rolled over the back of the sofa and plopped down beside Quentin, who didn't take his eyes from the TV.

Her mother had been making her way through the crowd behind the poker table, but now she stopped and felt in her bag for her phone. "Sweetie, what a delightful surprise!"

"How's Branson, Missouri?" Sarah asked.

Her mother looked around the casino. "An absolute circus."

"Mom," Sarah said, "I'm watching you on TV."

"Oh." Sarah's mother touched her hair, then gave a small wave to the wrong camera. "Sweetie, I *was* headed to Branson. I was standing in the Birmingham airport with my ticket. But Branson is such small potatoes. I had been there and done that, as you say. I'm a Diamond Life Master, I need forty-four hundred more points to make Grand Life Master, and I may never make it in my lifetime if I keep drawing partners like that— What *was* that unfortunate woman's name?"

"Beulah."

"Yes, Beulah," her mother repeated, the name dripping with derision. "So, as I was standing in the airport a few mornings ago, I decided I'd trade in my ticket and try my hand at Vegas."

"You seem to be doing okay," Sarah said. "Did you know they call you Hell's Belle?"

"I do declare," her mother said innocently. Then, with a not-so-innocent smile, she asked, "What do you think of Frank?"

Sarah eyed the white-haired gentleman who seemed to own the poker table. "As an adversary or a date?"

Her mother cupped her hand over the phone and whispered, "The next stop for the *World Poker Tournament* is San Juan. He wants me to fly to the coast and sail to San Juan with him on his yacht." She looked toward the table as Tennessee Frank motioned to her that the hand was over. In her normal voice she said,

"Sweetie, I have to go. I have another few days here. I'll call you from the boat. Give my regards to your Quentin." She put the phone back in her bag and walked toward the poker table. Tennessee Frank jumped up to pull out her chair for her.

Erin giggled. "That was an awfully short explanation of how your mother got to the featured table in the *World Poker Tournament*."

"My mother doesn't have time for me," Sarah said. "But in a good way." She turned to Quentin, who still refused to look at her. "Quentin, thank you!"

"What'd he do?" Erin asked, cheerful and suspicious.

"We played bridge with my mother," Sarah gushed before she thought. This date sounded decidedly unromantic. But maybe it would seem serious to Erin that Quentin had met her mom. "My mother's been unhappy, and Quentin goaded her into making a big change in her life, a switch from bridge to poker. At least, *she* thinks Quentin goaded her."

She scooted across the couch until her knee touched Quentin's. Despite his uneasy look at her, she said, "Whether you did it on purpose or not, thank you for resuscitating my mother." Tenderly she kissed the corner of his mouth.

She still didn't understand what the problem was, but she expected him to thaw at the good news about her mother. But he didn't respond to her kiss. As she drew away, he put one hand to his temple like he had a headache, green eyes flat. Then, without a word, he vaulted over the back of the sofa and went outside to the patio.

If he was falling for Sarah instead of Erin, as Wendy had suggested in her e-mail, he had a funny way of showing it.

Erin watched her sympathetically. Yet again, Sarah felt that she and Erin could be good friends. If. If only.

"He's really mad," Erin said. "You'd better go after him."

Sarah didn't particularly want to take relationship advice from Erin about Quentin. "He'll get over it. I don't even know what he's mad about."

"Have you been toying with him?" Erin asked. "Q doesn't like to be toyed with."

"Yes he does," Sarah protested. "He likes games."

"To a point," Erin said. "Listen. Lord knows I don't want to help you with Q. But he sings sharp when he's distracted. I want to keep the peace and finish this album today. So I'm going to give you a hint."

Sarah was stuck on the fact that Erin didn't want to help her with Quentin, and had admitted this, as if throwing down the gauntlet. Erin was jealous. Soon Erin would take Quentin back. This was just what Sarah had wanted all along. So why had her heart stopped beating?

The door down to the studio opened and Martin walked into the room. He said to Erin, "Tag. Your turn."

Erin gave Sarah one more quiet warning. "Q puts on, but he only gets really mad once a year or so. Well,

I take that back. This year he was mad after he got out of the ICU in Thailand, and he was mad after you convinced him to drive. And now. Hmmm, you've caused two out of three. You'd better go after him."

Sarah was tempted to stay and argue with Erin about who exactly had made Quentin mad after she convinced him to drive. But if *Erin* wanted Sarah to appease Quentin, there must be a genuine problem. Uneasy, Sarah stepped outside into the bright, hot morning.

Quentin stood in the shade of a crepe myrtle tree, bees buzzing wildly in the white flowers. Strong arms folded across his chest, protecting himself, he looked out over the panorama of Birmingham.

After Sarah approached him, he stood silently for several more minutes. She began to wonder whether he would acknowledge her at all. Finally he said slowly, "I don't want to play this game with you anymore."

"Okay," Sarah said. Wendy had thought, and Sarah had wanted to believe, that Quentin had picked Sarah over Erin. Now Sarah realized that it was the other way around. He felt that he was cheating on Erin, and he wanted Erin back after all. That's what he'd said: it wasn't a good idea for Quentin and Sarah to have sex, because of Erin.

What Sarah had revealed to Erin about the hand job must have freaked him out further. To him, it was a disaster. But from the perspective of the plan, it was perfect.

Never mind *Sarah's* perspective. Sarah had fainted, and Natsuko took over.

She said, "You're right. We've made Erin jealous enough. Why don't you try her?"

He turned the flat black-green eyes on Sarah. "*What?*"

She felt her resolve falter at the violence of his expression, but she stood her ground. "Why don't you ask her to dump Owen and get back together with you?"

He put his hand firmly behind her head and kissed her hard on the mouth. She tried to pull away, but he pressed himself closer to her. His erection teased her through her pants. Now his tongue in her mouth imitated his cock inside her, and she parted her lips for him.

She heard the kitchen door close. Out of the corner of her eye, she saw Martin glance briefly in their direction, then sit down at the table. Quentin reclaimed her attention by sliding his hand down to her crotch, and she didn't care this time whether Martin liked to watch. Quentin pushed her a few steps under the buzzing crepe myrtle, and as his head brushed the lower branches, white blossoms showered them both.

Sarah jerked and slapped her hand to her shoulder before she even registered the pain. "Ow!" she squealed. Her lust drained away all at once.

"What?" Quentin asked. He peered at her shoulder,

picked at it briefly, and pushed her out from under the crepe myrtle and across the patio. "Ice on it," he muttered.

"What is it?" Martin asked as they passed the table. Quentin said, "Bee sting."

"Oh," Martin said. "In the context, I thought it must be Cupid's arrow."

"Or Vulcan's spearhead," said Sarah, "where appropriate."

In the cold kitchen, Quentin lifted her up to sit on the counter. He put ice in a rag and held the bundle to her shoulder. He still gazed at her with dark, serious eyes, without speaking.

She stared back at him, fascinated. The air around his head had begun to scintillate, and her skin tingled insidiously. Her mind ran in circles. She forgot where she was and looked around in alarm, then remembered she was on a job at the Cheatin' Hearts' mansion, then forgot again.

The idea grew, and fell. It couldn't be. The realization returned and blossomed into terror. She hadn't seen a bee. She had only felt the sting. Quentin had *told* her she'd been stung by a bee, but really he'd shot her up with something awful. He had drugged, just like Nine Lives had drugged her. She whispered, "What have you done to me?"

She jumped down from the counter and ran for the door to the garage, processing even as she moved that her car keys were the other way, upstairs in Quentin's room, in her bag.

Before she'd made it five paces, he caught her around the waist. "Sarah! What's the matter?"

"Don't touch me!" She twisted away from him and dashed for the kitchen again, pausing to pound quickly on the door out to the patio, to catch Martin's attention. She spun against the kitchen counter and grabbed a long knife out of the block. When Quentin came around the corner, she pointed it at him.

He stopped in surprise. Keeping his eyes on her, he reached to open a drawer and pull out a pen. He put his other hand to his neck. "Is your throat closing up?"

Her throat was closing up. *Her throat was closing up.* He hadn't gotten her high for fun. He'd poisoned her. "What did—" she started, but she could hardly form the words. She swallowed with difficulty. "Tell me what you gave me or I'll kill you."

Martin opened the door from the patio. She looked in that direction. Suddenly Quentin grabbed her wrist and twisted it. She dropped the knife. He wrapped her in a wrestling hold with one arm and both legs while he struggled with the pen.

In a desperate burst, she pulled away and dashed across the marble floor as the dark room closed in on her.

"Grab her!" Quentin said.

She ran full-force into Martin, who caught her and held her firmly. Quentin came at her with the pen.

"Don't let him," she tried to say, but her voice was gone, her throat was closed, sparkles flashed in front of her eyes. She whispered, "Martin, don't let him."

"Put her down," Quentin said.

They pushed her, pulled her, manhandled her down to the cold marble floor while she tried to scream. Nine Lives' full weight was on her chest. His knees pinned her arms. He yelled at her, "Sarah! Hold still and let me give you this shot, or you're going to die!"

"Martin," she mouthed desperately.

Martin said soothingly in her ear, "Sarah, I used to be a nurse. I wouldn't do anything to hurt you. You're allergic to bees. You're going into shock. Your blood pressure has dropped, and you're seeing things and thinking things that aren't real. This shot will help you. We keep it here because Q is allergic to everything. Hold still. Okay, you're passing out, but you'll come back. There she goes."

~

"—was just putting ice on the sting, and she started looking at me like I was the devil," said Nine Lives. "When I go into shock, I get this feeling of doom like the world's about to end, but I never think someone's trying to kill me!"

"You're wheezing, Q," Martin said behind Sarah. "Would you get *off* her? You've scared the hell out of her. It doesn't matter why right now. Go call 911 and use your inhaler."

Nine Lives lifted his weight off her chest and walked back into the kitchen. He made a terrible noise each time he breathed.

If he was still walking around, he could still hurt

her. She reached down and yanked off her shoe and threw it in the direction of the retreating blur—

~

"—is going to be okay. Everything is fine. It's over now. You're fine. Everything is okay," Martin recited as he rubbed her hand insistently, too hard, so she knew she was alive. The room jumped, jarring dangling cords and tubes. She lay on a stretcher in an ambulance, with Martin sitting beside her.

The siren sounded shrilly, a few chirps. She must not be important enough for the full-blown constant wail. She must be okay.

"Everything is okay," Martin said.

She looked into his vacant eyes and wondered if he recited this litany to himself as he let the drugs take over.

"Don't worry, kid," he murmured, stroking a lock of hair away from her face. "I've got your back."

~

Quentin sat behind a crash cart with a defibrillator on top. Sarah couldn't see him, but he could hear her if something went wrong. In the last two hours, everyone he'd worked with at the hospital had walked by and made a comment: "Heard you panicked over a bee sting." "Heard your girlfriend got stung by a bee and you lost it." "Heard you didn't have your shot with you in Thailand and had to go to the ICU. That was stupid." "How come Martin wins Grammys and you don't?"

He had a response for the last: "How many hit singles have *you* written?" But the rest he deserved. And although he normally would take the ribbing in the good-natured way in which it was intended, today he held his head in his hands and wished he could sink into the linoleum.

Over and over he reviewed the weird scene in his mind. He was holding an ice pack to Sarah's shoulder, and she was there with him, perfectly sane. And then, all of a sudden, she wasn't. She was like a racehorse that reared back at being pushed toward the starting gate, her muscles taut and strong and moving under her skin, fear and anger making her eyes wild and unseeing. Well, she *seemed* unseeing, up until she beaned him in the back of the head with her shoe.

He was touching the scab in his hair when Owen and Erin finally came away from Sarah's bedside. Owen slapped his shoulder supportively and Erin rubbed his back.

Then came Martin. "She wants to see you. Hell if I know why. She was panicking. You panicked, too, and strong-armed her and made it worse. *You can't panic, Q.*" He launched one of his impressive cussing performances.

"Martin, he feels bad enough already," Owen said over the cussing. Erin put a soothing hand on Martin's chest, to no avail.

Finally the attending hollered across the room, "Martin, get out of my emergency room if you're going to talk like that. I'm sure Q deserves it, but you need to take it outside."

Martin flung a few more choice words at Quentin before finishing, "Don't you *touch* her again." He stormed out of the room. Owen and Erin gave Quentin sympathetic looks, then went after Martin.

Ignoring the stares that followed him, Quentin stood up, popped his neck, and walked to Sarah's bed. The privacy curtains were drawn on either side, leaving only the end of the bed open to the bustling room. Her knees were drawn up to her chest, her arms encircling them. She was a small spot of vibrant color in a field of white. As he sat down in the chair drawn up to the bed, he glanced at the monitor and saw that her heart rate, blood pressure, and pulse-ox were back to normal. She watched him with her poker face.

He said, "Tell me what happened in Rio." He glanced at the monitor again. Her heart rate was going up.

"Martin told me you went into anaphylactic shock like this in Thailand," she said quickly. "I believe you now, that you don't do drugs, and allergies and asthma have been sending you to the hospital all along."

"Great," he said flatly. "Tell me what happened in Rio."

She swallowed. "Martin told me this is what happened to your mother, too."

Quentin nodded grimly. "Rio."

She shook her head.

"I used to work here," Quentin said. He moved his finger in a circle in the air. "These people are my friends. They all think I panicked when you went into shock. You don't panic if you work in the emergency room." He leaned close to her. "You and I know I didn't panic. Or"—he gave a small laugh, despite himself—"I didn't panic *first*. People with allergies tend to lose it the first time their throats close up, but on top of that you were having some kind of flashback, like you thought I was out to get you. Tell me what happened in Rio. For the sake of our friendship, you have to tell me."

She put her chin on her knees and looked down at her bare feet. "I can't tell you. I haven't told anyone. I even lied to Wendy about the scar, because I don't want to get her involved when she has the baby to worry about. I told her I was mugged in Rio."

"You just jacked me off and threatened me with a knife in the space of an hour and a half. I'd say that makes us close." He raked his hands back through his hair and took a deep breath before he leaned forward to ask her the question quietly. "Did he rape you?"

"No," she said without looking up.

"Did he try?"

"Maybe."

He narrowed his eyes at her. "Did he give you drugs you didn't want?"

"He put something in my drink a few times," she murmured. Then she squared her shoulders and sat up straight, as if suddenly ready to face it. Or, not, because she told the story in the second person, distancing herself. "The high you can deal with. The bad part is that you don't know what he's given you, or how much. He's high when he gives it to you. You can't trust his dosing.

"You can't go to the hospital, because they'll call the police. You can't call the police, because you're on drugs. You can't reach your friend in Moscow. You can't call your pregnant friend in America, and you can't call your mother, because what can they do? It will only wig them out. All you can do is lock your hotel room door until you're not high anymore, expecting to OD the whole time, and passing the hours watching *Bewitched* reruns in Portuguese, which somewhat exacerbates a bad trip."

"Why didn't you leave?" he whispered.

"Oh, this stuff was later." She waved it away with the hand stuck with the IV needle. The tube tapped gently against the monitor. She gazed vaguely at the equipment before continuing. "It was fine at first. Nine Lives and his entourage were a mess, but I kicked them into shape. He got his album written and re-corded. Slowly. He'd go on a binge and I'd have to pull him back out. But we got it done."

She slipped back into the second person. "You want to be like them, so they'll trust you. You have to do what they do. Like I did with you guys that first night."

Quentin nodded, though he suspected that blend-ing in with Nine Lives meant more than tequila and strip poker.

She went on, "You have to decide what you're

going to do, and you have to decide when you're finally going to say no. Toward the end, he wanted me to do something I wasn't willing to do, and I said no. It was lucky that I was cool with his bodyguard and his driver. If they had to choose between us, they'd pick Nine Lives, because he was paying them. But they held him off me a couple of nights."

Quentin stared at her, the pretty, brown-eyed woman telling this horrible story frankly, as if recounting a jog down the road. "And you still didn't leave," he said in disbelief.

"Well, no," she said as if it were obvious. "You don't understand. My husband told me he didn't want a baby, moved out, and got a girlfriend. I dyed my hair pink and wore leather and went to whip up trouble in Rio like I was the anti-mother, you know? I couldn't have the family life that people want. So, hell, I was going to have the opposite life, *so there*.

"After about a month, I realized what paradise it would be to have my job back, and my friends back, and to spend my weekends alone in my apartment, eating Cheetos and downloading romance movies and letting myself go. But I'd lose everything if I fouled up the Nine Lives album. I'd lose my job, and no one else would hire me for this kind of work after I blew such a high-profile case."

She shifted uncomfortably on the bed and tried to stretch her arms over her head, but the IV tube pulled taut and stopped her. She put her arms back down.

"He finally finished the album, I sent it back by courier, and I was ready to get out of there. He had his people bribe the airline to cancel my flight reservation back to the States."

"So you were stuck there with him." Feeling sick, Quentin added, "He fell in love with you."

"I'm not sure that's possible, considering his mental state," she said, so calmly. "And then he comes on to you when his bodyguard and driver are mysteriously absent, as if he's upped their pay to get his way."

"And then what happens?" Quentin tried to hide his horror. He needed to keep her talking.

With one finger, she traced the scar under her chin. "With what?"

"He was wearing a skull ring. I think this was the crossbone," she said woodenly. "So what do you do?"

"What do you do?" Quentin repeated.

"You do what you can." She looked down at her bare toes. "You wield your shoe as a weapon."

Quentin laughed shortly and bitterly. "You use that thing like a Chinese throwing star."

She showed him the poker face. "Did I hurt you?"

"Rio," he said. He would not allow her to change the subject before he got the whole story.

"Rio," she agreed. "The hotel hears the commotion and calls the police. Of course, it's your job to go with Nine Lives and get him out of jail. But you're not going to take this, right?"

"Right," Quentin said.

"And you can't stay trapped in Rio, right?"

"Right."

"You know he can have all the charges against him dropped with a bribe and come after you again." She looked at Quentin with her dark-fringed eyes. "But not if you bribe first."

Quentin blinked. "You used your money to bribe the police in Rio to keep him in jail?"

"No," she said. "I used *his* money. I had access to his bank accounts because he gave me power of attorney one of the times he went to rehab. I set up payments so the police would keep him in jail indefinitely."

She embraced her knees, curling into a ball again. "If he gets back to New York and tells Manhattan Music what I did, I'll be fired from Stargazer for sure. And if Wendy knew about the whole thing, she'd try to cover for me. I can't ask her to do that. The truth would come out eventually, and she'd go down along with me.

"But if I get your album first, and your concert goes smoothly, I'll have enough clout at Manhattan Music that they'll believe me over him. I can threaten to have him dropped from the label if he crosses me. He doesn't have a lot of friends there." Her chin went back down onto her knees. "And now he's out of jail."

Quentin frowned. "You don't *know* he's out, do you?"

She shrugged.

"Is there someone in Rio you could ask?"

She shook her head. "I don't want to make a call

like that from the States. His lawyers might trace it and use it to blackmail me. I'm acquainted with his lawyers."

"It's a good thing you have a lot of hair," a passing nurse remarked to Quentin. By the time he turned around, the nurse was gone. He realized he had his hands in his hair again. He extracted his fingers with some difficulty.

Then he sat on the edge of the bed and hugged Sarah around the IV tube and the monitor cable. She didn't hug him back, but that was okay. He held her in his arms and kissed the top of her head.

"Sarah, I'm sorry," he whispered. "I'm sorry for being rough with you. When I worked here, I saw a lot of things that human beings shouldn't have to see. But today was the first time I ever panicked. Martin's so pissed at me. You can't panic in this line of work." He hugged her harder. "People do die of shock from bee stings. Not often, but it happens. And I saw you were about to pass out . . ." He pressed his lips to her silky pink locks again and tried to appreciate the reality of Sarah, and breathing, and Sarah breathing.

"I'm sorry, too," she said into his shirt. "I'm sure being threatened with a knife was an unpleasant surprise, especially juxtaposed with the hand job." Something in his face prompted her to add, "Don't you dare ask me what *juxtaposed* means."

"Sarah." He rubbed her knee, trying to rub some of the life back into her. "You're not alone anymore. If something like this ever happens to you again, you can always call me, wherever you are in the world, and I'll come get you."

"That's sweet, Quentin," she said sincerely, looking into his eyes. "But you'll move on. You'll get married and have kids and forget all about this day."

Not likely, Quentin thought. He said, "So will you. But if it's another one like that Harold Fawn jackass, how much good is he going to do you? I mean it. If you ever need help, call me. I'll bring Owen and Martin and Mad 'Red' Mud if I have to, and we'll come get you."

He turned at a rattling behind him. The attending leaned past him with a tin, offering Sarah a homemade cookie.

"No, thanks," Sarah said, putting a hand to her stomach.

"You should eat something," said the attending.

"Kind of queasy," Sarah murmured.

The attending offered the tin to Quentin as an afterthought.

"Do they have nuts in them?" Quentin asked.

"What do you think I'm trying to do, *kill* you?" the attending asked. "Don't answer that." She moved around the curtain to the next bed.

Sarah stared after the attending, then turned to Quentin. "Tell me what happened in Thailand."

He'd known this was coming. "Tit for tat," he muttered. "Well, it was the end of the tour. We were tired. We wanted a vacation. I should have known better, because everything went wrong that day. Martin found some heroin right away. Karen and I were getting on each other's nerves. I'm supposed to keep an asthma inhaler and an adrenaline shot—that shot Martin gave you—with me all the time. They were in Erin's purse. But Erin went in a market by herself and got her purse stolen. Owen and I tried to kill us a Thai guy, but he'd already passed her purse to somebody else. I didn't think anything about the inhaler and the shot, which were probably halfway to Udon Thani by then.

"We gave up and went to the beach. It was this beautiful beach. Let's just say it put spring break at Panama City to shame. There were these enormous rocks jutting out of the ocean."

"Like Chimney Rock?" Sarah asked.

"No. And then I felt myself start to pass out. I try to be careful what I eat, but sometimes when we're on tour, I slip up, because I don't know where all the ingredients are coming from.

"I passed out. Then there was a motorcycle with a cab on the back for passengers. They use them as taxis. A ride in that thing would've shocked *anybody* back into consciousness. At the hospital, I remember there were cats running down the halls, and the medical equipment looked like the computers in the first *Star Trek* TV series, very sixties.

"I was glad I'd had a nice day at the beach, because I was about to die. It got hairy in the ICU in Oklahoma

City last January, but I never thought I was going to die. This time was different. This was it. The doctor told me they were inducing a coma until my lungs recovered. The way I felt, I did not expect to wake up. Erin will tell you that it got very weird. I took her hand, and then Martin's hand, and Owen's hand, and Karen's hand, and said good-bye to them one last time."

He was back in the ICU. Karen clung to one hand and wailed, as if *he* was supposed to be strong for *her*, even though he couldn't breathe. Erin held his other hand firmly and chewed gum. That's what he concentrated on as they were putting him to sleep: the grip of Erin's hand, the sound of her gum smacking, and the strange concentric square pattern of the foreign ceiling tiles.

"And then, a few days later, I did wake up."

Sarah pulled at him. She wanted him to lie down with her. He tried to settle beside her on the bed, but the IV tube and the monitor cable got in the way. He moved to her other side and lay behind her, his front to her back. Careful not to touch her stung shoulder, he put his arm across her chest. He inhaled the scent of her hair: shampoo and Sarah.

She asked him, "Were you beckoned by the light?"

"Are you making fun of me for being near death?" he demanded. "Why does everybody make fun of me for being on a ventilator?"

"Because you love it. It helps you cope." She looked back over her shoulder to show him a genuine smile. "Just trying to lighten the mood here."

"Oh." He forced a laugh. "No, I was under heavy sedation. The propofol pretty much took care of anything like that."

She smoothed her hand up and down his arm. He felt his hair stand on end, and the IV tube swayed. She asked, "Why'd you fire Karen?"

The excuse he'd given himself was that he didn't want her to find out about Martin's drug use. There was more to it than that. "I fired her because I broke up with her. I didn't think I could break up with her and still have her as a manager, because hell hath no fury." Instantly he was sorry for quoting Shakespeare. But idiot Quentin didn't have to read Shakespeare. It was a common expression. Albeit probably not one idiot Quentin would use.

Sarah let it slide. "Why'd you break up with her?"

"Because . . ." He wasn't sure of the answer himself. "I don't know. I've been sick a lot. But before this, I never really expected to die at thirty. I thought I'd finish school and have kids. I thought I'd change the world with the research foundation we started. And I thought that when I died, I'd be with somebody I was in love with."

Sarah's hand halted on his arm. "What about Erin?"

He was able to stop himself from saying, "What *about* Erin?" He'd made enough mistakes today. He said truthfully, "When Erin and I are together, we don't get along. We argue."

"Do you love her?"

He wished Sarah would move her hand on his arm

again, but there was no chance of that now. He was damned either way. If he said he didn't love Erin, Sarah would leave him. She would think she'd gotten too close to him and he had chosen her over Erin, wrecking her plan to keep the band together. If he lied and said he was in love with Erin, that would ruin any slim chance he might have at a real relationship with Sarah later, if he ever figured out how to swing it.

He said carefully, and again truthfully, "Yes, I love her." *Just not the way you mean.*

Sarah sat up suddenly. The cable pulled out of the monitor, and the alarm sounded.

"I've got it," Quentin called over the beeping so that ten nurses wouldn't rush in. He rolled off the bed and bent to plug the cord back in.

"So, Martin used to work here, too?" Sarah asked conversationally, poker-faced.

"Yeah. Martin was a terrific nurse. The job kept him sober, because the hospital makes employees take drug tests. And Erin worked here as an ultrasound tech. We never were sure what Owen did. He has an MBA, and he worked up in accounting."

"*Owen* has an *MBA*?"

"Pretty good for a dumbass." Quentin grinned.

"What did *you* do?" she asked.

"Helped out." Quentin cupped his hands and called, "King to queen seven," to a passing paramedic.

"Shit," the paramedic exclaimed without stopping.

Quentin glanced up at the almost empty IV bag, then at his watch. "We can still finish your album by the deadline tonight. But we won't finish it before your courier's flight back."

"I'll take it to New York myself tomorrow morning," she said.

Quentin's heart skipped a beat. "Are you coming back down after that?"

"Of course," she said. "I'll just go up for the day. We still need to get you and Erin together. And I have to keep you out of trouble until the Nationally Televised Holiday Concert Event."

"I'll go with you to New York," he said suddenly.

Her eyes brightened, then darkened. "I don't think that's a good idea."

"We don't know whether Nine Lives is on the loose. It's bad to have the thing I have, the disabled— What did you call it?"

"Disabling codependence?"

"Yeah. It's bad to have that. But it's okay to ask for help."

She half smiled. "I don't want you to bite the head off a dove in the record company office."

"I'll behave," he promised.

"That's not the only thing I want to do while I'm in town. I need to visit Wendy's baby. This may be all the baby I ever get."

"Oh, honey," he said, taking her hand. "You should have told me it meant that much to you. We could have finished the album days ago, and you could have been there when the baby was born."

He really *was* idiot Quentin. He didn't realize what he'd admitted until her poker face began to fissure. She seethed, "You mean to tell me that all this time, you've been holding back, delaying the album *on purpose*—"

He clapped his hands. "Okay, let's get you out of here. We have an album to record." He caught a passing nurse and gestured to the IV. "Has she had enough of this? I'm taking her home."

Quentin hadn't expected what was left of the Birmingham paparazzi to be waiting on the sidewalk outside the emergency room, plus ten extra reporters and photographers in town early for the Nationally Televised Holiday Concert Event. But come to think of it, an ambulance pulling up to his house three days before the concert *was* a scoop.

He pushed through the photographers like a bodyguard to clear a path for Sarah, but Sarah stopped and gave a statement to the reporters. With a feeling of foreboding, he listened to her tell the truth. When they finally reached his big-ass truck, he told her reprovingly that she should be careful what she told the press, because it might come back to sting her.

"How can it possibly matter to anyone that I'm allergic to bee stings?" she asked.

"You're going to be sorry," he said as he drove back to the house.

He tucked her into his bed and went downstairs to the recording session made frantic by his bandmates' fears that they might miss the deadline. Several times he went upstairs to check on Sarah and found her sound asleep in the quiet room.

But at about eight in the evening, she stumbled down the stairs to the studio. It was a far cry from the first day he'd known her. Barefoot, she wore his boxers and T-shirt. She'd knotted them to take up some slack, but they still hung off her. A blanket was hunched around her, and her tousled hair fell in stripes to frame her ashen face. Wandering behind the technicians and stepping around the Timberlanes, to whom she didn't give a glance, she lay across the empty chairs at the back of the control room and curled into a ball. He had thought he'd never see it, but here it was: Sarah undone.

Erin nodded in Sarah's direction, as if Quentin needed prompting. He set his bass in its stand and walked out of the sound booth. Kneeling in front of Sarah, he pushed a pink strand away from her furrowed brow. "What can I get you?"

She opened her eyes and closed them again. "Nothing, thank you," she murmured. "Couldn't sleep."

"You're sure as hell not going to get any sleep down here."

"I wanted to be with you."

He wished this were true. *You mean you wanted to make sure we got your album done*, he thought, but he didn't have the heart to argue with her. He smoothed her hair again, squeezed her shoulder, kissed her forehead, and went back into the sound booth.

He switched off the sound to the control room and turned his back on the spectators. He wouldn't put it past Sarah to be able to read lips. "Sarah's taking the master copy to New York herself tomorrow," he told the band, "and I'm going with her."

"The hell you are," growled Owen.

"She knows a lot of our secrets," he said pointedly to Owen. "We don't want her to tell the record company. I think we should keep her happy."

Owen looked away.

Quentin explained to Erin and Martin, "We're only going up for a few hours. She wants to see her friend who just had a baby, and I'll check on the medical foundation. I won't have time to break Rule Three."

"It probably wouldn't take you very long," Martin remarked.

"I'm tired of your stamina jokes," Quentin said. "Erin, tell Martin about that time in Valdosta."

Erin smiled. Owen, adjusting a cymbal, didn't look the least bit jealous. What a relief.

But then Erin said, "Sarah won't tell the record company about us now that she has the album. You can check on the foundation some other time. There's no good reason for you to go." She ran through a fiddle lick as if that were the end of the discussion.

Quentin stepped over to Martin and said quietly, "Nine Lives is more likely to come after Sarah up there than down here. I'd appreciate it if you could help a brother out on this one."

Martin said, "I'll talk to Erin later."

The Timberlanes went home, the technicians went home, and at 11:47 p.m., the Cheatin' Hearts completed *Buns of Steel*. They crowded around Sarah, who was still curled in a ball on the control room chairs. They sang "Strip Poker Blues" a cappella as they presented her with the master copy of the album. She called the head honcho at Manhattan Music and yelled to him over the jubilant singing that the first part of her mission was accomplished.

13

FINALLY a chance to e-mail you. Can't wait to see you this afternoon! We are all well rested for your visit! HAHAHAHA gotta go baby crying again

Wendy Mann
Senior Consultant
Stargazer Public Relations

"How'd your meeting go?" Quentin asked as he opened the taxi door for Sarah and stepped back to let her in the car.

She gave the driver the address of Wendy's loft in Tribeca and waited for Quentin to slide in beside her. As the taxi moved into traffic down Sixth Avenue, she said happily, "Manhattan Music was very impressed that I turned in your album at all. They were *ecstatic* that it's so *good*. What have you been doing to those poor people?"

"Nothing they didn't deserve," Quentin said.

She relaxed against the seat, watching midtown Manhattan flash by. "I just wish I had longer in the city. I didn't expect my meeting to run over. Now I'll hardly have time to exclaim over the baby and stop in at my apartment before our flight."

"Oh, by the way," Quentin said offhandedly, "I called Stargazer and talked to the lady who handles your travel reservations. I postponed our flight until noon tomorrow."

"*Really*," Sarah said, hoping she looked irritated rather than delighted. She scrolled down her contacts to the travel desk and held the phone to her ear. "Voice mail," she informed Quentin. "This chick is just digging herself a deeper hole." After the beep, she said, "It's Sarah. Just calling to remind you that you don't work for Quentin Cox. You work for Stargazer. *For now*."

As she clicked the phone off, Quentin said, "That was harsh. She was a nice lady."

Sarah felt a flash of guilt, but she brushed it off. "That nice lady was totally taken in by your act. She probably gazed moonily into space while you serenaded her with 'Naked Mama.' And I'm afraid you're about to find out what *harsh* is. You're supposed to be back in Birmingham tomorrow for a run-through of the concert. Erin will call you."

"I'll make it in time," he said. "The run-through

isn't until tomorrow night. But you're right. She'll still call me. I left a message with Martin about what I was doing and then turned my phone off. Turn yours off."

"I can't do that," Sarah said. "There might be a PR catastrophe while I'm gone."

"They'll leave a voice mail, I promise."

"And that's another thing," Sarah protested. "I don't want to talk to an angry Erin on the phone, but I don't want to listen to a bunch of voice mails from an angry Erin, either."

"She won't leave you a bunch of messages. She'll leave *me* a bunch of messages. She'll leave you *one*."

"I'll bet it's a doozy."

"It'll be worth it," he said.

She glanced over at him. His brown curls danced behind his ears in the blast from the air conditioner vent. He bent his head to the bottom of the taxi window and squinted up at the tops of the passing skyscrapers, as Alabamians who had never lived in New York were wont to do, she remembered from her freshman year at college. He wore his poker face. It was impossible to tell whether he intended innuendo when he told her it would be worth it.

She wanted innuendo, and she didn't. She wanted him, but she couldn't entertain the possibility of stealing him from Erin. If the group broke up, even with the album completed, she might lose her job. Nine Lives would tell Manhattan Music what she'd done to him, Manhattan Music would tell Stargazer, and she'd never work in PR again. Quentin eventually would break up with her because she was an unemployed loser. And then she'd be one of these guys wandering in the busy street, spraying and wiping windshields and demanding five dollars.

Quentin lowered his window and stuck his head into the wind like a happy dog. Apparently Sarah didn't have to make a decision about sex, because there was no innuendo. He said innocently, "You get to spend some quality time with your friend. And when you're done, I can drop you off at your apartment and visit the foundation. We've been on tour so long, I haven't been by in a year. Since Thailand, I'd like to make sure they're on top of this allergy thing."

Sarah nodded. "So it's a real foundation."

"Of course it's a real foundation. Did you think it was a fake foundation?"

"Word around Manhattan Music is that it's a red herring to draw attention away from your cocaine addiction."

"That *does* sound like something we'd do." He laughed. "But that would be one expensive fish. No, the foundation is real. I don't want anyone else to have to go through what I went through when I was a kid."

"What gives you the kind of allergic reaction I had to bees?"

"Most nuts," he said. "I'm allergic to a lot of foods, but nuts are the one that's hardest to avoid."

"Yeah, I imagine it's hard to avoid nuts," Sarah commented provocatively, "you being a man and all."

Quentin sighed the longest sigh. "Are you making

a *nut joke*? Don't even start with me. I've had allergies since I was born. I had allergies in middle school. I've heard all the nut jokes. I made up all the nut jokes so I could tell them before someone else told them."

"Is that why you never eat out? Because of your food allergies?"

"I never eat out because I'm a great cook."

"And so humble," she teased him.

"Have you tried my aloo gobi?"

She smiled. "Do you mean that in the carnal sense?"

"No, it's vegetarian." He laughed. "Seriously, you're right. I never eat out because cooking meals myself is the only way I can be sure they won't kill me." He inhaled the city deeply through his nose. "And then there's the asthma. I have to exercise carefully."

"Thus you flaked out on me in the lake."

"I didn't flake out, see," he protested. "I knew I *would* flake out. When I was a kid, I didn't know my limits. Or I didn't want to know them. I went out for high school football with Owen one year. *That* was interesting."

He waved to a group of Japanese tourists on the sidewalk, and several of them waved back. Sarah turned around and watched through the back window as they gestured excitedly to each other, realizing who Quentin was, and started chasing the car. She was about to give the driver a twenty to lose them when a hole opened in traffic and he sped ahead.

"Other things trigger my asthma, too," Quentin went on. "Cigarette smoke is the main one. And once you're triggered, getting upset can make asthma worse, but that's only happened to me twice, thank God. The second time was yesterday, when you threatened to shiv me."

"Again, I'm sorry about that."

"It's okay. It actually wasn't as bad as the first time. I was mortified."

"You, mortified?"

"It does happen."

"Let me guess," she said. "Was it when Vonnie Conner turned you down?"

"If I'd had an asthma attack because Vonnie Conner turned me down, I would never have shown my face at high school again," he said. "No, it was at my granddad's funeral."

"Oh." She covered her lips with two fingers and said through them, "I'm so sorry."

"Don't be sorry. The whole spectacle is pretty funny in retrospect."

She cut her eyes sideways at him, unable to imagine what was so funny about having an asthma attack at his grandfather's funeral. "This was pretty recently, right?"

"A little over two years ago," he confirmed, "right before we signed with the record company. I was a pallbearer, which was somebody else's mistake, because I was pretty devastated when he died . . ."

As he trailed off, she nodded sympathetically. She knew how he'd felt.

"After we got our shoulders under the casket, the

closer we got to the church, the more upset I got. I guess I could pretend it wasn't happening before that, and I was at just another family reunion, but this was final.

"Well, somebody was smoking outside the church, and as we were crossing the threshold, I got a lungful. I couldn't reach for my inhaler in my pocket because, hello, I was carrying a casket. Normally I could have made it all the way down the aisle without it, but I was so upset already. On top of that, I was terrified of passing out in front of all those people. A lot of them were friends of my granddad's from Nashville, country music insiders. None of them could have gotten the Cheatin' Hearts a contract, but I didn't know that at the time. I was as tense as I've ever been, and that's when I"—he clapped his hands, one on top of the other—"hit the aisle."

"Oh!" Sarah gasped.

"And then the casket"—he clapped his hands again—"hit the aisle, tumbled end over end, and landed upside down."

"Oh my God!" Sarah squealed. "Why couldn't the other five guys hold it up?"

"That's what *I* said at the emergency room later!" Quentin exclaimed. "They're all like, 'Give a dude a nudge when you're about to faint like a girl, Q,' and I'm like, 'There are *six pallbearers*. I was holding up the whole thing myself? You can't hold it up yourselves if a guy has to pass out? Jesus.'" He paused. "My granddad would have loved it, though."

"No!" Sarah covered her mouth again to hold her laughter in.

"Oh yes. The casket was closed, and they did *not* open it after that to see what had happened to him. But he would have said, 'You should have left it open, and I would have gone flying! *That's* showmanship.'" As Sarah fought to stop giggling, Quentin reached across the car and poked her gently in the ribs. "All this can be yours now that you know you have allergies, too. You're just joining the club. Did they tell you in the emergency room that you need venom therapy?"

"Something sinister like that was mentioned, yes."

"It's not bad," he said. "They just give you a shot with a tiny bit of bee venom every few weeks, and increase the dose a little each time. Before long, you're not allergic to bees anymore. That is, not fatally allergic. That is, if you don't have an adverse reaction—"

"*That is*, spare me," she said. "I saw your adrenaline shot with your asthma inhaler in my bag. So I'm covered for now. I'll just stay out of Central Park."

She stole another look at him, so handsome and relaxed, friendly green eyes taking everything in. She asked him, "Do you ever think about upping the profile of the foundation? Coming out of the asthma and allergy closet, so to speak? You could do a lot of good. Celebrities are always raising awareness by admitting that they have medical conditions."

"I've been admitting it from the start," he said.

"All I got for my trouble was rumors about a cocaine addiction. And a multimillion-dollar recording contract." He chuckled. "I'm not ruling it out, but I'm not too sure how it would go over at this point. You're the PR expert. Picture this." He struck a pose as if speaking into a camera. "Hi, I'm Quentin Cox of the Cheatin' Hearts. You may know me for hit songs like 'I Want a Leia' and 'Honky-tonk Hell.' What you may not know is that shellfish gives me hives." He laughed again. "Maybe after the sixth album."

"Maybe after the Nationally Televised Holiday Concert Event," she suggested. "Your profile will be much higher. I'll even get you on a late-night talk show." She reached over and patted his thigh encouragingly.

He put his warm hand over her hand.

They continued to chat. She wondered whether he had a hard time concentrating on the conversation, as she did. Her whole body centered on her hand touching his hand.

Finally the taxi dropped them off in front of Wendy and Daniel's restored high-rise. As they waited for the doorman to call upstairs, she exclaimed, "Oh, man, I forgot all about their cat. Are you allergic to cats?"

"No!" he said, pointing at her and beaming.

"Congratulations. How about turtles?"

"I guess we'll find out."

In the ride up the elevator, she thought to warn him, "Wendy looked okay when I left, but she claims she gained three hundred pounds in her last week of pregnancy. Expect the worst, Jabba the Hutt." And by the time she knocked on the door of the loft, it had occurred to Sarah that she should have been warning Quentin about lots of things, a whole drive's worth, but now she heard footsteps.

Daniel flung open the door and embraced her. Sarah was vaguely concerned about what Quentin might think, but Daniel's muscles were tense. He needed this hug. She hugged him and rubbed his back.

Eventually, when he let her go, she examined him. He was handsome as ever, but he had dark circles under his eyes. He hadn't shaved, and Daniel *never* skipped shaving. She thought his dark hair might even be a little mussed, but her eyes could have been playing tricks on her. Finally she laughed. "You look tired."

"You look—" Daniel began in the sexy British accent he slipped into when he was stressed. He shook his head at Quentin. "You didn't see the before photo, but this is *some* makeover."

"Shut up," Sarah said, whacking his arm.

A baby's high wail sounded closer and closer, and Wendy appeared in the doorway. "Make it stop!" she exclaimed.

Sarah took the baby. The others introduced themselves and baby Asher and herded her out of the foyer to sit on the couch in the living room, but she hardly noticed, lost in the baby who shared her birthday.

She made some attempts at amusing faces, because

this was what she'd seen other people do with babies. Asher had his eyes squeezed shut to wail and couldn't see her. Wendy and Daniel were talking to Sarah, telling her about Asher. She couldn't hear anything they were saying over the wail.

Finally she said loudly, "At first I intended to tell you that he's adorable and tiny, but the screaming is really what you notice."

"He's hungry," Quentin said.

"Don't even go there, cowboy," Wendy said. "I just fed him. That's pretty much all we do around here."

"You look great," Sarah told Wendy to draw her off Quentin. It was true. She looked puffy, for Wendy, but far from Jabba-sized.

"Tell me another," Wendy said disdainfully. "This is Daniel's shirt. I'm still in maternity pants. And if the grocery store has a rule against bedroom slippers, I'm in trouble."

Sarah sympathetically examined Wendy's swollen feet, then gasped in fear. "Where's the baby?" She looked around frantically. Quentin was holding Asher and jiggling him in his arms. "Give me that!" she said. She took Asher back carefully. When he started wailing again, Sarah wondered whether Quentin was actually good at this.

"The baby's hungry," Quentin repeated.

"Stuff it," Wendy said.

"Have you had help?" Sarah shouted. She didn't want to yell and upset Asher further, but she wouldn't be heard otherwise.

"I was sorry to see Daniel's mother go," Wendy said. "How sick is that?"

Sarah could barely hear Wendy over the screaming. She asked, "Isn't this what pacifiers are for?"

"The Lactation League says you're not supposed to use a pacifier or a bottle for the first month, because it results in *nipple confusion*." Wendy relished the term. "The baby prefers the pacifier and the bottle and won't go back to the breast. Personally, I think it is a front for a misogynist group making up terms like *nipple confusion* to thwart me."

Sarah could tell that Quentin was about to have one of his laughing spells. He was holding his breath and turning red. He cast a wary glance at Daniel.

"And they want you to *express* the milk," Wendy said. "*Express* it, like it's going to flow gently out. There is no gentle flow here. If I spun around in circles, I'd look like a lawn sprinkler."

Quentin snorted. He was about to lose it. Even cool Daniel looked taken aback. Sarah stifled a laugh of her own. This was part of what made their marriage work. After two years, Daniel still wasn't used to Wendy.

Wendy went on, "And if your boobs hurt from this—shocking!—the Lactation League suggests that you slice up some cucumber and put it on your tits, or should I say *teats*? Can you *believe* this? As far as I'm concerned, there is only one thing a cucumber is good for—"

Sarah and Daniel were both shaking their heads gravely. *Don't make that joke.*

Wendy finished, "—and that's salad."

Quentin exploded. He removed himself into the hallway, but his musical laugh rang out through the house.

Daniel, lips pressed together grimly, put his arm around Wendy, hugged her close, and put his hand over her mouth.

She looked up at him with pitiful blue eyes. "I'm sorry," she mumbled through his fingers.

"Really?" he asked.

"No."

Quentin's laughter only intensified as he reentered the room and witnessed this. Wiping his eyes, he said, "I don't do this for just anybody, but I'm going to help y'all out. Give me the baby."

Sarah shot Wendy a look of disbelief as Wendy motioned for her to give Quentin the baby.

"I don't have a lot to lose at this point," Wendy explained. "Child-rearing lessons from a childless bachelor? Sounds fine."

Quentin took Asher. "When you're trying to feed the baby," he said, "you probably hold him across you, like this."

Sarah protested again. "I can't believe you're going to take advice on breast-feeding from this—"

Wendy slapped Sarah's knee and growled at her, "What the hell do you know, Pink? Go on, cowboy."

"When there was nothing to do at the hospital, sometimes I hung out in the neonatal unit," Quentin told Sarah self-righteously. She started forward and suppressed a scream of alarm as he gestured easily to the three of them with the arm holding Asher. "But there's going to be trouble if it gets out that the lead singer of the Cheatin' Hearts came to your house and held your baby up to his man-boob."

Sarah laughed. Daniel laughed. Wendy laughed uproariously, because this was her brand of humor.

"Try holding the baby like a football—okay, you've never played football. This doesn't mean anything to you. Hold the baby like you'd hold your purse if you were downtown, tucked under your arm, like this." He laid Asher down with Wendy again. Then he turned to Daniel and said, "Let's go make some snacks."

Daniel stared at him, uncomprehending. "What?"

Wendy patted Daniel's knee. "Go with him, lovah, and you can have a man-chat while I nurse."

"No, I really make snacks," Quentin said at the same time Sarah said, "No, he really makes snacks."

"Oh," Daniel said, standing up slowly. "I thought it was some Southern term for takeout on speed dial." He followed Quentin into the kitchen.

Wendy unbuttoned her shirt and held Asher as Quentin had suggested. Asher latched on, and the wailing stopped instantly. Sarah's ears rang in the silence.

"I think the baby was hungry," Wendy said. She caught Sarah staring. "I scoff at your cleavage. You and that Erin chick don't have anything on me."

In her amazement at Wendy, Asher, and Quentin, Sarah had forgotten all about Erin. She should never forget Erin, she scolded herself.

Wendy gazed down at Asher. "It's bizarre, isn't it?"

"Let's just say I'm glad you're going first."

"This is so great," Wendy said. "Quiet. Contentment. You don't understand what I've been through. Well, yes you do. Picture that screaming nonstop for seventy-two hours. I would feed him and feed him and feed him and take him off and he'd be screaming again in fifteen minutes. Poor baby! It's so much easier on him now. I can feel it working better. What's up with your boyfriend the lactation consultant?"

"Hell if I know. He also plays bridge and speaks Hindi."

"Nice piece of ass, too."

Sarah grinned. "We shouldn't curse around the baby."

"Oh yeah, the baby," Wendy said. She looked down at Asher again and smiled serenely. "Sometimes when I hold him, the most wonderful, peaceful feeling comes over me, like in a made-for-TV movie on the Lifetime channel. But then . . . I don't know. I feel like I'm a milk machine and there's nothing left of what I used to be."

Wendy seemed the same to Sarah. "Tell me about the breast-feeding. Do you feel orgasmic, like we read in the Lactation League book?"

"Not so much orgasmic. More nauseated."

"*Really*," Sarah said, disappointed. "Well, it's only day four."

"It's day four," Wendy agreed, much calmer now that the baby was calm. "Enough about me and my life-altering event. What about you? Have you had word from the unsinkable Mr. Fawn?"

Sarah flared her nostrils in distaste. "He's supposed to drop off some papers at my apartment."

"Aw, I think it's so *sweet* the dickhead wants you back. He called here yesterday to find out whether you were coming to town to see the baby. And oh yeah, by the way, to wish me joy. This new cowboy is infinitely more fun. He's so cheerful."

"Like Ernie on *Sesame Street*."

"No, not like that at *all*." Wendy stroked Asher's hair absently, motherly. "I got a call from Archie just now. Stargazer's very pleased to hear you got the Cheatin' Hearts' album out of them. You're off the hook for the Nine Lives fiasco, as long as you don't screw anything else up."

"There's the rub."

"I also got a call from one of my contacts at Manhattan Music. He said your cowboy propositioned an old lady down in Payroll, then stood on a desk and serenaded a girl in Foreign Rights."

Sarah swallowed. "Oh, I hadn't heard that. We did lose track of him for a while."

"Was he—" Wendy touched her nose: *cocaine*.

Sarah shook her head. "No, he's just *like* that. Get this. The Cheatin' Hearts were telling the truth about him all along. He's *really* not a drug addict."

Wendy looked at her skeptically.

"That's what *I* thought at first." Sarah nodded. "We have no further comment." This was Sarah and Wendy's code phrase for *I have to keep my act's secrets, but I will dish everything when we turn fifty.*

Wendy's eyes widened. "Then what's stopping you? You get some, do you understand me? Get some for me—indeed, for sexless new mothers everywhere!" The passion was intact, but the loud voice and wild gestures she normally would have used were toned down out of deference to Asher. Even their boss, Archie, hadn't been able to make Wendy stop shouting in the office. This was to be the first of the baby's many amazing feats.

Sarah said sadly, "I don't think I'm getting any."

"What do you mean, you don't think you're getting any?"

Sarah shrugged. "Like I said yesterday, he acted weird after I made him come. I think he's still in love with Erin."

"Are you listening to this?" Wendy asked Asher. She looked back at Sarah. "Surely you don't believe that, after he came to New York with you."

"I just wouldn't count on it, Wendy."

"But I *am* counting on it!" Wendy cried. "The thought of you having fun sustains me, and if I didn't have that, I'm not sure I could get through this."

"Oh, Wendy," Sarah said, putting an arm around her friend. "It's a huge adjustment. The biggest. You'll get the hang of it. I'll come babysit. More country music stars will drop by to give you child care tips. And have you seen the way Daniel looks at you?"

Wendy shook her head, but she gazed at Sarah with new hope.

Sarah patted Wendy's hand. "Heal up quick."

As if in answer, Daniel's hushed voice filtered in from the kitchen, then Quentin's soft chuckle. Daniel appeared in the doorway. He gazed at Wendy nursing Asher for a moment. Wendy gazed placidly back. Then he rounded the end of the sofa and bent toward her. She turned her head, offering her cheek for a kiss. A peck on the cheek wasn't what Daniel had in mind. He cupped her chin in one hand, turned her face to him, and kissed her deeply on the lips.

PDAs weren't typical behavior for the two of them. Wendy had an outrageous mouth but otherwise was the picture of propriety at work. Daniel was reserved, even haughty, except when Wendy made him laugh. At office parties the two of them looked more like the handsome, fashionably dressed famous couples they represented than PR reps, and they held hands and grinned at each other in a way that made women less lucky in love, like Sarah, wistful with envy. Even Sarah hadn't seen them kissing like this, though. She should have turned away. She didn't.

Finally Daniel kissed Wendy once more, chastely, on the lips, and gave Sarah a knowing glance. Then he sighed, set his forehead against Wendy's, and told her, "I'm going to take a nap."

"Did Quentin kick you out of the kitchen?" she asked.

"He suggested I leave the cooking to him. I tried to cut something with a spoon." He kissed her again and stroked Asher's hair.

Then he moved down the sofa to face Sarah. "How long are you in Alabama?"

"Just a few more days," she said brightly in case Quentin could hear her, "assuming the Cheatin' Hearts' Fourth of July concert goes smoothly." She held up one hand and crossed her fingers, knowing as she did so that she was wishing away more time with Quentin—the thing she wanted most.

Watching the doorway, Daniel whispered, "He's not really crazy. Or stupid."

"I know," Sarah said.

"And he's *very* into you." He eyed Sarah, waiting for her acknowledgment, until she nodded. He asked, "Is that okay with you?"

She didn't want to admit it. Not to him, with Wendy watching. Because that made it so. But she swallowed and heard herself saying, "Yeah."

Sarah and Daniel got along great—ever since the night two years ago when he saved Wendy's life. But he wasn't warm to anyone but Wendy, and that's why what he did next seemed so strange. He put his hand on Sarah's and said softly, "Call me if you need me."

"Okay," she said, watching him disappear down the hall. But she wouldn't call him. Not to help her with Quentin, not to get her out of the mess with Nine Lives. PR reps couldn't be associated with unsavory activity, because the press might latch onto a negative rumor and link it to the rep's client. She wouldn't jeopardize his career with the senator that way, and risk the stability of his little family, any more than she would tell Wendy the whole story of Nine Lives and ask her to cover for what Sarah had done.

She wished, once again, that her fellow Stargazer rep Tom was not in Moscow.

But Wendy had no idea how lost Sarah felt. She seemed awed only at Daniel's intensity as she said, "I'm telling you, you'd better take advantage of this Quentin thing." She handed Asher to Sarah and buttoned her shirt. She stretched out on the sofa, put her head on Sarah's thigh, and was snoring softly in thirty seconds.

Sarah rubbed Asher's back until she heard a belch, like she had seen people do on TV, then cradled him in one arm. He really was a beautiful baby. Not the least bit red or misshapen, like lots of the babies who had been brought to the office for show-and-tell. And he had the tiniest fingernails. She examined him for several minutes, coveting, contemplating how cool it would be to have one of these someday. Then she used the remote to turn on the TV to her mother playing poker.

After a while, Quentin brought in a bowl of salsa with tortilla chips and set it on the coffee table where Sarah could reach it and not disturb Wendy. He took Asher from Sarah expertly without waking him and sat in the chair beside her.

Suddenly starving, she crunched into a chip, then clapped one hand over her mouth in surprise. "The chip's hot," she whispered.

"Sorry," he said, concerned. "I should have warned you."

"No, not *too* hot. I'm not burned, just surprised. Did you *cook* these?"

"Yes! I told you I was making snacks."

"You made the salsa, too," she said, tasting it. "I expected something like homemade salsa, but not fried-before-your-eyes tortilla chips." She tried another. "*God*, you're good."

"They had a brand of tortillas in the fridge that I trust not to kill me," he explained. "When I start making my own tortillas, you can call an intervention." He reached over without moving Asher and tried a chip himself. "Yeah, I did good this time. But don't spoil your big dinner, now."

Sarah wondered if he meant sex. Big dinner equaled a big steaming pot of sex. No, of course that was ridiculous. She'd been around Wendy too long. Quentin wasn't subtle. If he wanted sex, he would say *sex*, not *dinner*.

She felt herself slipping into one of her vicious Quentin circles again. He said *dinner*, not *sex*. But he'd had his hand on her hand in the car. But he hadn't made a move on her on the airplane. But he'd flown up here with her. But she didn't want to have sex with him anyway. But she did.

It didn't matter. After all, even if there *was* sex with Quentin in her future, it was just sex, not love. Other tough broads probably took a dip with a heartthrob every ten days or so. It was casual.

Flanked by Quentin and Wendy, her two dearest friends, Sarah was able to relax a little, enjoy the baby and the lazy afternoon, and watch her mother on TV win three hundred thousand dollars.

~

Quentin stared at the pack of condoms on the shelf. He was not going to have sex with Sarah. He hadn't come to New York to break Rule Three. He'd come to protect her from Nine Lives and to visit the foundation. Now he would collect ingredients from this market, walk the block to her apartment, and cook her the best Indian she'd ever had. And get some shut-eye.

But what if an asteroid hit the earth? Surely that would override Rule Three. If he and Sarah were the last two people on the planet, he would have sex with her. And it would be better that she didn't get pregnant until they were settled.

It was only a question of how many condoms he needed. Here was a pack of thirty-six. How many times a day would they do it? Maybe three times on average, between the hunting and gathering? So, this pack would last twelve days, and by then they would have found a reliable food source.

He laughed. Then he realized that the other customers were staring at him. If they'd known he was from Alabama, they would have assumed he was an idiot. If they'd known he was a recording artist, they would have assumed he was on coke. They knew neither, so he tossed the box in his basket and moved on.

As he picked through the potatoes, he reflected on how Sarah had looked when she was with Wendy.

Open, unguarded, *happy*, with no trace of the poker face. He wanted to make her look like that with him. He'd already seen her like that a few times.

He moved into the spice aisle and thought about that beautiful, laughing look she had. The first time he'd seen it, he remembered foggily, was when he'd drunkenly kissed her against the refrigerator in his kitchen. He'd seen it again when he sang to her in the sound booth.

And she'd looked like that pretty much the whole day on her birthday. Not when she'd slapped him, but after that. And again the next morning, when he made her come in the shower. *That's* what he wanted to see again, the way she looked at him when he made her come—

A bell rang as a customer pushed open the door of the market. Quentin realized with a start that he was having a professional-wrestling-style staredown with a jar of garam masala.

No. All thirty-six condoms were in case of an apocalypse, he vowed as he walked down the street with the groceries. He was not going to break Rule Three.

Her apartment building was within long walking distance of the hospital where the foundation was based. As Quentin unlocked the street door with the key she'd given him, he looked around and pictured what it would be like if he quit the Cheatin' Hearts and went to work full-time for the foundation, even applied to medical school again, and moved in here with her.

That was his long walk, and this was his street. This was his classy lobby with enormous plants. This was his mirrored elevator, an interesting place to seduce her on their way back from a symphony concert some night.

This was a dangerous game he was playing, and he knew he was getting carried away, but he couldn't help himself. This was his hallway. This was his door, with his key in the lock. This was his apartment—

Sarah leaned with her elbows on the kitchen bar and her chin in her hands, perfect ass thrust out casually, examining a sheaf of papers. Across from her stood what could only be her jackass ex-husband.

When Sarah heard Quentin come in, she straightened and beamed at him, but then her face fell.

Quentin dropped both sacks of groceries on the wood floor. "Get out," he told the jackass.

"Quentin," Sarah said, recovering a nervous smile, "this is my ex-husband, Harold—"

"I know who he is."

"And we just need to work out some—"

"No," Quentin said. "Get out."

"Quentin—"

"I said no," Quentin shouted. "Would you like him to go out the door or the window?"

Quentin had never seen Sarah point both toes in and fidget, pressing the side of her high-heeled shoe down to the floor and back up. She looked small and vulnerable without her poker face. And this hurt more, because seeing her unguarded was a big part of what he wanted.

"Just a second," she murmured to the jackass. She clopped across the wood floor and touched Quentin's elbow. "Can I talk with you privately for—"

"No, you can't talk to me privately for a second and make it okay," Quentin said. "It's not okay. He has to go." Quentin was about to add, *I can't believe you'd give this guy the time of day after he sent you flowers and divorce papers on your birthday*, but that was just an excuse. It went way beyond that.

Sarah raised one eyebrow at Quentin. She whispered, "If you're doing this to make him jealous, that's nice, but you can stop now. I really need to talk to him about some retirement funds." She watched Quentin carefully, and her eyebrow went back down. "You're not bluffing." She turned to the jackass and said, "You'd better go."

The jackass took his papers, crossed the room, and paused at the door. Quentin was waiting for the jackass to touch Sarah, to lay one careless finger on her. But the jackass knew better. Avoiding Quentin's eyes, he said to Sarah, "I'll call you."

"No you won't," said Quentin.

Sarah told the jackass, "Just call my lawyer, okay?"

She closed the door behind him and turned to Quentin, laughing. "Were you bluffing? Because that was really great." Her smile faded when Quentin didn't smile.

"I don't want him back here," Quentin said. "Do you understand me?"

She said, "Not really."

He snatched the box of condoms out of the grocery sack and tossed Sarah over his shoulder.

14

Sarah had been a fool to tell Quentin she didn't like to be picked up and carried around. Because she did. She felt her nipples hardening, straining against her bra, as she watched the hardwood floors pass under her, through the living room, down the hall, into the bedroom. He threw her roughly onto the bed and pulled off her sandal.

Only, he wasn't full of fun as he'd been the other times he'd carried her. "Quentin," she said, but he was gone, just a body sliding his hands over her body. He wasn't looking at her face. Her other sandal was off. He tugged her shirt over her head, then pulled off his shirt with one motion of his thick muscled arm.

"Quentin, what's the hurry?" She tried to keep her voice even. "Let me catch up with you."

His black-green eyes finally flicked up to meet her eyes. Holding her gaze, he said in a voice so low that she could hardly hear him, "I can't pretend this is casual anymore." He brushed a strand of pink hair out of her eyes. His hand was shaking.

He kissed her, a deep, dark kiss that possessed her. Her body rushed to meet him.

He continued to kiss her as his hands moved over her. He pulled at her bra, her pants, her panties. He pressed two big, callused fingers inside her.

"*Quentin,*" she cried out.

His shorts were down, the condom was on, he was inside her. Then deeper inside her, then deeper inside than she was prepared for. She gasped as he slid as deep as possible and stopped, like a dead bolt sliding home in a lock.

Her sweat cooled on her skin. Shivering, she slicked her hands down the sweat on his back. She whispered, "Your eyes turn dark when you're angry."

He moved a little inside her, making her jump.

She began to be afraid. "Smile," she said.

"Can't."

"Have you gone over to the Dark Side?"

"Maybe."

Sarah thought she knew what was going on. He wasn't jealous about Harold. He felt guilty again for cheating, so to speak, on Erin. "Well, you done done it now," she said, imitating the hick line from "Come to Find Out." Anything to bring back his laugh. "You might as well enjoy it."

He put his hand to her cheek. His callused fingers

still trembled. He whispered, "When I saw that guy, I just . . . It was this animal thing. I had to have you. *Mine.*"

She decided to believe him, for now, because it was *so good*.

He moved again, long and hard inside her, and kissed her while he made slow love to her. The chill of cooled sweat on her skin turned hot once more. The late afternoon sun filtered through the curtains and bathed them both in its orange glow. She listened to cars passing and people laughing in the street as his tongue caressed her mouth. His cock rocked her gently, yet pushed her beyond where she'd thought her limits had been, deep into her. He held her hand with his big hand.

She thought it was her moan each time he pressed far into her that changed the tone. The languid afternoon honed a sharp edge as his mouth grew more insistent on her mouth and his cock massaged her harder and faster. She felt herself rising. She turned her head so his tongue played in her ear and she could talk. She wasn't sure what she said, but it involved Quentin and it was dirty.

She came just at the moment he began to climb. Her orgasm went on and on and folded over on itself as he thrust into her. Finally he squeezed her hand, and she watched the hard muscles of his stomach tense as he came.

He collapsed onto her and kissed her gently, so

slowly. Kissed eyelids. Cheek. Neck. Breast. A pause to suck her nipple. Kissed her shoulder. Inside of elbow. Wrist. Each finger of the hand he held. Then back to her mouth again, a sexy grind of his tongue inside her mouth. Still holding her hand, he propped his chin in his other hand and gazed at her.

"The dark look remains," she said. "This happened after the hand job, too. Coming makes you vacant. The porch light's on, but no one's home."

"No," he said. "It makes me think, which is a real scary thing for me to be doing." His hand played with her hand, tracing up and down her fingers and circling in her palm. "I want you to know something. That first night, and the next morning, I never forgot your name."

She laughed. "So you're full of shit. Which I knew."

He gave her a lopsided grin. "Can't a man be serious for once?"

Natsuko said, "No," while Sarah whimpered.

He dropped her hand and smoothed his hand across the flat of her belly. Her sex began to ache for him again.

But instead of moving his hand lower and rubbing there, abruptly he rolled away and stood. "Back in a few."

"Mm. 'Kay," she managed. She had hoped he would take her again. Harder, if possible. Surely that wasn't all? No, of course that wasn't all. He'd said he would be back.

Staring at the ceiling, she breathed deeply and let

out long sighs of satisfaction. She ought to be worried about what they'd done, what this meant for his relationship with Erin and her job with Stargazer. Her mind kept hitting this problem and skipping over it like a song on a scratched CD. The lyrics that played in her head, strong and loud, were that she'd had sex with *Quentin Cox the country singer*. It had been excellent. And on some level, she had known all along this would happen.

A noise in the hallway brought her attention back to the reality of her apartment. Bags rustled and cans clanked together as he picked up the groceries he'd dropped at the front door. The sounds came again as he set the groceries down on the kitchen counter. Then, in her bathroom, the shower and the fan turned on.

She rubbed her thighs lightly with her fingertips, thinking of her last shower with him. Maybe this was an invitation for an encore.

Or he just wanted to take a shower. And if she went in after him, she would be the groupie slut that she'd pretended to be at the lake.

As she moved her fingertips up to caress her nipples, she decided that she could not possibly be a groupie slut when *he* was in *her* apartment. So she slipped from the tangled sheets and padded into the bathroom after him.

Through the steam, she saw that a single condom packet sat waiting on the bathroom counter. That was her answer.

She'd passed through this bathroom plenty of times while Harold was taking a shower. She paused with her hand on the shower door, taking in the dark blur of Quentin's body behind the wet glass, so much taller and more powerful than Harold's body. She opened the door.

Quentin was watching her already, green eyes intent, as he worked a bar of soap in his hands. As soon as she clicked the door shut behind her, he reached for her, smoothing the suds across her chest. He circled her nipples with his thumbs. Every part of her body responded, wanting him close to her, on top of her, inside her. His hands traveled down her hips and kneaded her thighs, and she opened her legs for him. His fingers found her curls and rubbed them clean, then pulled her into the hot shower stream to rinse her. She pressed her face into his rock-hard biceps and tried her best to hold on as he massaged her.

Remembering that she owed him one, she moved her mouth to his nipple, circled it with her tongue, bit gently. He made a noise, something between a grunt and a laugh. She licked her way down his sternum. But with a quick glance up at his face, she saw that he followed her movements with his green eyes hard and his strong jaw locked. He was waiting patiently for one thing.

He held her by the elbows as she eased down to her knees on the tile. She reached for his erection.

She opened her mouth wide to slip the thick ridge of his head past her lips. There she paused, both hands gripping his solid thighs, and thought about what she was doing: giving the front man of the Cheatin' Hearts a blow job. Then she rose up on her knees and took as much of him into her mouth as she could, feeling his head bump against the back of her throat.

Even over the sounds of the fan and streaming water, she heard him gasp and try to keep control with hard, short breaths through his nose. One of his hands fisted her hair and the other supported her chin, guiding her where he wanted her to go. She loved that he knew what he desired, and he took it from her. That made her want to pleasure him even more. She opened wider but pressed him with her lips. As she pictured what she must look like to him, she felt her nipples beading in the hot water, and her sex was slick and ready.

Stroking into her mouth and out, holding her head steady, he growled, "Remember what I told you would happen if you tried to get me off in the shower?"

She did remember, and her body flashed hot at the threat.

He released her and pulled away from her. Then he grabbed her up from the floor and kicked the shower door open so hard that it banged against the wall. He hauled her out of the hot spray into the cool bathroom. Throwing a towel down on the edge of the counter, he forced her down onto it and held her there with one heavy hand. She was able to see his blurry reflection in the mirror as he picked up the condom packet with the other hand and tore it open with his teeth. He watched himself unroll the sheath. And then he watched himself guide his dick inside her.

She let out a cry as his head stretched her. His green eyes flicked up to meet her gaze in the steamy mirror, then back down. With a long, quiet groan of pleasure, he eased the ridge of his head through her opening and buried himself inside her.

In this position, the feeling was so intense that she tried to wiggle away from him, down, forward, anywhere. He slapped his hands to her buttocks and held her still as he began to pump rhythmically into her. His dick pressed along the front wall of her vagina and found her G-spot, she knew, because now she felt her face flush hotter and the hair on her arms stand up. A few more strokes and she fell into a black abyss.

She spasmed around his solid member, aching for him to pull out, and still he pumped into her. Bending over her to whisper closer to her ear, he said, "You look so sweet when you come, Sarah. I'll bet you can come again for me."

She wasn't so sure. Trying to work past her discomfort, she raised herself on her tiptoes to give him a slightly more open angle, and she squeezed herself around him.

He gasped sharply, slapped both hands to her ass, gripped her hips hard as he impaled her. Her discomfort vanished, replaced by a desire for him to get as far as he could inside her, empty himself into her. Every thought centered around one spot, the place where he joined with her.

"Quentin," she cried as she felt herself rising again. This time they came together, his hardest thrusts timing perfectly with her loss of control.

And then, as her orgasm trailed away but he still pumped himself hard inside her, the tiniest sense of panic grew in her belly. She watched his reflection making love to her, taking up a huge part of her mirror. This was a famous singer, one of the spoiled stars she'd been sent to whip into shape, and *he had fucked her*.

He placed one hot hand on her lower back, where her tramp stamp would be if she really were a tramp—which she was beginning to have some second thoughts about. "My God, Sarah," he said, "could you get any hotter?" He took a long, steadying breath that ended in a small laugh. "I need to lie down for a minute. How about you?"

"Uh." She was speechless.

He helped her up from the counter, then rubbed her dry with the towel that had cushioned her. He dried himself while she dialed the shower off. Then he led her by the hand through the apartment, back to her bed. The afternoon light filtering through the window had tired and softened as they slid into the sheets, facing each other.

He put his hand on her hip and closed his eyes.

She put her hand on his chest and closed her eyes.

She rested. Blanked. It felt like a long time, but glancing at the beside clock, she saw only a quarter hour had passed when she woke and saw he was watching her.

His hand stroked her hip. "I'm sorry," he said. "You won't be able to wear that bikini for a few days. This is going to bruise."

"It was worth it." The panic rose inside her again, but she knew her words were true. Whatever the consequences of this day with him, she would cherish the memory.

"You don't want me to get too close," he whispered. "You still don't want me to tell you."

Tell me what? cried Sarah, but she knew. She said, "No."

"But we done done it, like you said," he protested, "and we might as well enjoy it for the rest of the day." Now his hand trailed from her belly up to her face, and his fingers traced her hairline. "You are so beautiful." He seemed to be staring at her, studying her genuinely. "Have I ever told you that I *really* like your hair?"

She smiled.

"See," he said, running his fingers down the damp strands, "like that, when it falls around your face. It could be a brown strand. It could be blond. It could be pink. It's different, unpredictable." He chuckled. "You think I sound like an idiot, like every other man . . ."

He was about to say *in love*. She helped him. "Making love," she suggested, and laughed lightly. "Declarations of a woman's beauty never sound idiotic. They always sound *good*."

He gazed at her seriously for a moment. Then he seemed to realize that it was no use. He laughed again. "Speaking of good," he said, and she thought he would make a comment about the excellent sex. "How about some naked Indian food?"

~

At sunset, they sat outside on her balcony, watching the lights of traffic. Quentin wore his boxers, Sarah a tank top and pajama pants. They looked like two people who'd just had long, hot sex over and over, and she loved it. She wished they could have hot sex and then flaunt the fact to her neighbors every evening, not just this one.

They swayed slowly on the porch swing. When Harold had lived here with her, he'd told her the swing couldn't be hung here. She had showed him how it could be hung. He had still refused to help her, saying it was stupid to hang a Southern-style porch swing on a New York City balcony. She'd called Tom to help her.

She was glad she had. And she was glad this part of her apartment wasn't tainted by the hand of Harold, so she could enjoy it with Quentin. Though she had to say that the hand of Harold was quickly fading. It had vanished from her kitchen. And her bathroom. And her bed.

She settled her head back against Quentin's solid chest. "That was so good," she said.

"The food or the sex?" he asked. The low notes of his voice vibrated through her body and gave her chills.

"Both," she said.

"What was your favorite?"

"The aloo gobi," she said. "And that time between

the chutney and the murg saagwala, when you had me turned around backward—"

"Oh yeah," he said knowingly. "That *was* good aloo gobi."

She hit his chest playfully, realizing as she did that this was exactly the move Erin was accustomed to executing on Owen. Shut *up*, Erin. Sarah asked, "What was *your* favorite?"

"*This* is my favorite. Sitting here with you, feeling like you're mine, like I've marked you as mine. I don't know where this caveman thing is coming from." He bent toward her and ran his hand along his eyebrow. "Is my brow ridge growing?"

What about Erin? she wanted to ask. She had a feeling this would not work out, but she didn't want to discuss it right now. She suspected this was all she would get, and she didn't want to ruin it.

She reached out one fingertip to trace one dark eyebrow, then the other. While he smiled and closed his eyes, she traced down his straight nose to his expressive lips and his square jaw, then up his cheek and into the tangled waves of his hair.

He opened his eyes and asked her gently, "You didn't grow up in Schenectady, did you? You grew up in Fairhope."

"Why do you say that?" she asked coyly.

"I can see you with big trees behind you, Spanish moss, watching the bay," he said. "I hear it when you say my name. And I hear it when you're about to come. You don't sound like Schenectady when you come. You sound like a Southern girl enjoying herself."

Sarah sighed as the last of Natsuko dropped away under Quentin's gaze. "Fairhope lost to your high school in the football playoffs once."

"I remember." Quentin nodded. "I came down for Owen's game."

"I wonder whether we saw each other." She envisioned sixteen-year-old Quentin, tall and thin, a head above the crowd, untamed hair, glasses, a coat in November, worn jeans, the deck shoes in comparatively mint condition. She asked, "Can you picture me with brown hair?"

"I didn't see you there," he said. "If I had, I would have known it right then."

Known what? she ached to ask. But she didn't want to know.

After the dusk faded, they went back inside. They had run out of ingredients for Indian food. Now, between bouts of making love, they talked, or one of them slept. Sarah thought each time surely *that* was the last time. And each time, after a pause, she felt Quentin rise into her again.

Late at night, when the noise of traffic outside her window had all but died away and Quentin had fallen asleep, Sarah fantasized about what it would be like to be with him, move in with him, marry him, have kids with him.

She could do the band's PR from home. She pic-

tured herself living in his Birmingham mansion, sur-
rounded by hills and trees. But he'd be gone on tour all
the time. And she'd always worry about what he was
doing on tour with Erin.

Okay, this was a fantasy. She didn't have to think
about Erin. She could pretend Quentin was faith-
ful and not interested in Erin. She pictured him
devoted to her. This was easy, after he'd made such
careful, caring love to her all afternoon and evening.
She pictured him as a guy she'd met at college, dated
in the vibrant city, moved in with, and eventually
married, like Harold. Like Wendy and Daniel, an
easy relationship with nothing more serious keeping them apart than Daniel being exacting, Wendy
talking out her ass, and the waterbed effect that had
winged her in pregnancy. And now they had a beautiful baby.

Sarah and Quentin would not.

She realized, heart sinking into her belly, that she
had fallen in love with him, and this was going to turn
tragic.

But not yet. Not tonight.

She felt his eyelashes flutter and his stubble scrape
against her cheek, and he stirred awake. In the soft
glow from the streetlights outside, he smiled his slow,
sleepy smile at her.

"What have you done to me?" she whispered.

He stirred against her down below. "Let me show
you."

~

They slept late in the morning, made love, ate one of Quentin's huge breakfasts, made love again, and hailed a taxi for LaGuardia. Sarah was hopeful. In the sunny morning, possibilities for the future seemed brighter. Natsuko was skeptical. What Sarah read as Quentin's enthusiasm this morning, Natsuko read as mania.

There *did* seem to be a marked increase in heavy petting when the airplane neared Birmingham and the *Fasten Seat Belts* light blinked on. And in the terminal, as they were about to pass through security, Quentin flattened her against the wall and pressed his lips to her chin. On her scar.

She shoved him away. "Did you check your phone?" she asked him suspiciously. "Did you get a message from Erin?"

He stepped out of the way of other travelers passing. "No, I haven't gotten a message from her at all," he said.

Sarah nodded. "That's the problem, isn't it?" She looked through the security checkpoint. "You think she's out there waiting for you, don't you?"

He put both hands in his hair. "Sarah—"

"You know each other so well." She turned on her high heel and stalked toward the gate.

"Sarah," he said above and beside her as she walked quickly. "Sarah, I don't want to leave it like this."

As they passed into the public section of the airport, Erin looked up from a bench. Her big, innocent blue eyes held a troubled expression, and she wrapped both arms around her abdomen. She looked strikingly like Wendy had looked sitting in the airport when she was pregnant.

Sarah went cold.

She supposed it could be Owen's baby.

And it could be Quentin's baby, from several weeks before.

Or Quentin could have had a relationship with Erin all along, unbeknownst to Sarah. Sarah didn't think so. She'd been with him so much. She didn't know where he'd find the time. He actually needed sleep at night. Besides, if he'd done it in the last few days, Erin wouldn't know she was pregnant this soon.

No, it was from before. *Erin hides sobriety from men.* She must have suspected all week, and now she knew for sure. It was Quentin's baby, all right. Otherwise, Erin wouldn't have come to fetch him from the airport.

Quentin called to Sarah, but she kept walking right past Erin. She wasn't going to look back. It took forever for her to reach the door to the parking deck where she'd left her BMW. Finally she couldn't stand it any longer. She looked back.

He was in the huddle stance again, a winded football player, fists on hips, head down. Like he was listening to Erin's plan. Not like he was in love with Erin.

Now he rocked back on one foot, hands still on hips, and watched Sarah go. And in that one glance, Sarah saw that she'd been fooling herself.

He *wasn't* in love with Erin. He'd told Sarah he was, out of habit. Now he was in love with Sarah.

She had sensed this, but Natsuko had been protecting her. Quentin had fathered Erin's child. When he found out, he would marry Erin, just as he'd talked about doing whatever Sarah wanted to do that first morning. Because he was a decent guy. A responsible man.

Mission accomplished. With Erin and Quentin on the mend, permanently this time, the band would never break up now. Sarah walked out of the terminal before she could cry.

～

"There is a *vibe*," Erin had said to Quentin at the airport. "But I'm not going to ask if you did her. In exchange, I want you to concentrate on this concert, and let the record company go on her way."

Tamping down his panic, Quentin had obeyed, for the time being. He'd watched Sarah's perfect ass in those tight pants exit the terminal. She'd looked back only once, wearing the poker face.

And now, poker face still on, she sat in the middle of the block of folding chairs set up in front of the stage beneath the statue of Vulcan, watching the run-through of the concert. The way her hair was pulled into a sophisticated ponytail down her back, it looked more brown than blond or pink. She wore the emerald necklace with a low-cut green dress. Her hemline was so short that he thought she might give everyone a peep show when she uncrossed and recrossed her legs.

He was very glad when they finished the rehearsal and she climbed the stairs to the stage. The TV people were trying to tell the band something about where the cameras would be. Quentin turned his back on all of them and held out a hand to Sarah.

Ignoring him, she called, "Remember, the FCC will be watching the broadcast, Erin, so no nipple."

Erin started to holler some very creative girl-obscenities at Sarah, but Owen covered her mouth and Martin tugged her away by the hand. Placidly, with the poker face, Sarah watched the scene she'd caused. Quentin's three bandmates piled into Owen's truck and roared out of the parking lot, honking the horn three times, a message: *Rule Three.*

After they'd driven off, Sarah turned to Quentin. "Did you know I've never heard the whole band sing in person before?"

"You listened to us finish the album that night after you got stung."

"I've never heard you sing in person while I was awake," she clarified. "And Quentin, you are *terrific*. You *all* sound *terrific* together. I thought so from hearing your albums, but there's no comparison to hearing you live. I've never worked with an act this talented. I feel privileged to have helped the Cheatin' Hearts stay together. It would be an absolute shame if something happened to break you up."

He put a hand on her soft elbow.

"Don't." She pulled away. "I don't want any. That's not what I meant. I honestly just wanted to let you know how talented I think you are. Musically."

"Sarah," he said reproachfully. "You're at my rehearsal. Dressed like that. Don't tell me you don't want some."

"I don't want anything from you," she said. Then her poker face broke into a wistful grin. "Well, maybe I do. I may want you to eat your heart out."

"You want some," he insisted. "I happen to have some that I can give you."

"Or loan to me," she snapped.

He sighed and ran his hands back through his hair. "Look, I really do have something in the big-ass truck that I need to give you. *Besides* that," he added at her expression. "Come on."

They walked across the parking lot to his truck. He closed the door behind her, rounded the truck, and slid into the driver's seat. It had been a good ploy to get her into the truck, but he didn't want to give her the bag just yet. That would definitely ruin any chance he had of getting her clothes off.

Apparently she had the same goal in mind, because she'd forgotten all about the ploy. "We really shouldn't," she said. "There are stagehands around."

He looked past her out the windows of the truck. "They're all gone for the night."

"There's a security guard around somewhere," she said. "One would hope."

"Down by the entrance," Quentin assured her.

"Anyway, isn't the chance of being caught part of the thrill of doing it in a pickup?"

"I wouldn't know."

"Me, neither. So let's go back and get something we both missed out on in high school."

He wasn't going to reach out and grab her. He was afraid she'd bail out of the truck and drive away in her BMW, and he'd never see her again. Instead, he waited.

"Do you happen to have any cheap cologne in the glove compartment, like boys wore in high school?" she asked. "Left from the former owner of the truck? Or planted for effect?"

"Cologne triggers my asthma," he told her.

"Pity." She rushed into him, kissing the corner of his mouth hungrily.

He turned his head to give her better access to his neck while he fumbled with one hand in the glove compartment for a condom. Then he laid her down on the seat, and quickly found that this was inconvenient. "Where the hell do you put your right elbow?" he complained.

"I don't know." She laughed.

"I reckon kids in high school are a lot skinnier." He pushed off her and fished for the lever to let down the seat back. In the process, he leaned on the horn and startled both of them.

"Sit up," she suggested. "Let me ride you."

Quentin didn't need any convincing. He sat up in the middle of the long seat and unfastened his shorts.

Then he pushed her panties aside and pulled her onto his cock. *Oh*, he'd been afraid he wouldn't get any more from her, ever. This was too good to be true.

She slid up and down him for a few moments, but he wasn't getting everything he needed. He put his hands on her back and pressed her tightness down onto him. She gasped and worked herself up and down, like she enjoyed this as much as he did.

He pulled the sleeves of her green dress off her shoulders and nipped at her breasts, then suckled her as he pulsed into her.

"Que'n," she gasped in that half-gone Fairhope accent. Her fingernails dug into his forearm.

He was going to have to do this again. Somehow he was going to figure out a way to do this with her again. And again.

She shuddered on his cock. He gave it to her harder and faster. Her hands, her lips, were everywhere on him, frenzied. With a final groan, he emptied himself into her.

He held her tight and still for a few minutes, with his cock inside her. The mountain breeze was cool on his skin, and the frogs were loud in the trees outside the open truck windows. He traced his fingers through the baby blond strands that had come loose from her ponytail and framed her face. He set his forehead against hers.

Finally he joked quietly against her cheek, "Now is when you cry and say you wish we hadn't done it."

"Wrong." She kissed his jaw and made the hair

on his arms stand up. "Now is when I say that felt fantastic, and I thank my lucky stars I'm such a loose woman."

She sounded like she was done for the night. He was not. He slipped a hand under the hiked-up skirt of her dress, onto her flat belly.

She jerked out from under him and moved away, across the seat, pulling up the sleeves and neckline of her dress to cover her breasts. "Don't do that," she said.

"But that's one of my favorite parts," he complained, fastening his shorts. "You made me think the first morning you were here that I might have gotten you pregnant. Seems like I could touch you there if I wanted." He blurted it out more angrily than he'd intended, and he wondered where all this emotion was coming from. He was logical, and he still had everything under control.

Then it occurred to him that he might not have everything under control after all. "Did you lie to me that first morning? Did we do it?" It came out hoarse: "Are you pregnant?"

"No," she said quietly, gazing down at her manicured hands in her lap.

He reached over and took her chin in his hand, so she had to look at him. He asked again, "Sarah, are you pregnant?"

"No," she said, glaring at him with dark-fringed eyes. She jerked her chin away.

"Then why do you act like you just saw a ghost?"

She huffed out a sigh. "What did you want to give me?" she asked coldly.

Reluctantly, he pulled the shopping bag from behind the seat. "I'm in a band. I have to get along with them. And sometimes that means doing things I don't want to do." He passed the bag to her.

She peered inside at her clothes from Quentin's dresser drawer, which Erin had packed up for her.

"But, Sarah," he began, taking her hand.

"'But, Sarah,'" she repeated woodenly, pulling her hand away.

"I want to be with you," he said in a rush. "Only you. But it will get me in big trouble. And I need to know how you feel about me."

"I feel more than I should," she said, meeting his gaze head-on.

"You think I'm in love with Erin," he said. "I'm not. There was a time when I was, but that was a long time ago, and way before you."

"You *told* me you were in love with her. In the emergency room."

"I never told you I was *in love* with her," he objected. "I told you I *love* her." He laughed shortly. "I love Owen, too, on a good day."

Sarah stared at him with the poker face.

"My God, Sarah," he said, feeling the anger rise again. "You don't still believe I'm on coke, do you?"

"No," she said. "I don't believe you're stupid, either."

Oh no.

She said through her teeth, "Why all this subterfuge? And if you pretend again that you don't know what *subterfuge* means—"

He opened his hands. "To keep you away."

She nodded. "Anything to protect yourself. You're used to doing what makes you feel good at the moment. That's fine when you're twenty-one. Or, at least, it's to be expected. But when you're thirty, it's irresponsible."

He folded his arms. "And you think that before the Cheatin' Hearts took off, I just worked at some shit job at the hospital, and never saved any money or did anything so I could support a family. The fact that I have money now doesn't count for anything."

"Of course it counts," she said. "Of course your success with the band counts. But you live the band lifestyle. You tour, and you start fights, and you have a girl in every port—"

"I don't have a girl in every port. We travel by bus or airplane."

"—and that's not what I want," she said more loudly. "You see, even now, you're not taking this seriously."

"I am!" he exclaimed. "I'm taking this *very* seriously! But the person you're describing is not me."

"How the hell would I know that?" Sarah asked.

Quentin didn't have an answer.

"This has been fun," she said. "I mean, *fun*. This has been the most fun I've ever had. But, long-term . . ."

"You're not really a pink-haired girl," he finished for her.

"I guess not." She reached behind her neck to unclasp the emerald necklace.

"*Don't do that*," he said in alarm.

She paused with her hands behind her head, watching him.

"Just give me until tomorrow," he said. "There's something I need to do."

Sarah shook her head. "It's not what you can do. It's what you *are*." She put her graceful hand on his knee. "You need to go back to Erin." Dragging the shopping bag after her, she jumped out of the big-ass truck and slammed the door.

He got out and followed her at a distance as the sharp crack of her shoes echoed across the parking lot. His crazy comic book villainess in high heels, abbreviated green dress, and brown ponytail striped with pink. Leaving him.

Think, Q. Think, Quentin. His mind was a blank. Just when he needed it most.

As she started the engine, he reached the BMW. He knocked once on the window and she lowered it.

He knelt on the asphalt so he was on her level. He asked her, "Are you bluffing?"

Her poker face remained motionless, but her dark brown eyes filled with tears.

"You're not bluffing," he breathed.

As she raised the window, her face was replaced with a reflection of Vulcan's ass. Quentin stepped back and she sped away.

He stood alone on the black asphalt in the black night for some moments, willing the black mood to lift so he could think again.

Finally he spun around and looked up to the spotlit iron man for inspiration. Vulcan mooned him, mocking him.

"Come on, big guy!" Quentin shouted. "Turn around and look at me when I'm talking to you!"

The cool mountain breeze swayed the trees, and the frogs chirped in answer.

With a dejected sigh, Quentin turned for his truck. And that's when it hit him. He had a big-ass truck! He was mobile. He could drive home to talk to his dad, the expert on falling headlong in love with the world's most inconvenient woman.

15

～

Yes, you're going to hell for knowingly having sex with the father of a pregnant woman's baby. No, you can't assign a numerical value to the great sex and insert it into an algorithm to figure out exactly how damned you are. It's no use. You're toast. If you get there first, save me a good seat.

Wendy Mann
Senior Consultant
Stargazer Public Relations

Sarah drove to the Galleria and packed her bags, because Nine Lives might be after her and she had no protector now. She moved to the hotel downtown where she'd played bridge with her mother and Quentin, but of course she couldn't sleep. She found the gym and went for a long run.

In the morning, she returned to the office at the Galleria and tied up loose ends. Hugged Amber and Beige and the men in the office good-bye. Gave Rachel some last-minute advice about life as a PR diva. Called the holiday skeleton crew at the Manhattan Music office to arrange for a replacement drummer to be put on standby in case Owen found out about Quentin and Erin's baby, freaked, and quit the band right before the Nationally Televised Holiday Concert Event. Then Sarah booked her own late afternoon flight back to New York.

Now she needed only to swing by the mansion and drop off Quentin's asthma inhaler and adrenaline shot, which he'd transferred from his truck to her bag before they left for New York. *And the necklace*, she thought to herself, fingering the heavy emeralds.

His truck wasn't in the driveway. The other two trucks and Erin's Corvette were home. Sarah balked at the idea of bursting in on them when Quentin wasn't there. But they were *all* her responsibility, not just Quentin. And if she didn't return his things now, what would she do? Sit around in lovelorn agony, awaiting his return? *Mail* the emerald necklace back to him? She compromised by knocking twice on the door from the garage before walking in.

Erin, standing barefoot in the kitchen, looked up from arranging ham on a slice of bread. She said in her sweet chipmunk voice, "Speak of the devil."

"I wanted to return a few things to Quentin," Sarah said. She hoped Erin would offer to take the inhaler, the shot, and the emerald necklace. That would rub in to Erin how close Quentin and Sarah had been. And shock Quentin when he received these items from girl-friend number two via girlfriend number one. All that was left of Sarah was a bitter shell.

Erin didn't offer to play courier. "He's not here. Can't you tell?" She gestured to the bread. "We can hardly boil water without him. He called last night to say he was going to see his dad. I don't know where he is now. He was a lot easier to keep track of before he could drive." She walked over to the open door of the studio and called down the stairs, "Sarah's here."

Owen climbed the stairs to the kitchen and put his hand on Sarah's shoulder. "We need to talk to you," he said pleasantly. "Can I get you a beer?"

Sarah glanced at her watch. It was two o'clock. She asked, "Do I *need* a beer?"

"You might," Martin said from the stairs. "Let's sit outside." He was pounding loudly on a pack of ciga-rettes. Sarah hadn't known he smoked.

This did not look good.

She'd thought PR for the Cheatin' Hearts was Ra-chel's problem from here on out, but now she wasn't so sure. She fished in her bag and turned off her cell phone, which had been ringing constantly all morn-ing.

Owen passed out bottles, and Sarah refrained from

pointing out that Erin's was a waste of a perfectly good beer. They filed outside and sat at the table in the palpable heat of mid-afternoon, despite the shade of a crepe myrtle. Hundreds of bees buzzed in the tree, and Sarah almost shied away. But she didn't fear anaphylactic shock—at least, not while the bees minded their own business, and she still had Quentin's rescue shot in her bag in the kitchen, and a nurse sat next to her. Albeit one wasted on heroin.

Owen leaned forward across the table. "Sarah, we're coming clean with you. We want to make you an offer, but we have to extract a promise from you first that this is in strictest confidence, and you won't tell the record company what we tell you."

"Okay." Sarah wasn't sure she could keep such a promise. It depended on what the secret was. She had a job to do, after all. But whether she could keep the secret didn't matter. She got the feeling that it had to do with Quentin's conspicuous absence. She needed to know.

Erin gripped her diamond cross pendant between her thumb and forefinger and slid it back and forth on its chain. "Two years ago, before we got the contract with Manhattan Music, we thought we were finally about to sign a different contract in Nashville. A record company executive had come to a show to recruit us." She put a hand on Owen's back. "And then Owen, in his infinite wisdom, slept with her. Somewhere between the first kiss and the blow job—"

Owen shrugged away from Erin's hand on his back. "Just the facts, ma'am," he said angrily.

"—he told her that Q has asthma. Well, there were other acts she could sign, with lead singers who never had a problem breathing. She couldn't get out of there fast enough. Needless to say, we didn't get our contract. In fact, to have any chance at all of signing with another company, we had to pay her to keep quiet about Q's asthma. We pooled our savings and scraped together twenty thousand dollars."

"Thus Owen earned the moniker *dumbass*," Martin said.

"We all had pretty good jobs at the hospital," Erin said, "but Q gave up more. He had a promising career, and he was about to quit the band to pursue it. We didn't think the Cheatin' Hearts could make it without him. For that, we were really pissed at him and . . ." She looked guiltily at Owen. "Behaved badly."

"Pitched fits," Owen confirmed. "Made him feel like he was betraying his three best friends."

Erin nodded. "We convinced him to stay and make one last push for a contract. And he wanted to make sure it was worth the risk of giving up his career."

Sarah tried to envision Quentin's promising career as head lactation consultant.

"So Q made three rules," Erin said. "If any of us broke them, we'd get kicked out of the band. Rule Three"—she touched her middle finger—"no sex with the record company, so there wouldn't be a repeat of a band member giving our secrets away. Since Manhattan Music sent you, you fall in that category, too. We've known all along that you and Q weren't doing it, and that y'all pretended to be together to get me back with Q."

Calmly, very calmly, controlling her hand to keep it from shaking, Sarah took a sip of her beer. "Really? That was a lot of good making out, all for nothing. Why didn't he just tell me about your rules?"

Owen said, "I assure you his intentions were completely dishonorable."

"Yeah," Erin said, "he's made it painfully clear to us the entire time that he thinks you're hot. In fact, I was afraid that y'all had really fallen for each other. Martin was sure you had. Yesterday I acted like I was getting back with Q in the airport to chase you off. But now we can see that you—that it was all business."

Sarah nodded knowingly.

"And he couldn't tell you about Rule Three because he didn't want you to find out about Rule Two"— Erin touched her index finger—"no sex between band members. Our relationship with the record company has been so difficult, and our badass image is so important to our success, that we didn't want to let on to you what straightlaced nerds we are. In reality, Owen and I have never done it, and Q and I never did it."

"Yes you did," Owen protested angrily, as if this were an old and rehashed argument.

"Okay, we *did*," Erin said to Owen, "*two years* ago.

But not since we made the rules and got the contract. Do you *mind*?" She turned back to Sarah. "That's why Q made the rule. Q and I fought like cats and dogs when we dated, and he didn't think the band could survive another relationship like that.

"And Rule One"—she touched her thumb—"no drugs. That's because Martin had a problem a long time ago." She glanced at Martin, who smoked his cigarette, seemingly oblivious, clearly high.

Sarah asked levelly, "Why tell me about your rules now?"

Erin said, "Because we want you to be our new manager."

Sarah's heart leaped, and her mind raced through the possibilities. A chance to be with Quentin almost constantly, to tour with Quentin. Who wasn't with Erin. Who was free after all.

He'd told her *so* many lies in the past ten days.

But he'd told his friends he thought she was hot.

She had to pull herself together. There was more to life than this man, such as the job the band was offering. Surely they planned to top her Stargazer salary. She wondered whether they understood what a gargantuan sum Stargazer paid her to put up with shit exactly like this. She should hint to Quentin privately.

And then she saw how uneasily Erin and Owen looked at her. And when she asked, "Why didn't you wait for Quentin to come back before you presented this to me?" Martin lit another cigarette.

Owen said, "We're kicking Q out of the band."

Sarah looked around at them. Owen and Erin were immeasurably sad. Martin toyed with a third cigarette on the ready.

"I can't believe you'd do that to him," Sarah said, unable to quash defensiveness for him. "You're such good friends."

"We're doing it *for* him," Owen said. At Sarah's raised eyebrow, he added, "You don't understand. Q's been so driven since his mother died. He was valedictorian in high school and summa cum laude in the respiratory therapy program in college. He aced the entrance exam and got into medical school. That's why we made the big push to get a contract when we did. He was about to leave the band so he could start medical school, research allergy and asthma, save the world, save himself, and go back and save his mother.

"I knew him before she died. He was sick a lot, but he didn't let it get him down. He was the class clown. He compensated. After she died, he was still the class clown, but there was always this drive working underneath.

"Five years ago, we formed the band, and I saw that kid again. I don't know if you've ever seen him in front of a live audience, Sarah, but he's different. Happy. He—" Owen stopped for loss of words.

"Lights up," Martin suggested, exhaling smoke.

"Yeah," Owen pointed at Martin, then waved smoke away. "I think Q felt that with the band, he could forget about dying for the first time in a long time. But we knew—or at least *I* knew—that the drive would come back. And then, after Thailand . . ."

Owen's voice trailed off, and Erin took up the story. "We really thought he was going to die in Thailand."

"I was trying to work out what I was going to say to his father," Owen confirmed.

Erin looked at Owen in horror, as if she hadn't heard this particular detail before. Then she went on, "Q thought he was going to die, too. We think he decided then that he needed to go to medical school after all. Only he won't admit it. It's like he wants both, he can't have both, and the two halves of him are driving each other crazy. I mean, he's always made us do nutty stuff. Did he tell you Owen didn't really get shot in Crete?"

Sarah shook her head and Owen said, "You don't have to *offer* that story, Erin."

"On our tour stop in Greece," Erin said anyway, "we went to the beach, and Owen fell on a rock—"

"A *javelin* rock," Owen corrected her.

Erin gave a little laugh. "It *was* a very sharp rock, and went deep in his shoulder. We knew it would leave a big scar like a gunshot wound, and that he wouldn't be able to play drums for days. Q decided we should use it. We bribed some locals to swear to the press that they'd seen Owen get shot in a bar fight. Then we turned around and systematically denied it. *That* I could handle, just barely.

"But since Thailand, it's out of control. He fired Karen without so much as consulting the rest of us. He made us put off recording the album. He decided that he and I should stop fake-dating, and I should pretend to be with Owen."

Watching Erin with concern, Owen added, "And he was really mean to Erin about her concert."

"He was *so mean* about my concert with the orchestra," Erin agreed. "It was something I'd wanted to do since I was a little girl, and he boycotted it. He said it was bad publicity for us. He said badass country music stars don't play with an orchestra until they're ready for their greatest hits album and liposuction. He only let me do it because it was a benefit for the foundation."

Sarah saw Quentin's point, but she also saw how much the concert had meant to Erin. Erin's eyes went cold as she talked about it, clearly recalling the argument she and Quentin had.

"Q basically left the band in Thailand," Erin said. "We think the best thing to do now is to kick him out and free him to do what he needs to do. Otherwise, he'll get crazier and crazier, and he'll bring the band down with him."

Martin lit his fourth cigarette.

Sarah sipped her beer to buy a few seconds while she tried and failed to reconcile this information. She couldn't do it. The ignorant, fun-loving lover who had lied to her was simply a different person from the would-be med student who had lied to her twice as much. Did the new Quentin love her like the old Quentin seemed to, or was that an act, too?

It didn't matter, she decided. She couldn't solve the Quentin conundrum right now, and she had to take care of herself. She needed to protect her job by keeping the band together.

"I appreciate the offer," she said, "and I'm flattered that you think I could handle this mess. But I can't be your manager, for a couple of reasons. First, you say you're coming clean with me, but you're lying to me even now. I'm not Karen. I can't work this way."

"What do you—" Erin began innocently.

"Oh, come *off* it, Erin," Sarah interrupted. "I would love to believe that kicking Quentin out of the band is purely altruistic on your part. But you and Owen"— she waved her fingers between the two of them—"are having sex with each other, and you both want to kick Quentin out before *he* kicks *you* out." She turned to Martin. "And you're so far gone on heroin that you're backstabbing your best friend. You're kicking him out of the band so you can do drugs without him hounding you."

Erin gaped at Martin, her eyes filling with tears. Owen slumped over with his elbow on the table and his chin in his hand. Martin flicked ash, too high to be particularly concerned.

Sarah didn't pause to let it sink in. While she had them off balance, she went on. "The other reason I won't be your manager is that the Cheatin' Hearts will never make it without Quentin. You could get a new lead singer, but you'd never recapture what you have now. I doubt Manhattan Music would even re-sign you without him.

"You could break up, and each of you could make it on your own. You could have long, successful careers in Nashville. Write songs. Join other bands. Produce albums for other people. But you can't go on as the Cheatin' Hearts. Each of you is integral to the group, but Quentin is—"

As she paused to find the words, Martin offered, "The life."

Sarah took a big swig of beer and banged the bottle down on the table with finality. "I have a flight to New York soon. Tell me how we're leaving this so I don't have to come down here again."

Erin said quietly, "You need the group to stay together to keep your job, right? So don't tell Q we had this conversation. Maybe he won't self-destruct, and we'll go back on tour like we always planned."

"Girlfriend." Sarah felt tough athlete Sarah rise up to subdue crafty Natsuko. "You are not *hearing* me. You're in denial. You can't go on tour and pretend nothing's happened. Martin is addicted to heroin, and you're pregnant with Owen's baby."

Erin watched Sarah for one, two, three beats, unmoving, expressionless, so long that Sarah thought she'd guessed wrong.

Erin burst, "You bitch!" at the same time that Owen exclaimed, "What?"

"Ouch," Sarah said, "and you haven't told Owen."

Owen and Erin jumped up from the table simultaneously. Erin screamed at Sarah, but Owen blocked her with his big body.

Sarah stood up and clacked across the flagstones. It was a relief to close the kitchen door on the screaming. She slid her bag from the counter.

When she turned around, Martin stood in the kitchen with his lit cigarette. "I've enjoyed having you spy on us, kid." Swaying a little on his feet, he took her hand.

"Me, too." She looked into his beautiful dark eyes behind the crooked glasses. She asked him, "Are you going to kick it now? You're the link between Erin and Owen on one side, and Quentin on the other. You're going to have to take some positive action to keep the band together. You'll lose everything you love if you don't."

Martin squeezed her hand. "Ask me again when I'm sober."

They stood in exactly the spot where Quentin customarily kissed her good-bye and banged his head on the door. Martin kissed her on the forehead. And then she walked through the garage to her car.

~

For the first few minutes of the drive to the airport, she felt numb, thought nothing. Then pieces of the puzzle began to fall out of the sky, littering the highway in front of her.

She was devastated. Last night, Quentin had tried to tell her. He'd basically asked whether she could take him as she thought he was, and she'd basically told him no. Having him turn out to be a brilliant college grad on a mission to save the children should have been a bonus. It was no good trying to explain to him now that she would have jumped at the chance if it hadn't been for Erin.

She was outraged. He'd lied to her over and over and over. He had pretended to her that he didn't know the word *renegotiate*.

But above all, she was hopeful. There would have been no reason for Quentin to pursue her last night *after* sex when he knew she was leaving for New York soon, unless he meant it. He loved her.

It was just a matter of finding him.

For the first time in nine months, she didn't have a plan.

Well, the plan definitely should not include a trip to the airport. She turned the BMW around at the next exit and headed back the way she'd come. And quickly ground to a halt in a traffic jam. She heard on the radio there was a collision up ahead between a busload of fans headed to the Nationally Televised Holiday Concert Event and a limousine.

She might as well make use of this downtime. Maybe Quentin had left her a message. She reached into her bag and switched her phone back on. As she drew it out, her eyes fell on Quentin's asthma inhaler, which she'd forgotten to leave at the mansion.

She flinched as the phone rang in her hand.

~

Quentin jumped down from his big-ass truck. He ran through the garage and into the kitchen.

And hit a wall of cigarette smoke.

"Q!" Martin exclaimed. He let out a stream of epithets, this time directed at himself, because he'd smoked in Quentin's path. "Man, I am so sorry!"

Quentin stumbled, coughing, out the back door to the patio. Erin and Owen's argument echoed against the house. He told them desperately, "Sarah checked out of her hotel last night, and she's not answering her cell."

Erin and Owen didn't even slow down. Quentin glanced over at Martin, who had sat down at the patio table, cigarette butts and ash around his chair. Quentin fleetingly wondered what could have stressed Martin out so badly that he needed to smoke even when he was high. In the name of self-preservation, when they roomed together in college, Quentin had convinced Martin to stop smoking. Or so Quentin had thought. But that could wait.

"Hey!" he said.

Erin paused in yelling at Owen just long enough to tell Quentin, "She came here and now she's gone."

Quentin stepped between Erin and Owen to stop the stream of vitriol. He took Erin by the shoulders and looked down into her big blue eyes. "When was she here?"

"She just left," Erin said, her eyes meeting his gaze for the first time. "Q, we're all aware that you need to use your inhaler. So go do it. You can't always be the center of attention." She laid into Owen *again*. Incredible.

"I need to be the center of attention right now," Quentin said, leading her by the hand to the chair beside Martin. Next he shoved Owen toward a chair, and Owen was so engrossed in his conflict with Erin that he didn't even shove Quentin back. Now they were all sitting down, with Quentin standing in front of them, about to make the smartest or the stupidest move of his life, and Erin and Owen were *still* going at it. Finally Quentin shouted, "Shut *up*!"

Erin and Owen shut up, shocked at being yelled at by someone other than each other.

"I slept with Sarah," Quentin said.

Owen's eyes narrowed. Erin's shoulders sagged. Martin let his head loll back on his chair to gaze at the treetops.

"I slept with Sarah," Quentin repeated in a rush, "and I love her, and I'm going to ask her to marry me. I have a ring and everything." He felt in his pocket to make sure the ring box was still there. "Well?" he asked impatiently when Erin and Owen continued to stare at him and Martin continued to be high. "Are you going to kick me out of the band?"

"We already tried that," Owen said, "but Sarah wouldn't let us."

It was Quentin's turn to stare in disbelief. "Sarah *told* you I broke Rule Three?"

"No, but—" Owen held his head in his hand now. "Martin broke Rule One."

"I know," Quentin said at the same time Martin said, "He knows."

Owen paused, then said, "And Erin and I broke Rule Two."

"I thought you did," Quentin said. "And then I thought you didn't."

"After you and Owen had that fight in the driveway," Erin said, "I told him not to look at me anymore when we were around you. And to be nice to Sarah, because he thought Sarah knew what was going on. That seemed to work."

"It did," Quentin acceded, turning to Owen. "*Dumbass*. You were supposed to *fake* doing her."

Owen shot Quentin the bird.

"And I'm pregnant," Erin said.

"Are you taking folic acid?" Quentin asked automatically.

Then his brain caught up. He had Owen down on the hot flagstones, vaguely aware of Owen's chair still skidding, metal across stone, into the pool. He gripped Owen's throat with one hand and swung the other fist back. Martin was shouting at him.

"I'm in love with her!" Owen choked out.

Quentin hesitated and eased his grip on Owen's neck.

"You don't understand," Owen went on breathlessly. "All those love songs I've written with Erin, I've written them *for* Erin."

"Even 'Only a Flesh Wound'?" Quentin asked.

"I mean it," Owen said. "I'm in love with her. I've been in love with her for so long. And I just can't *stand* it anymore that you're with her—"

"For God's sake, Owen," Erin broke in, "that ended two years ago. I keep saying this."

"But you've been making out with him ever since," Owen called to her.

"That was the act!" she protested. "How was I supposed to know that it made you jealous? I didn't even know you liked me! You acted like I was about as attractive as Martin!"

Martin murmured to the sky, "Please don't drag me into this."

"And you had sex with that girl from the record company in Nashville!" Erin wailed.

"Only to make you jealous," Owen said. "I know that's terrible. Except I did enjoy the blow job."

Quentin gave him a warning look. Dumbass.

Owen got the message. "Completely terrible," he repeated. "Erin, I would have done anything. I'll still do *anything*." He looked up at Quentin with pleading eyes. "I love her, man."

Quentin stood and helped Owen up with one hand. Then he pointed Owen's shoulders in Erin's direction. "Say it to *her*."

"I'm in love with you," Owen said softly. He crossed the patio to kneel in front of her chair. "I love you," he said, looking up at her. He laid his head in her lap. "I love you so much."

After five years of Owen and Erin acting in private like no more than friends, this was so strange. Quentin turned to Martin to see what he thought. Martin rolled his eyes and let his head loll back on the chair again.

"Baby, I love you, too," Erin cooed, stroking Owen's hair. "I wouldn't have done it with you if I didn't. There was too much to lose." She glared at Quentin.

Quentin clapped his hands. "Enough of this touchy-feely shit. I've got my own woman to grovel to. Where did Sarah go?"

"I think . . . the airport," Erin said uneasily.

"The *airport*!" Quentin said. "Y'all sold me down the *road*! What is she doing at the *airport*? What did you tell her?"

Owen turned around to sit on the flagstones with his back against Erin's legs. He gave a man-sized sniff. "We asked her to be our manager," he said hoarsely.

"What'd she say?" Quentin asked in horror.

"She said no."

"That's not a good sign."

"And in the process of asking her," Owen explained, "we told her everything."

"What do you mean, *everything*?"

"Q, you're wheezing," Martin said without moving his head from the back of his chair.

"We told her we've known all along that the two of you weren't really doing it," Erin said helpfully, winking.

"Did you tell her I got into med school?"

"Yes, but she didn't act surprised," Erin said confusedly.

"She pulled the Obi-Wan Kenobi on you and made you *think* she wasn't," Quentin said.

"I didn't get that at all," Erin said slowly. She looked to Martin. "What about you?"

"I don't know," Martin said, lifting his head. "My perception may be a little off because I'm a heroin addict."

Both Erin and Owen stared at Martin like he'd grown a second head. Erin backed away from Martin, over the arm of her chair, across to Owen's other side.

"It's heroin, Erin," Martin grumbled, "not cooties."

Quentin smacked his fist into his hand. "Y'all focus! Did you screw me over or didn't you?"

Owen had both his arms around Erin now. From the depths of the bear hug, Erin said, "She knew everything, Q. She knew I was pregnant. In fact, the bitch told *Owen* I was pregnant."

Quentin struggled to stay upright as a wave of dizziness swept over him. "Oh no!" he said. "No wonder she was so pissed at me last night! She thought it was my baby!"

"Well, now she knows it isn't," Erin said simply. "What's the problem?"

"The problem is that she *went to the airport anyway*!"

"What are you so stoked about, Q?" Owen protested. "Don't you think she'd rather date—"

"Marry," Quentin said. "Don't you get it? I want to keep this one!"

"Don't you think she'd rather *marry* a college graduate than a hospital orderly?" Owen asked. "You'd have been able to hide that from her for about two more days. Too many people know."

"I realize that," Quentin said. "Things weren't going well last night, and I didn't want to piss her off any more than I already had. But I wanted to be the one to tell her. Otherwise, she'll think I've been trying to fool her the whole time."

"But you *have* been trying to fool her," Erin pointed out.

"I *realize* that!" Quentin said again before yielding to a fit of coughing, having traveled the full circle of emotion and returned to desperation.

"Outsmarted yourself," Owen muttered.

"Q, you're wheezing," Martin said again. "Go get your inhaler."

It really was becoming hard to breathe. Quentin stomped across the patio and up the steps. The cigarette smoke had aired out of the kitchen, but he'd let the attack go on too long. He tripped and almost fell on the step on the way in, then fumbled in the drawer for the inhaler.

No inhaler. He'd used it up the day they'd used the adrenaline shot on Sarah.

He had another inhaler in the big-ass truck.

No, he didn't have another inhaler in the truck. He'd put it in Sarah's bag at the airport before they flew to New York. Sarah had it.

The kitchen began to close in with his throat. He could get breaths in, but he couldn't get them back out, so he couldn't take more in. He felt in his pocket again, took out the ring box, and held it like a talisman.

A phone would be more helpful. His phone was in the truck. He looked around the kitchen for Martin's, and then somehow he was lying on the cold marble tile.

Owen's silhouette filled the doorway to the patio. He called back over his shoulder, "Q's on the floor."

"The inhaler's in the drawer," Martin yelled from outside.

Quentin heard Owen rummage in the drawer. By now, Erin and Martin were in the doorway. Martin said, "No, he used the last of it the day Sarah went to the hospital."

"Where's another?" Erin asked Quentin over the wheezing.

Quentin made a scribbling motion with one hand. When someone handed him a pad and pen, he wrote *Sarah has it* and tore off the sheet for them.

"Why does Sarah have it?" Erin shrieked. "You mean to tell me you're a respiratory therapist with asthma and you only have one rescue inhaler to your name and, duh, your *girlfriend* has it?"

Quentin scribbled *Help, dumbass,* and tore the paper off for Owen.

Owen read it and said, "No shit, Sherlock."

Quentin wrote *911,* handed it to Martin, and waited until he actually saw Martin punching buttons on the phone before he started scribbling a message to Sarah. He noticed with passing interest that his finger-nails were turning blue.

16

Liar, schmiar! Who cares? He's a hot med student country star! And he goes down on you! And he can't breathe and he needs you! I don't see a problem.

Wendy Mann
Senior Consultant
Stargazer Public Relations

The agony Sarah endured while stuck in traffic and e-mailing with a horny and irate Wendy was a complete waste, because when she finally arrived at the emergency room, the large receptionists wouldn't let her back to see Quentin. "We know who you are," they said, eyeing her hair. "Martin said no."

"But Martin *called* me!" Sarah exclaimed.

"He told you Quentin had an asthma attack," one of the receptionists said. "He asked you not to get on your plane, because Quentin insisted. But did Martin tell you to come down here?"

"He was getting in the ambulance," Sarah said. "He hung up on me."

As if that should serve as the answer, the receptionists turned back to their computer screens.

Sarah paced close to them in her high heels and shot them dirty looks. They were unfazed. She thought she heard Quentin's voice, hoarse, down the hallway. Then Owen's voice, angry. A series of crashes and women's screams.

"You let me back there," Sarah told the receptionists, beating the flat of her hand on the counter.

"Martin said no," one of them repeated.

"I'm going!" Sarah yelled at the woman, who was about a hundred pounds heavier than her. She moved toward the hallway.

The *schlop*, *schlop*, *schlop* of flip-flops sounded double-time ahead of her, and Erin appeared in the waiting room with an armload of crumpled plastic bags.

"Do you realize they won't let me back there?" Sarah asked as she passed Erin.

"Stop her," Erin said to a receptionist, who stepped into Sarah's path. When Sarah turned to give Erin a piece of her mind, Erin lasered her with blue eyes. "Shut up for just a minute," she said, dumping her armload on the counter.

She picked up Sarah's bag from a nearby chair, slid

it onto the counter, unzipped it, and began stuffing it with the plastic bags: inhalers, adrenaline shots. It was full to bursting and still she was poking in more shots. Finally satisfied, she zipped it, pressing the edges together so it would close. She took the handle in one hand, grabbed Sarah with the other, and led her to a bank of chairs on the far side of the waiting room.

She leaned close to Sarah and said, "Don't ever, ever, *ever* let him be without an adrenaline shot and an inhaler. He's usually pretty good, but you have to be better." She told the empty air in front of her, "Q, you are the stupidest genius I know!"

Sarah must have been looking at Erin like she'd lost it, because Erin turned back to her and explained, "It's easier to argue with him when he's not here. He's so pissed with us for telling you everything this afternoon. A few minutes ago, he tried to punch Owen and knocked over a crash cart and passed out again."

Sarah winced. "I heard." She stood up. "Call off your dogs and let me see him."

Erin shook her head and pulled Sarah back down to sit. "Look, Sarah, he breathed a lot of Martin's cigarette smoke, and then he got upset about you, and then he tried to kill Owen. He's getting meds, but his lungs are very twitchy. We need to keep him calm. We can't give him a tranquilizer because those drugs suppress the respiration. We just want you to stay out of there right now. It would be better if y'all worked this out after the concert, so he doesn't have a relapse. He's doing a lot better."

"You mean he's *allergic* to me?"

"No, it's just—"

Another realization hit Sarah. "You mean you're going to go *on*?"

"Hell," Erin said, looking at her watch, "it's only four. The show doesn't start until seven. We had him on in three hours after he had an attack in St. Louis. We're *professionals*."

They eyed each other uneasily as a shout from Martin and another crash echoed up the hallway.

"I need you to do me a favor," Erin said. "And if you do this for me, you and I can call it even."

Sarah's heart leaped, because she wanted Erin to be her friend. Skeptical Natsuko calculated who had actually committed more offense against whom.

"Q wrote you a note as he was passing out at the house," Erin said, "and he gave it to me for safekeeping. He thinks I'm out here giving it to you now. Truth is, I lost it somewhere on the kitchen floor in the confusion." A note of pleading entered her high voice. "I need to you to go back and find it for me. Q is so mad at me already."

"You're just trying to get rid of me," Sarah said.

"That, too." Erin nodded. "But you *do* want to read this note. And I thought I saw something else on the kitchen floor that might interest you."

"Okay," Sarah relented.

"Thank you so much," Erin gushed. They embraced each other warmly, all awkwardness gone.

Sarah allowed herself a deep sigh with her arms around her friend. After a few moments, she sat back. "Did he really act with Karen like he acts with me?"

Erin stared at Sarah for a second, then remembered what she'd said that day at her guesthouse. "No." She smiled. "I've never seen him act this way. Definitely not with me. That's why Martin and Owen and I tried to collar him. Guess what? You can't collar Q."

They grinned at each other as they stood. But Erin's smile faded as Sarah headed for the reception desk rather than the exit. The receptionists stood at the ready.

"Where are you going?" Erin wailed.

"I'm not leaving until I see him," Sarah said.

Erin ran to insert herself between Sarah and the emergency room. "*Girlfriend,*" she said pointedly, "this is still *my* band. This is *my* Nationally Televised Whatever Whatever. At least for five more hours, until nine o'clock, when the show's over and the fireworks start, this is *my* band, and Q is *mine.*" Her expression softened. "And then you can have him."

~

Sarah escaped the paparazzi without making a statement except to say that the Nationally Televised Holiday Concert Event would go on as planned. With a sigh of relief, she slipped into the BMW, exited the parking deck, and accelerated onto Eighth Avenue

South, the usually bustling thoroughfare all but deserted for the holiday. After five minutes, she pulled into Quentin's driveway.

The door into the kitchen was ajar, with air-conditioning seeping out and hot humidity flooding the dark room. The usually maid-clean marble floor was littered with the leavings from the paramedics, plastic bags marked *STERILE* and ripped open. There were also a few small white sheets of paper.

She picked up one sheet. On it was scrawled, *Sarah has it.*

Sarah went cold, even with warmth from outside swirling around her. Quentin must have written this, and he meant the inhaler. Surely this wasn't what Erin had wanted Sarah to see. If she was trying to make Sarah feel guilty, she'd succeeded.

Frantically Sarah grabbed up the other notes. *911,* one said, and the next, *Help, dumbass,* which didn't make her feel any better.

Her high-heeled sandal kicked something solid under the plastic bags. She stooped to find a jewelry store ring box.

Poised to open it, she saw that her hands shook, and Natsuko slapped Sarah around. There was no telling whether it was meant for her.

Inside was a *freaking enormous* diamond flanked by hefty emeralds.

It was for her.

She slipped its cool weight onto her finger.

That's when she saw the last note, which had drifted under the cabinets.

SARAH
I love you
Don't leave

Sarah sat down on the floor with the note. She read the six words over and over, ran her fingertip over the messy handwriting, touched *I love you*.

"Found something?" Nine Lives asked behind her.

~

Tonight would be a first for the Cheatin' Hearts since they became famous. They would tell the truth.

In the emergency room, they'd all agreed—the rest of them talking, Quentin writing on a pad—that they would mention Erin's pregnancy in the act.

Then Owen had suggested they nix the cowboy hats. Everyone heartily seconded this idea. Erin had always complained that the hats messed up her hair, and Quentin found them bothersome and sweaty at an outdoor concert.

Martin had told them that he would check himself into rehab as soon as the concert was over tonight. And when they'd arrived at Vulcan Park, he'd taken his long-sleeved shirt off in the heat, revealing the purplish track marks snaking up both arms. Quentin wondered whether he would keep the shirt off for the concert. He thought Martin might have gone off the deep end. But he hoped this was step one toward recovery: admitting to the world that he had a problem.

It was Martin's turn to get drunk. He didn't bring it up, and the rest of them were reluctant to push him, considering. Quentin didn't volunteer because he planned to have a lot going on with Sarah after the concert. He figured Owen felt the same way about Erin. This would be their first completely sober concert in two years.

Quentin looked forward to the concert. He looked forward to playing it naked, so to speak, revealing their real strengths and flaws. It was nice to be himself again after two years of deceit. Even if, at the moment, being himself meant lying in the payload of Owen's truck, flattened by asthma, staring up at Vulcan's butt, pining for Sarah.

They wouldn't let him go look for her. He needed to rest and recover as best he could for the concert. And Owen had taken his cell phone away so he wouldn't be tempted to talk. Which was just as well. He'd left Sarah three voice mail messages before he had the attack, when he was searching for her. If he left her ten more, he might start to look pitiful.

He sat up for the millionth time and scanned the parking lot for Sarah's BMW. Spaces were filling up fast for the Nationally Televised Holiday Concert Event, but security had been instructed to look for Sarah's pink hair and let her back here, past the barriers. There wasn't a sign of her. No flash of pink in the crowd. He waved halfheartedly to the Timberlanes and their butler, whom he'd gotten front-row seats.

Surely Sarah would show. If not before the concert, during. But he needed a plan in case she didn't come. Maybe there was a red-eye flight from Birmingham to New York, or—hey, he had a big-ass truck! He could drive to Atlanta to catch a flight. He wondered how much it would cost to charter a flight himself. Usually he didn't waste money on flashy stuff like that, but this was important.

Why didn't she call?

Maybe there was something wrong with her cell phone. He could leave her an e-mail message in case she checked her laptop. He slid out of the truck bed and headed for the large trailer functioning as a dressing room so he could retrieve his phone from Owen.

Inside the trailer, Martin reclined on a sofa with his eyes closed, lost in something he was composing on his acoustic guitar, shirt still off. Erin laughed with the woman piling and spraying her hair on top of her head. Owen sat in a chair across the room from Erin, grinning at her unabashedly.

Quentin pulled up a chair next to Owen and sat down. Without taking his eyes away from Erin, Owen handed over Quentin's cell phone so Quentin could make sure it was set to ring and that Sarah hadn't left a message. Quentin let out a frustrated sigh and started coughing again.

The hairdresser spun Erin around to spray the back

of her hair. Now Erin faced Owen. Erin beamed at him. Owen's smiled broadened.

Quentin tried to climb out of his mood to be happy for them. They both were so content, sharing sappy looks with each other across the room. But he only sank deeper into the funk, contemplating how he'd prevented them from being together for five years. Unknowingly, but he should have known.

After a few minutes of silence except for Martin's guitar and Erin's animated laughter, Owen said quietly to Quentin, "Don't be sorry. I should have said something or done something. I was afraid of chasing her off, and I wanted to be near her. Anyway, it doesn't matter now."

Quentin typed a text message on his phone and handed it to Owen: *Vonnie Conner.*

Owen looked at the screen and handed the phone back to Quentin. "Vonnie Conner," Owen muttered in disgust. "Q, Sarah is nothing like that. Vonnie Conner led you on. Behind that poker face, Sarah feels and sees. She had my number from day one. That's why I avoided her. Every time she looked at me, I felt like she was coming up and punching me in the chest."

Quentin nodded, because he knew what Owen meant.

"I thought all along that it was a shame you couldn't break Rule Three," Owen said. "You're perfect for each other. Surely she sees that, too. You'll have a great life together. She's just held up somewhere."

Quentin sighed and nodded again.

Owen said, "I like it a lot better when you can't talk."

The trailer door opened. Quentin sucked in his breath, knowing it was Sarah at last.

Then coughed, because he'd breathed too deeply. It was only Rachel.

She stopped and put her hand through Martin's hair. Then she came to stand in front of Quentin.

"Did you find her?" he whispered.

She shook her head no. "But I have a confession." She eyed Owen, and then her gaze slid back to Quentin. "I'm the one who called her down here."

"What?" Owen asked sharply.

She turned to make sure Martin hadn't heard, then gave Owen a reproving look. Quietly she told Quentin, "I really did agree with you that we couldn't get Martin in rehab secretly if he didn't want to go. And if we went to Owen and Erin to talk about an intervention, they would kick him out of the band, which would be the end of him."

Owen's mouth twisted in guilt.

"What I didn't agree with," Rachel said, "was that the problem would work itself out. I had to do something. I'd heard of a PR crisis manager who'd saved Lorelei Vogel's career a couple of years ago—remember what a mess that girl was? But I didn't want to call this PR lady and explain Martin's problem. My contract says you guys could sue me if I did that."

"I wouldn't—" Quentin started to protest.

Rachel held one finger up to his lips. "You haven't been yourself since Thailand. I wasn't going to take that chance, not when I'm supporting my sister and my brother. Anyway . . ." She took a deep breath. "I called Manhattan Music and told them the band was about to break up because you were jealous of Erin and Owen. They panicked, predictably. I made them promise not to say who called, just to convey that message, and I suggested the crisis manager. I figured when she came down to straighten you out, she would discover Martin's problem and solve it. If anybody could have finagled a way out of that mess, it was her. But she was on maternity leave, so her company sent Sarah."

"Was it Wendy Mann?" Quentin asked hoarsely. When Rachel nodded, he looked up at the metal ceiling and sent a silent thanks to baby Asher for entering the world at just the right time, so Sarah would be sent to save them all.

"I just wanted you to know," Rachel said sadly. "I'm glad it all worked out for us, more or less. But Sarah's thought the whole time that you're in love with Erin. And if she's angry about being lied to, that might be why she's still missing."

Quentin hugged Rachel, letting her know without words that she'd done the right thing, and she was a lot smarter than him.

Then he crossed the trailer, stepped into the setting sunlight, and slammed the flimsy door behind him. With one last glance around the parking lot for the BMW, he slid into the payload of Owen's truck and composed an e-mail message to Sarah.

17

Sarah, I love you. Please come back to me. I'm so sorry. Rachel was the one who called you down to help Martin. The story about me was fake. She didn't tell me any of that until just now. And I'm sure the denouement you witnessed at my house was a freak show. I didn't mean for you to find out that way. I was going to tell you everything about me this afternoon, and all the rules, but you weren't at your hotel or my house, and you didn't answer your cell. I had no idea Erin was pregnant. If I had, I wouldn't have let you go on thinking the baby was mine. I swear I had nothing to do with it. I last had sex with Erin two years ago, on Memorial Day. I remember this specifically because we played a gig in Auburn, and there was a row. I do love her, but not the way you meant the day you asked in the emergency room. Honestly, Sarah, I know I've hurt your feelings over and over in the last ten days, because I thought I had to for the band. It's killed me every time. Please don't go to New York. If you're there, please come back. If you don't come back, I'll come get you, but tell me your travel plans so we don't chase each other back and forth across the continent. You know I could take that Fawn guy, and he will never, ever make you aloo gobi. They're waving to me. I have to go. I'm getting a little desperate here, Sarah. I'd skip the Nationally Televised Holiday Concert Event to come find you, but then I'd be in worse trouble with you if you got fired. Right? Now I really have to go. This is driving me out of my freaking mind. I need you back. Where are you? Please come.

For long periods, Sarah would lie on one of the sofas in Quentin's den with her head in Nine Lives' lap, staring up at the cat-eye contacts that hid his pupils, dilated from methamphetamine. His story, terrifying the first time she'd heard it almost nine months ago, was familiar enough now that she could tune it out. She was out to get him, Manhattan Music had it in for him, the proceeds from his album sales were being used to bribe the TV entertainment news shows into calling him a has-been. He flipped through the channels, trying to find one of these shows to make his point to her. For some reason, each time he gave up, he stopped the TV on a NASCAR race. Whenever he paused, Sarah responded calmly, "Mmmm-hmmm. I understand what you're saying."

Then he would jump up, take a swig of vodka from his flask, and pace around and around the coffee table as if he couldn't figure out how to escape the *U* of sofas, ranting about the very real offense Sarah had committed against him. The food was bad in jail, and it was hard to get sushi and meth brought in when Sarah had cut off his money.

The cycle went on for hours while Sarah plotted a way out of this. There wasn't a phone in the house. Her phone was in her bag in the BMW. That was her only hope, really: 911. There was no escaping in the BMW. Even if she managed to dash out to the driveway and slip into the convertible without Nine Lives catching her, his bodyguard would be waiting down at the gate. With a crowbar, because the bodyguard planned ahead.

Nine Lives pounced on the sofa. "How long did you think they'd keep me in Rio, Sarah?" he purred close to her face. "It's fine to bribe the police, but when you leave, they start taking bribes from someone else." His hot breath was on her cheek. He was near enough to bite her.

She tried to concentrate on NASCAR. "I was scared, Bill," she said. "You cut me with your ring when you hit me."

He smiled grimly and rubbed the scar in his plucked eyebrow. "And you need to be more careful with that shoe." He leaned even closer. His lips touched her cheek as he growled at her, "Have you ever gotten stitches in a Brazilian jail?"

His soft hand with the long fingernails filed to points grazed her rib cage and headed south. She tried not to tense. This NASCAR race was actually pretty exciting.

His fingers reached her hand guarding her lap. His nails rasped across the diamond-and-emerald ring. He started back, then picked up her hand to examine the stone more closely. "Speaking of rings," he said. "You're in the national gossip columns with this singer from the Cheatin' Hearts. And they call me your *ex*-boyfriend. Did he give you this ring?" He moved his soft hand to her throat. "And the necklace? What happened to the ankhs I gave you?"

"You know it's not like that, Bill," she said with reproach. "I've told you I never date musicians." This wouldn't have been a lie ten days ago. "It's business. New musicians, new jewelry."

Nine Lives sniffed. "I have something special for you, too." He pulled a tiny bottle and a packaged syringe from his pocket and showed them to her. "Kryptonite."

Sarah hoped this wasn't a new delusion. She said carefully, "I'm not Supergirl."

"Figuratively, Sarah," he said. "Do you think I'm *crazy*? It's bee venom. You made the local paper with your little problem."

"Bee venom," Sarah repeated emotionlessly. "Where did you get bee venom?"

"Hospital," he said simply. "They bottle it and give it to people with the allergy, to build up a tolerance. You'd be amazed what you can get *anywhere* for four thousand dollars and some crystal."

Sarah laughed. "You're going to shoot me up with *bee sting*?" Wait until she told Wendy about this. The gasoline-huffing boy band Wendy had handled last year didn't hold a candle to Nine Lives and his bee venom.

He popped the sterile wrapping around the syringe. He was serious.

"You know that'll kill me," she breathed.

He said offhandedly, "If I give you enough."

She vaulted over the back of the sofa and half ran, half fell down the stairs, then dashed down the hall to Martin's room. Slammed the door, locked it, jerked out the top left-hand drawer of the dresser, and opened the gun case.

It was empty.

The door boomed next to her, and something slammed into her shoulder. She fell on Martin's bed in a mass of wood splinters and plaster dust, with Nine Lives' bodyguard heavy on top of her.

"Hello, Goonie," she groaned.

"Hello, Sarah," he said pleasantly. He stood her up and brushed her off casually enough. But he gripped her upper arm hard as he pulled her up the stairs.

"Please don't let Bill play around with that bee venom," she whispered to him. "It could kill me."

He stopped her on the stairs and turned to her,

his pupils dilated. He'd started using, too. "You and me used to be cool, Sarah," he told her. "You used to be all right. But while you were keeping Bill in prison, we were all stuck in Rio without a paycheck. Let him pass the bee shit to me, and I'll shoot you up myself."

Nine Lives was waiting in the kitchen. The two of them escorted Sarah down the driveway and held her while she recited the code for Nine Lives' driver to open the gate. She glanced hopefully toward the bushes, but of course all the paparazzi were at the Nationally Televised Holiday Concert Event. She gazed the other way, toward the Timberlanes' driveway, but their large car was gone.

Nine Lives' driver, Fred, stood next to the open back door of a limo with a wrecked front end. Before Sarah slid onto the seat, she looked into his eyes. Dilated pupils. "Et tu Brute?" she asked.

Fred said, "Shut up and get your little Caesar ass in the car." Even though she got in without protest, he gave her a shove across the seat, muttering, "Et tu Brute."

"Come on, Fred," she coaxed. "Bill could kill me with that bee venom. You're not mad enough at me to kill me, are you? You're not willing to kill a girl over a few paychecks?"

"It ain't the paychecks so much," he said. "It's what happens to you in Rio when your cash is cut off. Why couldn't you just let him fuck you?" He slammed the door.

Sarah pressed her cold hands to her face. She was about to cruise Birmingham in the methmobile. She was going to die here in the methmobile of an induced allergy attack at the hands of a demented rock star while the man she loved played a country concert under Vulcan's bare buttocks. And it wasn't funny if she couldn't e-mail it to Wendy.

The doors opened on both sides. All three men reached out to her. Goonie sat on her legs and held her wrists while Fred put his knee on her throat.

"This isn't necessary," she croaked.

"I seen what you did to Bill with that shoe," Fred told her.

Beyond Fred's leg, Nine Lives stuck the needle into the small bottle again.

"Thank you for using a clean syringe," she said.

Nine Lives assured her, "I wouldn't do anything to hurt you, Sarah."

Fred and Goonie laughed.

"How do you know how much to give me?" she asked.

"I'll give you just a little at first," Nine Lives said.

"And if your head gets swole up," said Fred, "we'll know that was too much."

She asked, "Can't I just have some meth?"

Goonie said, "Bet you fifty she keeps a straight face through this."

"You're on," said Fred.

"I wouldn't take that bet," said Nine Lives as he jabbed the needle into her shoulder.

～

She watched several red-ringed white hives pop up on her arms, and she gripped the limo seat hard as her throat began to close. Nine Lives on one side and Goonie on the other just watched her, amused. It got worse and worse, and then it didn't get any worse. She wouldn't die from this dose.

Through the sparkles flashing in front of her eyes, she tried to watch the Cheatin' Hearts concert on the small TV hanging from the ceiling of the limo. Quentin wore the green college T-shirt with the fire-breathing dragon, sleeves rolled up to expose his tanned biceps. The cameras seemed to take perverse pleasure in cutting to his ancient deck shoes as he adjusted the sound of his bass guitar with a pedal. But through song after song, most of the broadcast zoomed in on his handsome face, the flash of his deep green eyes, his tangled waves of brown hair.

His hair. The Cheatin' Hearts weren't wearing their characteristic cowboy hats.

He hit the money note at the end of "Party in the Double-Wide," but after that, his voice grew raspy. He traced a circle in the air with his finger, grabbed a water bottle at the base of his mike stand, and walked offstage. The other three began an instrumental without him.

The camera swung to Erin, who looked especially beautiful tonight, in her way. Her boobs were enormous in the bustier she wore with her Daisy Dukes, her blond curls were equally enormous and bouncy, and her carefully made-up frosted pink lips shone in the spotlights. She looked happy. The camera flashed to Owen, who looked happy. The camera flashed to Martin, who focused on his guitar.

Martin's shirt was off.

The instrumental ended quickly and Quentin returned, fist to his mouth, still coughing a little. "Sorry about that, folks," he said. "Y'all may have heard I had a little problem this afternoon. It ain't a party until somebody pulls out the beta-agonist." The crowd cheered like he'd named a beer brand. He smiled his lopsided smile and shook his head at Erin.

"Now he's going to mention you again," Nine Lives said, absorbed in the show. "I swear, if he mentions you again—"

"Sarah," Quentin said into the microphone, "if you don't show up, we might just release our third album free on the Internet." The crowd cheered again.

Sarah thought, *There goes my job.*

Throughout "Honky-tonk Hell," Sarah focused on the TV, Quentin's smiling green eyes, his smooth lazy voice. He was so happy and comfortable onstage, a joy to watch. Nine Lives stared at her.

The song ended. Nine Lives said, "He'd better not mention you again."

Quentin asked, "Have y'all been watching the *World Poker Tournament*?" He paused for the crowd's cheer. "Y'all know Hell's Belle, the poker queen? That's Sarah's mother, and this song's for her." The band began "Naked Mama."

Sarah thought, *There goes Christmas in Fairhope*.

"I *hate* country music," said Nine Lives.

"Me, too," said Goonie.

Sarah said, "I used to."

The song ended. The camera caught Quentin mouthing to Martin, "Where is she?"

Nine Lives leaned forward with his chin in his hands, pointed fingernails pricking his face. "You made that guy fall in love with you," he murmured. "Just like you did me. And you fucked him, when you wouldn't fuck me."

"Oh, did you think he was talking about *me*?" Sarah laughed. "No, he's talking about a different Sarah."

"Sarah," said Quentin, "you need to get your purty pink-haired self up here."

Nine Lives watched her, waiting for her to crack. She concentrated on Quentin, who had his hands in his hair.

"Sarah pointed out to me that this next song could be interpreted as being about backdoor action," he said. "So we're dedicating it to Nine Lives, who's in prison in Rio." The band started "Come to Find Out," and the crowd roared.

Nine Lives scratched his cheekbone with one pointed fingernail, leaving a red mark. Then he looked at his watch. "Fred," he called, "the concert will be over in a few minutes. Let's go get him."

"What do you mean, 'go get him?'" Sarah asked, trying her best to sound calm. "Do you mean the singer? What do you want with him?"

"He's got a little coke problem, right?" Nine Lives asked. "OD'd recently in Thailand? If you've been on his ass, he hasn't done it since. I'll bet he's really bluesing for some coke. It just so happens that I *have* some coke. I thought I'd get him good and hopped up. And then I'll let him watch while I show you what really happens in a Brazilian prison."

Sarah looked at Goonie. Goonie smiled at her.

She watched trees and buildings and signs spin by out the windows of the limo for a few moments while it sank in.

She said quietly, "The thing is, Bill, he's not really on coke. You know how you'd collapse at nightclubs in Rio and I'd start a rumor in the press that you had diabetes? Well, the Cheatin' Hearts are the opposite. Quentin has asthma and allergies. He doesn't do coke."

"Wow, you can lie with a straight face," said Nine Lives.

"Bill, you have to believe me. Quentin's never done drugs. He was in the ICU in Thailand because of an allergy. If you coke him up like he's an addict, he really will OD. You'll kill him."

"Sarah," Nine Lives said condescendingly, "if we don't give him enough, he won't get off." He pointed to the TV. The camera focused on Martin's hands as he played the intricate guitar solo in "Heavily Sedated." Black track marks marred both arms. Nine Lives said, "The Cheatin' Hearts don't do drugs. Right!"

"Allergies," Goonie said, shaking his head and laughing.

Sarah recalled what Quentin had told her: *Be careful what you say to the press. It might come back to sting you.* She'd better keep her mouth shut. Nine Lives had become an avid news reader of late. Cocaine was bad enough, but if she wasn't careful, she'd persuade Nine Lives to feed Quentin an almond.

It was difficult to act alluring to a greasy rock icon while she was having an allergic reaction, but she gave it a go. She leaned over to him and whispered in his ear, "We don't have to do it like this. It's no fun if we're angry with each other. Do you have your plane here?"

He nodded.

"You and I can ditch Goonie and Fred and fly to Monte Carlo. Or Cannes. Monaco." Sarah tried to think of more resort towns where French was spoken. She was fluent in French, and she didn't want to get stuck in another Portuguese situation.

"No dice," he hissed. "You'd just be trying to get away from me the whole time. No, I think I'd rather get revenge."

"Me, too," said Goonie.

Fred leaned through the window between the front and back seats. "Me, too,"

"Turn around and drive the car, Fred!" Goonie boomed. "That's how we wrecked this morning."

"How do you feel after that shot?" Nine Lives asked her.

"Itchy."

"How about some more?" He patted her in a friendly way on the shoulder where he'd injected her. "I don't think I gave you enough before."

Not even Natsuko could see her way out of this now. When Sarah showed up at the concert with Nine Lives, Quentin would come to rescue her, and Goonie and Fred would take him. She had to keep him out of this. It wasn't his fight. She couldn't go to the concert. She would let them kill her instead.

"Holy shit," Nine Lives gasped. "Goonie, give Fred his fifty bucks back. Sarah's crying."

"*That's* what we like to see," said Goonie. "Don't wreck, but you gotta look at this, Fred. There's a girl in there."

Fred glanced through the window between the seats. "There's a *bitch* in there, more like it."

"There, there," Nine Lives purred, rubbing Sarah's knee. "We don't want to hurt you, Sarah. Not unless you make us mad. We just want to soften you up for our big night. Or do we? Goonie, maybe you like a fighter."

Goonie said, "I want her softer than *that*."

"Okay," she said, sniffling and dabbing carefully under her eyes with her fingertips. "Do you mind if I lie down?"

Nine Lives patted his thigh amiably. Sarah stretched out across the seat with her head in his lap. Goonie rubbed her feet in the high heels soothingly. Out the sunroof, the clouds were violent pink with the sunset, and so clearly defined. The sunroof was open, she realized. The ultimate opulence in Alabama: windows open with the air-conditioning on.

"I made up this song a couple of days ago," Quentin said on the TV, "watching Sarah work out in the gym of the hotel at the Galleria."

He'd been *watching* her? Sarah had some hard questions for her creepy fiancé.

He had better be glad she would never see him again.

If she turned to look at him on the TV she would cry harder, so she stared out the sunroof and let his voice soothe her as Nine Lives felt around in his pockets for the little bottle of venom.

"Now I wish I hadn't written this one," Quentin said, "because I'm trying to get Sarah back, not make her run some more. It was supposed to be a surprise for her, and she's not here. But Erin's giving me that *look*. It's next on the playlist, so I guess we have to do it. 'Pink-Haired Sarah.'"

The easy, funky little beat was unlike anything Sarah had heard the Cheatin' Hearts play before. She thought analytically that Quentin might get his first Grammy from this one.

> *Pink-haired Sarah in the sun.*
> *I wonder what makes Sarah run?*

Or not, Sarah thought. *Sun* and *run*. Good one. Nine Lives had found the bottle.

> *What does Sarah have to lose?*
> *Pink-haired Sarah has the blues.*

Sarah thought about Wendy. She thought about her mother.

Nine Lives unwrapped another syringe.

> *What does Sarah know is coming?*
> *What keeps pink-haired Sarah running?*

She thought about Quentin standing with his father in the gravel parking lot of the Highway 280 Steak House, which rarely served steak. Quentin and his father opened the hood of his truck and peered into the engine. They straightened and laughed together, and Quentin looked so proud. Then he saw Sarah watching from the doorway of the restaurant. He gave her the lopsided grin. Quentin would be fine without her.

Nine Lives stuck the needle into the bottle and pulled back the plunger.

> *Sarah laughing in the sun.*
> *I wonder what makes pink-haired Sarah run?*

Then came the chorus, with Erin, Martin, and Owen in a soaring three-part harmony: "Run, Sarah, run."

"Run," sang Quentin. "Pink-haired Sarah, run."

She took a deep breath and held it as Nine Lives pulled back her sleeve to expose her shoulder.

"Run, Sarah, run," sang the chorus.

Quentin sang, "Hon, what are you running from?"

Sarah leaped up from the seat, caught hold of the edge of the sunroof, and hauled herself through the small opening.

And braced herself as Fred made a sharp turn into the nearest parking lot.

"Help!" she screamed at the top of her lungs, realizing the futility of the exercise even as she did so. Of all the luck, they'd pulled over at a much-advertised strip club. It was probably an hourly occurrence here for a pink-haired woman in a low-cut shirt and an emerald neck-lace to scream for help out the open sunroof of a limo.

They had both her ankles, but she kicked violently and managed to grasp the side of the car. She was al-most out.

Then, with one hard jerk from inside the limo, she bounced onto the seat beside Nine Lives again.

Goonie grabbed her, putting his full weight on her arms while Fred sat on one of her legs. She jammed the other high heel into an unknown part of Nine Lives and ground in. Not because this would help, but be-cause she was pissed.

"Would you hold her?" Nine Lives yelped. One of his cat-eye contacts had fallen out. He turned his furi-ous gaze on her: one cat eye, the other eye with the pupil blown out almost to the edge of his hazel iris. He sat on her, too, and felt around on the seat for the lost bottle.

"Don't do it, man," Goonie advised. "The concert is around the corner, and we need her conscious to get us past security."

Everything is going to be okay, she recited Martin's litany in her head. *Everything is fine. I'm fine. Everything is okay.* And then, Quentin's words: *It's okay to ask for help.*

~

"Pink-Haired Sarah" neared its end, and Quentin prepared to repeat the first verse. He signaled to Martin to signal to Erin to signal to Owen to change the lyrics, replacing *run* with *come*. He'd sung it this way for them in the album sessions, but Erin nixed this version because she thought Sarah would hate them for the dirty double entendre. It seemed appropriate now, and Quentin had nothing to lose. The crowd whooped its approval at the change as Quentin sang,

> *Sarah laughing in the sun.*
> *I wonder what makes pink-haired Sarah come?*
> *Come, pink-haired Sarah, come.*

A limo with a smashed fender made its way slowly through security to park at one side of the stage. Quentin had thought all the professional wrestlers were in the audience already, but sometimes Mad "Red" Mud liked to be flamboyantly late.

They ended the song to the loudest applause of the night, which Quentin barely registered. Martin had predicted that "Pink-Haired Sarah" would win Quentin his first Grammy. But who cared, if the song's eponym ran to another hemisphere to disentangle another codependent band? If she was really angry with him, she might do just that. She might instruct her office not to tell him where she'd gone.

In that case, he could fly to New York tomorrow and do some snooping. He already had an in with the lady in the Stargazer travel office. Or he could sweet-talk Wendy. Or have a man-to-man with Daniel.

Something thwacked him in the back of the head, and Owen's drumstick rolled in front of Quentin's toes. Owen kept a stash of extra drumsticks for this purpose. Quentin must have been daydreaming. "Martin wrote this next song," Quentin said quickly, "'Barefoot and Pregnant.' You may notice that Erin is taking her shoes off."

The audience moaned, and Erin grinned defiantly. She tossed one of her low-class high-heeled shoes into the crowd.

"We had to talk Erin into making the announcement," Quentin went on, "because she hasn't told her grandma out in Irondale. Sorry, Lillie Mae. And because Erin and Owen haven't gotten married yet."

Martin played the first few notes of the wedding march that launched "Barefoot and Pregnant." These were easy lyrics and it was an easy bass line, so Quentin could think ahead while he went through the motions. At the end of the song, which slowly devolved into a long fiddle solo, Mad "Red" Mud would jump up onstage, grab the mike from Quentin, and holler that Erin was pregnant with *his* baby. The other professional wrestlers would follow him onstage and start the fake fight extravaganza.

Erin, Owen, and Martin were concerned about the extravaganza. Really there wasn't anything fake about it. They would have to punch each other hard because they hadn't rehearsed it. But Quentin had insisted on this. It was bad enough that they had to warn security not to intervene. If they practiced with the wrestlers, too, the plan would definitely leak to the press. Besides, the fake fight couldn't *look* fake. To avoid the fray, Erin would climb up on one of the enormous speakers and play her version of Jimi Hendrix's version of "The Star-Spangled Banner" while the fireworks started.

And then, as soon as the cameras turned off and Quentin could extricate himself from the tussle, he would see about that flight to New York.

Or not. Just as he stepped back in feigned surprise to let Mad "Red" Mud take the mike, Sarah climbed the stairs to stand behind the speakers at the side of the stage. Thank God!

With Nine Lives. And two enormous goons.

Quentin lifted off his guitar strap and swung the guitar behind his head to use as a weapon. And then stopped short as Nine Lives motioned to the syringe stuck in Sarah's shoulder, plunger out.

Oh God. What was that maniac doing to her?

Someone tackled Quentin from the back. Quentin landed heavily on his ribs. The guitar went flying. He struggled to stand and make it over to Sarah, but a wrestler jerked him into the fight center stage.

"Would you stop a minute?" he yelled to Red. "There's a—"

Red socked Quentin in the jaw, and Quentin reeled back toward Sarah. The two goons were coming for him.

Then one of the goons skidded back into a speaker. Owen had fallen into him.

"Owen!" Quentin said, bending over him. "Help me! There's a—"

The goon was up, and he had Quentin by the shirt. Then a wrestler punched Quentin in the gut, and punched the goon hard enough in the head that the goon went down, on top of Quentin.

Quentin winced at the pain in his hip as he hit the stage. That was his plastic asthma inhaler breaking in his pocket. He was flat on his back, looking up at Erin high on the speaker with her eyes closed, blissfully fiddling "The Star-Spangled Banner." Several booms sounded. The fireworks were starting.

He pulled himself out from under the unconscious goon and scrambled up just in time to see Martin and the other goon fall off the back of the stage. Maybe Quentin could reach Sarah now that more people were comatose. He punched and got punched, punched and got punched, homing in on her as he went.

The syringe was out of her shoulder. She'd kneed Nine Lives in the groin and elbowed him in the eye. Nine Lives kept coming after her. He pinned her face-down on the stage. Then he put his arm around her throat, jerked her up, and backed her down the stairs, toward the open door of the limo.

Quentin rushed for her. He had to grab her before

Nine Lives disappeared with her again. He'd almost reached her when Owen tackled him. *No!*

A shot rang out, high and sharp, separate from the fireworks.

"Dumbass!" Quentin yelled, tossing Owen off him. Sarah was gone.

He found her crumpled at the foot of the stairs.

Pulling her high-heeled shoe free of Nine Lives' grip, Quentin picked her up off the ground and sat down on the stairs with her. "Where are you hit?" he coughed, looking desperately at her arms, pulling up her shirt.

"Everything is fine, I'm fine, everything is okay," she recited. "It's not me. It's him." She pointed to Nine Lives howling on the ground.

Martin, hunched over, walked toward them under the stage. He shoved his gun into his pocket and pulled at Nine Lives' arm to flatten him on the asphalt. A hole in the thigh of Nine Lives' black jeans oozed dark blood.

Martin pressed his hands over the wound. He said over his shoulder, "Q, you're wheezing."

"Where's your inhaler?" Sarah breathed.

Quentin pulled it out of his pocket and showed her the broken plastic. He bulleted it at Nine Lives, who screamed, "Ow!"

Between fireworks blasts, running footsteps sounded behind Quentin on the stage. He started around, ready for another wrestler, but it was only Erin. "Q," she cried desperately, "Owen's stitches came out."

"Put pressure on it," Quentin called as best he could. "I'll be there in a minute."

Erin bent down and handed a plastic-wrapped inhaler to Sarah. "Wedding present," she said. "You owe me." She ran away again.

While Quentin inhaled the meds, Sarah climbed off his lap and descended the stairs. She bent over Nine Lives, whispering in his ear. He spoke back to her, too low for Quentin to hear over the fireworks finale. Apparently Nine Lives said the wrong thing, because Sarah slapped his face hard and whispered to him again.

Pocketing the inhaler, Quentin stood behind Martin and snapped his fingers. Martin handed him the gun. Quentin shoved it in his waistband and headed behind the dressing room trailer. He motioned for Sarah to follow him.

He looked around to make sure they were alone. The huge crowd sounded distant, and the only witness to their conversation was Vulcan himself. "Do you think any TV cameras caught Martin shooting Nine Lives?" he asked Sarah hoarsely.

"There's no way," she said. "The cameras were all in front. Martin was on the ground behind. He shot Nine Lives through the skirt at the base of the stage."

"How about people in the audience filming with phones?"

"No. Wrong angle."

"Good. You didn't see anything," he instructed her.

"I've got the gun. If you have to tell the cops something, tell them I shot Nine Lives."

"I can't do that to you," she said, looking up at him with her big brown eyes. "Even for Martin."

"You have to," he insisted. "If they take Martin to jail and test him right now, they'll find the junk. That will ruin a self-defense plea."

"No, it—"

"It was my fight," he insisted, taking in her mussed hair and a small scrape on her cheek.

"Maybe it won't come to that," she said. "I told Nine Lives to blame it on his bodyguard. They won't be able to prosecute the bodyguard, because they won't find the gun on him, but at least that will keep them off Martin's trail. And I told Nine Lives that all of them have to go to rehab and make it stick. My job is safe after this hullaballoo, and I'll have more clout with Manhattan Music to get him dropped from the label if he crosses me again."

"You're good at this." He chuckled. "You're better at this than *I* am." He stepped close to her and took her hands. His fingers hit diamond. "You found the ring!" he exclaimed. "You're *wearing* the ring."

He traced his thumb down his fiancée's cheek, across the scar below her chin, and back into her soft, crazy hair. He kissed her, then kissed her harder, amazed all over again at the force of the longing and the love that had overcome him in ten days. The way she responded had him wondering how soon he could possibly do her.

He broke the kiss reluctantly at the wail of sirens. "I forgot about Owen's stitches."

Sarah squeezed his hand. "I'd better go help Rachel and the art school girls. It's going to be another long night."

"Whatever time we get through, meet me back at Owen's big-ass truck," Quentin told her. "We're not sleeping. Not tonight."

18

I accept your resignation. Archie is not going to like this after the Nationally Televised Holiday Concert Debacle. I hear online sales for the Cheatin' Hearts AND Nine Lives are through the roof already, and Manhattan Music is going to be upset that Stargazer let you get away. But working for the Cheatin' Hearts will be a good fit for you, *if you know what I mean.* Tell your green-eyed hick-hunk— Well, never mind. You don't have to tell him anything. Now that things are settling down with the baby, I have some work at home to keep me busy. *If you know what I mean.* ;)

Wendy Mann
Senior Consultant
Stargazer Public Relations

Vulcan's butt glowed majestically in the orange light of sunrise. Sarah would have thought any view was picturesque from a blanket in the back of Owen's truck, with Quentin's arms wrapped protectively around her. Even the trash littering the empty park looked quaint. The police had finally given up and gone home. She and Quentin had the park, the trash, the sunrise, and Vulcan's butt all to themselves.

She told him what her evening had been like. After a few moments of peaceful silence, Quentin let her go and slid to the side of the truck bed.

"Where are you going?" she asked.

"To kill Nine Lives." His eyes were black.

"Quentin." She reached over and put a hand on his arm.

"I've worked at the hospital for years, and I've picked up a few tricks. I can kill him in such a way that no one would ever know he was murdered."

"Someone would see you go into his hospital room," she reasoned.

"The folks at the hospital would cover for me."

She sighed. She understood what Erin meant about arguing with him. "We think we've thrown the police off Martin's scent, but if Martin *were* to get in trouble, he'd be in a lot more trouble if Nine Lives died. I've had enough drama for one day. I only told you what happened because I want us to be honest with each other from now on. I didn't expect you to go *kill* him. I've got him covered. It's okay for you to delegate some of the responsibility of manipulating people. It's okay to ask for help."

He grimaced and rotated his neck. Sarah heard a pop. "I'm in caveman mode," he told her.

"I know!"

"It's just that Martin kept telling me Nine Lives would come after you, and I wasn't there for you."

"Yes you were," she said. "That's what you have friends for. You have Martin's back. Martin has yours. And mine."

"Right. You're right." Quentin relaxed a little.

She scooted across the blanket and pressed herself against him until he hugged her. He put his hand protectively over the bandage that covered the hole Nine Lives had gouged in her arm with the needle.

She kissed his hand. "There's the Quentin I've just met. A respiratory therapist who's been admitted to med school. A brilliant, eloquent, sensitive man, everything I want. And then there's the Quentin I've dealt with for ten days, who breaks the law for fun and profit, chases skirts, manipulates his friends, uses double negatives, and threatens to murder people."

He laughed.

"Not that I'm any better," she said. "The real Sarah is a meek athlete with a closet full of sweatpants. Then there's the persona I call Natsuko, modeled after this badass publicist I saw at the Grammys last year. She's never afraid to do what she likes and take what she wants. If we're going to have a relationship, there isn't room in this truck bed for all four of us."

He wrapped both arms around her waist and squeezed. "All right. I'll suppress Mad Dog Quentin, for now. I'm not promising I won't call him back up if I need him."

"You won't need him with me."

"Which Sarah do I get?"

She smiled up at him. "Which one do you want?"

"I want them both. And I'm not sure Sarah and this other persona are clearly differentiated. I saw Sarah from the beginning. And I saw that she had a little bit of Nat-whatever running through her. I ain't choosing."

She raised one eyebrow at him.

"I'm not choosing," he corrected himself, laughing. "I'm sorry. I'm so used to doing the burly hick act around you." He fingered strands of her hair and flipped them this way and that, lovingly experimenting.

"But, Sarah," he said. "And this is gainfully employed Quentin talking now. I know you may have some dealings with Stargazer and Manhattan Music and Nine Lives for a few more weeks while you're wrapping things up with your old job. But you need to do that with Nine Lives' manager, over the phone. If Nine Lives ever comes within a mile of you, I will do my best to kill him."

She glanced up at Quentin again. His eyes looked

like murder. She put her hands into his curls and tugged. "Would you come back from the Dark Side?"

He laughed his musical laugh again. They settled more comfortably on the blanket and gazed up at the glowing statue.

"So, Dr. Cox." She sighed happily.

"I don't think so," he said. "I see a future for me as the lead singer of a country band called the Cheatin' Hearts. But I want to spend more time on philanthropy from now on, particularly for the foundation in New York. I'm moving in with you. I'd like to experience the Big Apple for a while. You can manage the band from there. And I'm bringing my big-ass truck with me. Of course, I'll have to come out of the asthma and allergy closet, like you suggested."

"Martin's real addiction more than makes up for your fake addiction."

He laughed shortly. "I'm not sure how much longer the Cheatin' Hearts Death Watch will last. The newspaper may decide we're going to live after all."

"They may." She rubbed her hand on his thigh.

He put his hand over her hand. "I can work with the foundation and stay with the band. The four of us talked about it yesterday. We're taking a year off touring, to let Martin get clean and repair whatever's left of his relationship with Rachel."

"I think there's a lot left of his relationship with Rachel," Sarah said thoughtfully.

Quentin went on, "And to let Owen and Erin have

their baby." He cleared his throat. "When are we going to have *our* baby?" He moved his warm hand under her shirt, on her belly.

She relaxed into him. "I'm not in such a hurry anymore. Give me a few years to get over *Wendy's* baby."

"Deal." He kissed her forehead. "Listen, we need to get the hell out of Dodge today, away from the reporters. Where do you want to spend a month?"

The gorgeous beaches of Thailand flashed across her mind, but she wasn't sure she could ever make that joke to Quentin. "How do you feel about Greece?" she suggested.

"I liked Greece, but I don't think it's a good idea. Ever since we faked Owen getting shot in Crete, we've had a rabid fan base in Greece." He twisted her hair around his finger. "How about Hawaii?"

"Don't you think it's awfully hot in Hawaii at this time of year?"

"Can't be any hotter than here."

"True," she said. "I could suffer through four weeks in Hawaii. With you." She grinned up at him. "This is so cool! Especially after yesterday. I had a *really* bad day yesterday. I guess things have a way of working themselves out, as long as you're not engineering a fistfight."

"And sometimes when you are," he said, bending to kiss her mouth.

And then he broke Rule Three.